HEINRICH HEINE: SELECTED PROSE

HEINRICH HEINE (1797–1856) was born of Jewish parents in Düsseldorf. After an unsuccessful attempt at a career in business, he entered Bonn University in 1819 to study law – though literature claimed more of his time. In 1820 Heine transferred to Göttingen University, where he graduated as a doctor of law in 1825. Two of the intervening years were spent amid cultivated and intellectual society in Berlin, where his first two books were published; he also began to write cultural and political journalism. Though his collection of lyric poetry, *Buch der Lieder*, published in 1827, was eventually to acquire worldwide fame, Heine was at first better known for his brilliant and witty prose. His major early work was the satirical *Reisebilder* (1826–31), sketches based on travels in Germany, Italy and England. In 1831, disillusioned with Germany and inspired by the July Revolution in Paris, Heine moved to France. For many years he made his living chiefly by the articles he wrote for German and French newspapers, informing the Germans about current affairs in France and explaining to the French the political significance of Germany's philosophical revolution and Romantic literature. The finest of his later poetic achievements are the mock-epics *Atta Troll. Ein Sommernachtstraum* (*Atta Troll: A Midsummer Night's Dream*, 1847) and *Deutschland: Ein Wintermärchen* (*Germany: A Winter's Tale*, 1844), and the collection of lyrics and narrative poems, *Romanzero* (1851). In 1848 his health collapsed, and for the remaining eight years of his life he was bedridden and in great pain, but he sublimated his sufferings both in poetry and in such prose works as his memoirs of his childhood.

RITCHIE ROBERTSON was born in 1952 and educated at Nairn Academy and the universities of Edinburgh, Vienna and Oxford. Since 1989 he has been a university lecturer in German and Fellow of St John's College, Oxford. He has published *Kafka: Judaism, Politics and Literature* (1985) and an introductory study of Heine in the series *Jewish Thinkers*, besides being co-editor of the yearbook *Austrian Studies*. His previous translations include E. T. A. Hoffmann's *The Golden Pot and Other Tales*.

HEINRICH HEINE

SELECTED PROSE

TRANSLATED AND EDITED
WITH AN INTRODUCTION AND NOTES
BY RITCHIE ROBERTSON

PENGUIN BOOKS

PENGUIN BOOKS

Published by the Penguin Group
Penguin Books Ltd, 27 Wrights Lane, London W8 5TZ, England
Penguin Books USA Inc., 375 Hudson Street, New York, New York 10014, USA
Penguin Books Australia Ltd, Ringwood, Victoria, Australia
Penguin Books Canada Ltd, 10 Alcorn Avenue, Toronto, Ontario, Canada M4V 3B2
Penguin Books (NZ) Ltd, 182–190 Wairau Road, Auckland 10, New Zealand

Penguin Books Ltd, Registered Offices: Harmondsworth, Middlesex, England

This edition first published 1993
1 3 5 7 9 10 8 6 4 2

Typeset by Datix International Limited, Bungay, Suffolk
Set in 10½/12 pt Monophoto Fournier
Printed in England by Clays Ltd, St Ives plc

CONTENTS

INTRODUCTION

DURING his own lifetime Heinrich Heine was at least as well known for his prose as for his poetry. The subsequent fame of his verse is due in part to the many composers who set poems, especially those in the *Book of Songs*, to music. Hence his early, lyrical verse became known at the expense of his later, predominantly satirical verse, and his verse has in turn overshadowed his prose. Yet Heine's prose is as rich in humour, satire, wit, lyricism, and anger as his best verse. It juxtaposes these modes with an agility that forces the reader to remain constantly alert. And, especially in the *Travel Pictures* from the 1820s, this range of tones is combined with narrative, fictional characterization, and elaborate techniques of self-presentation to achieve a complexity of which verse is seldom capable. I have chosen a selection of prose works both for their brilliance and the interest of their subject-matter: three self-contained works from the *Travel Pictures* series, a short essay on 'Differing Conceptions of History', the long political interpretation of German religion and philosophy which Heine wrote for French readers in the 1830s, and finally the *Memoirs* in which, near the end of his life, he recalled (and mythicized) his childhood.

Heine was born on 13 December 1797 in Düsseldorf, a town of some 16,000 inhabitants, the capital of the Duchy of Jülich-Berg on the Lower Rhine. During his boyhood, as he recounts in the autobiographical section of *Ideas: The Book of Le Grand*, it kept changing hands. Its absentee ruler, Maximilian Joseph, the Elector Palatine and King of Bavaria, informed his Düsseldorf subjects on 21 March 1806 that he was abdicating; the Duchy was ceded to Napoleon and made into a French state. The new Grand Duke, Joachim Murat, Napoleon's brother-in-law, entered Düsseldorf on 24 March. Napoleon himself visited Düsseldorf in November 1811, though Heine, in describing the occasion, evokes a springlike atmosphere. In 1815, after the fall of Napoleon, the Duchy was assigned to Prussia, and Heine became a Prussian citizen.

Not a great deal is known about Heine's parents and early childhood beyond the information given in the *Memoirs*. He was the eldest child, and had two brothers and a sister. Their father, Samson Heine (1764–1828), was a dealer in textiles. Their mother, Betty Heine (1771–1859), came from a distinguished family of court Jews, the van Gelderns: Heine occasionally and unjustifiably writes this as 'v. Geldern', as though the 'v.' stood for the aristocratic 'von'. One of his maternal ancestors, his great-uncle Simon van Geldern (1720–88), was an exotic character who travelled through Palestine and North Africa (though he was never a robber chief, as Heine imagines), toured the courts of Europe, met Voltaire and Casanova, and finally helped the Abbé Grégoire to argue for the emancipation of the French Jews.

Among the Düsseldorf people Heine mentions, 'mad Alouisius' and 'drunken Gumpertz' are independently recorded. A possible original has been traced for Red Sefchen, the early girlfriend described in his *Memoirs*, but it is likely that to a large extent she and her spell-working aunt the Göcherin are circumstantial fictions, testifying to Heine's intense interest in folk-tales and his desire to align himself with social outcasts.

Although Heine's family were Jewish, they seem to have felt no strong commitment to Judaism. In early childhood Heine was taught some Hebrew, but little remained with him beyond some verb conjugations. Thereafter he attended Catholic schools in a former Franciscan monastery. He recalled the headmaster, Ägidius Jakob Schallmeyer, with respect, and the French teacher, the Abbé Daulnoy, with irritation.

The young Heine's identification with his exotic great-uncle no doubt strengthened his feeling of being an outsider in the commercial setting in which he was brought up. His father went bankrupt in 1819, and thereafter the family was dominated by Heine's uncle Salomon, a multi-millionaire and leading citizen of Hamburg; Heine tried all his life to acquire some of Uncle Salomon's fortune, alternating between the gross encomium in the *Memoirs* and such outbursts as his remark: 'The best thing about you is that you bear my name.' Salomon Heine set his nephew up in business, but Heine was dragged down in his father's bankruptcy, and the family concluded that he was fit only to study at university.

Heine went first, in the autumn of 1819, to the University of Bonn, which had been founded the year before. His main subject was law, but he also attended lectures on history and literature, including those by the great critic August Wilhelm Schlegel. It was normal practice for German students to move between universities, and after a year Heine moved to the Georgia Augusta University of Göttingen, so called after the Elector Georg August II of Hanover, who founded it in 1734. In the late eighteenth century Göttingen had been Germany's outstanding university, renowned for advances in physics, philology, and biblical criticism, and it still had a high reputation for law, Heine's enforced specialism, but in general its intellectual atmosphere had declined. Student societies (ancestors of the 'fraternities' at American universities) were prominent: Heine lists the archaic names ('Vandals', 'Frisians', etc.) of the *Landmannschaften* or regional fraternities, associating them with Dark Age barbarism. Students' duelling and drinking were governed by a rule-book called the *Komment*; these activities, along with whoring and rioting, in which professors' windows were often broken, were as standard a part of student behaviour as Heine indicates. There were also 'beer-states' whose subjects were ranked by their drinking capacities: Heine mentions the Kingdom of Cyprus maintained by the students at Halle. During the wave of nationalist enthusiasm that accompanied the defeat of Napoleon, attempts had been made to reform these fraternities by establishing *Burschenschaften* or patriotic student societies whose main activities should be gymnastics and debate; Heine joined one in Bonn, and the Brocken episode of *The Harz Journey* shows his lingering fondness for its patriotic atmosphere. He also joined one in Göttingen, but was expelled, probably because of the growing mood of antisemitism.

For this and other reasons, Heine disliked Göttingen. His law studies were not only boring but dominated by the approach of the Historical School of law, which traced legal institutions back to the local traditions from which they had evolved and attacked the liberal ideas inspired by the French Revolution. Nor did Heine like the fact that Göttingen, being located in the Kingdom of Hanover, was under the rule of the Kings of England, which he saw as a reactionary power. Heine's antipathy to Göttingen finds its most famous expression early in *The Harz Journey* and appears also in *Ideas*, especially in the anecdote about Professor Saalfeld.

Soon after his arrival at Göttingen Heine got into trouble for challenging another student to a duel. Though duels frequently took place, university authorities were trying to suppress them, and Heine was rusticated for six months. He transferred to the University of Berlin, founded in 1810 during the short-lived period of liberal reform in Prussia, and was far happier there. Berlin was an outstanding university. Heine attended lectures by the eminent though arch-conservative legal historian Friedrich Karl von Savigny, the great Homer scholar F. A. Wolf, the Sanskrit scholar Franz Bopp who was founding the new discipline of comparative philology, and, in philosophy, the charismatic though barely intelligible Hegel. How much Heine knew about Hegel's philosophy is uncertain: Hegel and especially his followers are ironized in *The Town of Lucca*, but *On the History of Religion and Philosophy in Germany* (henceforth *History*) ends by describing Hegel as 'the greatest philosopher Germany has produced since Leibniz', and as we shall see, its structure is largely borrowed from Hegel.

Berlin gave Heine access to cultivated society, notably the salon maintained by the gifted Rahel Varnhagen (a convert from Judaism) and her husband, the diplomat and writer Karl August Varnhagen von Ense. Heine's first volume, *Poems*, appeared in Berlin in 1822, followed in 1823 by *Tragedies with a Lyrical Intermezzo*. The tragedies were *Almansor*, dealing with the oppression of the Moors in medieval Spain, and *William Ratcliff*, which belonged to the currently fashionable genre of fate-tragedy and is set in a thinly imagined Scotland. An extract from *Almansor* is quoted in *Ideas*. The poems eventually reappeared with the rest of Heine's early poetry in the *Book of Songs* (1827), not Heine's greatest work but the one on which his international reputation was to be founded, as more and more of its contents were set to music by Schubert, Mendelssohn, Schumann, Liszt, and Brahms.[1] Before then Heine had returned to Göttingen to complete his studies. After mugging up law for much of 1824, he made a three-week walking tour in the nearby Harz Mountains which provided the basis for *The Harz Journey*, his first major prose work. He gained his law degree in July 1825 after sitting a written examination and conducting a Latin disputation, at which the examiner, Professor Gustav Hugo, complimented him on his poetry.

Heine, however, did not want to use his law degree. The only salaried profession that seems seriously to have attracted him was university teaching, but in Prussia this profession had been barred to

Jews since 1822. This seems to have been the main reason why Heine converted to Lutheranism in June 1825. His mixed feelings about his Jewish allegiance are apparent from *The Harz Journey*. Here we find the snide references to Jewish money-making that are also frequent in Heine's letters and are no doubt prompted partly by his oppressively rich uncle; but we also find a veiled apologia for Heine's conversion in the incident where the narrator grasps the cross on top of the Ilse Rock. This text contains, too, a mention of Christian Gumpel, who reappears briefly in *Ideas*, features at more length in *The Town of Lucca* as the ennobled and Italianized Marchese di Gumpelino, and is a major character in its companion-piece, *The Baths of Lucca*. Although Heine uses him to typify the pretentious social climbing of the wealthy and would-be assimilated Jew, he is loosely based on a real character, a Hamburg banker called Lazarus Gumpel; though the real Gumpel remained loyal to Judaism, and was deeply hurt by Heine's caricature. On the other hand, the narrator of *The Harz Journey* dislikes the commercial antisemitism of the young Frankfurt merchant, and takes revenge by pretending to be a sleepwalker. And there is also revenge of a kind in the comparison of Catholic chanting to Jewish dialect or *Mauscheln* in *The Town of Lucca*, and in the assurance that only Jewish converts keep Christianity going. In Chapter 13 of this text, and elsewhere, we find another view of Judaism: the judgement that Judaism was an antiquated religion, leading a ghostly existence since its supersession by Christianity.

Heine's conversion did him little good. Having proved his incapacity for business, and unwilling to use his degree, he drifted. His only job – indeed, the only regular employment he ever had – was as editor of a periodical in Munich in the winter of 1827–8. Otherwise he lived in Hamburg, topographical details of which, including Unbescheiden's oyster restaurant and Heine's rooms on Düster ('Gloomy') Street, reappear faithfully in *Ideas*; or travelled, sometimes at his Uncle Salomon's expense and sometimes at his publisher's, to North Sea resorts, to Italy, and in the summer of 1827 to London and the Kent coast. But all this time he was establishing a reputation as the most gifted writer of prose and poetry to have emerged since the beginning of the century. The first volume of *Travel Pictures* appeared in 1826, followed by others in 1827, 1830 and 1831; his collected early poetry appeared as the *Book of Songs* in 1827. They were not runaway successes, but they sold steadily and were often reprinted. The *Book of Songs* appeared thirteen times in Heine's lifetime.

Although Heine was deservedly seen as a political writer, his political standpoint is not easy to describe. The closer one looks, the more one perceives inconsistencies, ambivalences, and genuine changes of mind which, to his dogmatic opponents, seemed like acts of betrayal. There is deep and justified ambivalence, for example, in his attitude towards the French Revolution. In the 1820s he quotes its slogans ('*Aux armes, citoyens!*') and calls as loudly as the censorship permits for a similar revolution in Germany. In the next decade, however, we find more doubts. 'I love the memory of the former revolutionary struggles and of the heroes who fought them,' he writes in 1832, 'yet I should not like to live under the rule of such sublime beings; I could not stand being guillotined every day.'[2]

Heine's attitude to Napoleon is similarly ambivalent. Napoleon's victories over the Central European powers, culminating in the humiliating defeat of Prussia, till recently the Continent's greatest military power, at Jena in 1806, enforced a political reorganization which, as Heine recalls in *Ideas*, made it extremely difficult to learn geography. The three hundred or so territories constituting the Holy Roman Empire, including many petty and ill-governed secular and ecclesiastical statelets, were reduced in 1803 to a small number of mostly sizeable states; the Empire itself was formally wound up in 1806. Napoleon established three satellite states where French law prevailed; one of them was a French state known as the Grand Duchy of Berg where Heine was brought up, so that he benefited from the relatively enlightened Napoleonic Code. Hence he regarded Napoleon as the main antagonist of the reactionary German princes and the heir of the French Revolution. Accordingly, Napoleon is equated with Prometheus in *The Harz Journey* and with Christ in *Ideas*. Later, Heine adopted a more sober view, considering that Napoleon had betrayed his cause by letting himself be anointed Emperor; a passage in *French Painters* even associates him with another emperor, Nero: 'Bonaparte, who could have become a Washington of Europe and became only its Napoleon, never felt quite at ease in his imperial purple mantle; freedom haunted him, like the ghost of a slain mother.'[3]

Heine is consistent in attacking the European order restored by the Congress of Vienna (1815). In *The Town of Lucca*, the three reactionary powers forming the Holy Alliance – Prussia, Austria, and Russia – are sarcastically identified with spectators at Christ's crucifixion, while in *Ideas* the restoration of the Bourbon dynasty in France after Napoleon's defeat at the Battle of Leipzig (1813) illustrates how close the ridiculous is to the sublime. In Germany, French domination inspired intellectuals with intense feelings of nationalism. The Rhinelander Joseph Görres undertook to express the deep emotions of the German people (*Volk*) whose identity, he argued, was based on a common language and culture transcending political fragmentation. Fichte's *Addresses to the German Nation* (1808) extolled the mystical profundity of the German language. F. L. Jahn tried to strengthen national feeling among young Germans by founding a gymnastic movement, which Heine alludes to in saying that 'the Germans became agile'. E. M. Arndt not only celebrated German nationhood but called for its political expression in a unified state which would be free both of revolutionary anarchy and princely despotism. Other, less democratically minded thinkers wanted to roll back the effects of the French Revolution; some, like Adam Müller, dreamed of restoring the medieval order of society. Once Napoleon was safe on St Helena, democrats like Arndt and Jahn fell into disfavour, while reactionaries like Müller enjoyed high positions. The German Confederation of thirty-nine states, dominated by the Austrian Chancellor Metternich, regarded even nationalism as tainted by 'demagogy'. The Carlsbad Decrees of 1819 were intended to suppress radicalism throughout the German Confederation by censoring publications and keeping the universities under close supervision.

Heine attacks all nationalists, whether radical or reactionary. He explodes the myth that the so-called War of Liberation of 1813 was a popular uprising. He repeatedly mocks the German nationalists and their pseudo-medieval costume. The student from Greifswald in *The Harz Journey* is one example; a better-known one is the description of his enemy, the classics professor Massmann, from *Journey from Munich to Genoa*:

> His headgear consisted of a cloth cap, similar in form to Mambrino's helmet, and his stiff black hair hung down at some length and was parted in front *à l'enfant*. On the front of this head, which claimed to be a face, the goddess of vulgarity had stamped her mark, so firmly that the nose there had been almost squashed; the downcast eyes seemed to be grieved by their futile search for this nose; a malodorous

smile was playing round the mouth. [...] His garb was an old German coat, admittedly somewhat modified in keeping with the most essential requirements of modern European civilization, but in its cut still recalling the coat worn by Arminius in the Teutoburg Forest, of which the primal form has been traditionally preserved by a patriotic society of tailors, as mysteriously as Gothic architecture was by a guild of mystical masons. The collar of this famous coat was covered by a white laundered rag, forming a deeply significant contrast with the bare old German throat; from its long sleeves there hung long, dirty hands, and between these a long, boring body could be seen, with short, amusing legs suspended from it – the entire figure would have made a cat laugh in its wretched parody of the Belvedere Apollo.[4]

This vitriolic caricature is also densely allusive. It connects Massmann with the ancient Germanic chieftain known to nationalists as Hermann (Heine pointedly retains the Latin name), who defeated three Roman legions in the Teutoburg Forest in A.D. 9, and with the Middle Ages – or rather, to examples of anachronistic pseudo-medievalism: 'Mambrino's helmet' is the name given by the deluded Don Quixote to the barber's basin kept by Sancho Panza, while the 'mystical masons' suggest Freemasonry. And in finally calling Massmann a parody of the Belvedere Apollo, Heine – writing in neoclassical Munich, on his way to Italy – establishes classicism as the master-discourse which frames and shames romantic nationalism.

Yet in some ways Heine seems disturbingly close to the nationalists. On the Brocken he joins in singing Arndt's 'Song of the Fatherland'; but the two lines quoted have a universal revolutionary significance. In *The Harz Journey* he laughs at the statues of German Emperors in the medieval town of Goslar, and in *History* he derides the medievalism of the 'young old German' who wanted revenge for the execution of a thirteenth-century Emperor; but in both works he also enthuses about the innate creativity of the German people. The difference is that Heine considers himself the true spokesman for the German nation, 'the sleeping sovereign' as he calls it in the preface to *History*, while the nationalists, even if not reactionaries, are fatally tainted with bourgeois philistinism. We may also detect, especially in the eulogy of Luther in Book I of *History*, some over-compensation for the insecurity of Heine's German identity. This insecurity had been exacerbated by the increasing antisemitism of the 1820s which made itself felt in repressive legislation, racist publications, and Heine's expulsion from the Göttingen *Burschenschaft*. Heine's fascination with German folk-tale and folk-song was one response; his political radicalism was another.

In the 1820s there was no way in which Heine's brand of political radicalism could find practical expression. Accordingly, *The Harz Journey* confines itself to hinting at the revolutionary potential as yet unrealized in the German people. However, a strange kind of visionary politics emerges when Heine, in one of the inset poems, calls himself a 'knight of the Holy Spirit'. This alludes to Cola di Rienzo, a lower-class revolutionary who in 1347 entitled himself 'a knight of the Holy Spirit' when he seized power in Rome and dreamed of making it the capital of a free republic. Heine probably took this tripartite conception of history from *The Education of the Human Race* (1777) by one of his favourite writers, the Enlightenment scholar, journalist and playwright Gotthold Ephraim Lessing (1729–81), to whom he pays ample tribute in *History*. In this work Lessing argues that God's revelation to mankind did not come at a single stroke but in stages. Moses represents the first stage; once mankind had absorbed his Law, it gradually became ready to receive Christ's teaching; and the third stage, Lessing surmises, is promised in the New Testament as 'the everlasting gospel' (Revelation 14:6) and was anticipated by the late medieval theologian Joachim of Fiore, who foretold a third age, that of the Holy Spirit, succeeding the ages of the Father and the Son. 'It will assuredly come!' says Lessing, 'the time of a new eternal gospel, which is promised us in the primers of the New Covenant itself!'[5] This scheme may lie behind Heine's reference to Christ as a democratic God in *The Town of Lucca*.

Around 1828 Heine learnt of strikingly similar doctrines among the Saint-Simonians of Paris. Henri de Saint-Simon (1760–1825) was regarded by his followers as the preacher of a third religious revelation, completing those of Moses and Jesus. He was a utopian socialist who deplored the exploitation of man by man and proposed a new social order with no hereditary distinctions of wealth or status. Women were to be emancipated, and artists were given an exalted position as visionary guides to the future. The attractions of this doctrine may have been one reason for Heine's move from Germany to Paris in 1831.

Another was the (largely) bloodless revolution there in July 1830, which put the last Bourbon king, Charles X, to flight and placed on the throne the citizen-king Louis Philippe. Once in Paris, Heine certainly had some personal contact with the Saint-Simonians, though their importance for him is still being debated.[6] They were largely eclipsed in 1832 after the prosecution of their leaders for offending public morality. In any case Heine soon became sceptical about the value of utopian projects set in the future, as is clear from his essay *Differing Conceptions of History*, probably written in 1833. The anecdote about the Saint-Simonians recounted in *History* is derisive.

Heine's life after settling in Paris can be surveyed very briefly. He wrote outstanding journalism, much of it published in the relatively liberal *Augsburg General News*. He specialized in mediating between cultures, explaining the French to the Germans and the Germans to the French. Thus *Conditions in France* reports on public events in the early years of Louis-Philippe's regime, while two substantial works, *The Romantic School* and *On the History of Religion and Philosophy in Germany*, inform French readers about the recent literary and philosophical revolutions in Germany, and subject cultural phenomena to a far-reaching political interpretation. These were intended as a counterblast to Madame de Staël's *De l'Allemagne* (1810), which had presented Germany as the stereotypical land of poets and thinkers and thus, in Heine's opinion, served the reactionary aims of Romantics and nationalists. Indeed the French versions of Heine's treatises were published together under the title *De l'Allemagne*.

Many other works date from the 1830s and 1840s: three unfinished novels, much poetry, and diverse prose, ranging from essays on Shakespeare to a study of German folklore concerning elemental spirits. As for his literary contacts, Heine immersed himself in French society and became acquainted with Balzac, Berlioz, Nerval, Gautier, George Sand, Meyerbeer, and many others of the eminent. He had only loose ties to the community of German exiles led by Ludwig Börne and to the more or less radical 'Young German' writers such as Karl Gutzkow and Heinrich Laube back home. His radical reputation, however, sufficed for the German Federal Diet to lump him together with the Young Germans in a decree of 10 December 1835 which forbade any of them to publish in the territories of the Confederation. The ban could not be rigidly enforced, but their efforts to circumvent it cost

Heine and his publisher much effort and anxiety. One should mention also Heine's marriage in 1841 to Crescence-Eugénie Mirat (known to him by the more pronounceable name Mathilde), with whom he had been living since 1836, and who looked after him until his death; his trip back to Germany in 1843, given poetic form as *Germany: A Winter's Tale* (1844); and his many quarrels, not least with his family, whom he accused of withholding that part of his Uncle Salomon's legacy that was rightfully his, and who in turn exercised all their influence to prevent him from defaming them in print.

That was nothing, however, compared to the disaster that overtook Heine in 1848, ironically at the very time when his radical political ideals were enjoying a short-lived triumph. His health had long been precarious, with recurrent headaches, eye strain, and latterly occasional paralysis; now it collapsed completely, and for the last eight years of his life he was bedridden and in frequent and extreme pain. Paralysis affected various parts of his body in turn; when it attacked his eyelids he had to hold his eyes open with his fingers in order to read. His illness was probably venereal in origin, though unusual in not impairing his mental capacities.

It was in this state that Heine underwent the return to religion described in the preface to the second edition of *History*. The pious, admonitory tone of that passage is somewhat misleading. Heine had never professed atheism; indeed, the narrator of *The Town of Lucca*, where religion receives its most profound and differentiated treatment, visibly tires of Lady Matilda's shallow blasphemies. The late Heine castigates his earlier self for being misled by Hegel's philosophy of perfectibilism into believing that human beings could become gods. He never puts forward a confession of faith, and he seems to have liked mystifying visitors, who were intrigued by exaggerated reports of his 'return'. In a letter to his publisher he insists that he has not become 'a Bible-thumper' or 'a pious lambkin', and adds: 'Great, sublime, terrifying thoughts have come over me, but they were thoughts, flashes of light, and not the phosphorous vapours of pious piss.'[7] And in recanting his earlier hubris, he emphasizes the value of having a God to address and even denounce when he is suffering:

> Yes, I am glad to be rid of the halo to which I aspired, and no philosopher will ever again persuade me that I am a god! I am only a

> poor human being, who moreover is no longer quite healthy, and is, indeed, very ill. In this condition it is a great benefit for me that there is someone in heaven to whom I can constantly whimper out the litany of my sufferings.[8]

Heine's style is digressive, dialogic, and allusive. Its digressions are modelled principally on those of Sterne's *Tristram Shandy* (1761–7) and *A Sentimental Journey* (1768), which were extremely popular in Germany and inspired a host of imitators. Heine resembles Sterne also in often addressing a fictive reader: the 'Agnes' at the end of *The Harz Journey*, the 'Madame' of *Ideas*, the 'dear reader' of *History*, and the 'dear lady' of the *Memoirs*. This device creates a space in the text for the reader and helps us to keep track of Heine's divagations. However, Heine differs from even the greatest of Sterne's German imitators, Jean Paul, in the meticulous and elaborate composition that underlies his seeming inconsequentiality. This applies especially to *Ideas: The Book of Le Grand*, at first sight a bewildering medley, on closer inspection a masterpiece of intertwined allusions and themes.

These allusions are not arbitrary or whimsical, as they often are in Sterne and Jean Paul. Heine claims to be disclosing the true meaning of historical phenomena, and for this activity he likes to use the concept of the 'signature'. In the speculative study of nature, the 'signature' of an animal or plant was those distinctive features that enabled a skilled observer to detect its essential nature. Such concepts appealed to the German Romantics, who regarded nature as a secret script or coded message which poetic insight could decipher. Heine improves on the Romantics by transferring his attention from the natural to the historical world and reading in it the 'signatures' which disclose an esoteric meaning. Similarly, his *Memoirs* undertake to reveal 'the *signatura* of my very being'. Even more grandly, he declares in *History* that 'the world is the signature of the word', the sign pointing to a hidden creative thought.

Allusiveness was in part forced on Heine by the censorship, which was not very strict – otherwise Chapter 12 of *Ideas* would hardly have been possible – but interfered enough to make Heine adopt the technique of esoteric reference that is parodied in *The Harz Journey*, when the narrator enlightens the naive young *Burschenschaft* member about the concealed political meaning of the Berlin ballet. To take just one example, *The Harz Journey* is filled with ironic allusions to Romantic medievalism. The student fraternities recall the barbarian tribes of the Dark Ages; the 'old, weary, worn-out man' revisiting his family vault in Quedlinburg represents the medieval Emperors, one of whom, Heinrich I, is buried there; the Emperor Heinrich reappears, making love instead of war, in the Princess Ilse's song, and this in turn picks up the motif of idle rulers from the poem about the herdsman. One could go on indefinitely, but it would be a pity to forestall the reader's pleasure in gradually picking up these allusions.

The Harz Journey

Heine's early prose works, published under the collective title *Travel Pictures*, depart from accepted models of travel writing. Instead of the objective style of travel writing exemplified by Goethe's *Italian Journey*, Heine practises a subjective mode of composition which subordinates the external world to the whimsical mental habits of the narrating persona.

All the *Travel Pictures* have some foundation in Heine's own experience. The walking tour on which *The Harz Journey* is based lasted three weeks, in September and October 1824, and covered some 280 miles. One of its high points was the ascent of the Brocken, the large mountain on whose flat top the German witches were said to assemble on Walpurgisnacht (30 April) for orgies like those depicted in the Walpurgisnacht scene of Goethe's *Faust*. Another high point, or at least Heine hoped it would be such, was a visit to Goethe himself in Weimar on 2 October; it is not recounted, but, as we shall see, Goethe's presence haunts the text. Events, however, are subordinated to the work's intricate thematic structure.

The introductory poem presents Heine's Harz journey as an escape from the town's social conventions into nature, from insincerity into true feeling, and from affected bourgeois society into the simplicity and depth of rural life. It thus introduces the three protagonists of *The Harz Journey*: the country people, the townspeople, and the narrator. The people enter the narrative most prominently when Heine visits the mining village of Klausthal and descends a mine. He celebrates their quiet, unchanging, contemplative way of life; the creativity which gave rise to German folk-tales recorded by the Grimms; their religious feeling; and their loyalty to their undeserving political overlords – in the case of the Klausthal miners, to the Duke of Cambridge, since the Kingdom of Hanover was in personal union with the British Crown. His tendency to idealize the *Volk* is counterbalanced by the realism with which he describes the mine. Mines appear frequently in German Romantic fiction (for example, in Novalis's fragmentary novel *Heinrich von Ofterdingen* (1802)) but as symbols of the descent into the depths of the soul or the cosmos, whereas the mine Heine describes is dirty, dangerous, and full of incomprehensible machinery.[9]

The antithesis to the country people are the philistine townspeople, especially those of Göttingen. Heine stresses their lack of imagination and their inability to appreciate nature or poetry. Thus the young merchant with whom Heine shares a bedroom in the Brocken inn expresses his admiration for the sunset by prosaically exclaiming: 'How beautiful nature is, by and large!' And the visitors' book at the inn on the Brocken is full of bad verses by every Tom, Dick and Harry. This part of the text is also a satire on tourism. In the late eighteenth century an ascent of the Brocken was still an adventurous hike; after the inn was built on the summit in 1800, however, the Brocken increasingly became a tourist attraction. By 1824 well over a thousand people ascended the mountain each year, and, as Heine indicates, one could even get up and down it by carriage. Heine's anti-philistine satire stands in a well-established German tradition, reaching back to Clemens Brentano's treatise *The Philistine before, in, and after History* (1811) and E. T. A. Hoffmann's *The Golden Pot* (1814), and forward to Thomas Mann's *Tonio Kröger*, where clumsy appreciation of nature and inept attempts at poetry are similarly derided.

The third protagonist of *The Harz Journey* is the narrating persona himself. He has many autobiographical features: most obviously, he is bored with studying law in Göttingen. But he is also a literary construct, and his development has been perceptively traced by Jeffrey Sammons.[10] First the narrator has to get clear of Göttingen, unloading his spite against the city and its repulsive inhabitants as he does so. Twice he performs the symbolic gesture of lightening his pack. His dreams record fears and anxieties, which he is slow to shake off; but as he becomes refreshed by nature, he becomes more and more independent of it: on the Brocken he is able to pass up the sight of the sunrise for the sake of his morning coffee. After the Brocken episode, sexual concerns come to the fore in symbolic form. From the Brocken the narrator descends into the valley of the river Ilse, and he tells how a legend concerning a princess named Ilse has grown up because of the river's name. Here he interpolates a poem in which Princess Ilse speaks, inviting the weary and careworn to be refreshed by her love; and after this the narrator comments: 'It is a feeling of infinite bliss when the visible world converges with that of our hearts.' He is so far restored by now that nature can act as a kind of sexual surrogate, infusing him with a feeling of well-being. Later, in the coda at the end of the text, the narrator returns to Heine's perennial theme of unhappy love, and he gives the woman the name Agnes. His heart, he declares, is like the aloe flower, which blooms only once in a hundred years; and though his past experience has been unhappy, his heart is restored and is now about to flower again.

Heine's visit to Goethe goes strikingly unmentioned. Indeed, hardly anything about the visit can be found in Heine's letters until the following May, when he rather unkindly stresses Goethe's decrepitude. Presumably Heine was disappointed by the visit. Moreover, although he greatly admired some of Goethe's works, such as *Faust Part I* and *The Sorrows of Young Werther*, he did not share in the Goethe cult practised by the Varnhagen circle in Berlin. Later in the 1820s Heine was extremely critical of the older Goethe for propagating a politically reactionary classicism, and identified Goethe with 'the artistic period' which was to be succeeded by a politicized literature. However, the text of *The Harz Journey* is shot through with allusions to Goethe's works. Goethe had himself climbed the Brocken in December 1777 and written a poem about it called 'Harz Journey in Winter'. The Brocken episode obviously recalls the Walpurgisnacht scene in *Faust*, and perhaps also the Auerbach's Cellar scene. In the poem, 'On the hillside stands the cottage . . .', the girl's question, 'Do you believe in God?' is the question put to Faust by Gretchen. The work by Goethe that Heine most often alludes to, however, is *Werther*. There, as in *The Harz Journey*, the protagonist is retreating from unpleasant entanglements into the solace and healing power of nature, and shows fondness for simple people and children. The two drunken youths, who recite Ossianic lyrical prose in the cupboard after bewailing the death of a beloved, parody Werther, who reads Ossian aloud. And the persona is very like a counterpart to Werther, for it appears at the end of the text that he is suffering from unrequited love, yet he recovers his spirits instead of shooting himself as Werther did. If his former beloved hears a shot, he announces, it will be the sound of his heart bursting into flower, like the aloe.

Ideas: The Book of Le Grand

In 1828 Heine foretold that the 'beautiful objective world' of Goethean classicism would be transformed by the new generation of writers into a 'realm of the wildest subjectivity'.[11] *Ideas: The Book of Le Grand*, written two years earlier, seems to exemplify this revolution. Its governing principle is that of incongruity, expressed in Napoleon's saying that 'from the sublime to the ridiculous is only a step'. It can be described accurately, but very inadequately, as a prose text of twenty chapters, which fall into four sections of five chapters each. The first five chapters turn on the familiar theme of unrequited love; the next five are autobiographical, recalling Heine's schooldays in Düsseldorf, his sight of Napoleon, and his friendship with a French soldier in Napoleon's army, the drummer Le Grand; the third section is a satire on writing and scholarship, and on the nature of ideas; and the fourth returns to the theme of unrequited love.

This description, however, conveys nothing of the bewildering experience of reading *Ideas: The Book of Le Grand*. The title itself is perplexing, since it sounds both like a philosophical treatise and like a book of the Old Testament (by analogy with the Book of Ruth or the Book of Job). The text is far less like a conventional narrative than was *The Harz Journey*. It subordinates the world to the imagination of a persona whose identity keeps shifting. He is the hero of the unspecified 'old play' and the person delivering a dramatic monologue to 'Madame'. He is also a jester, for he mentions his cap and bells. Soon he declares himself to be the Count of the Ganges – an impossible mixture of a European title with an Indian location – and he is also a Venetian knight. Similarly, different locations – ancient India, Venice, and modern Hamburg – are all superimposed on each other. And this apparent confusion is presented as a faithful mimesis of the world, which is nothing more than the dream of an intoxicated god.

Commentators have tried to approach the text via the personal references. Rejection in love is the dominant theme of Heine's early work; the *Book of Songs* is held together by the gradual assimilation and acceptance of this traumatic experience. It seems to go back to Heine's rejection at the age of eighteen by his cousin Amalie, and several scholars have surmised that he also made advances to and was rebuffed by Amalie's sister Therese. The evidence of Heine's feelings for Therese is scanty, but not negligible: it consists mainly of some powerful and bitter poems he wrote after she had visited him in Paris many years later. As for his rejection by Amalie, we can hardly suppose that the experience retained its intensity for ten or more years; he seems to have used it to construct a Byronic persona, a suffering, world-weary, cynical character at odds with the philistine environment which, in the person of his beloved, has rejected him. With this proviso, we may accept the conjecture that the 'She' of Chapter 2 and the Signora Laura of Chapter 18 refer to Amalie. 'Madame' is generally assumed to be Friederike Robert, a beautiful Jewish society hostess in Berlin, to whom Heine wrote many personal letters and several poems, and who fits the description in Chapter 16. It is impossible to identify Gertrud, Katharine, Hedwig, and Johanna, though since Andernacht is not far from Bonn, this part may well be founded on some events that occurred when Heine was studying at Bonn.

'Little Veronika' is wholly mysterious; but Heine uses the notion of transmigration of souls to suggest that when little Veronika died, her soul passed into the body of 'Madame', who was born that same day; and 'Madame' is then revealed to be also a reincarnation of the Sultaness of Delhi. The narrator's various personae – Count of the Ganges, Venetian knight, and inhabitant of modern Hamburg – may also be seen as successive incarnations which occasionally get muddled up. The Venetian setting is perhaps motivated by the fact that Hamburg, like Venice, was a commercial and maritime republic; Signora Laura's garden on the River Brenta, which flows into the Venetian lagoon, would then correspond to Heine's uncle's country estate beside the Elbe. Thus Heine universalizes his experience of rejection in love by representing it as something that happens repeatedly, in every age and country, as well as in the imaginary 'old play'. As for the dedicatee, Evelina, she assists this universalizing process. Elsewhere, in *The North Sea*, Heine uses the name 'Evelina' to imply 'women in general'; and it is an anagram of *vielen* ('many', in the dative plural) followed by a feminine suffix. Biographical interpretation is therefore somewhat unrewarding, except in directing attention back to the intricacy of Heine's literary composition.

The Town of Lucca

Heine's Italian travel books show his skill in creating fictional characters – better, indeed, than do his three unfinished novels. The best-known is *The Baths of Lucca*, with its comic characters, the converted Marchese Christophoro di Gumpelino, formerly Christian Gumpel of Hamburg, and his obstinately Jewish servant, Hirsch-Hyacinth. I have chosen to translate *The Town of Lucca* instead, partly because much of *The Baths of Lucca* is taken up with a polemic against Count August von Platen which disagreeably displays Heine's homophobia, and partly because *The Town of Lucca* combines vivid characterization with a more interesting set of themes.

Lady Matilda, a character briefly encountered in *The Baths*, is here developed and used to embody a religious standpoint, that of extreme freethinking and irreverence. The opposite standpoint, that of naive devotion, is represented by the dancer Francesca, whose beauty had already enchanted the narrator in *The Baths*. The narrator himself represents an intermediate set of attitudes: he enjoys Matilda's blasphemy but eventually finds it irritatingly shallow; Francesca's devotion seems almost preferable, even though it is a product of the most abject ignorance. There is little point in speculating about whether Matilda and Francesca are based on real originals. Heine spent September 1828 in Lucca, but we have no independent information about what he did there. Some references in the text suggest that he met Matilda in Ramsgate during his English trip the year before, and had a brief affair with her; there is no knowing.

However, by making the narrator visit Lucca Cathedral in the company of two former lovers, Heine ironically establishes a conflict between religion and the senses. This conflict is developed in various ways throughout the text. A version of it is present in the initial conversation with the philosophical lizard about man's relationship to nature, which is one of both familiarity and estrangement. Another version appears in the account of how the Greek religion of joy was displaced by a religion of suffering, which, however, suits the needs of oppressed humanity better than the callous sensuousness of Olympus.

Yet Heine also suggests that sickness and suffering are not the inevitable human lot: the pleasures of love and art are already incarnated in the dancer Francesca; and religion is shown to be hand in glove with political oppression, both in the narrative and in the open polemic which ends the work. It is astonishing how many aspects of religion Heine manages to introduce, in vivid and memorable shapes, into this brief text.

Differing Conceptions of History

Heine probably wrote this text in 1833; it was found among his papers after his death and published in 1869. The title was given to it by the editor. In it Heine distances himself from two philosophies of history: the conservatism he associated with the Historical School of law and with the later Goethe, and the perfectibilism he found among the Saint-Simonians and in Hegel. Though he found the latter more sympathetic, he points out that one directs us to the past, the other to the future; one promises pie in the sky, the other promises jam tomorrow; neither can help to enrich people's lives here and now.

On the History of Religion and Philosophy in Germany

As an exposition of philosophy, this light and popular survey ought to speak for itself, though its accuracy should not be trusted too far. It also sets out Heine's understanding of history. He fits his material into a historical scheme in which religion is superseded by philosophy, which in turn serves as the prelude to politics. Hence the first of the three Books comprising *History* deals with Christianity and with the primitive religion which the Christian missionaries encountered in Germany and which survives in folk legend. It culminates in the figure of Martin Luther, who is presented as embodying a quintessentially German version of Christianity. The second Book turns to philosophy proper. It takes the work of Descartes as the fountainhead of modern philosophy, from which sprang the diverse schools of Leibniz, Spinoza, and Locke. The thought of Leibniz in particular, having been publicized in Germany by Christian Wolff, provided the foundation for the German Enlightenment. Heine surveys the thinkers of the

Enlightenment period, from Philipp Johannes Spener and August Hermann Francke, the leaders of the Protestant renewal movement known as Pietism, via the clergyman who sought to extract the supernatural components from Christianity, to the two protagonists of the Berlin Enlightenment, King Frederick the Great of Prussia and the book-seller and journalist Friedrich Nicolai. This section culminates in Lessing. Though still famous as a playwright and aesthetician, Lessing is important to Heine chiefly as a critic whose writings promoted freedom of thought and reduced Christianity to deism – the belief in a God who, having created the world, refrained from intervening in its workings by miracles or incarnation. The third Book begins with Kant, who, by showing that the existence of God could not be proved, is said to have destroyed deism and thus swept away the last remnants of religion. The post-Kantians are treated with considerable satire: Fichte, with his theory that nothing exists but the self; and Schelling, according to whom the mind is ultimately identical with nature, and whose system is therefore called the 'philosophy of nature' or 'philosophy of identity'. Schelling is also satirized for the conservatism which made him feel at home in the reactionary atmosphere of Catholic Bavaria, whose capital, Munich, was known as 'Athens on the Isar' because of the neoclassical building programme. Finally, Heine presents Hegel as the culmination of German philosophy, yet tantalizingly avoids any exposition of Hegel's thought. Instead, he ends by drawing the political consequences of his narrative and foretelling a German revolution which will mobilize the energies hitherto devoted to philosophy.

It will be apparent from the above summary that Heine's narrative proceeds via conflict and reconciliation, and that each reconciliation falls apart and produces a new conflict; it will also be apparent that his history focuses on a number of great men, particularly Luther and Lessing. Both these features reveal Heine's debt to Hegel, and especially to the lectures on the philosophy of history which Hegel delivered in Berlin in the winter of 1822, when Heine was a student there. Hegel's history likewise proceeds via conflict, resolution, and further conflict – that is, dialectically; it too is focused on great men who become 'world-historical figures'; but, as with Heine, its real protagonists are ideas, and its development is towards the realization of freedom. 'The history of the world,' says Hegel, 'represents the successive stages in the development of that principle whose substantial content is the consciousness of freedom.'[12]

The ideas whose conflict underlies the history of philosophy, as Heine recounts it, are Spiritualism and Sensualism. Heine uses these words in a particular sense which he is at pains to make clear. 'One of them,' he says, 'seeks to glorify the spirit by striving to destroy matter, while the other tries to assert the natural rights of matter against the usurpations of the spirit.' The term Spiritualism applies to all those doctrines which are hostile to the material world, nature, the senses, the body, and physical enjoyment, and urge us to adopt a self-denying, ascetic way of life in the hope of attaining an incorporeal heaven; while Sensualism asserts the claims of the body and the senses and the value of food and drink, sensual love, and sensuous art like that of the Greeks and the Renaissance. Heine uses these concepts in a highly flexible way. He sees Christianity as a version of Spiritualism (emphasizing, and doubtless exaggerating, its Gnostic element), but he describes Luther as putting forward a strongly Sensualist variety of Christianity. And, in true dialectical fashion, he treats the two concepts as so intertwined that neither is viable on its own. The ancient Germanic religion, understood as nature-worship, was a form of Sensualism, but it needed Christianity to refine and humanize it. The Germans, in Heine's view, have a natural affinity with Sensualism, which is shown in their primitive religion, in the figure of Luther, in the German reception of Spinoza's pantheism, and in the success of Schelling's pantheistic philosophy of nature; and his book ends grimly and ominously by anticipating a resurgence of pantheism in the coming German revolution. When this happens, and the German people at last claim the material well-being which their rulers have tried to deny them, their revolution will necessarily be violent and brutal, because it will be a revolt of Sensualism against Spiritualism. Many readers have been struck by Heine's prescience, not least Thomas Mann, who in 1951 wrote to the Heine critic Ludwig Marcuse:

> You rightly describe his prophecy of a German revolution as rather too patriotic. But the breaking of the cross in it, and the vision of the unleashing of primeval Germanic paganism, could astonish one in 1933.[13]

Memoirs

Heine wrote about his own life in several different ways. The autobiographical element in *Ideas: The Book of Le Grand* provides an account of recent history from an individual perspective. The *Confessions* form a partial intellectual autobiography, in which Heine explains his enmity to Madame de Staël, describes his early years in France, and, above all, accounts for his rejection of Hegel and his return to a religious outlook. The *Memoirs*, written in the same period (1853–4), are sharply focused on Heine's family and his childhood experiences. Heine planned them from at least 1837 onwards, and often tried to blackmail his relatives into providing him with money by threatening to satirize them in print. This worked: in 1846 his cousin Carl agreed to pay him an annual pension on condition that he would say nothing critical of his Uncle Salomon, Carl's father, who had died in 1844. The *Memoirs* were not published until 1884, a year after the death of Heine's widow, and for a long time it was believed that Heine's relatives had interfered with the text and removed offensive passages; however, the most recent editor, Gerd Heinemann, treats this story sceptically.

The *Memoirs* are intended to disclose the origins of Heine's later 'intellectual and spiritual development'. Thus he tells us how his education predisposed him to become a free-thinker; how he reacted against his mother's plans by becoming a poet; how his fascination with his great-uncle, the Easterner, animated his imagination; how his curiosity about his paternal grandfather made him aware of his Jewish background and gave him the experience of being an outsider; how he acquired an interest in superstition and folk legend; and how his calf-love for Red Sefchen inspired his sympathy with the downtrodden and his attachment to the French Revolution.

They also, however, introduce us to a strange and dark imaginative world, similar to that of Heine's later poetry. This is especially the case when the Göcherin appears. She is a kind of evil mother-figure, contrasted with, but also resembling, the good figure of Heine's mother: by her spells, the Göcherin controls (and sometimes mismanages) young people's lives, as Heine's mother tried to organize his. The Göcherin's method of inducing impotence with 'magic knots' is recognizable as a widespread superstition.[14] It makes explicit the theme of impotence vs. potency which has already been touched on in

Heine's description of his father and in the latter's catch-phrase: 'One must tap another barrel.' It also introduces the theme of physical dismemberment, which is developed in the account of the burial of the sword that has cut off a hundred heads, and in the folk-song about Otilje, who is offered a choice of deaths. Thus Heine's own illness enters the text metaphorically. The culminating episode in which the young Heine kisses Red Sefchen, however, sets love and life against death and dismemberment, and as their relationship is approved by Heine's father, the most positive figure in the text, the *Memoirs* end in a light, hopeful, and humorous tone.

NOTES

1. See *The Penguin Book of Lieder*, ed. and tr. S. S. Prawer (Harmondsworth, 1964).
2. *Französische Zustände* ('Conditions in France'), in Heine, *Sämtliche Schriften*, ed. Klaus Briegleb (6 vols., Munich, 1968–76), iii, 207.
3. *French Painters*, tr. David Ward, in Susanne Zantop (ed.), *Paintings on the Move: Heinrich Heine and the Visual Arts* (Lincoln and London, 1989), p. 150.
4. *Reise von München nach Genua* ('Journey from Munich to Genoa'), in *Sämtliche Schriften*, ii, 322.
5. *Lessing's Theological Writings*, ed. and tr. Henry Chadwick (London, 1956), p. 96.
6. Contrast E. M. Butler, *The Saint-Simonian Religion in Germany* (Cambridge, 1926), and Robert Holub, 'Heine and Utopia', *Heine-Jahrbuch*, 27 (1988), 86–112.
7. Letter to Julius Campe, 1 June 1850, in Heine, *Säkularausgabe*, vol. 23 (Berlin and Paris, 1972), p. 43.
8. *Geständnisse* ('Confessions'), in *Sämtliche Schriften*, vi, 476.
9. See Theodore Ziolkowski, *German Romanticism and its Institutions* (Princeton, 1990), Ch. 2.
10. Jeffrey L. Sammons, *Heinrich Heine: The Elusive Poet* (New Haven, 1969), Ch. 4.
11. Review of Wolfgang Menzel's *Die deutsche Literatur*, in *Sämtliche Schriften*, i, 455.
12. Georg Wilhelm Friedrich Hegel, *Lectures on the Philosophy of World History, Introduction*, tr. H. B. Nisbet (Cambridge, 1975), pp. 129–30.

13. Letter of 14 October 1951, quoted in Volkmar Hansen, *Thomas Manns Heine-Rezeption* (Hamburg, 1975), p. 262.
14. On 'magic knots', cf. 'Das Tagebuch' ('The Diary'), in Goethe, *Selected Poems*, tr. David Luke (Harmondsworth, 1964), p. 207, and see Emmanuel Le Roy Ladurie, 'The Aiguillette: Castration by Magic', in his *The Mind and Method of the Historian*, tr. Siân and Ben Reynolds (Brighton, 1981), pp. 84–96.

NOTE ON THE TEXT

I HAVE used the text in Heinrich Heine, *Historisch-kritische Gesamtausgabe der Werke,* edited by Manfred Windfuhr and published by Heine's old publishers, Hoffmann und Campe of Hamburg. Besides the Düsseldorfer Heine-Ausgabe (as it is generally known), I have referred to the edition by Klaus Briegleb: Heine, *Sämtliche Schriften* (Munich, 1968–76). The Düsseldorf texts of *History* and *Memoirs* differ considerably from those in other editions. As the textual history of the former work is extremely complicated, the Düsseldorf editor has gone back to Heine's original manuscript of 1834. The Düsseldorf text of *Memoirs* likewise follows Heine's manuscript. My own divergences from the Düsseldorf text are indicated in the notes: I have included in *History* part of a passage on Protestantism which Heine added as an afterthought and which the Düsseldorf edition prints separately, and I have omitted a long passage on the relations among Fichte, Kant, and Goethe which could not have been of much interest to the present-day reader. In addition, I have silently corrected one wrong date and adopted a variant reading which locates student vandalism in the Weender Street in Göttingen and thus links this text to *The Harz Journey*.

FURTHER READING

ALL Heine's poetry is now available in a well-annotated English translation which can on the whole be warmly recommended: *The Complete Poems of Heinrich Heine*, tr. Hal Draper (Oxford, 1982). For commentary on the *Book of Songs*, see S. S. Prawer, *Heine: Buch der Lieder* (London, 1960), and as a companion to the later poetry, the same author's *Heine, the Tragic Satirist: A Study of the Later Poetry 1827–56* (Cambridge, 1961).

The most comprehensive (though not complete) attempt at translating Heine's prose is *The Works of Heinrich Heine*, tr. C. G. Leland and others (12 vols., London, 1891–1905). Selections from this and other nineteenth-century translations are sometimes reissued, but they cannot be recommended. Fortunately, Heine's reflections on the French Salon of 1831 are now available in a good translation by David Ward, accompanied by informative essays and coloured illustrations: Susanne Zantop (ed.), *Paintings on the Move: Heinrich Heine and the Visual Arts* (Lincoln and London, 1989).

Ritchie Robertson, *Heine* (London, 1988), is intended as a brief introduction to Heine's work as a whole. The outstanding general studies in English are Jeffrey L. Sammons, *Heinrich Heine: The Elusive Poet* (New Haven, 1969), and Nigel Reeves, *Heinrich Heine: Poetry and Politics* (Oxford, 1974). Sammons has also written an excellent biography, on which I have drawn heavily: *Heinrich Heine: A Modern Biography* (Princeton, 1979).

On the history of Heine's time, James J. Sheehan, *German History 1770–1866* (Oxford, 1989), is now indispensable. Literature and history are skilfully related in Eda Sagarra, *Tradition and Revolution: German Literature and Society 1830–1890* (London, 1971). On the situation of Jews in Germany, see Jacob Katz, *Out of the Ghetto: The Social Background of Jewish Emancipation, 1770–1870* (Cambridge, Mass., 1973); and S. S. Prawer, *Heine's Jewish Comedy* (Oxford, 1983).

FURTHER READING

For more rigorous guides to the philosophy discussed in *History*, see Norman Hampson, *The Enlightenment* (Harmondsworth, 1968), and Julian Roberts, *German Philosophy: An Introduction* (Cambridge, 1988).

TABLE OF DATES

1797 *13 December* Born in Düsseldorf.

1819 Attends University of Bonn, studying law as his principal subject.

1820 Transfers to University of Göttingen; rusticated for planning to fight a duel.

1821 Moves to University of Berlin.

1822 Publishes *Poems*.

1823 Publishes *Tragedies with a Lyrical Intermezzo*.

1824 Returns to Göttingen to complete his studies.
September–October Walking tour through the Harz Mountains.
2 October Meeting with Goethe in Weimar.

1825 Conversion to Protestantism; graduation from Göttingen.

1826 *The Harz Journey* published in book form as part of *Travel Pictures* I.

1827 Publishes *Book of Songs*; *Travel Pictures* II, including *Ideas: The Book of Le Grand*.

1830 July Revolution in Paris.

1831 *The Town of Lucca* published as part of *Supplement to the Travel Pictures* (later reprinted as *Travel Pictures* IV).
Heine moves to Paris, where he lives for the rest of his life.

1835 *On the History of Religion and Philosophy in Germany* published in book form; *The Romantic School*.
10 December Heine's writings, along with those of the so-called 'Young German' school of writers, are officially banned throughout Germany.

1841 Marries Crescence-Eugénie Mirat ('Mathilde').

1842 Writes *Atta Troll: A Midsummer Night's Dream*, a romantic and humorous narrative poem, satirizing many targets including German political poets (published 1847).

1843 Revisits Germany.

1844 Friendship with Karl Marx; publication of *Germany: A Winter's Tale*, a fictionalized account of his visit, and of *New Poems*.

1848 Outbreak of revolutions in Berlin, Paris, Milan, Naples, Vienna, Prague. Heine collapses with a painful and paralysing illness; bedridden for the last eight years of his life.

1851 Publishes *Romanzero*, a major collection of poems.

1853 (probably) Heine writes the *Confessions* and much of the *Memoirs*.

1854 Publishes *Poems 1853 and 1854*.

1856 *17 February* Dies; buried at Montmartre.

THE HARZ JOURNEY

Nothing is permanent but change; nothing is constant but death. Every heartbeat inflicts a wound upon us, and life would be a perpetual process of bleeding to death, were it not for poetry. It grants us what Nature denies us: a golden age that does not rust, a spring that does not fade, cloudless happiness and everlasting youth.

Börne[1]

NEAT black coats and silken stockings,
Spotless cuffs and social arts,
Gentle words and fond embraces –
Oh, if only they had hearts!

In their bosoms, hearts – and love,
Love that in the bosom glows –
Oh, they kill me with their whining
About fancied lovers' woes.

To the hills I shall ascend,
Where the huts are meek and low,
Where the breast expands in freedom,
And the breezes freely blow.

To the hills I shall ascend,
Where the fir-trees darkly loom,
Brooks are plashing, birds are singing,
Clouds are racing through the gloom.

Farewell, ye polished drawing-rooms,
Polished company in town!
To the hills I shall ascend,
And I'll laugh as I look down.

The town of Göttingen, famous for its sausages and university, belongs to the King of Hanover, and contains 999 hearths, sundry churches, a lying-in hospital, an observatory, a lock-up, a library, and a beer-cellar, where the beer is very good. The stream that flows past is called the Leine, and serves for bathing in the summer; its water is very cold, and at some points so wide that Lüder[2] had to take a very long run when he jumped over it. The town itself is beautiful, and looks its best when you turn your back on it. It must have been in existence a long time; for I remember that when I matriculated there five years ago, shortly before being rusticated, it had the same grey look, like an old head on young shoulders, and was already fully equipped with proctors, bulldogs, dissertations, *thés dansants*, washer-women, reference-books, roast pigeons, Guelph Orders,[3] graduation-day coaches, blockheads, Aulic Counsellors, Judicial Counsellors, disciplinary committees, eccentrics, and many other tricks. Some people even claim that the town was built at the time of the Germanic migrations and that every Germanic tribe deposited an unbound copy there; these specimens were the ancestors of all the Vandals, Frisians, Swabians, Teutons, Saxons, Thuringians and other student societies who may even today be seen in hordes in Göttingen, distinguished by the colours of their caps and the tassels on their pipes, parading along Weender Street, and perpetually fighting on the bloody battlefields of the Grass Mill, Ritsch's Tavern, and Bovden; they still observe the manners and customs of the Dark Ages, and are governed partly by their *Duces*, who are called Head Cocks, and partly by their ancient law-book, which is called the *Komment* and deserves a place among the *legibus barbarorum*.

By and large the inhabitants of Göttingen may be divided into students, professors, philistines, and cattle; which four classes are by no means sharply distinct. The cattle are the most important class. It would take too long to list the names of all the students and all the Ordinary (and disorderly) Professors; besides, I cannot call to mind all the students' names at this moment, and many of the professors have not made a name for themselves. The number of philistines in Göttingen must be very great, like the sands, or rather the mud, of the sea; truly, when I used to see them in the mornings, planted outside the gates of the academic court, with their dirty faces and clean accounts, I wondered how God could have created such a pack of scoundrels.

Fuller information about the town of Göttingen may be conveniently obtained from the topography of the same by K. F. H. Marx.[4] Although I am under the most sacred obligations to the author, who was my doctor and did me many kindnesses, I cannot recommend his work unreservedly, and I must deplore his failure adequately to rebut the erroneous view that the women of Göttingen have excessively large feet. Indeed, I have been at work for many a long day on a serious refutation of this view, and have therefore attended lectures on comparative anatomy, taken notes from the rarest books in the library, and spent hours studying the feet of the ladies passing along Weender Street. In the work of profound learning which will embody the results of these studies, I discuss: (1) feet in general, (2) feet in the ancient world, (3) elephants' feet, (4) the feet of Göttingen women, (5) I collect everything that has been said about these feet in Ullrich's Beer-Garden, (6) I examine these feet in their context, and add an extensive discussion of calves, knees, etc., and finally, (7), if I can find any paper large enough, I shall add some copperplate engravings with facsimiles of the feet of Göttingen ladies.

It was still very early when I left Göttingen, and the learned —[5] was no doubt still in bed and dreaming, as usual, that he was walking in a beautiful garden where the flower-beds produced nothing but slips of white paper with quotations written on them, gleaming delightfully in the sunshine; and now and then he would pull up a handful and laboriously transplant them to a new bed, while the nightingales rejoiced his old heart with their sweetest notes.

Before the Weender Gate I met two little schoolboys, Göttingen born and bred, one of whom said to the other: 'I don't want anything more to do with that Theodor, he's a good-for-nothing scamp, for yesterday he didn't even know the genitive of *mensa*.' Trifling though these words may sound, I cannot but record them, indeed I should like to have them inscribed on the gate as the town's motto; for the child is father to the man, and these words convey all the narrow, desiccated, pedantic pride of the erudite Georgia Augusta University.

A fresh morning breeze was blowing on the highway, and the birds were singing most cheerily, and gradually my spirits too became lively and cheerful. This refreshment was sorely needed. For some time past I had been confined to the Pandects' stable,[6] the Roman casuists had enfolded my mind like the grey toils of a spider's web, my heart felt wedged between the iron paragraphs of selfish legal systems, names like Justinian, Hermogenian, Tribonian, and Pickled-Onion were ringing in my ears, and I even mistook a pair of lovers sitting under a tree for an edition of the *Corpus Juris* with the publisher's symbol of linked hands.

Things were livening up on the highway. Milkmaids went past, as did donkey-drivers with their grey pupils. Beyond Weender I met the Shepherd and Doris.[7] This is not the idyllic couple of whom Gessner sings, but two well-fed university proctors, who must see to it that no students fight duels in Bovden and that no new ideas are smuggled into Göttingen by some speculative lecturer instead of spending several decades in quarantine. The Shepherd greeted me as a colleague; for he too is a writer, and has often mentioned me in his half-yearly reports. He has often cited me, as well, and when he found me not at home, was always kind enough to write the citation in chalk on the door of my room. The occasional one-horse carriage rolled past, packed to the brim with students who were leaving for the holidays, or for good. In a university town like this there is an incessant coming and going, and a new generation of students is found every three years; it is a ceaseless stream of humanity, in which one term's wave supplants another, and only the old professors remain standing amid this general flux, firm and immovable, like the pyramids of Egypt – except that these academic pyramids contain no hidden wisdom.

At Rauschenwasser I saw two likely youths on horseback emerging from the myrtle bowers. A female, who plies her horizontal trade there, accompanied them as far as the highway, and patted the horses' skinny thighs with a practised hand. When one of the horsemen paid her a gallant compliment with the whip on her broad posterior, she burst out laughing and sauntered off Bovden-wards. The youths, however, galloped off to Nörten, bawling most wittily, and giving a charming rendering of Rossini's air 'Drink beer, Lizzie my dear!'. I could still hear their notes when they were a long way off, but I soon lost sight of the sweet singers, especially as they spurred and whipped their horses, which seemed to have a slow and steady German character, most violently. Nowhere are horses worse treated than in Göttingen, and when I saw a poor lame broken-down nag, drenched in sweat, earning its scanty feed by being tormented by our knights of Rauschenwasser, or by pulling a carriage full of students, I often thought: 'Poor beast, your forefathers must have tasted forbidden oats in Paradise!'

I met the two youths again in the inn at Nörten. One of them was devouring a herring salad, and the other was chatting with the leathery yellow maid known as Fusia Canina[8] or the Debt-Collector. He showed his common touch by uttering a few proprieties to her and touching her more and more commonly. To lighten my knapsack, I unpacked my blue trousers, which are of great historical significance, and gave them to the little waiter known as Humming-Bird. Meanwhile Bussenia, the old landlady, brought me a buttered roll and complained that I visited them so seldom; for she is very fond of me.

Beyond Nörten the blazing sun was high in the sky. It wanted to do me a good turn, and warmed my head so that all the unripe thoughts in it became fully ripe. The Sun Inn in Nordheim is not to be despised either; I stopped there and found lunch already on the table. All the dishes were tastily cooked and pleased me much better than the tasteless academic dishes, the leathery, unsalted dried fish with old cabbage, which had been set before me in Göttingen.

After I had appeased my stomach somewhat, I noticed in the same parlour a gentleman and two ladies who were on the point of leaving. The gentleman was dressed all in green, and even wore a pair of green spectacles which made his red copper nose seem covered in verdigris; he looked as King Nebuchadnezzar[9] must have done in his later years, when, as legend tells us, like a beast of the forest, he ate nothing but lettuce. The green man wanted me to recommend a hotel in Göttingen, and I advised him to ask the first student he met the way to the Hotel de Brühbach. One of his companions was his lady wife, a large and ample lady, who had a red ten-acre face with dimples in her cheeks that looked like Cupid's spittoons, a long, fleshy, pendulous double chin like an inferior sequel to her face, and a high-stacked bosom defended by stiff lace and scalloped collars as though by turrets and bastions. The other lady, her sister, was the complete opposite of the one just described. If the first was descended from Pharaoh's fat kine,[10] this one was descended from the lean kine. Her face was no more than a mouth between two ears, her bosom was as desolate as the Lüneburg Heath; her whole figure seemed to have been boiled down to nothing, like a free dinner for poor divinity students. Both ladies asked me simultaneously if the Hotel de Brühbach had respectable guests. I assured them with a good conscience that it did, and as the gracious trio departed, I waved to them from the window. The landlord of the Sun had a sly grin; he doubtless knew that the Hotel de Brühbach is what Göttingen students call the lock-up.

Beyond Nordheim the ground rises, and fine-looking hills are to be seen here and there. On the way I met mainly shopkeepers going to the Brunswick Fair, and a swarm of women, each carrying a huge cage, almost as big as a house, and draped in white linen, on her back. In the cages were all manner of song-birds, incessantly whistling and twittering, while their bearers tripped along merrily chattering. I found it very funny to see one bird carrying another to market.

It was pitch dark by the time I got to Osterode. Having no appetite for dinner, I went straight to bed. I was dog tired and slept like a god.

In my dream I found myself back in Göttingen, in its library. I was standing in a corner of the law library, rummaging through old dissertations, absorbed in reading, and when I stopped I noticed to my astonishment that night had fallen and that the room was lit by crystal chandeliers. The nearby church clock was just striking twelve as the door slowly opened, and in came a huge, majestic woman, reverently attended by the members and hangers-on of the Law Faculty. Although the giantess was well stricken in years, her countenance retained traces of a severe beauty. Her every glance proclaimed the Titaness, mighty Themis.[11] Her sword and scales were borne negligently in one hand, while in the other she held a roll of parchment, and two young *Doctores juris* held the train of her grey, faded robe. On her right the skinny Aulic Counsellor Rusticus, the Lycurgus of Hanover, sprang nimbly to and fro, declaiming from his most recent draft legislation; on her left her gallant and good-humoured *cavaliere servente*, Privy Counsellor Cujacius, hobbled along, constantly cracking legal jokes and laughing so heartily at them that even the grave goddess bent down to him with a smile, tapped him on the shoulder with her roll of parchment, and whispered kindly: 'Naughty little rascal, who clips the trees from the top down!' The other gentlemen now came forward one by one, each with a remark and a smile, whether about a little system he had newly excogitated, or a little hypothesis, or a similar misshapen product of his little mind. Through the open door there entered some strange gentlemen who announced themselves as the other great men of the illustrious order; they were mostly angular, lurking fellows, who with immense self-satisfaction instantly began producing definitions and distinctions and disputes about every jot and tittle of a pandect. And new figures kept coming in: old jurists in outmoded costumes, with white full-bottomed wigs and long-forgotten faces, very astonished that they, the celebrities of the previous century, were now held in no particular esteem; and they joined in, after their fashion, in the general chattering and shrieking and yelling, which rose like the surge of the sea, louder and more bewildering in each moment, around the lofty goddess, until she lost her patience and cried in gigantic tones of terrible agony: 'Silence! Silence! I hear the voice of my beloved Prometheus, unjustly chained to his rock of torments by mocking strength and dumb violence, and all your chattering and squabbling cannot lave his wounds or break his fetters!' Thus spake the goddess, tears streaming from her eyes; the whole assembly howled as though in mortal terror, the ceiling groaned, books tumbled from their shelves, it was in vain for old Münchhausen[12] to step out of his picture-frame and call for quiet, the raving and shrieking grew wilder and wilder – From this Bedlamite uproar I escaped into the History Room, to that blessed spot where sacred pictures of the Apollo of Belvedere and the Medicean Venus stand side by side. I fell at the feet of the goddess of beauty, and the sight of her made me forget all the wild goings-on I had fled from; my delighted eyes drank in the symmetry and the eternal charm of her blessed body, Greek peace entered my soul, and the sweetest notes of Phoebus Apollo's lyre descended upon my head like heavenly benedictions.

When I woke I could still hear a pleasant tinkling. The cattle were going to the pasture and their cow-bells were ringing. The dear golden sun was shining through the window and illuminating the pictures on the walls of my room. They represented the War of Liberation, and faithfully showed how we were all heroes; there were also execution scenes from the French Revolution, Louis XVI on the guillotine, and other choppings-off of heads. Such pictures make you thank God that you are lying peacefully in your bed, drinking good coffee, with your head reposing comfortably on your shoulders.

After I had drunk my coffee, dressed, read the graffiti scratched on the window-panes, and settled my account in the inn, I left Osterode.

This town has a certain number of houses, and various inhabitants, including several souls, as you may learn in more detail from Gottschalk's *Guide for Visitors to the Harz*. Before I went on to the highway, I ascended the ruins of the ancient castle of Osterode. The ruins consist only of one-half of a large tower with thick walls that seem eaten away by cancer. The road to Klausthal led me downhill again, and from one of the first acclivities I looked back into the valley, where Osterode with its red roofs peeps out of the green pine forests like a moss-rose. The sun lit the landscape with childlike charm. From here you have an impressive view of the surviving rear half of the tower.

After walking some distance I fell in with a journeyman coming from Brunswick, who told me a rumour current there, that the young Duke, on his way to the Promised Land, had been captured by the Turks, and could only be freed in return for a large ransom. The

Duke's long journey may have given rise to this legend. Our common people still think in the traditional fabulous manner that is so charmingly recorded in the popular epic *Duke Ernest*.[13] The person who told me this news was an apprentice tailor, a dainty young fellow, so thin that the stars could shine through him, as they do through Ossian's wraiths, and altogether a man of the people, in whom whimsy and melancholy were eccentrically mingled. This was particularly apparent from the drolly touching way in which he sang the wonderful folksong: 'A beetle sat upon a fence; hmm, hmm!'. That is a nice characteristic of us Germans: however crazy any of us may be, he can always find someone still crazier who can understand him. Only a German can respond to the feeling in this song, while splitting his sides and crying his eyes out. I also noticed how deeply Goethe's words have entered the popular mind, for my skinny companion also trilled to himself now and again: 'Full of joy, full of sorrow, but thought's always free!'[14] Such textual corruption is usual among the people. He also sang the song in which 'Lotte mourns at her Werther's grave'.[15] The tailor almost melted with sentimentality at the words:

I weep alone amid the roses' glade,
Where oft we whispered in the pale moonlight!
I wander mournful by the silver spring,
That murmured once of beauty and delight.

Soon, however, he became frolicsome, and told me: 'In our hostel at Kassel we have a Prussian who makes such songs himself; he cannot sew a stitch to save his life; if he has a penny in his pocket, he has twopence-worth of thirst, and when he is well oiled, he thinks the sky is a blue camisole, and weeps buckets, and sings a song with double poetry!' I asked him to explain this last phrase, but my little tailor hopped to and fro on his matchstick legs and kept exclaiming: 'Double poetry is double poetry!' Finally I worked out that he meant poems with alternating rhymes, especially Italianate stanzas. Meanwhile, the exertion and the contrary wind had made the knight of the needle very tired. He made a great show of stepping out vigorously, and boasted: 'I'm just getting into my stride!' But soon he complained that he had blisters, and that the world was much too big; and finally he sank down gently under a tree, shook his delicate head like a sorrowful lamb's tail, and cried with a melancholy smile: 'Poor devil that I am, I'm dead beat!'

Here the mountains grew steeper; beneath me the pine forests were swaying like a green ocean, and above me the white clouds were sailing through the blue sky. The wild landscape was tamed, so to speak, by its unity and simplicity. Nature, like a good poet, dislikes abrupt transitions. However bizarrely shaped the clouds may sometimes appear, their white or at least soft colouring harmoniously matches the blue sky and the green earth, so that all the colours in a landscape melt into one another like gentle music, and every prospect of nature cures fretfulness and calms the spirit. (The late lamented Hoffmann[16] would have painted the clouds in garish colours.) Like a great poet, nature also knows how to produce the greatest effects with the utmost economy of means: nothing but sun, trees, flowers, water, and love. Of course, if the latter is absent from the beholder's heart, the whole landscape will be an unpleasing sight; then the sun is merely so many miles in diameter, and the trees provide good firewood, and the flowers are classified according to the number of their stamens, and the water is wet.

A little boy who was collecting brushwood in the forest for his sick uncle pointed out to me the village of Lerbach, whose grey-roofed cottages stretch for a good half-hour's walk through the valley. 'There are stupid people with goitres there,' said he, 'and white Moors' – this is the popular name for albinos. The little boy seemed to be on the best of terms with the flowers; he greeted them as friends, and they seemed to rustle in reply to his greeting. He whistled like a finch, the other birds all around answered by twittering, and before I knew what was happening, he had scurried off with his bare feet and his bundle of twigs into the thick of the forest. 'Children are younger than we are,' I thought, 'and can still remember how they too used to be trees or birds, and understand what these are saying; but we are already old, and our heads are too full of worries, jurisprudence, and bad verses.' The time when things were otherwise came vividly into my memory as I entered Klausthal, a pleasant mountain village, which you do not notice until you are standing right in front of it. I arrived on the stroke of twelve, as the children were pouring out of school with loud cries. The boys, almost all with rosy cheeks, blue eyes and flaxen hair, were jumping and whooping, and made me recall with mingled amusement and sadness my own early days in a dreary Catholic monastery school at Düsseldorf. There I had to remain seated on a wooden bench for the whole morning, enduring such a lot of Latin, beating, and geography, and I too likewise whooped and rejoiced immoderately when the bell of the Franciscan monastery finally struck twelve. From my knapsack the children noticed that I was a stranger, and they greeted me most hospitably. One of the boys told me they had just been having religious instruction, and showed me the Royal Hanoverian Catechism, with which they had been answering questions on Christianity. The book was very badly printed, and I fear this means that the sacred teachings will leave a disagreeably thick and smudgy impression on the children's minds. I was also much displeased to see that the multiplication table, which conflicts dangerously with the doctrine of the Holy Trinity, was printed on the last page of the catechism, so that the children could be led at an early age into sinful doubts. We are much wiser in Prussian territories; in our zeal to convert those people who are so good at counting, we take care not to print the multiplication table just after the catechism.

I had lunch in the Crown Inn at Klausthal. They served me fresh green parsley soup, violet-blue cabbage, a joint of roast veal like a model of Chimborazo, and also a kind of smoked herrings called *Bückinge* after their inventor, Wilhelm Bücking, who died in 1447. On account of this invention Bücking was so revered by the Emperor Charles V that in 1556 the latter made the journey from Middelburg to Bievlied in Zeeland for the sole purpose of seeing the great man's grave. How splendid such a dish tastes if you know the historical background to it and are eating it yourself! Only the coffee after lunch was spoiled for me by a talkative young man who sat down beside me and indulged in such monstrous bragging that the milk on the table turned sour. He was an eager young travelling salesman with twenty-five brightly coloured waistcoats and an equal number of golden rings, seals, breast-pins, etc. He looked like a monkey that had donned a red jacket and said to itself: 'The tailor makes the man.' He knew a vast number of riddles, as well as anecdotes which he always told at the most unsuitable moment. He asked me what was the latest news from Göttingen, and I told him that before my departure the University Senate had issued a decree forbidding anyone, on pain of being fined three dollars, to cut off dogs' tails; the reason being that in the dog-days mad dogs put their tails between their legs and can thus be distinguished from the sane, which would be impossible if they had no tails. – After the meal I set off to visit the mines, the silver works, and the mint.

In the silver works I failed, as so often, to see any silver being extracted. In the mint I had more luck, and was able to stand by and watch money being made, though that was as far as I got. I have always been a bystander on such occasions, and I am sure that if it ever rained silver dollars I would only get holes knocked in my head, while the children of Israel would collect the silver manna with great delight. Looking at the gleaming new-born dollars, I felt a comical mixture of reverence and sentiment; I took one that had just been minted in my hand, and addressed it thus: 'Young dollar! What destinies await you, how much good and how much evil you will cause! You will protect vice and patch up damaged virtue, you will be first loved and then cursed, you will help in revelry, procurement, lies and murder! You will wander restlessly for centuries, through clean hands and dirty ones, until at last, burdened by guilt and weary of your sinful career, you will be gathered to your kindred in Abraham's bosom, where you will be melted down, purified, and made fit for a new and better existence.'

My descent into the two principal mines in Klausthal, the Dorothea and the Carolina, was extremely interesting, and I must recount it in detail.

Half an hour's walk from the town you arrive at two large blackened buildings, where you are immediately received by the miners. They wear loose jackets hanging down to their thighs, dark, usually steel-blue, in colour, with trousers of the same hue, a leather apron tied at the back, and small green felt hats without brims, like skittles with their tops cut off. The visitor puts on a similar costume, only without the leather apron, and a miner, a deputy, lights his lamp and takes you to a dark opening which resembles the mouth of a chimney. He descends into this until only his head and torso remain visible, instructs you to keep a firm grip of the ladder, and asks you to follow him and not be afraid. In fact there is no danger; but you don't believe that at first, if you are completely ignorant of mining. It feels strange enough to have to undress and put on a kind of prisoner's outfit. And now you have to climb down on all fours, and the dark hole is so very dark, and God only knows how long the ladder may be. But soon you notice that it is not a single ladder extending into black infinity, but several ladders, each with fifteen to twenty rungs, and each ending on a small platform on which you can stand, and from which another hole leads to another ladder. The first mine I descended was the Carolina. She was the dirtiest and most disagreeable Carolina I have ever encountered. The ladder's rungs are wet and muddy. And down you go, from one ladder to the next, with the deputy ahead of you, constantly assuring you that it is not at all dangerous, so long as you keep a good grip of the rungs, and don't look down, and don't become dizzy, and on no account step on the platform to one side where the pulley whirs up and down, and where, a fortnight earlier, some careless person fell and broke his neck. Down below there is a confused swishing and humming; you keep bumping into beams and ropes which wind the barrels containing ore or coagulated water up to the surface. From time to time you arrive in tunnels cut out of the rock, known as adits, where the ore can be seen growing, and where the solitary miner sits all day, laboriously hacking lumps of ore out of the wall with his hammer. I did not penetrate to the lowest depths, where some say you can hear people in America shouting 'Hurrah for Lafayette!'[17] But, between you and me, the place I got to seemed quite deep enough: there was a perpetual roaring and humming, with machinery in constant uncanny motion; you could hear underground springs flowing and see water trickling down the walls on every side, while clouds of vapour arose from the earth, and the twinkling of the miner's lamp looked fainter every minute amid the darkness and solitude. It was really deafening; I found it hard to breathe, and had trouble in keeping hold of the ladder's slimy rungs. I felt no trace of what people call fear, but, strangely enough, down there in the depths I remembered being on the North Sea in a gale, about the same time a year earlier, and I now felt how pleasant and cosy it is when the ship rolls from side to side, the winds perform on their trumpets, the merry shouts of seamen can be heard, and God's free air blows freshly all around. Yes, air! Gasping for air I ascended several dozen ladders, and the deputy led me through a very long narrow tunnel cut into the mountain to the Dorothea pit. This mine is more fresh and airy, and the ladders are cleaner, but also longer and steeper than in the Carolina. Here my spirits revived, especially as I again saw signs of living people, for down below only moving gleams could be seen. Miners with their lights were climbing up; as they passed us they called out the traditional miners' greeting, 'Good luck!', which we returned. Young and old alike looked at us directly and thoughtfully. Their faces in the mysterious light of their lamps were grave, pious, and somewhat pale, and I felt the presence of peaceful and familiar memories, but also of painfully perplexing ones, as I beheld these men who had been working all day in their dark, lonely shafts and now longed to return to the daylight and to the eyes of their wives and children.

My cicerone himself was German to the core and as honest as the day. He took intense pleasure in showing me the adit where the Duke of Cambridge,[18] when visiting the mine, had dinner with his entire retinue. The long wooden dinner-table is still standing there, along with the great chair made of ore on which the Duke sat. The latter, according to the good miner, was to be an everlasting monument; and he told me enthusiastically about the many festivities which had taken place. The whole tunnel was decorated with lights, flowers and foliage; a pitman sang and played the zither; the dear stout Duke enjoyed himself hugely and drank a great many healths; and my guide told me how many miners, especially himself, would happily lay down their lives for the dear stout Duke and the entire House of Hanover. My heart is always stirred when I see this feeling of loyalty being expressed in simple and natural tones. It is such a beautiful feeling! And it is such a truly German feeling! Other nations may be more dexterous, wittier and more entertaining; but none is so faithful as the faithful German people. If I did not know that this faithfulness is as old as the world, I would suppose that it had been invented by a German heart. German faithfulness! This is not just a modern cliché. At your courts, you German princes, you should never cease singing the song of faithful Eckart[19] and the evil Duke of Burgundy, who had Eckart's dear children killed and yet found him as faithful as ever. You have the most loyal people of all, and you are wrong to think that the intelligent, faithful old dog has suddenly gone mad and is snapping at your sacred ankles.

Like German faithfulness, the miner's little lamp had guided us quietly and safely, without much flickering, through the labyrinth of shafts and tunnels; we emerged from the stifling darkness of the mountain into the radiant sunlight – Good luck!

Most of the miners live in Klausthal and in the adjacent mountain village of Zellerfeld. I visited several of these worthy people, viewed their modestly furnished homes, and heard some of their songs, very charmingly accompanied on the zither, their favourite instrument. At my request they recounted old legends about the mountains, and recited the prayers which they utter together before descending into the dark shaft; and many a good prayer did I pray with them. An old deputy even suggested that I should stay with them and become a miner; and when I took my leave, he gave me a message for his brother, who lives near Goslar, and asked me to deliver many kisses to his dear niece.

Although the life these people lead may appear calm and immobile, it is none the less a genuine, living life. The ancient, tremulous woman who was sitting behind the stove opposite the big cupboard may have sat there for a quarter of a century, and her thoughts and feelings are closely interwoven with every corner of the stove and every carving on the cupboard. And the stove and cupboard are alive, for part of a human soul has entered into them.

Only such a deep contemplative life, such direct empathy, could have given rise to the German fairy-tale, which is characterized by the presence not only of animals and plants, but even of supposedly inanimate objects as speakers and actors. It was to meditative, inoffensive people, in the quiet seclusion of their lowly cottages amid the mountains and forests, that the inner life of such objects was revealed. Hence these people necessarily acquired the appropriate character, a pleasing mixture of imaginative whimsy and pure humanity; and so their fairy-tales present us with wondrous events in a perfectly matter-of-fact way. A needle and a pin leave the tailors' hostel and lose their way in the dark; a piece of straw and a lump of coal try to cross the river and are drowned; a shovel and a broom, standing on the staircase, quarrel and come to blows; the mirror, in reply to a question, shows the image of the fairest woman of them all; even drops of blood begin to speak, uttering dark and fearful words of concern and compassion.

It is for the same reason that during childhood our lives are so full of significance. At that time all things are equally important to us: we hear everything, we see everything, and all our impressions carry equal weight; but later we become more purposeful, attend more exclusively to single things, exchange the pure gold of contemplation for the hard-earned paper currency of book-definitions, and gain in breadth what we lose in depth. Now we are grand, grown-up people;

we keep moving house, and the maidservant tidies up every day, altering the position of the furniture just as she sees fit; and our furnishings are of little interest to us, for either they are new, or else they are Hans's today and Isaac's tomorrow. Even our clothes are alien to us: we scarcely know how many buttons there are on the coat we are wearing at this moment; we change our garments so often that none of them retains any connection with the history of our minds and our bodies. We can barely remember the appearance of that brown waistcoat that once made us a laughing-stock, even though the dear hand of our beloved once rested so sweetly on its broad stripes!

The old woman sitting opposite the big cupboard, behind the stove, was wearing a flowered skirt of some long-disused material, which had been the bridal dress of her late mother. Her great-grandson, a fair-haired boy with flashing eyes, dressed as a miner, was sitting at her feet and counting the flowers on her skirt, and she has doubtless told him many tales about this skirt, serious and charming tales, which the boy will not forget in a hurry; they will cross his mind when he is a grown man and is working alone at night in the tunnels of the Carolina, and he may tell them again long after his dear great-grandmother's death, when he himself, an ancient, silver-haired man, is sitting surrounded by his grandchildren, opposite the big cupboard, behind the stove.

I stayed the night in the Crown. During the day Aulic Counsellor B.[20] had arrived there from Göttingen, and I had the pleasure of paying my respects to the old gentleman. When I had written my name in the visitors' book and was leafing through the pages for the month of July, I found the precious name of Adalbert von Chamisso,[21] the biographer of the immortal Schlemihl. The landlord told me that this gentleman had arrived in indescribably bad weather and had left again in equally bad weather.

The following morning I had to lighten my knapsack again by throwing overboard the pair of boots that I had packed, and I lifted my feet and went to Goslar. How I got there I cannot tell. All I remember is that I sauntered up hill and down dale, and gazed into many a verdant valley; the silver waters rippled, the birds twittered in the woods, the cow-bells tinkled, the golden rays of the dear sun shone on green trees of every kind, and the blue silk covering of the sky overhead was so transparent that one could look right through into the holy of holies, where the angels sit at the feet of God and learn the *basso continuo* from studying his face. But I was still wrapped up in the dream I had had that night, which I could not banish from my soul. It was the old fairy-tale in which a knight descends into a deep well where the most beautiful of princesses is lying in an enchanted sleep. I was myself the knight, and the well was the dark pit of Klausthal, and suddenly there appeared a great many lights; the watchful dwarfs rushed from holes on every side, grimaced with anger, slashed at me with their short swords, and blew such piercing blasts on their horns that more and more of them hastened to the scene, wagging their broad heads in a terrifying fashion. Only when I struck them and drew blood did I realize that they were the thistles, with red blossoms and long beards, whose heads I had knocked off with my stick as I was walking along the highway the day before. Once they had all been driven away, I came to a magnificent and brightly lit hall; in its midst, wearing a white veil and as motionless as a statue, stood the beloved of my heart, and I kissed her lips, and, by the living God! I felt with rapture the breath of her soul and the sweet trembling of her lovely lips. It was as though I heard God calling: 'Let there be light!' A dazzling ray of the everlasting light darted down; but at that same moment night again fell, and everything dissolved into the chaos of a vast, turbulent sea. A vast, turbulent sea! The ghosts of the departed flew in terror over the foaming waters, their white shrouds fluttering in the wind; in pursuit, cracking his whip, came a harlequin in a motley costume, and that was me – and suddenly the monsters of the deep thrust forth their misshapen heads from the dark waves, and stretched out their claws to seize me, and my terror woke me.

How the most delightful fairy-tales can sometimes be spoilt! The knight who finds the sleeping princess is supposed to cut out a piece of her precious veil; and when his bold deeds have roused her from her magic sleep, and she is once more seated on the golden throne in her palace, the knight is supposed to walk up to her and say: 'Fairest of princesses, do you recognize me?' And she replies: 'Bravest of knights, I do not recognize you.' And then he shows her the piece cut out of her veil, which fits exactly, and the two of them embrace tenderly, and the trumpets blow, and they celebrate their wedding.

It is really a peculiar misfortune that my dreams of love seldom come to such a beautiful end.

The town of Goslar has such a pleasing name, and has so many ancient imperial associations attached to it, that I expected it to be a stately and majestic place. But this is what always happens when you look closely at a famous object! It turned out to be a miserable hole with a labyrinth of crooked streets, mostly narrow, through which flows a rivulet, presumably the Gose; the whole place was fusty and decayed, and the paving was as rough as Berlin hexameters. Only the antiquities round its edge – remnants of walls, towers, and battlements – lend the town some character. One of these towers, known as the Keep, has walls so thick that chambers have been carved out in them. The area outside the town where the famous assembly of marksmen is held is a fine large meadow from which the mountains can be seen all around. The market-place is small and has a fountain in its centre whose waters pour into a great metal basin. When fires break out, people strike the basin, which gives off a resounding clang. Nobody knows where the basin came from. Some say the Devil put it in the market-place one night. In those days people were stupid, and so was the Devil, and they gave each other presents.

The town-hall at Goslar is a guard-room painted white. The guild-hall beside it has a better appearance. About midway between the ground and the roof stand statues of German emperors, blackened by smoke but with some gilding left; they hold a sceptre in one hand and the globe in the other, and look like roasted proctors. One of the emperors holds a sword instead of a sceptre. I could not work out what this distinction meant; yet it must have some meaning, since the Germans have the curious habit of never doing anything without thinking about it.

I had read a great deal in Gottschalk's *Handbook* about the ancient cathedral and the famous imperial throne at Goslar. When I wanted to inspect them, however, I was told that the cathedral had been demolished and the throne removed to Berlin. We live in portentous times: cathedrals a thousand years old are torn down, and imperial thrones are consigned to the lumber-room.

Some curios from the late lamented cathedral are now displayed in St Stephen's Church. There is some very beautiful stained glass, as well as some bad paintings, one of which is said to be by Lukas Cranach; also a wooden crucifix and a pagan sacrificial altar made of some unknown metal. The altar is shaped like a long rectangular drawer and is borne by four crouching caryatids who hold their hands above their heads and grimace unpleasantly. Still more unpleasant, though, is the large wooden crucifix, mentioned earlier, which stands nearby. The head of this Christ, with real hair and thorns and a face smeared with blood, is a masterly representation of the death agony of a man, but not that of a divine saviour. Physical suffering alone has been carved into this face, not the poetry of pain. Such a picture would be more suitable for an anatomy lecture than for the house of God.

I lodged in an inn near the market-place, where I would have enjoyed my lunch more if I had not been joined by the landlord with his long superfluous face and his tedious questions. Fortunately I was soon relieved by the arrival of another traveller, who had to undergo the same catechism: 'Who? What? Where? How? Why? When?' This stranger was an old, weary, worn-out man, who, to judge from his remarks, had roamed all over the world, lived for a long time in the Dutch East Indies, acquired a large fortune and lost it all, and was now returning to Quedlinburg, his home town, after thirty years' absence; 'for,' he added, 'our family vault is there.' The landlord made the enlightened observation that where the body is buried can be of no concern to the soul. 'Have you got that in writing?' replied the stranger, looking so sly that sinister wrinkles formed around his meagre lips and colourless eyes. 'But,' he added, evidently anxious to reassure us, 'let me say nothing against other people's graves. The Turks bury their dead in much more attractive places than we do; their churchyards are proper gardens, where they sit in their turbans on the white gravestones, in the shadow of a cypress, gravely stroking their beards, and calmly smoking their Turkish tobacco in their long Turkish pipes; and as for the Chinese, it is a real pleasure to see them tripping daintily across the resting-places of their loved ones, where they pray, and drink tea, and play the fiddle, and adorn the graves very prettily with gilded palings, porcelain figures, scraps of brightly coloured silk, artificial flowers, and coloured lanterns – all very pretty – how far is it to Quedlinburg?'

The churchyard in Goslar did not much appeal to me. Hence I was all the more taken by the beautiful curly-haired girl who was smiling out of a rather high ground-floor window as I arrived in the town. After dinner I sought the dear window again; but all it contained was a glass of water with white bell-flowers. I climbed up, took the dainty flowers out of the glass, and calmly stuck them on my cap, paying small heed to the gaping mouths, petrified noses and goggling eyes with which the people on the street, especially the old women, watched this qualified act of theft. As I passed the same house an hour later, the fair one was standing at the window, and on noticing the bell-flowers on my cap she blushed bright red and turned hastily away. I had taken a more careful look at her beautiful face: it was a sweet, transparent incarnation of the summer evening's breeze, the moonlight, the nightingale's song, and the rose's fragrance. – Later, when darkness had fallen, she stepped out of the door. I came – I approached – she withdrew slowly into the dark hallway – I took her by the hand and said: 'I am a lover of flowers and kisses, and if anything is not given me freely, I steal it!' – and I kissed her quickly – and as she was about to flee, I whispered reassuringly: 'I'm leaving tomorrow and will probably never return' – and I felt the furtive answering pressure of her charming lips and her delicate hands – and I hastened away, laughing. Yes, I cannot help laughing when I recall that I had unwittingly spoken the magic words with which our redcoats and bluecoats conquer women's hearts more often than with their moustached amiability: 'I'm leaving tomorrow and will probably never return!'

My lodgings had a splendid view of the Rammelsberg. It was a fine evening. Night was galloping on her black horse, its long mane fluttering in the wind. I stood at the window and contemplated the moon. Is there really a man in the moon? The Slavs say that his name is Clotar, and that he makes the moon grow by pouring water on it. When I was small, I heard that the moon was a fruit which, when it was ripe, was plucked by God and placed with the other full moons in the great cupboard far away, where the world is closed by having planks nailed across it. As I grew bigger, I noticed that the world was not so closely bounded, and that the human mind had broken through the wooden barriers and unlocked all seven heavens with a huge key of St Peter – the idea of immortality. Immortality! Beautiful idea! Who was the first to think of you? Was it an honest citizen of Nuremberg, sitting outside his front door one mild summer evening with a white night-cap on his head and a white clay pipe in his mouth, thinking comfortably how nice it would be if his pipe and his vital spark (such as it was) never went out and he could go on vegetating in all eternity? Or was it a young lover who thought up the idea of immortality in his sweetheart's arms, and thought it because he felt it, and because he could think and feel in no other way? – Love! Immortality! – my breast suddenly grew so hot that I thought the geographers had misplaced the equator and it was now running straight through my heart. And feelings of love flowed from my heart, flowed yearningly into the distant night. The flowers in the garden beneath my window emitted a stronger fragrance. Fragrances are the flowers' feelings, and just as the human heart feels more strongly at night, when it thinks itself alone and unobserved, so the clever and modest flowers, too, seem to wait for the cover of darkness before surrendering to their feelings, which they breathe out in sweet fragrances. – Flow forth, fragrance of my heart! and seek beyond those mountains for the beloved of my dreams! She is already lying asleep; angels are kneeling at her feet, and when she smiles in her sleep, it is a prayer which the angels pray after her; heaven lies in her bosom with all its raptures, and when she breathes, my heart trembles far away; the sun has set behind her silken eyelashes, and when she opens her eyes again, it is day, and the birds are singing, and the cow-bells are ringing, and the mountains are gleaming in their emerald garments, and I tie up my knapsack and set off.

During the night I spent in Goslar, something extremely strange happened to me. Even now I cannot recall it without a shudder. I am not timorous by nature, but I am almost as afraid of ghosts as the *Austrian Observer*.[22] What is fear? Does it proceed from the intellect or from the heart? I used to argue about this question so often with Dr Saul Ascher[23] whenever we ran into each other in the Café Royal in Berlin, where for a long time I was in the habit of lunching. He always maintained that we fear something because we recognize it as fearsome through rational inferences, and that only the reason had any power; the heart had none. While I ate well and drank well, he kept demonstrating to me the advantages of reason. Towards the end of his demonstration he would often glance at his watch, and he always concluded with the words: 'Reason is the supreme principle!' – Reason! Whenever I hear this word now, I still see Dr Saul Ascher with his abstract legs, his tight-fitting surtout of transcendental grey, and his rugged, chilly face, which could have served as an engraving in a geometry textbook. This man, in his late fifties, was a personified straight line. In striving after the positive, the poor man had argued away all life's splendour, all the sunbeams, all the faith and all the flowers, leaving nothing but the cold, positive grave. The Belvedere Apollo and Christianity were the objects of his particular ill-will. He even wrote a pamphlet against the latter, proving that it was irrational and untenable. Indeed, he wrote a vast number of books, in which reason was always bragging of its own excellence; the poor Doctor's intentions were perfectly serious, and, as far as that goes, deserved full credit. But the best part of the joke was that he put on such a serious and silly expression when he could not understand something that every child understands, precisely because it is a child. Now and again I visited this rational doctor in his home, where I found him in the company of pretty girls; for reason does not forbid sensuality. One day, when I wanted to pay him another such visit, his servant told me: 'The Doctor has just died.' I felt little more than if he had said: 'The Doctor has moved house.'

But to return to Goslar. 'Reason is the supreme principle!' I said to myself reassuringly as I got into bed. However, it did not help. In Varnhagen von Ense's *German Tales*,[24] which I had brought from Klausthal, I had just been reading the dreadful story about the son whose own father intended to murder him, and who received a warning at night from the ghost of his dead mother. The story was so marvellously told that it made deep horror send shivers down my spine as I was reading it. Besides, ghost-stories are even more blood-curdling if you are reading them on a journey, especially at night, in a town, in a house, in a room, where you have never been before. How many horrific events may already have taken place on the very spot where you are lying? – that is what you cannot help wondering. Moreover, the moon was now shining into the room so equivocally, all manner of uninvited shadows were moving on the wall, and as I sat up in bed to look more closely, I caught sight of –

There is nothing more uncanny than unexpectedly glimpsing one's own face by moonlight in a mirror. At the same moment a ponderous, yawning bell struck, so lengthily and so slowly that after the twelfth stroke I was convinced that twelve full hours had passed and it would have to start striking twelve all over again. Between the penultimate and the last strokes of the bell another clock struck, very quickly, with a piercing sound like the voice of a nagging woman; perhaps it was annoyed by its neighbour's slowness. When both iron tongues had fallen silent, and a deep, deathly stillness reigned throughout the house, I suddenly thought I heard something shuffling and shambling in the corridor outside my room, like the uncertain gait of an old man. At last my door opened, and the late Dr Saul Ascher slowly entered. A cold fever slid through my every limb, I trembled like an aspen leaf, and scarcely dared to look at the ghost. He looked just as he always did, the same transcendental grey surtout, the same abstract legs, and the same mathematical face; but the latter was somewhat yellower than before, and his lips, which had previously formed two angles of $22\frac{1}{2}$ degrees, were pressed together, and the hollows of his eyes had a greater radius. Swaying, and leaning on his rattan cane as in the past, he approached me and said amiably in his usual slurred dialect: 'Don't be afraid, and don't imagine I'm a ghost. It's an illusion of your imagination if you think you're seeing my ghost. What is a ghost? Give me a definition. Deduce for me the conditions under which a ghost is possible. What rational connection would such an apparition have with reason? Reason, I say reason –' And now the ghost proceeded to an analysis of reason, quoted Kant's *Critique of Pure Reason*, Part 2, Division 1, Book 2, Chapter 3, on the distinction between phenomena and noumena, then constructed the problematic belief in ghosts, placed one syllogism upon another, and concluded with the logical proof that there are absolutely no such things as ghosts. Meanwhile cold perspiration was running down my back, my teeth were chattering like castanets, my mortal terror made me nod in unqualified agreement with every sentence in which the disembodied doctor proved the absurdity of being afraid of ghosts, demonstrating this so energetically that at one point he absentmindedly pulled a handful of worms out of his fob instead of his gold watch, and, on perceiving his error, thrust them back with comically anxious haste. 'Reason is the supreme –' – then the clock struck one and the ghost vanished.

From Goslar I continued my journey the following day, partly at random, partly aiming to visit the brother of the miner in Klausthal. Beautiful, charming Sunday weather once more. I ascended hills and mountains, watched the sun trying to dispel the mists, wandered cheerfully through the shivering woods, and the bell-flowers of Goslar tinkled around my dreaming head. The mountains were wearing their white nightdresses, the fir-trees were shaking sleep from their limbs, the fresh morning breeze was combing their long green hair, the birds were at prayer, the meadows in the valley gleamed like cloth of gold studded with diamonds, and the herdsman marched across it to the sound of cow-bells. In fact I had probably got lost. You keep taking side-roads and footpaths, thinking these will bring you nearer to your goal; the Harz mountains are like life in general. But there are always kind souls who lead us back to the right path; they are glad to do it, and it gives them additional pleasure if they can inform us with a self-satisfied countenance and a loud, benevolent voice how far we went out of our way, what chasms and marshes might have swallowed us up, and how fortunate it is that we met such expert guides as themselves in the nick of time. Near the Harzburg I found someone who set me right in this way. He was a well-fed citizen of Goslar with a shining, paunchy, stupidly artful face; he looked as if he had invented cattle disease. We walked together for some distance, and he told me all manner of ghost-stories which could have been very enjoyable, except that they all ended with the discovery that it wasn't a real ghost, that the white figure was that of a poacher, and that the whimpering voices came from the newly-born young of a wild sow, and the noise on the floor from the pet cat. 'It's only when people are ill,' he added, 'that they think they see ghosts; but as for me, if you'll pardon my mentioning myself, I'm hardly ever ill, except that sometimes my skin comes out in a rash, and then I always cure myself with spittle.' He also drew my attention to the practical and useful qualities of nature. Trees are green because green is good for the eyes. I agreed with him, and added that God created cattle because beef soup builds up people's strength, that he created donkeys to provide people with comparisons, and that man was created to eat beef soup and not be a donkey. My companion was delighted to find a kindred spirit, his countenance shone yet more joyously, and he was deeply moved at our parting.

As long as he was at my side, all of nature seemed robbed of its magic, but as soon as he was gone the trees again started to speak, and the sunbeams rang and the flowers danced on the meadow, and the blue sky embraced the green earth. Yes, I know better; God created man so that he might admire the splendour of the world. Every author, be he never so great, wants his work to be praised. And in the Bible, God's memoirs, it is said in so many words that he created man to glorify him and praise his works.

After wandering to and fro for a long time I found my way to the home of the brother of my friend from Klausthal, spent the night there, and had an experience which produced the beautiful poem that follows:

I

On the hillside stands the cottage
Of the miner wise and old;
There the tall green fir-tree whispers,
And the moon shines bright as gold.

In the cottage stands an armchair,
Richly carved and wondrously,
On it sits a happy man,
And that happy man am I!

On the stool the young girl sits,
In my lap her arms repose;
Her eyes are like two blue stars,
Her lips are like a crimson rose.

And the two blue, precious stars
Gaze at me, so large and close,
And she lays her lily finger
Smiling on the crimson rose.

No, her mother isn't looking,
Busy at her spinning-wheel,
And her father's playing his zither,
Singing an old melody.

And the young girl whispers softly,
Soft and gentle as can be;
Many's the important secret
She's already told to me.

'But we can't go any longer,
Now that granny's dead and gone,
To the marksmen's fair at Goslar
Where we used to have such fun.

Here, however, it's so lonely,
On the mountain's chilly brow,
And in winter we are buried
In the heavy falls of snow.

And I'm such a timid girl,
And I've such a childish fright
Of the wicked mountain spirits,
Who do their evil work at night.'

Suddenly the girl falls silent –
Did those words make terror rise? –
And with both her little hands
She conceals her precious eyes.

Louder now the fir-tree whispers,
And the spinning-wheel is groaning,
And the zither sounds as well,
And we hear its tune intoning:

'Never fear, my dearest child,
Let the evil spirits play;
At your side, my dearest child,
Angels guard you night and day!'

II

Fir-tree with its fingers green
Taps the casement small and tight,
And the moon, the yellow spy,
Lights us with its gentle light.

Father, mother in their chamber
Gently snore in slumber deep,
But the two of us are talking,
Never want to fall asleep.

'Though you say you've often prayed,
To believe you I don't dare;
For that twitching of your lips
Surely doesn't come from prayer.

Yes, that cold and wicked twitching
Never fails to frighten me,
But my fears and doubts are calmed
When your pious eyes I see.

And I don't think you have faith,
Not the faith that we inherit;
Do you believe in God the Father,
God the Son and Holy Spirit?'

'Even as a little boy,
Cradled in my mother's arms,
I believed in God the Father,
Who preserves the world from harm;

He who made our comely earth,
And the comely human race,
He who gave sun, moon and stars
Each its true and destined place.

When I was a little older,
Then my thoughts could further run,
And I reached the age of reason,
And believed too in the Son;

In the dear and loving Son,
With his loving benediction,
Which was met, as often happens,
By the cruel crucifixion.

Now that I have read and travelled
I can truly judge of merit,
And with all my swelling heart
I believe in the Holy Spirit.

He performed the greatest wonders;
Greater wonders yet remain:
For he broke the tyrant's castle,
Broke the bondsman's heavy chain.

He can heal wounds old and deadly,
And restore old liberty;
All mankind are born as equals,
All are noble, all are free.

He dispels the mists of evil,
Drives dark fantasies away
That have spoiled our love and pleasure,
Leering at us night and day.

The Holy Spirit has selected
A thousand knights to do his will;
He has filled their souls with courage,
Armed them well with strength and skill.

How their precious swords are gleaming,
How their noble banners wave!
I dare say, my child, you'd like to
See a knight so proud and brave?

Well then, look at me, my child,
Kiss me hard and look your fill;
I myself am such a knight,
I do the Holy Spirit's will.'

III

Quietly the moon is hiding
There behind the fir-tree green,
In the room our candle flickers,
Scarce an object can be seen.

But my two blue, precious stars
Shine with brightness clear and pure,
And the crimson rose is blazing,
And she speaks in tones demure:

'Little people, little brownies,
Steal from us our bread and bacon;
Though at night it's in the larder,
In the morning it's been taken.

Little people sip the cream
From the milk, they like that best;
Leave the dish without its lid,
And the kitten drinks the rest.

And the kitten is a witch,
And upon the witching hour
Creeps off to the haunted mountain,
To the ancient ruined tower.

That was once a lofty castle,
Full of joy and weapons bright;
Knights in armour, squires and ladies
Danced in torches' flickering light.

Then a sorceress bewitched them,
Castle, knights, and all the rest;
Only ruins now are standing,
Where the screech-owl makes her nest.

But my granny used to say:
If you speak the word of power,
Standing at the proper spot,
At the true and witching hour:

Then the ruins will be changed
To the castle fair and bright,
Knights and squires and ladies fair
Dancing in the torches' light.

And whoever speaks that word
Owns the castle old in story;
Drums and trumpets then will pay
Homage to his youthful glory.'

Thus the fairy-stories flower
From her rosy lips so fair,
And above, her eyes pour out
Their blue starlight rich and rare.

Now she twines her golden hair
Round my hands, like precious twill,
Calls my fingers pretty names,
Laughs and kisses; then she's still.

All things in the quiet room
Look at me like friends of yore;
And the table, and the cupboard,
Did I see them long before?

Now I hear the cheerful chatter
Of the clock; the zither seems
Quietly to play itself,
And I sit there lost in dreams.

This is now the proper place,
And the true and witching hour;
Don't you think that my bold lips
Will pronounce the word of power?

Look, my child, the midnight's gloom
All around us now is quaking,
Louder whisper stream and fir-trees,
And the mountain's slowly waking.

The zither's notes, the goblins' songs
Are sounding from the mountain cave,
Like a madcap spring, there blossoms
An array of flowers brave;

Flowers, bold and magical,
With broad leaves of foreign fashion;
Fragrant, stirring, many-coloured,
Like embodiments of passion.

Roses red like furious flames,
Scatter petals from the throng;
Lilies, high as crystal columns,
Rise to meet the sky ere long.

And the stars, as big as suns,
Gaze below with ardent yearning;
In the lilies' giant petals
You can see their radiance burning.

But the two of us, sweet child,
Suffer changes more amazing;
Gold and silk and light of torches
Shine around us two embracing.

You have turned into a princess,
And this hut's a castle rare;
All around us are rejoicing
Knights and squires and ladies fair.

I, however – I have you,
And the castle old in story;
Drums and trumpets now are paying
Homage to my youthful glory!

The sun rose. The mists fled, as ghosts do when the cock crows for the third time. I continued on my way up hill and down dale, and before me floated the beautiful sun, always casting its light on new beauties. The spirit of the mountains was obviously well disposed towards me; he must have known that a poet like me can tell many pretty tales, and this morning he showed me his Harz as not many people have seen it. But the Harz saw me, too, as only a few people have seen me; pearls were glittering in my eyelashes, as precious as those in the grass of the valley. My cheeks were wet with the dew of love, the rustling fir-trees understood me, their twigs parted and moved up and down like dumb people who convey their joy with their hands, and from the distance came a wondrous, mysterious tinkling, like the bells of a church lost in the forest. They say these are the cow-bells, which in the Harz have such a clear, pure and delightful tone.

It was noon, judging from the position of the sun, when I came upon one of those herds of cattle, and the herdsman, a friendly, fair-haired young man, told me that the mountain at whose foot I was standing was the old Brocken, famous throughout the world. For many hours' walk all around there is not a single house, and I was glad that the young man asked me to share his lunch. We sat down to a *déjeuner dînatoire* consisting of bread and cheese; the lambs picked up the crumbs, the heifers with their gleaming hides gambolled around us, ringing their bells mischievously, and laughing at us with their large, contented eyes. We feasted royally; indeed my host seemed to me to be a true king, and since he is the only king who has given me bread so far, I shall sing about him in royal fashion.

Yes, the herdsman is a king,
With a green hill for his throne;
And the sun above his head
Is his heavy golden crown.

Flattering courtiers are his sheep,
Decorated all in red;
And his cavaliers are calves,
Strutting with conceited tread.

The goats are his court theatre,
And the cattle and the birds,
With their little bells and flutes,
Are his chamber orchestra.

And so pleasant is their singing,
And such pleasant murmuring keep
Waterfall and faithful fir-trees,
That the king drops off to sleep.

Then his kingdom must be governed
By his minister, the dog,
Who by barking and by growling
Scares away each passing rogue.

In his sleep the young king mutters:
'Governing has always been
Very tiring – how I wish
I were home, beside my queen!

In her arms my head rests softly,
And within the loving eyes
Of my dear, my precious consort,
There my boundless kingdom lies!'

We parted on friendly terms, and I climbed the mountain cheerfully. Soon I was received by a spinney of lofty firs, for which I have all possible respect. These trees, you see, have not found growing altogether easy, and in their youth they had a hard time of it. This part of the mountain is strewn with large granite boulders, and most of the trees had to creep round these rocks with their roots, or force them out of the ground, and seek laboriously for the soil from which to draw nourishment. Here and there the rocks lie on top of one another, forming a kind of gateway, and the trees stand on top of them, stretching their naked roots over the stone gate, and reaching the soil only at its foot, so that they seem to be growing in mid-air. And yet they have risen to that lofty height, and, as though they had become one with the stones they clasp, they are more firmly rooted than their easygoing fellows in the soft forest soil of the lowlands. That is also, in life, the stance of those great men who have gained strength and secured their position by overcoming early obstacles and impediments. Squirrels were climbing on the branches of the fir-trees, and the fallow deer were strolling beneath them. When I see such a dear and noble animal, I cannot understand how cultivated people can take pleasure in harrying and killing it. One of these animals had more compassion than human beings, and suckled Sorrowful, the starving son of St Genevieve.[25]

It was delightful to see the golden sunbeams darting through the dense greenery of the firs. The roots of the trees formed a natural staircase. Swelling mossy banks were everywhere; for the rocks are covered almost ankle deep by the most beautiful species of moss, as if upholstered in bright green velvet. Pleasant coolness and the dreamy murmuring of the springs. Here and there you see the silver gleam of water trickling from under the stones and splashing the bare roots and fibres of the trees. If you bend down to look more closely at what is going on, you seem to be eavesdropping on the secret history of the plants' growth and the quiet heartbeat of the mountain. In many places the water gushes from the stones and roots, forming small cascades. These are pleasant places to sit. There is such a wonderful murmuring and babbling, the birds sing fragmentary sounds of yearning, the trees whisper like a thousand girls' tongues, the strange mountain flowers gaze at us like a thousand girls' eyes, stretching out to us their wondrous broad leaves with their comical serrations, the merry sunbeams flash playfully to and fro, the wise herbs tell one another green fairy-tales, everything seems enchanted, the sense of cosy seclusion grows ever stronger, an ancient dream comes to life, the beloved appears – but alas, she soon disappears again!

As you climb further up the mountain, the fir-trees become shorter and more stunted; they seem to be gradually shrivelling up, until only bilberry bushes and mountain plants remain. It also becomes perceptibly colder. Here the curious groups of granite boulders become prominent; they are often of an astonishing size. No doubt they are the balls which the evil spirits toss to one another on St Walpurga's Night, when the witches come riding up on broom-handles and pitchforks, and their weird and wicked pleasures begin, as the credulous old nurse recounts, and as may be seen in Retzsch's charming illustrations to

Faust. Indeed, a young poet on his way from Berlin to Göttingen, who rode past the Brocken on the night before the first of May, even saw some literary ladies holding their aesthetic tea-party in a nook of the mountain, convivially reading the *Evening News*[26] aloud, lauding their poetic billy-goats, who were prancing and bleating around the tea-table, as universal geniuses, and passing their definitive judgements on all phenomena of German literature; but when they got on to the subject of *Ratcliff* and *Almansor*, and described the author as devoid of piety and Christianity, then the young man's hair rose on his scalp, terror seized hold of him – I put spurs to my horse and galloped away.

Indeed, when you ascend the upper half of the Brocken, you cannot prevent yourself from recalling the delightful tales of the Blocksberg, and especially the great, mystical, German national tragedy of Dr Faustus. I kept thinking I could hear the cloven hoof climbing at my side, and someone humorously puffing and panting. And I am sure even Mephisto must gasp for breath when he ascends his favourite mountain; it is an extremely exhausting climb, and I was glad when at last I caught sight of the yearned-for Brocken House.

This house, which, as many pictures have shown, consists only of a single storey and stands on the summit of the mountain, was built in 1800 by Count Stolberg-Wernigerode, for whom it is managed as an inn. The walls are astonishingly thick, because of the winds and the cold in winter; the roof is low, with a look-out point resembling a tower in the middle, and next to the house there are two small outhouses, the first of which formerly provided shelter for visitors to the Brocken.

On entering the Brocken House I had an unusual sensation, as though I were stepping into a fairy-tale. After long scrambling among fir-trees and rocks, you suddenly find yourself in a house among the clouds; towns, hills, and forests remain below, and on the summit you find a motley gathering of strangers, who receive you, as is natural at such places, almost as though they had been expecting you, with a mixture of curiosity and indifference. I found the house full of visitors, and, as a wise man should, I was already thinking about how to spend the night, and the discomfort of a straw bed; in a faint voice I promptly asked for tea, and the landlord of the Brocken had sense enough to realize that somebody as poorly as I must have a proper bed for the night. This he provided for me in a tiny room where a young merchant, a long emetic in a brown coat, had already ensconced himself.

In the inn parlour all was life and motion. Students from various universities were there. Some had just arrived and were refreshing themselves, others were preparing to set off, tying up their knapsacks, writing their names in the visitors' book, and receiving bunches of flowers from the maidservants; cheeks were pinched, songs were sung, with leaping and shouting, questions and answers, good weather, good walking, cheers, cheerio. Some of those leaving were pretty drunk, and they could enjoy the fine view twice over, since a drunk man sees everything double.

Once my strength was more or less restored, I ascended the look-out point, where I found a diminutive gentleman with two ladies, a young one and an elderly one. The young lady was very beautiful. She had a magnificent figure, and, on her curly head, a black satin hat resembling a helmet, with whose white plumes the breezes were playing; her slender limbs were so tightly encased in a black silk coat that their noble forms were clearly discernible, and with great free eyes she was gazing calmly down into the great free world.

When I was still a boy I had nothing in my head but tales of magic and miracles, and I took every beautiful lady with ostrich plumes on her head for an elf-queen, and if I noticed that the train of her dress was wet I took her for a water-nixie. Now I think differently, since I know from natural history that those symbolic feathers come from the stupidest of birds, and that the train of a lady's dress can get wet by perfectly natural means. If I had seen this beautiful young lady in the above-mentioned posture on the Brocken with my boyish vision, I would undoubtedly have thought that she was the mountain fairy and had just uttered the spell that made everything down below appear so wondrous. Indeed, the first time we look down from the Brocken everything appears wondrous in the extreme, our minds receive new impressions from all sides, and these diverse and even contradictory impressions combine in our souls to form a great emotion which we cannot yet disentangle or understand. If we succeed in analysing this emotion we can recognize the character of the mountain. Its character is entirely German, both in its weaknesses and its strengths.

The Brocken is a German. With German thoroughness it displays to us, in a sort of gigantic panorama, the many hundred towns, townships and villages, mostly to the north, and all the hills, forests, rivers, and plains for an infinite distance all round. But, for that very reason, the whole scene resembles a clearly drawn and distinctly coloured map; nowhere is the eye pleased by a beautiful landscape in the strict sense; just as our German compilers of reference works always want to present their entire material with honest precision and therefore never think of presenting individual details in an attractive manner. The mountain is also rather German in its calm, sensible, tolerant character, because it can take such a wide, clear survey of things. And when such a mountain opens its giant eyes, it may well see more than we dwarfs can, who scramble about on it with our foolish little eyes. Many people, indeed, claim that the Brocken is decidedly prosaic, and Claudius sang: 'The Blocksberg is a great big philistine!'[27] But that is an error. Its bald pate, which it sometimes covers with a cap of white cloud, does give it a somewhat philistine air; but, as with many other great Germans, this results from pure irony. It is notorious that the Brocken occasionally goes in for wild, fantastic revelry, e.g. on the first night in May. Then it throws its cloudy cap in the air with a jubilant yell, and, like the rest of us, goes crazy in a truly German and romantic manner.

I immediately tried to engage the beautiful lady in conversation: for one enjoys the beauties of nature all the more if one can give one's opinion of them on the spot. She was not witty, but attentive and thoughtful, with truly well-bred manners. I do not mean the usual stiff, negative good-breeding which knows exactly what not to do, but the much rarer free, positive good-breeding, which tells us exactly what to do and gives us the utmost social self-assurance along with a perfectly relaxed demeanour. To my own surprise, I displayed a great deal of geographical knowledge, told the fair inquirer the names of all the towns we could see, and sought and showed them to her on the map, which I spread out on the stone table in the middle of the look-out point, with a real lecturer's air. There were many towns I could not find, perhaps because I was searching more with my fingers than with my eyes; the latter were meanwhile finding their way around the face of the lovely lady, where they found more attractive regions than 'Schierke' and 'Elend'.[28] Her face was one of those that never charm, seldom delight, and always please. I like such faces, because their smiling brings peace to my stormy and suffering heart.

I could not work out the relationship between the ladies and the diminutive gentleman who was with them. He was a strange, skinny figure of a man. His small head was scantily covered with grey hair which stretched across his narrow forehead and down to his greenish dragonfly eyes; his bulbous nose projected for some distance, while his mouth and chin retreated timidly towards his ears. His little face seemed to consist of delicate yellowish clay which sculptors use for their first models; and when he pursed his narrow lips, thousands of tiny, fine, semicircular lines ran across his cheeks. The little man did not speak a word, but now and again, when the elder lady whispered some friendly remark to him, he smiled like a pug-dog with a cold.

The elder lady was the younger one's mother, and she too had extremely well-bred manners. Her eyes suggested an unhealthily emotional and melancholy disposition; round her lips lay severe piety, yet I fancied they had once been very beautiful, and had laughed a great deal, and had received and returned many kisses. Her face resembled a palimpsest where the half-erased verses of an ancient Greek love-poet peep from under the monastic black letters of a text by a Father of the Church. The two ladies and their companion had been to Italy this year, and told me all manner of delightful things about Rome, Florence, and Venice. The mother had much to say about Raphael's paintings in St Peter's; her daughter talked more about the opera in the Fenice Theatre.

As we were talking, dusk began to fall: the air grew still colder, the sun sank nearer the horizon, and the look-out point began filling up with students, apprentice craftsmen, and some honest citizens together with their spouses and daughters, all wanting to see the sunset. It is a sublime moment, which moves the soul to prayer. All stood in solemn silence for a good quarter of an hour, watching the lovely ball of fire gradually sinking in the west; our faces were illumined by the red light of evening, we automatically folded our hands; we seemed to be a silent congregation standing in the nave of a gigantic cathedral, while the priest raised aloft the body of the Lord, and Palestrina's immortal chorale flooded down from the organ.

While I stood thus lost in devotion, I heard someone next to me exclaiming: 'How beautiful nature is, by and large!' These words came from the fervent bosom of my room-mate, the young merchant. Thus restored to my workaday mood, I was now able to say many fine things about the sunset to the ladies, and to accompany them back to their room as calmly as though nothing had happened. They also permitted me to converse with them for another hour. Like the earth itself, our conversation revolved round the sun. The mother observed that the sun setting amid mist had looked like a red rose which the gallant sky had thrown into the outspread white bridal veil of its beloved earth. The daughter smiled and remarked that the more you saw of such natural phenomena, the less of an impression they made. Her mother corrected this erroneous opinion by citing a passage from Goethe's letters of travel, and asked me if I had read *Werther*? I think we also talked about Angora cats, Etruscan vases, Turkish shawls, macaroni, and Lord Byron, from whose poems the elder lady recited some passages about the sunset with charming lisps and sighs. Since the younger lady did not know English and wanted to read these poems, I recommended the translations by my beautiful and ingenious fellow-countrywoman Baroness Elise von Hohenhausen;[29] nor did I miss this opportunity to rant, as I always do with young ladies, against Byron's godlessness, lovelessness, cheerlessness, and heaven knows what else.

After this task I went for a walk on the Brocken; for it is never completely dark there. The mist was not thick, and I looked at the outlines of the two hills known as the Witches' Altar and the Devil's Pulpit. I fired my pistols, but there was no echo. Suddenly, however, I heard well-known voices, and felt myself being embraced and kissed. It was my fellow-countrymen, who had left Göttingen four days after me and were most astonished to run into me all alone on the Blocksberg. Stories were told, surprise expressed, appointments made, with laughter and memories – what a joyful encounter!

Dinner was served in the large room. A long table with two rows of hungry students. Normal university talk to begin with: duels, duels, and more duels. Most of the company came from Halle University, and so Halle was the main topic of conversation. Counsellor Schütz's[30] window-panes were exegetically illuminated. Then it was recounted how brilliant had been the last court held by the King of Cyprus, how he had chosen a natural son, arranged a marriage between a Princess of Liechtenstein and his left leg, and dismissed his official mistress, and that the entire Ministry had been deeply moved and shed the regulation tears. I hardly need explain that all this refers to beer-house titles in Halle. Next we talked about the two Chinamen who had displayed themselves in Berlin two years earlier and were now being trained in Halle as lecturers on Chinese aesthetics. This gave rise to joking. Suppose a German were to display himself for money in China? A poster for this purpose was devised, with a certificate from the mandarins Ching-Chang-Chung and Hi-Ha-Ho attesting that he was a genuine German, with a list of his tricks, consisting mainly of philosophizing, pipe-smoking, and patience, and ending with the remark that no dogs were allowed at twelve o'clock, the feeding-time, because dogs generally snatched the best morsels from under poor Germans' noses.

A young member of a patriotic society, who had just been in Berlin for purification, talked a lot about that city, but very one-sidedly. He had been to see Wisotzki[31] and the theatre, and misjudged both. 'The tongue of youth is quick to utter words . . .' etc.[32] He talked about lavish costumes, scandals involving actors and actresses, and so on. The young man did not know that in Berlin it is the appearance of things that counts, as the common expression 'put on a show' sufficiently indicates, and so this cult of appearances must flourish especially on the stage. The theatre management must therefore pay particular heed to the 'colour of the beard it is best to play in',[33] and to the accuracy of the costumes, which are sketched by accredited historians and sewn by academically qualified tailors. And this is necessary. For if Mary Queen of Scots wore an apron that belonged to the age of Queen Anne, the banker Christian Gumpel would quite rightly complain that the whole illusion was destroyed; and if Lord Burleigh had inadvertently put on Henry IV's trousers, then the good lady of Military Counsellor von Steinzopf, *née* Lilientau, would not take her eyes off this anachronism all evening. The management's minute attention to illusionistic detail extends, however, not only to aprons and trousers, but also to the people in them. Thus Othello is to be played in future by a genuine blackamoor, whom Professor Lichtenstein[34] has already engaged to come from Africa for this purpose; in *Hatred and Penitence*[35] Eulalia is to be played in future by a genuine female runaway, Peter by a genuine stupid boy, and the Unknown by a genuine unwitting cuckold; and there is no need to send to Africa for any of those.

If the above-mentioned young man had misunderstood the circumstances of the Berlin theatre, he was even more unaware that Spontini's Janissary opera,[36] with its drums, elephants, trumpets and tom-toms, is a heroic device for imbuing our effete nation with warlike energy, a device recommended with political shrewdness by Plato and Cicero. Least of all did the young man grasp the diplomatic significance of the ballet. I was at pains to point out that there is more political skill in

Hoguet's feet than in Buchholz's head,[37] that all his steps signify diplomatic negotiations, and that each of his movements has a reference to politics. For example, when he leans forward yearningly and spreads out his arms, he means our Cabinet; when he spins round a hundred times on one foot, without moving from the spot, he means the Federal Diet; when he minces about as though his feet were bound, he has the petty princes in mind; when he sways to and fro like a drunkard, he is signifying the European balance of power; when he bends and entwines his arms as though tying them in a knot, he is indicating a Congress; and finally, when he gradually rises on tiptoe, maintains this posture for a while, then suddenly breaks into the most frightful capers, he is representing our outsize friend in the East.[38] The scales fell from the young man's eyes, and he now realized why dancers receive more honours than great poets, why the ballet is an inexhaustible subject of conversation among the diplomatic corps, and why a beautiful dancer is often kept *privatim* by a minister, who doubtless labours day and night to win her for his special political system. By Apis! how great is the number of exoteric and how small the number of esoteric theatre-goers! The stupid populace stands gaping, admiring leaps and bounds, studying anatomy in Lemière's postures, applauding Röhnisch's *entrechats*,[39] and chattering about grace, harmony and thighs – and none of them notices that the dances are a code for the fate of the German fatherland.

While such talk flew to and fro, we kept utility in mind and did full justice to the large dishes which were honestly filled with meat, potatoes and so on. However, the food was bad. I mentioned this casually to my neighbour, but he replied most impolitely, in an accent from which I recognized a Swiss, that we Germans knew as little of true frugality as of true freedom. I shrugged my shoulders and remarked that the real time-servers and sweetmeat-makers everywhere were Swiss and deserved that name, and that the present heroes of Swiss freedom, who favoured the public with so much bold political talk, reminded me of cowards firing pistols at fairgrounds, astonishing all the children and peasants by their boldness, and yet remaining cowards.

The son of the Alps had undoubtedly meant no harm; 'he was a fat man and therefore a good man,' says Cervantes.[40] But my neighbour on the other side, who came from Greifswald,[41] was much offended by his remark; he declared that German energy and simplicity were not yet extinct, struck himself a resounding blow on the chest, and emptied an enormous glass of beer. The Swiss said: 'Now, now!' But the more soothingly he said this, the more the student from Greifswald warmed to his subject. This man dated from the days when lice had a good time and hairdressers were afraid of starving. He had long hair which hung over his shoulders, a knightly beaver cap, a black coat of old German cut, a dirty shirt that also performed the office of a waistcoat, and under it a medallion containing a lock of hair from the mane of Blücher's white horse.[42] He looked like a life-size reproduction of a fool. I like taking some exercise at dinner, and therefore let him draw me into a patriotic dispute. He was of the opinion that Germany should be divided into thirty-three districts or *Gauen*. I maintained, however, that it should be forty-eight, because one could then write a more methodical handbook on Germany, and it was necessary, after all, to make learning relevant to life. My friend from Greifswald was also a German bard, and confided in me that he was working on a national heroic poem, celebrating Hermann and his victory over the Romans. I gave him many useful hints for this epic. I pointed out that he could convey the log-roads and swamps of the Teutoburg Forest onomatopoeically by rough and watery verses, and that it would be a fine patriotic touch to make Varus and the other Romans talk nothing but nonsense. I hope this artistic device will enable him, like other Berlin poets, to achieve an overwhelming illusion.

Conversation at our table kept growing louder and more familiar, beer gave place to wine, punch-bowls steamed, we drank, swore brotherhood, and sang. 'The Father of our Country'[43] rang out, as did glorious songs by Wilhelm Müller, Rückert, Uhland and so on. Fine tunes by Methfessel. Best of all were the German words of our Arndt: 'The God who planted iron, He did not make us slaves!' And outside the wind howled as though the old mountain were joining in our singing, and a few unsteady friends even declared that he was joyfully shaking his bald head and thus moving our room to and fro. Bottles were emptied and heads were filled. One bawled another sang falsetto, a third recited from Müllner's *Guilt*,[44] a fourth spoke Latin, a fifth preached moderation, and a sixth got up on his chair and lectured: 'Gentlemen! The world is a cylinder, people are individual pins, seemingly scattered innocently on it; but the cylinder revolves, the pins strike one another and make a noise, some more than others; this produces a wondrous and complicated music, which is called world history. We shall therefore deal first with music, then with the world and finally with history, dividing the latter into positive and Spanish flies.' And so it went on with sense and nonsense.

A cheerful fellow from Mecklenburg, who had dipped his nose into his glass of punch and was sniffing the steam with a blissful smile, remarked that he felt as if he were standing in front of the theatre bar in Schwerin. Another held his wine-glass in front of his eyes like a telescope and seemed to be observing us attentively, while the red wine ran down his cheeks into his gaping mouth. The man from Greifswald was suddenly inspired to embrace me and exclaim jubilantly: 'Oh, if only you knew how I feel, I'm in love, I'm a happy man, she loves me too, and, God damn me, she's a cultivated girl, for she's got big breasts and wears a white dress and plays the piano!' But the Swiss was weeping, kissing my hand tenderly, and constantly whimpering: 'O Bäbeli! O Bäbeli!'

Amid these wild goings-on, where the plates were learning to dance and the glasses to fly, there were two youths sitting opposite me, pale and handsome as marble statues, one resembling Adonis, the other Apollo. The rosy glow which the wine had cast on their cheeks was barely visible. They were gazing at each other with infinite love, as though each could read the other's eyes, and their eyes were as radiant as though some drops of light had fallen from the dish of flaming love that a pious angel above bears from one star to the other. They were speaking softly, their voices trembling with yearning, and telling sad stories in a wondrous melancholy tone. 'Now Lore's dead too!' said one, sighing; and after a pause he told the story of a girl in Halle who was in love with a student. When the latter left Halle, she no longer spoke to anyone, ate little, wept day and night, and kept looking at the canary which her lover had once given her. 'The bird died, and soon after that Lore died too!' was the end of the story, and the two youths again fell silent, and sighed as though their hearts would burst asunder. At last the other spoke: 'My soul is sad! Come out with me into the dark night! I would feel the clouds' breath and the moon's beams. Companion of my sorrow! I love thee, thy words are like the sighing of the reeds, like gentle flowing streams; they echo in my bosom, but my soul is sad!'

The two youths now rose, one put his arm round the other's neck, and they left the room and its uproar. I followed them and saw them enter a dark room, where one of them opened a large wardrobe instead of a window. Both stood in front of it with arms outstretched in yearning, speaking alternately. 'Breezes of dim night!' cried the first, 'how refreshingly ye cool my cheeks! How delightfully ye play with my fluttering locks! I am standing on the mountain's cloud-capped pinnacle; beneath me lie the sleeping towns of man and the glittering blue waters. Hark! down in yon vale the fir-trees are whispering! Over yon hill the spirits of our forefathers pass in misty shapes. Oh, would that I might hunt with you, on the cloudy steed, through the stormy night, over the rolling sea, up to the stars! But alas! I am laden with sorrow and my soul is sad!'

The other youth had likewise stretched out his arms yearningly towards the wardrobe; tears gushed from his eyes, and he addressed a pair of yellow leather trousers, which he took for the moon, in melancholy tones: 'Fair art thou, daughter of the heavens! Gracious is the repose of thy countenance! Thou walkest in beauty! The stars follow thy blue paths in the east. At the sight of thee the clouds rejoice, and their gloomy shapes are lightened. Who in the heavens is like unto thee, child of night? In thy presence the stars are abashed, and turn away their sparkling green eyes. Whither dost thou flee from thy path, when thy countenance grows pale at morn? Hast thou halls like unto me?[45] Dost thou dwell in the shadow of sorrow? Are thy sisters fallen from the heavens? Are they no more, who once roved joyously with thee through the night? Yes, they are fallen, O fair light, and thou often hidest thy face to mourn them. But at last there will come a night when thou also hast vanished, leaving thy blue paths above. Then the stars will raise their green heads that were once abashed in thy presence; they will rejoice. But now thou art clad in thy radiant splendour and dost gaze down from heaven's gates. Rend asunder the clouds, O ye winds, that the child of night may shine forth, and the bosky mountains may gleam and the sea roll its foaming billows in the light!'

A well-known, not very slender friend, who had drunk more than he had eaten, although this evening he had as usual devoured a helping of beef that would have satiated six guardsmen and an innocent child – this friend came rushing past in high good humour, i.e. hog-whimpering, pushed the two elegiac friends somewhat roughly into the cupboard, went thundering to the front door, and kicked up a hideous din outside. The noise in the main room also kept growing more confused and muffled. The two youths in the wardrobe wailed and lamented that they were lying dashed to pieces at the foot of the mountain; the noble red wine was pouring from their throats, they were inundating each other with it, and one said to the other: 'Farewell! I feel myself bleeding to death. Why dost thou wake me, breeze of spring? Thou toy'st with me, saying: "I drop on thee the dew of heaven." But the time is at hand when I must fade, the gale is at hand that shall scatter my petals! Tomorrow the wanderer will come, who beheld me in my beauty; his eye will seek me all through the field, and will not find me.' But everything was drowned by the well-known bass voice outside the front door, which was yelling and cursing and blasphemously complaining that there was not a single street-light burning along the whole length of the dark Weender Street, and you couldn't even see whose windows you had smashed.

I can carry a lot – modesty forbids me to say how many bottles – and I reached my bedroom in fairly good condition. The young merchant was already in bed, wearing a chalk-white night-cap and a saffron-yellow flannel jacket for the sake of his health. He was not yet asleep, and tried to engage me in conversation. He was from Frankfurt on the Main, and therefore he immediately began talking about the Jews, who had lost all sense of beauty and nobility, and sold English goods 25 per cent below cost price. I took a fancy to pull his leg, and so I told him that I was a sleepwalker and must apologize in advance in case I should disturb his sleep. Hence the poor fellow never slept a wink all night, as he confessed to me the following day, since he was afraid that while sleepwalking I might do some damage with my pistols, which were lying beside my bed. In fact I fared little better than he did; I slept very badly. Wild, terrifying phantoms. Dante's *Inferno* arranged for piano. Finally I dreamt that I was watching the performance of a legal opera called *Falcidia*,[46] with a score by Gans, based on the law of inheritance, and music by Spontini. A mad dream. The Roman Forum was magnificently illuminated, Serv. Asinius Göschenus was seated on his chair as praetor, his toga wrapped proudly around him, uttering thunderous recitatives; Marcus Tullius Elversus, displaying all his feminine charm as *prima donna legataria*, sang the languishing bravura aria *Quicunque civis romanus*; trainee solicitors in brick-red make-up formed a roaring juvenile chorus; lecturers dressed as genii, in flesh-coloured tricots, danced an ante-Justinianic ballet and placed garlands of flowers on the Twelve Tables; amid thunder and lightning the offended spirit of Roman legislation arose from underground, followed by trombones, tom-toms, and a rain of fire, *cum omni causa*.

I was pulled out of this tumult by the landlord, who woke me so that I could see the sunrise. On the tower I found some people already waiting, rubbing their cold hands, while others, with sleep still in their eyes, were staggering up to join us. At last the quiet congregation of the previous evening was again assembled, and we watched in silence as the small crimson ball rose above the horizon, a wintry twilight spread, and the mountains seemed to float in a white surging sea, with only their peaks visible, so that we fancied we were standing on a small hill in the middle of a flooded plain from which only the occasional dry patch of soil emerged. In order to put down in words what I had seen and felt, I wrote the following poem:

Light is dawning in the east
As the sun begins to glimmer,
Far and wide the mountain peaks
In the misty ocean shimmer.

If I had seven-league boots,
Faster than the wind I'd whirl
Where beyond the mountain peaks
Lives my dear and precious girl.

Gently I would draw the curtains
From the lovely sleeper's bed,
Gently kiss her ruby lips,
Gently kiss her dreaming head.

Gently, gently I would whisper
In her little lily ear:
'Dream that we are lovers still,
And our love is always dear.'

Meanwhile, my yearning for breakfast was just as great, and after making some polite remarks to the ladies I hastened down to drink coffee in the warm parlour. Not before time; my stomach was as bare as St Stephen's Church in Goslar. But with the Arab beverage the heat of the Orient ran through all my limbs, I was enfolded by the scent of Eastern roses, I heard the sweet song of the bulbul, the students turned into camels, the maidservants, with their pyrotechnic eyes, became houris, the philistines' noses became minarets, and so forth.

However, the book that lay beside me was not the Koran. It contained plenty of nonsense, all the same. It was the Brocken visitors' book, in which all the travellers who climb the mountain write their names, and most of them add a few thoughts or, failing that, their feelings. Many even express themselves in verse. In this book you can see what horrors are produced when the great army of philistines takes advantage of such handy opportunities as the Brocken and resolves to be poetic. The Prince of Pallagonia's palace[47] does not contain such monstrosities as this book, where excisemen display their mouldy feelings of exaltation, office-boys their stagy outpourings of emotion, old German amateur revolutionaries their gymnastic platitudes, Berlin schoolmasters their ill-considered clichés of delight, and so on. Thomas, Richard and Henry want to show their literary talents for once. Here the majestic splendour of the sunrise is described; there are complaints about bad weather, unfulfilled expectations, and the mist that hides the view. 'Saw nothing coming up, saw double going down!' is a standing joke, repeated by hundreds. The whole book smells of cheese, beer, and tobacco; it is like reading a novel by Clauren.[48]

While I was drinking coffee and leafing through the visitors' book, as I have described, the Swiss came in with fiery red cheeks, and told me enthusiastically about the sublime spectacle he had enjoyed on the tower, as the pure, calm light of the sun, the symbol of truth, did battle with the nocturnal mists; he said it looked like a battle between spirits, where raging giants brandish their long swords, armoured knights gallop on rearing horses, chariots, fluttering banners, fantastic beasts emerge from the wild throng, till at last they all coil into the craziest grotesque shapes, turn paler and paler, and vanish without a trace. I had missed nature's display of demagogy, and if there is an inquiry I can affirm on oath that I know nothing about anything except the taste of the good black coffee. Alas, the latter was to blame for making me forget about my fair lady, and now she was standing outside the door, with her mother and their companion, about to climb into their carriage. I scarcely had time to hurry to her and assure her that the weather was cold. She seemed annoyed that I had not come earlier; but I soon wiped away the lines of displeasure from her fair brow by presenting her with a remarkable flower which the previous day I had risked life and limb to pluck from a steep rock face. Her mother wanted to know the name of the flower, as though she considered it unseemly for her daughter to pin a strange, unknown flower on her bosom – for the flower did indeed obtain this enviable position, which would certainly have been beyond its wildest dreams when still on yesterday's lonely height. The ladies' taciturn companion now suddenly opened his mouth, counted the flower's stamens and said drily: 'It belongs to the eighth class.'

It always annoys me to see that God's dear flowers have been divided into castes, just like ourselves, and according to similar external features like differing stamens. If there has to be classification, people should follow the suggestion made by Theophrastus,[49] who wanted to classify flowers in a more spiritual manner, that is, by scent. As for me, I have my own system of natural history, according to which I classify everything as eatable or uneatable.

However, the elder lady was far from insensitive to the mysterious nature of flowers, and she could not help declaring that she took great pleasure in flowers when they were still growing in the garden or in pots, but that her bosom trembled with slight pain, a sense of dream-like anxiety, when she saw a flower that had been picked – for such a flower was really a corpse, and the delicate corpse of a picked flower hung down its withered head so sadly, like a dead child. The lady was almost terrified by the dismal implications of her remark, and it was my duty to dispel them with some lines from Voltaire. How a few words of French can always return us immediately to the proper conventional tone! We laughed, hands were kissed, gracious smiles were given, the horses neighed, and the carriage jolted slowly and toilsomely down the mountain.

The students were also preparing to leave, tying up their knapsacks and settling their bills, which proved unexpectedly cheap; the responsive maidservants, their faces showing signs of happy love, brought us bunches of flowers, as is customary, helped us to fasten them to our caps, and were rewarded with a few kisses or small change; and so we all descended the mountain, some of us, like my acquaintances from Switzerland and Greifswald, taking the path to Schierke, while the others, twenty or so strong, including my fellow-countrymen and myself, led by a guide, headed towards Ilsenburg via what are known as the Snow-Holes.

It was a breakneck descent. Students from Halle march faster than the Austrian militia. Before I knew where I was, the bare region of the mountain with boulders scattered about on it was already behind us, and we were going through a wood of fir-trees such as I had seen the day before. The sun was already pouring down its festive rays to light the young men in their comically bright-coloured clothes as they forced their way cheerfully through thickets, disappearing here and reappearing there, running along the tree-trunks laid over swamps, holding on to tree-roots at the edge of precipices, raising their voices in joyous shouts, and receiving equally merry answers from the twittering birds, the rustling firs, the streams plashing out of sight, and the resounding echo. When light-hearted young people come in contact with beautiful nature, each takes pleasure in the other.

The further down we came, the more attractive was the murmuring of underground springs; only occasionally, amid rocks and bushes, could the gleam of water be seen, as though it were listening to know if it were safe to appear; finally a little wave sprang resolutely forth. Then the usual phenomenon could be seen: a bold spirit takes the first step, and the great train of timorous followers suddenly pluck up courage, to their own surprise, and hurry to join their leader. A host of springs tripped hastily from their hiding-places, uniting themselves with the first to appear, and soon they all formed a sizeable streamlet, murmuring down the valley in innumerable falls and curious windings. This is the Ilse, the sweet, charming Ilse. It flows through the blessed Ilse Valley, at either side of which the mountains gradually rise higher, and they are mostly covered, right down to the valley floor, with beeches, oaks and ordinary shrubs, instead of firs and other conifers. For the latter type of tree is found chiefly on the Lower Harz, as the east side of the Brocken is called, in contrast to its west side, which is known as the Upper Harz, and is indeed much higher and hence more suited to the growth of conifers.

It is impossible to describe how joyfully, freshly and delightfully the Ilse plunges over the strangely shaped rocks that it encounters in its course, so that at one spot the water fizzes up wildly or overflows in foam, while elsewhere it flows in pure curves from all manner of cracks in the rock, as though from mad watering-cans, and further down it trips lightly over the pebbles like a cheerful girl. Indeed, the story is true that the Ilse is a princess who runs down the mountain in the bloom of laughing youth. How her white foamy dress gleams in the sunshine! How her silver ribbons flutter in the wind! How her diamonds sparkle and flash! The lofty beech-trees stand beside her like grave fathers, watching the antics of the charming child with concealed smiles; the white birches sway in aunt-like pleasure, yet also alarmed by the child's daring leaps; the proud oak-tree watches like a surly uncle who will have to pay for the fine weather; the birds in the air applaud jubilantly, the flowers on the banks whisper tenderly: 'Oh, take us with you, take us with you, dear little sister!' – but nothing can delay the merry girl as she bounds on, and suddenly she seizes hold of the dreaming poet, and a flowery rain of ringing rays and radiant ringing comes streaming down upon me, and I faint with sheer splendour, and hear only her sweet voice fluting:

'I am the Princess Ilse,
And I live beneath the hill;
Come with me to my palace,
With joy your heart I'll fill.

There in my crystal waters
I'll bathe your brow so wan;
You shall forget your sadness,
You sick and sorrowful man!

Let my white arms embrace you,
And on my breast so white
You shall lay your head while dreaming
Of fairy-tale delight.

I will kiss and caress you,
As once I kissed and caressed
The dear, dead Emperor Heinrich,
He too lay on my breast.

The dead stay dead for ever,
And only the living live;
And I am fair and flourishing,
With my laughing heart to give.

Come down into my palace,
My palace of crystal bright,
Where merry squires are singing
As ladies dance with their knights.

There's a rustling of silken dresses
And a rattling of iron mail,
And drums and trumpets are sounding,
And fifes and bugles wail.

But like the Emperor Heinrich
My arms shall embrace you too;
I stopped his ears with my fingers
When the martial trumpet blew.'

It is a feeling of infinite bliss when the visible world converges with that of our hearts, and green trees, thoughts, birdsong, melancholy, the blue of heaven, memory and fragrance are twined together in sweet arabesques. Women know this feeling best, and perhaps that is why a lovely, sceptical smile hovers about their lips when we boast with academic pride of our feats of logic, classifying things so neatly into objective and subjective, and fitting our heads with thousands of compartments, like a chemist's shop, with reason in one, intellect in another, wit in the third, bad jokes in the fourth, and nothing at all, or rather the idea, in the fifth.

As though walking in a dream, I scarcely noticed that we had left the Ilse Valley and were going uphill again. It was steep and toilsome, and many of us were gasping for breath. But, like our late cousin who is buried at Mölln,[50] we thought in advance about going downhill, and felt much happier. Finally we got to Ilse Rock.

This is an enormous granite rock, rising loftily and boldly from the valley. On three sides it is enclosed by high, tree-covered mountains, but the fourth side, to the north, is free, and from it you can see

Ilsenburg below and the river Ilse, far into the lowlands. On the towering pinnacle of the rock stands a large iron cross, and there is just room for four feet.

As nature has endowed Ilse Rock with fantastic charms, owing to its shape and position, legend has also cast its rosy glow upon it. According to Gottschalk, 'It is said that there was once an enchanted palace here, in which the rich and beautiful Princess Ilse lived, and that she still bathes in the Ilse every morning; anyone fortunate enough to catch the right moment is taken by her into the rock where her palace is, and royally rewarded.' Others tell a pretty story about the love between Miss Ilse and the Knight of Westenberg, which one of our best-known poets has celebrated romantically in the *Evening News*.[51] Others tell a different story: it was the old Saxon Emperor Heinrich who enjoyed his most imperial hours with Ilse, the beautiful water-fairy, in her enchanted rocky castle. A recent writer, Mr Niemann, has written a guide-book to the Harz in which he has devoted praiseworthy diligence to listing the heights of the mountains, the deviations of the compass needle, the debts of the towns, and suchlike, and he maintains: 'The stories told about Princess Ilse belong to the world of fable.' That is what all those people say who have never set eyes on such a princess, but we, who are specially favoured by fair ladies, know better. Emperor Heinrich knew it too. Not for nothing were the old Saxon emperors so attached to their native Harz. You need only leaf through the pretty Lüneburg Chronicle,[52] where the good old gentlemen are depicted in old-fashioned loyal woodcuts, clad in armour and mounted on their steeds, with the sacred crown of the Empire on their beloved heads, sceptre and sword in their firm hands. From their dear faces with Van Dyck beards you can clearly tell how often they yearned for the sweet heart of their Harz princesses and the familiar murmuring of the Harz forests, when they sojourned in foreign parts, especially in Italy, land of lemons and poison, where they and their successors were so often lured by the desire to call themselves Roman emperors. This love of titles is truly German, and it ruined the emperors and the Empire.

However, I advise whoever stands on the pinnacle of Ilse Rock not to think about emperors and the Empire, nor about the fair Ilse, but simply about his own feet. For as I was standing there, lost in thought, I suddenly heard the subterranean music coming from the enchanted palace, and I saw the mountains all around standing on their heads, and the red slate roofs of Ilsenburg began to dance, and the green trees flew about in the blue air so that everything went blue and green before my eyes, and my giddiness would undoubtedly have made me plunge into the abyss, if in my spiritual distress I had not clung tight to the iron cross. I am sure no one will think the worse of me for doing this in such an awkward position.

The Harz Journey is and remains a fragment, and the colourful threads so prettily woven into it to form a harmonious whole are suddenly cut off, as though by the shears of inexorable Fate. Perhaps I shall continue weaving them in future songs, and what is now left in meagre silence will then be said in full. In the long run it does not matter when and where something is uttered, so long as it is uttered. Individual works may remain fragments, so long as they form a whole when put together. By placing them together, deficiencies may be made good, rugged passages softened and acerbic remarks rendered milder. This may apply to the opening pages of *The Harz Journey*, and they might seem less sour if it is made clear elsewhere that my dislike of Göttingen in general, though even greater than I have stated, is far less great than my regard for some individuals there. And – why should I conceal it? – I refer especially to the beloved man who in early days was so concerned for my welfare, imbued me even then with a deep love for the study of history, and strengthened my enthusiasm later. He thus led my mind along more peaceful paths, suggested more salutary directions for my energies, and provided me in general with those historical consolations without which I could never endure the tormenting events of the day. I am speaking of Georg Sartorius,[53] that great historian and great man, whose eye is a bright star in our dark times, and whose hospitable heart is open to all the joys and sorrows of other people, to the cares of the beggar and the king, and to the last groan of disappearing nations and their gods.

Nor can I refrain from indicating, at this point, that the Upper Harz, the region of the Harz which I have described as far as the beginning of the Ilse Valley, is far less pleasing to the eye than the romantic and picturesque Lower Harz, and the wild, rugged beauty of its sombre fir woods forms a marked contrast to the latter; just as the three valleys of the Lower Harz formed by the Ilse, the Bode and the

Selke contrast charmingly with one another, if one is able to personify the character of each. They are three female figures, and it is no easy matter to decide which of them is the most beautiful.

I have already spoken and sung about the dear, sweet Ilse and how sweetly and charmingly she welcomed me. That sombre beauty, the Bode, gave me no such gracious welcome, and when I first caught sight of her in Rübeland, dark with smithies, she seemed surly, and hid herself in a silver-grey veil of rain. But she cast aside her veil with sudden love as I reached the summit of the Rosstrappe, her countenance shone on me with sunny splendour, all her features breathed forth colossal tenderness, and her rocky bosom, now conquered, seemed to utter sighs of yearning and sounds of melting melancholy. I found less tenderness but more cheerfulness in the fair Selke, the beautiful and amiable lady, whose noble simplicity and serene calm wards off any sentimental familiarity, though she betrays her love of teasing by a half-hidden smile. That must be why I was afflicted by many minor mishaps in the Selke valley: when I tried to jump over the water, I fell splash into the middle; afterwards, when I had replaced my wet footwear with slippers, I mislaid or rather mistrod one of them; a gust of wind carried off my cap; my legs were scratched by brambles, and so on and, alas, so forth. But I gladly forgive the beautiful lady for all these mishaps, for she is beautiful. And now she stands before my mind's eye in all her quiet charm, and seems to say: 'Even if I laugh, I don't mean you any harm, and I beg you to make a poem about me.' The magnificent Bode likewise appears in my memory, and her dark eyes say: 'You resemble me in pride and in pain, and I want you to love me.' The beautiful Ilse, too, comes tripping along, dainty and enchanting in face, figure and movements; she is exactly like the lovely being who confers bliss on my dreams, and she looks at me, just as She does, with irresistible indifference and yet with such deep, eternal, transparent truth – Well, I am Paris,[54] the three goddesses are standing in front of me, and I give the apple to the beautiful Ilse.

Today is the first of May. Spring is flooding the earth like a sea of life, the white foam of flowers hangs on the trees, a warm, translucent mist spreads everywhere. In the town the window-panes of the houses are gleaming joyfully, the sparrows are again building their nests in the eaves, people are walking along the street and wondering why the air so affects them and why they feel so strange; brightly-clad girls from Vierlanden are carrying bunches of violets; the orphan children, with their little blue jackets and their dear illegitimate faces, march in procession along the Jungfernstieg[55] and are as happy as though they were going to regain their fathers today; the beggar on the bridge looks as pleased as though he had won first prize in the lottery, and the sun with her most tolerant rays even shines on the dark broker who, not yet hanged, is hurrying along with his villainous factory-goods face – I shall take a walk outside the city gate.

It is the first of May, and I am thinking of you, beautiful Ilse – or should I call you Agnes, since you like this name best? – I am thinking of you, and I would like to see you again running down the mountain and shining as you go. Most of all, though, I would like to stand in the valley below and catch you in my arms. It is a fine day! Everywhere I see green, the colour of hope. Everywhere, like lovely miracles, the flowers are blossoming, and my heart is ready to blossom again. This heart too is a flower, a very strange one. It is not a modest violet, not a laughing rose, not a pure lily, or any other flower that delights girls with its dainty charm and can be placed prettily on their pretty bosoms, and withers today and blooms again tomorrow. This heart is more like the heavy, exotic flower from the forests of Brazil, which, according to legend, blooms only once in a hundred years. I remember seeing such a flower when I was a boy. One night we heard a shot as though from a pistol, and the following morning the children next door told me that it was an 'aloe' which had suddenly burst into bloom with such a crack. They took me into their garden, and there, to my astonishment, I saw that the low, tough plant with the comically broad, jagged leaves, on which you could easily cut yourself, had suddenly shot up and was bearing aloft the most magnificent blossom, like a golden crown. We children could not see so high, and old chuckling Christian, who was fond of us, built a wooden stair round the flower, and we climbed up it like cats, and peered inquisitively into the flower's open calyx, from which the yellow stamens and exciting, unfamiliar fragrance came forth with unheard-of splendour.

Yes, Agnes, this heart blooms seldom, and not easily; so far as I recall, it has bloomed only once, and that must be a long time ago, at least a hundred years. However magnificently it displayed its flowers then, I seem to remember that they were compelled to wither wretchedly from lack of sunshine and warmth, if indeed they were not violently destroyed by a dark winter gale. But now something is stirring and moving in my bosom, and if you suddenly hear a shot – don't be frightened, my girl! I haven't shot myself, it is my love bursting its bud, and shooting up in radiant songs, in eternal dithyrambs, in the most joyous wealth of song.

But if this exalted love is too high, my girl, then take an easier way, ascend the wooden stair, and from it look down into my blossoming heart.

It is still morning, the sun has hardly traversed half its course, and my heart is already giving off such a fragrance that it is going to my head and making me so giddy that I can no longer tell when irony stops and the sky starts, I populate the air with my sighs, and I myself should like to dissolve into sweet atoms, into the uncreated divinity; what will happen when night falls, and the stars appear in the sky, 'the unhappy stars, that can tell you –'

It is the first of May, today the meanest shop-boy has the right to be sentimental, and would you deny it to the poet?

IDEAS:
THE BOOK OF LE GRAND

Stalwart race of Örindur,
Stoutest pillar of our hall,
Shall from age to age endure,
Though the stars decree its fall.

Müllner[1]

May
Evelina
accept these pages
as a sign
of the author's friendship and love

CHAPTER I

> She was lovable, and he loved her; but he was not lovable, and she did not love him.
>
> (Old Play)

MADAME, do you know the old play? It is a quite extraordinary play, only somewhat too melancholy. I once played the leading role in it, and all the ladies wept; there was only a single one who did not weep, she did not shed a single tear, and that was precisely the point of the play and its true catastrophe. –

Oh, that single tear! It still torments my thoughts; when Satan wants to destroy my soul, he whispers in my ear a song about that unwept tear, a dreadful song with a yet more dreadful tune – oh, it is only in hell that this tune is heard! —

— — — — — — — — — — — — — — — — — — — —

You can probably imagine, Madame, how people live in heaven, especially as you are married. People have a splendid time there, they have every possible amusement, they live in joy and delight, like pigs in clover. They dine from morning to night, and the cuisine is as good as Jagor's,[2] the roast geese fly about with sauce-boats in their bills, and are flattered to be consumed; cakes gleaming with butter grow wild like sunflowers, there are streams of bouillon and champagne everywhere, and trees with napkins fluttering from them, and people dine and wipe their mouths, and dine again, without upsetting their stomachs, they sing psalms, or they jest and dally with the dear, dainty little angels, or they go for walks on the green Hallelujah meadow, and their white flowing robes fit very comfortably, and nothing spoils the feeling of blessedness, no pain, no discomfort; indeed, even if you accidentally tread on someone's corns, and cry 'Excusez!', the other person gives a beatific smile and assures you: 'You did not hurt me, brother; *au contraire*, you only heightened my heart's heavenly bliss.'

But about hell, Madame, you have not the least idea. Of all the devils you probably know only the smallest, the little Beelzebub Amor, the civil croupier of hell, and as for hell itself, you know it only from *Don Giovanni*, and you never think it hot enough for that seducer, who sets such a bad example, although our admirable stage-managers are as lavish with flames, fiery rain, gunpowder and colophonium as any good Christian can ask for in hell.

All the same, hell is a much worse place than our stage-managers realize – otherwise they would not put on so many bad plays – the heat in hell is quite hellish, and when I once visited it in the dog-days, I found it unbearable. You have no idea of hell, Madame. Not much official news reaches us from it. That the poor souls down there must spend the whole day reading all the bad sermons that are printed up here – that is a slander. Hell is not as bad as that; Satan will never devise such fiendish torments. Dante's description, on the other hand, is rather too moderate, and, on the whole, too poetic. Hell seemed to me like a huge kitchen in a town house, with an immensely long stove on which were three rows of iron pots, and in these the damned were sitting and being roasted. In the first row were the Christian sinners, and, believe it or not, their number was by no means small, and the devils were working especially hard to stoke the fire under them. In the next row were the Jews; they kept screaming and were sometimes teased by the devils, and it was very comical when a fat, puffing pawnbroker complained of the excessive heat, and a little devil poured a few bucketfuls of cold water over his head, to show him that baptism was a true refreshment to the soul. In the third row were the pagans, who, like the Jews, cannot be admitted to salvation, and must burn for ever. I heard one of them calling angrily from the pot, as a burly devil was adding fresh coal: 'Spare me, I was Socrates, the wisest of mortals, I taught truth and justice and laid down my life for the sake of virtue.' But the burly, stupid devil went on with his work, muttering: 'Stuff and nonsense! All pagans must burn, and we can't make an exception for one single individual.' – I assure you, Madame, the heat was frightful, with screaming, moaning, groaning, wailing, and whimpering – and through all these hideous sounds could be heard the dreadful tune of the song of the unwept tear.

CHAPTER 2

> She was lovable, and he loved her; but he was not lovable, and she did not love him.
>
> (Old Play)

MADAME! the old play is a tragedy, though its hero neither kills himself nor is killed. The heroine's eyes are beautiful, very beautiful – Madame, do you not smell the perfume of violets? – yet polished to such a point that they pierced my heart like glass daggers and must certainly have peeped out of my back – these murderous eyes failed to kill me. The heroine's voice is also beautiful – Madame, did you not hear a nightingale singing just now? – a beautiful, silken voice, a sweet fabric spun from the sunniest sounds, and my soul was entangled in it, choking in torment. I myself – it is the Count of the Ganges who is now speaking, and the story is set in Venice – I myself had once had my fill of such torments, and even in the first act I was thinking of putting an end to the play and blowing not only my brains out but also my fool's cap, and I went to a haberdashery on the Via Burstah,[3] where I found a pair of handsome pistols displayed in a case – I can still remember the case very well, it also contained many pleasing trinkets of mother-of-pearl and gold, iron hearts on golden chains, china cups with tender mottoes, snuff-boxes with pretty pictures, such as the divine story of Susannah,[4] the swan-song of Leda, the rape of the Sabine women, Lucretia, that plump paragon of virtue with the bare bosom into which she plunges the dagger when it's all over, the late lamented Bethmann, *la belle ferronière*, alluring faces one and all – but I bought the pistols all the same without haggling, and then I bought bullets, and then gunpowder, and then I went to Signor Unbescheiden's restaurant and ordered oysters and a glass of Rhine wine –

I could not eat, far less drink. My hot tears fell into my glass, and in the glass I saw my beloved home, the blue sacred Ganges, the everlasting gleam of the Himalayas, the vast banyan forests in whose broad arcades the wise elephants and the white-clad pilgrims were quietly walking; strange, dreamy flowers gazed at me with concealed admonitions, wondrous golden birds uttered cries of wild jubilation, flickering sunbeams and the sweet, mad cries of laughing monkeys teased me delightfully, the pious prayers of the priests sounded from distant pagodas, and in their midst could be heard the melting lamentation of the Sultaness of Delhi – she was running furiously up and down in her tapestried chamber, tearing her silver veil, thrusting to the floor the black slave-girl with the peacock fan, weeping, raving, shrieking – but I could not understand what she was saying, for Signor Unbescheiden's restaurant is three thousand leagues away from the harem at Delhi, and besides, the beautiful Sultaness had been dead for three thousand years – and I hastily drank my wine, the clear, joyful wine, and yet my soul grew even darker and more sorrowful – I was condemned to death —

As I left the restaurant, I heard the death-knell ringing for a criminal about to be executed, and a crowd of people surged past; but I took up my position at the corner of the Strada San Giovanni[5] and delivered the following monologue:

'Old legends tell of golden palaces
Where harps are played and lovely maidens dance,
Smart servants do their bidding, and the scent
Of jasmine, myrtle, roses fills the air –
And yet a single disenchanting word
Turns all that splendour instantly to dust,
And nought remains but piles of ancient rubble
And marshes haunted by nocturnal birds.
Thus I, by uttering a single word,
Have disenchanted all of flowering Nature.
She lies recumbent, lifeless, cold and pale,
Like to a royal corpse in painted state,
Whose cheeks have had their pallor coloured red
And in whose hand a sceptre has been placed,
But with a yellow, withered pair of lips,
Since they forgot to paint them likewise red;
And mice now gambol round the royal nose,
And insolently mock the golden sceptre.'

It is a truth universally acknowledged, Madame, that one must deliver a monologue before shooting oneself. Most people use Hamlet's 'To be or not to be' on such occasions. It is a good speech, and I would gladly have quoted it; but you must take care of Number One, and if, like me, you have likewise written tragedies containing speeches by people graduating from life, such as the immortal *Almansor*, then it is quite natural to give your own words preference even over Shakespeare's. At any rate, such speeches are a very useful custom; at least one gains time – And so it befell that I remained at the corner of the Strada San Giovanni for rather a long time – and as I was standing there, condemned and consigned to death, I suddenly caught sight of *Her*!

She was wearing her blue silk dress, and her pink hat, and her look was so mild, so death-conquering, so life-bestowing – Madame, you probably know from Roman history that when the Vestal Virgins in ancient Rome met a criminal who was being led to execution, they had the right to pardon him, and the poor rogue remained alive. – With a single look she saved me from death, and I stood before her as though brought back to life, as though dazzled by the solar radiance of her beauty, and she went on – and let me live.

CHAPTER 3

AND she let me live, and I am alive, and that is the main thing.

Let others enjoy the pleasure of having their tombs adorned with the beloved's flowers and wetted with her tears – O women! hate me, scorn me, reject my advances, but let me live! Life is too, too comically sweet; and the world is so delightfully confused; it is the dream of an intoxicated god, who took French leave from the company of divine wine-bibbers, and lay down to sleep on a lonely star, and does not know himself that he creates everything he dreams of – and his dream-images are sometimes a wild, motley throng, sometimes harmonious and rational – the Iliad, Plato, the Battle of Marathon, Moses, the Medici Venus, Strasbourg Cathedral, the French Revolution, Hegel, steamships, and so on, are individual bright ideas in this god's creative dream – but it will not be long before the god wakes up, and rubs his sleepy eyes, and smiles – and our world will fade into nothingness, indeed it will never have existed.

Never mind! I'm alive. Even if I am only the shadowy image in a dream, that is still better than the cold, black, empty nothingness of death. Life is the highest good, and the worst of evils is death.[6] Let lieutenants in the Berlin Guards sneer and call it cowardice for the Prince of Homburg to recoil in terror on seeing his open grave – Heinrich Kleist nevertheless had just as much courage as his high-chested, well-corseted fellow-soldiers, and, alas, he proved it. But all strong people love life. Goethe's Egmont is sorry to leave 'this pleasant habit of existing and acting'. Immermann's Edwin is as attached to life as 'a babe to its mother's breasts' and although it is hard for him to owe his life to someone else's mercy, he nevertheless pleads for mercy,

For living, breathing are the highest good.

When Odysseus in the underworld sees Achilles as the leader of dead heroes, and lauds him for his fame among the living and the regard in which he is held even by the dead, the latter replies:

'O shining Odysseus, never try to console me for dying.
I would rather follow the plough as thrall to another
man, one with no land allotted him and not much to live on,
than be a king over all the perished dead.'[7]

Indeed, when Major Duvent challenged the great Israel Löwe[8] to a duel with pistols, saying: 'If you don't face me, Mr Löwe, you are a dog,' the latter replied: 'I would rather be a living dog than a dead lion!' And he was right – I have fought enough duels, Madame, to be entitled to say this – Thank God! I'm alive! Red life is boiling in my veins, the earth is quivering under my feet, I clasp trees and marble statues with ardent love, and they come to life in my embrace. To me, every woman is the gift of a world, I revel in the melodies of her face, and with a single glance from my eye I can enjoy more than others can with their whole bodies in all their lives. To me, every moment is an eternity; I do not measure out time by the Brabant ell or the small Hamburg ell, and I need no priest to promise me a second life, for there is enough experience for me in this life when I live backwards, in the life of my ancestors, and conquer eternity in the realm of the past.

And I'm alive! Nature's great pulse is beating in my breast too, and when I rejoice, a thousandfold echo replies. I hear a thousand nightingales. Spring has sent them to rouse the earth from her early-morning doze, and the earth shivers with delight, her flowers are the hymns that she sings in rapture to the sun – the sun is moving much too slowly, I'd like to whip its fiery steeds to make them gallop faster – But when the sun sinks into the sea with a hiss, and the great night arises with her great yearning eyes, O! then indeed I tremble with true pleasure, the evening breezes lie against my surging heart like girls fondling me, and the stars beckon, and I rise, and hover over the tiny earth and the tiny thoughts of mankind.

CHAPTER 4

But at last the day will come when the heat in my veins is extinguished, winter dwells in my bosom, its white flakes flutter scantily round my head, and its mists obscure my sight. My friends will lie in storm-beaten graves, I alone shall remain, like a solitary blade of grass forgotten by the reaper; a new generation will have sprung up with new desires and new thoughts, in astonishment I hear new names and new songs, the old names have faded away, and I myself have faded away, perhaps still respected by a few, scorned by many, and loved by none! And the rosy-cheeked lads hasten to me, and press my old harp into my trembling hand, and say with laughter: 'You have been silent for a long time, you lazy greybeard; sing us songs again about the dreams of your youth.'

Then I shall grasp the harp, and my old joys and sorrows awaken, the mists depart, tears flower again from my dead eyes, spring returns to my bosom, sweet sounds of melancholy quiver in the harp-strings, I see once more the blue river and the marble palaces, and the lovely faces of women and girls – and I sing a song about the flowers of the Brenta.

It will be my last song, the stars will gaze at me as they did in the nights of my youth, the lovelorn moonlight will again kiss my cheeks, the ghostly choirs of dead nightingales will flute from the distance, my eyes close drowsily, my soul dies away like the sounds of my harp – fragrance rises from the flowers of the Brenta.

A tree will give shade to my gravestone. I would have liked a palm, but they do not thrive in the North. It will doubtless be a linden-tree, and on summer evenings lovers will sit there and caress; the siskin listening on the branch knows how to keep a secret, and my linden rustles familiarly above the heads of these happy people, who are so happy that they do not even have time to read the writing on the white gravestone. But later, when the young lover has lost his sweetheart, he will return to the well-known linden, and sigh and weep, and gaze long and often at the gravestone, and read the inscription on it: 'He loved the flowers of the Brenta.'

CHAPTER 5

MADAME! I have been lying to you. I am not the Count of the Ganges. I never saw the holy river in my life, nor the lotus-flowers that are mirrored in its devout waves. I never lay dreaming under Indian palms, I never lay praying before the diamond god of Juggernaut, though he could have been of great help to me. I was never in Calcutta, any more than the Calcutta chicken that I had for lunch yesterday. But I come from Hindustan, and that is why I feel so at ease in the vast poetic forests of Valmiki,[9] the heroic sufferings of the divine Rama move my heart like a familiar pain, from the flowery songs of Kalidasa spring forth my sweetest memories, and a few years ago, when a kind lady[10] in Berlin showed me the pretty pictures her father had brought from India, where he was Governor-General for a long time, the delicately painted, quiet and devout faces seemed so well known, and I felt as though I were looking at my own ancestral portraits.

Franz Bopp[11] – Madame, you have of course read his *Nalus* and his *The Conjugation System in Sanskrit* – gave me much information about my forebears, and I now know that I sprang from the head of Brahma, and not from his corns; I even suspect that the entire *Mahabharata* with its 200,000 lines is merely an allegorical love-letter sent by my first forefather to my first foremother – oh, they were very much in love, their souls kissed, they kissed with their eyes, they were both one single kiss –

An enchanted nightingale is sitting on a red coral tree in the Pacific and singing a song about the love of my ancestors; the pearls are peeping curiously from their mussel cells, the wondrous water-flowers are shivering with melancholy, the wise sea-snails, with coloured china towers on their backs, are crawling closer, the sea-roses are blushing bashfully, the yellow pointed starfish and the glassy jellyfish with their thousand hues are stirring and stretching, and all are thronging to listen –

But, Madame, this nightingale's song is much too long to be inserted here: it is as long as the world itself; even the dedication to Anangas, the god of love, is as long as all Walter Scott's novels, and there is an allusion to this in a passage from Aristophanes which goes in German like this:

Tiotio, tiotio, tiotinx,
Totototo, totototo, tototinx.
(Voss's translation)[12]

No, I was not born in India; I came into the world on the banks of the beautiful river where folly grows on green hills and in autumn is picked, trodden, poured into barrels and sent abroad – Truly, at dinner yesterday I heard someone utter a piece of folly which in 1811 was in a grape that I then saw growing on the Johannisberg. Plenty of folly is consumed in the region itself, and the people there are like people anywhere: – they are born, eat, drink, sleep, laugh, weep, repeat slanders, are anxiously concerned about propagating the species, try to seem what they are not and to do what they cannot, do not shave until they have beards, often have beards before they reach the age of reason, and when they have reached it, they get drunk again on white and red folly.

Mon dieu! if I had enough faith to move mountains, then I would make the Johannisberg follow me everywhere. But since my faith is not strong enough, imagination must come to my aid, and it transports me to the beautiful Rhine.

Oh, that is a beautiful region, full of charm and sunshine. The blue river reflects the hills along the bank with their ruined castles and forests and ancient towns – On summer evenings the townspeople sit outside their front doors, and drink out of big jugs, and chat familiarly, saying how well the vines are doing, praise be! and how the law-courts should be open to the public, and how Marie Antoinette was guillotined without so much as a by your leave, and how the tobacco monopoly makes tobacco dearer, and how all men are equal, and what a splendid chap Görres[13] is.

I never troubled myself about such conversations, and preferred to sit with the girls in the bow-window, where I would laugh at their laughter, and let them strike me in the face with flowers, and pretend to be angry, until they told me their secrets or some other important story. The beautiful Gertrud was almost mad with pleasure when I sat down beside her; she was a girl like a flaming rose, and once when she embraced me I thought she would burn up and be consumed in my arms. The beautiful Katharine would melt away in gentle music when she talked to me, and her eyes were a pure, deep blue such as I have never before found in people or animals, and only rarely in flowers; it was pleasant to look into them, and they inspired all kinds of sweet thoughts. But the beautiful Hedwig was in love with me; for when I went over to her, she would bend her head so that her black curls fell over her blushing face, and her shining eyes gleamed like stars in a dark sky. Her bashful lips did not utter a word, and I could not say anything to her either. I coughed and she trembled. Sometimes she would send me a message by her sister, telling me not to climb the rocks so quickly, and not to bathe in the Rhine when I had heated myself by running or drinking. I once overheard her devout prayer to the statue of the Virgin which stood in a niche in the hallway, adorned with tinsel and lit garishly by a small lamp; I distinctly heard her asking the Mother of God 'to stop him from climbing, drinking and bathing'. I would certainly have fallen in love with the beautiful girl, if she had been indifferent towards me; and I was indifferent towards her, because I knew she loved me – Madame, anyone who wants to be loved by me has to treat me like dirt.

The beautiful Johanna was the cousin of the three sisters, and I enjoyed sitting beside her. She knew the most beautiful folk-tales, and when she pointed with her white hand out of the window at the mountains where all the stories she told had taken place, I felt quite enchanted: the old knights arose visibly from the ruined castles and cut one another's iron clothing to shreds, the Lore-Ley once again stood on the mountain peak and sang her sweet, pernicious song, and the Rhine murmured so sensibly, so reassuringly, and yet at the same time in a teasingly sinister way – and the beautiful Johanna looked at me in such a strange, intimate, bafflingly familiar manner, as though she herself were part of the tales she was telling. She was a slender, pale girl, pensive, and afflicted by a fatal illness; her eyes were as clear as truth itself, her lips were piously curved, the features of her face contained a great story, but it was a sacred story – perhaps a love-legend? I do not know, and I never had the courage to ask her. Whenever I looked at her for long, I became calm and serene, I felt as though it were a quiet Sunday in my heart and the angels there were holding a divine service.

At such happy times I told her stories from my childhood, and she always listened seriously, and it was strange! whenever I was no longer able to remember names, she reminded me of them. When I asked her in surprise how she knew the names, she replied with a smile that she had learnt them from the birds that nested on the slates outside her window – and she even tried to persuade me that these were the very same birds that as a boy I had bought with my pocket-money from the hard-hearted peasant lads and then allowed to fly away freely. I think, though, that she knew everything because she was so pale and did indeed die soon. She also knew when she was going to die, and wanted me to leave Andernacht the day before. When I left she gave me both hands – they were white, sweet hands, and as pure as the Host – and she said: 'You're very good, and when you are angry, think of little Veronika who is dead.'

Did the garrulous birds betray this name to her as well? At times when I was haunted by memories, I had often racked my brains without managing to recall this dear name.

Now that I have it again, my earliest childhood blossoms in my memory, and I am a child again, playing with other children on the Castle Square at Düsseldorf on the Rhine.

CHAPTER 6

YES, Madame, that is where I was born, and I point this out expressly just in case after my death seven cities[14] – Schilda, Krähwinkel, Polkwitz, Bochum, Dülken, Göttingen, and Schöppenstadt – compete for the honour of being my birthplace. Düsseldorf is a town on the Rhine; 16,000 people live there, and many hundreds of thousands more lie buried there. And among these there are many of whom my mother says it would be better if they were still alive: for example, my grandfather and my uncle, old Herr v. Geldern and young Herr v. Geldern, who were both such famous doctors, and saved so many people from death, and yet had to die themselves. And pious Ursula, who carried me as a child in her arms, lies buried there as well, and a rose-bush grows on her grave – she loved the scent of roses so much when she was alive, and her heart was pure rose-perfume and kindness. The shrewd old Canon lies buried there too. Goodness, how wretched he looked when I saw him for the last time! There was nothing left of him but mind and bandages, and yet he studied day and night, as though he were worried lest the worms might find too few ideas in his head. Little Wilhelm[15] lies there too, and that is my fault. We were school-fellows in the Franciscan monastery and were playing at the side of the building where the Düssel flows between stone walls, and I said: 'Wilhelm, do save the kitten that has just fallen in' – and he climbed down cheerfully on to the plank that lay across the stream, pulled the kitten out of the water, but fell in himself, and when they fished him out, he was wet and dead. The kitten had a long life.

The town of Düsseldorf is very handsome, and it is a strange feeling to think of it in foreign parts, if you happen to have been born there. I was born there, and I feel as though I should go straight home. And when I say home, I mean Bolker Street and the house where I was born. One day this house will be very noteworthy, and I have told the old lady who owns it that she must not sell the house on any account. The price she would get for the whole house would scarcely amount to the tip that noble Englishwomen in green veils will one day give to the maidservant who shows them the room where I was born, and the chicken-coop where my father used to lock me up when I had eaten grapes on the sly, and the brown door on which my mother taught me to write the alphabet with chalk – goodness me! Madame, if I become a famous writer, it will have cost my poor mother plenty of effort.

But my fame is still sleeping in the marble quarries of Carrara, the laurel-leaves of scrap paper with which my brows are wreathed have not yet spread their fragrance throughout the world, and when noble Englishwomen in green veils visit Düsseldorf now, they leave the famous house unvisited and go straight to the market-place and look at the colossal black equestrian statue that stands in the middle. This is supposed to represent the Elector Jan Wilhelm.[16] He wears a black suit of armour and a full-bottomed wig that hangs down his back. As a boy I heard the tale that the artist who cast this statue had been alarmed to observe, while doing so, that he had not sufficient metal, and the townspeople hastened to his aid and brought their silver spoons to complete the casting – and now I spent hours standing in front of the statue and racking my brains to work out how many silver spoons it contained, and how many apple tarts you could buy with all that silver. Apple tarts, you see, were my passion at that time – now it is love, truth, freedom, and crab soup – and not far from the Elector's statue, at the corner of the theatre, there used to stand the oddly-shaped, bow-legged fellow with the white apron and a basket round his waist full of delightfully steaming apple tarts, which he would commend in an irresistible treble voice: 'The apple tarts are quite fresh, just out of the oven, they smell so delicious' – Truly, when later in my life the Tempter wanted to win me over, he spoke in just such an alluring treble voice, and I would not have stayed twelve hours with Signora Giulietta if she had not struck the sweet, fragrant note of the apple tarts. And truly, apple tarts would never have attracted me so much if crooked Hermann had not concealed them so mysteriously with his white apron – and it's the aprons that – but they are carrying me away from my context; I was talking about the equestrian statue that contains so many silver spoons, and no soup, and represents the Elector Jan Wilhelm.

He is said to have been a fine gentleman, and very fond of art, and very skilful himself. He founded the picture-gallery in Düsseldorf, and in the observatory there they still show a very artful set of wooden drinking-mugs, all fitting into one another, that he carved in his leisure hours, of which he had twenty-four each day.

In those days the princes were not harassed as they are now, and the crowns were firmly attached to their heads, and at night they pulled night-caps over their crowns and slept soundly, and their subjects slept soundly at their feet, and on waking up in the morning they would say, 'Good-morning, father!' and the prince would answer: 'Good-morning, dear children!'

But suddenly things changed: one morning, when we woke up in Düsseldorf and wanted to say, 'Good-morning, father!', our father had gone away, and the whole town had a vague feeling of anxiety, there was a kind of funereal mood everywhere, and people crept silently to the market-place and read the long paper poster on the wall of the town-hall. The sky was overcast, and yet Kilian the skinny tailor was standing there in his nankeen jacket, which he normally only wore indoors, and his blue woollen stockings were hanging down so that his bare legs peeped out mournfully, and his narrow lips were quivering as he muttered to himself the words on the poster. An old soldier from the Palatinate was reading in a louder voice, and at many of the words a bright tear trickled into his honest white moustache. I was standing beside him and weeping in sympathy, and I asked him why we were weeping? And he replied: 'The Elector thanks his subjects.' And then he read some more, and at the words: 'for their proven loyalty', 'and releases them from their duties', he wept even harder – It is strange to see such an old man with a faded uniform and a scarred soldierly face suddenly weeping so hard. While we were reading, the electoral coat of arms was being removed from the town-hall; everything was so gloomy and alarming, as though we were expecting an eclipse of the sun; the Town Councillors went about with such a slow, abdicated step, even the all-powerful policeman looked as though he had no more orders to give, and was standing there with an air of peaceful indifference, although mad Alouisius was again standing on one leg, pulling idiotic faces, and rattling off the names of the French generals, while the drunken hunchback Gumpertz was rolling in the gutter and singing 'Ça ira, ça ira!'[17]

I went home, however, and wept and lamented: 'The Elector thanks his subjects.' My mother was at her wits' end, I knew what I knew and it was no use telling me otherwise; I went to bed weeping, and during the night I dreamed that the world was coming to an end – the lovely flower-gardens and green meadows were taken from the ground and rolled up like carpets, the policeman climbed up a long ladder and took the sun down from the sky, Kilian the tailor stood watching and said to himself: 'I must go home and put on some decent clothes, for I'm dead, and I'm to be buried this very day' – and it kept getting darker, a few scanty stars were gleaming above our heads, and even these fell down like withered leaves in autumn. Gradually people vanished, and I, poor child, roamed about in terror. Finally I was standing in front of the willow hedge outside a deserted farmstead, where I saw a man digging up the earth with a spade, and beside him a hideous spiteful woman holding something like a human head in her apron, and it was the moon, and she placed it with anxious care in the open pit – and behind me stood the old soldier from the Palatinate, sobbing and spelling out: 'The Elector thanks his subjects.'

When I woke up, the sun was once more shining through the window as usual, drums were beating in the street, and when I entered our living-room and said good-morning to my father, who was having his hair cut and was wrapped in a white cloth to keep the powder off his clothes, I heard the nimble hairdresser telling him the hair-raising news that today at the town-hall homage would be paid to the new Grand Duke Joachim, and that he belonged to the best of families, and had married the Emperor Napoleon's sister, and had excellent manners, and wore his beautiful black hair in curls, and was about to make his official entry, and would certainly be liked by all the women. Out in the street, meanwhile, the drums went on beating, and I went and stood outside the front door and watched the French troops marching in, the joyful nation of glory that went through the world with music and song, the serene and serious faces of the grenadiers, the bearskin caps, the tricolour cockades, the gleaming bayonets, the *voltigeurs* full of merriment and *point d'honneur*, and the big, all-powerful drum-major with silver embroidery, who could throw his stick with its gilded knob up to the first storey, and his eyes up to the second storey – where beautiful girls were looking out of the window. I was pleased that we were having soldiers quartered on us – my mother was not pleased – and I hurried to the market-place. It looked completely different, as though the world were being newly painted; a new coat of arms was hanging on the town-hall, the iron rails on its balcony were draped with sheets of embroidered velvet, French grenadiers were on sentry duty, the old Town Councillors had put on new faces and were wearing their Sunday suits, and looking at one another in French and saying 'Bonjour'; ladies were peeping from all the windows, inquisitive townsfolk and spotless soldiers filled the square, and I and some other boys clambered on to the Elector's great horse and looked down at the motley bustle in the market-place.

Peter-next-door and big Kurz nearly broke their necks in this escapade, and that would have been no bad thing; for one of them afterwards ran away from his parents, joined the soldiers, deserted, and was shot in Mainz; the other, however, conducted geographical researches in other people's pockets, was accordingly made an active member of a public reformatory, tore apart the iron fetters that bound him to it and to his fatherland, succeeded in crossing the water, and died in London from wearing a tie that was too narrow and pulled itself tight when an officer of the Crown drew the plank from under his feet.

Big Kurz told us that there was no school today, because of the ceremony of homage. We had a long wait before the ceremony began. At last the balcony of the town-hall filled up with brightly-clad gentlemen, flags, and trumpets, and the Mayor, in his famous red coat, delivered a speech that was rather long-drawn-out, like elastic or a knitted night-cap into which someone has thrown a stone – though not the philosopher's stone – and I could make out many phrases quite clearly, for example, that they wanted to make us happy – and at the last word the trumpets were blown, and the flags were waved, and the drums were beaten, and 'Vivat' was shouted – and as I shouted 'Vivat' I held on tight to the old Elector. And that was necessary, for I felt quite dizzy, I thought people were standing on their heads, because the world had turned upside-down; the Elector's head with its full-bottomed wig nodded and whispered: 'Hold on to me tight!' – and only the cannon-fire from the ramparts brought me back to my senses, and I climbed slowly down from the Elector's horse.

As I went home I again saw mad Alouisius dancing on one leg, while he rattled off the names of the French generals, and the hunchback Gumpertz rolling drunk in the gutter and howling 'Ça ira, ça ira', and I said to my mother: 'They want to make us happy, and so there's no school today.'

CHAPTER 7

NEXT day the world was back in order and there was school again, just as before, and we learnt our lessons by heart, just as before – the kings of Rome, the dates, the nouns with *im*, the irregular verbs, Greek, Hebrew, geography, German language, mental arithmetic, – goodness! it still makes my head swim – this had all to be learnt by heart. And much of it came in handy subsequently. For if I had not known the kings of Rome by heart, I wouldn't have cared a jot afterwards whether or not Niebuhr[18] had proved that they really never existed. And if I had not known dates, how could I afterwards have found my way around the great city of Berlin, where any two houses are as similar as two peas or two grenadiers, and where you cannot find your acquaintances unless you know the number of their house; for every acquaintance I thought of a historical event of which the date matched the number of his house, so that I could easily remember the one by thinking of the other, and hence a historical event always came into my mind whenever I caught sight of an acquaintance. For example, on meeting my tailor, I immediately thought of the Battle of Marathon; if I met the smartly-dressed banker Christian Gumpel, I immediately thought of the destruction of Jerusalem; if I caught sight of a Portuguese friend who was deep in debt, I immediately thought of Muhammad's flight from Mecca; if I saw the university judicial officer, a man whose strict probity is well known, I immediately thought of the death of Haman;[19] on seeing Wadzeck[20] I immediately thought of Cleopatra – Oh, dear God, the poor brute is dead now, his tear-ducts are dried up, and we may say with Hamlet: 'Take him for all in all, he was an old woman, we shall often look upon his like again!'[21] As I said, dates are quite indispensable, I know people who have nothing in their heads but a couple of dates, and thus managed to find the right houses in Berlin, and are already university professors. At school, though, I had a terrible time with all those numbers! Arithmetic, in the strict sense, was even harder. I found it easiest to subtract, where there is a very practical rule: 'Four from three won't go, so I must borrow one' – but I advise everyone in such cases to borrow a few pence extra; for you can never tell.

But as for Latin, you have no idea, Madame, how complicated it is. The Romans would never have had time to conquer the world if they had first had to learn Latin. These happy people already knew in their cradles which nouns took the accusative in *im*. I, however, had to learn them by heart in the sweat of my brow; still, it is just as well that I know them. For on 20 July 1825, when I held a Latin disputation in public in the great hall at Göttingen – Madame, it was well worth hearing – if I had said *sinapem* instead of *sinapim*, the first-year students present might have noticed it, and I should have been disgraced everlastingly. *Vis, buris, sitis, tussis, cucumis, amussis, cannabis, sinapis*[22] – These words, which have attracted so much attention in the world, did so by entering a distinct class and yet remaining an exception; I greatly respect them for it, and to have them at hand in case I should require them unexpectedly has given me inward solace and reassurance in many dark hours of my life. But, Madame, the irregular verbs – they differ from the regular verbs because they lead to more beatings – they are frightfully difficult. In the gloomy cloisters of the Franciscan monastery, near the classroom, there was then hanging a large crucified Christ made of grey wood, a dreadful image that still sometimes marches through my dreams, and gazes sorrowfully at me with fixed, bloodstained eyes – I would often stand in front of this image and pray: 'Oh, you poor God who was tortured like me, if you possibly can, please make sure that I remember the irregular verbs.'

I shall say nothing about Greek; it would annoy me too much. The monks in the Middle Ages were not far wrong when they maintained that Greek was an invention of the Devil. God knows the sufferings that I endured in learning it. Hebrew was easier, for I always had a soft spot for the Jews, even though they crucify my good name to this day; but I could not learn as much Hebrew as my pocket-watch, which had much intimate contact with pawnbrokers, and thus acquired many Jewish habits – for example, it wouldn't go on Saturdays – and learnt the sacred language, and practised its grammar afterwards; for in sleepless nights I would often be astonished to hear it ticking to itself: *katal, katalta, katalti – kittel, kittalta, kittalti – pokat, pokadeti – pikat – pik – pik*[23] –

Still, I understood much more of the German language, and that isn't exactly child's play. For we poor Germans, as if we weren't sufficiently plagued by having soldiers quartered on us, doing military service, and paying poll-taxes and a thousand other dues, have also saddled ourselves with Adelung's grammar,[24] and torment one another with the accusative and the dative. I learnt a great deal of German language from old Rector Schallmeyer, a fine cleric, who had looked after my welfare ever since I was a child. But I also learnt something of the sort from Professor Schramm, a man who had written a book on perpetual peace, and in whose class my fellow-brats did most squabbling.

While writing away without a pause, and having all sorts of ideas, I have started telling old school stories without noticing it, and I take this opportunity to point out to you, Madame, that it was not my fault that I learnt so little geography that afterwards I could not find my way around in the world. For at that time, you see, the French had moved all the frontiers, countries were given new colours every day, those that had been blue suddenly became green, some even became blood-red, the numbers of souls listed in the textbooks were moved about and mixed up until the Devil himself couldn't get them right; the natural products likewise changed, chicory and mangel-wurzels now grew where there had previously been nothing to see but rabbits and country squires chasing them; national characters also changed, the Germans became agile, the French no longer paid compliments, the English no longer threw their money away, and the Venetians were not cunning enough; among the princes there was plenty of promotion, the old kings acquired new uniforms, new kingdoms were baked and went like hot cakes, yet many potentates were chased out of house and home, and had to try to earn their living by different means, and some took to a trade and made sealing-wax or – Madame, this period is about to end, I'm almost out of breath – to cut a long story short, in times like these you can't get very far in geography.

Natural history is easier, there are not so many changes going on, and you have engravings of monkeys, kangaroos, zebras, rhinoceroi, and so on. Since I remembered these pictures vividly, it often happened subsequently that people would seem on first sight like old acquaintances.

Mythology was easy too. I greatly enjoyed the rabble of gods who ruled the world in such cheerful nakedness. I doubt if any schoolboy in ancient Rome learnt the main articles of his catechism, such as Venus's love-affairs, better than I did. To be quite honest, since we had to learn the ancient gods by heart, we should have kept them too, and we are probably little better off with our neo-Roman tritheism, let alone our Jewish monidolatry. Perhaps that mythology was not really so immoral as people have claimed; for example, it was a very proper idea of Homer's to give the much-loved Venus a husband.

I did best, however, in the French lessons of the Abbé Daulnoy, a French émigré, who had written lots of grammars and wore a red wig, and sprang to and fro very slyly when he was lecturing on his *Art poétique* and *Histoire allemande* – In the whole school he was the only person who taught German history. French, though, has its own difficulties, and to learn it you need many soldiers quartered upon you, much drum-beating, much *apprendre par cœur*, and above all, you mustn't be a *bête allemande*.[25] There were many harsh words, and I remember as if it were yesterday how I got into trouble because of *la religion*. I must have been asked six times: 'Henri, what is the French for faith?' And six times, more tearfully each time, I answered: 'It's *le crédit*.' And the seventh time the enraged examiner, cherry-red in the face, cried: 'It is *la religion*' – and blows rained down, and all my schoolmates laughed. Madame! from that time on I have never been able to hear the word *religion* mentioned without my back turning pale with fright and my cheeks going red with shame. And quite honestly, in my life *le crédit* has been more use to me than *la religion* – It suddenly occurs to me that I still owe five dollars to the landlord of the Lion in Bologna – And truly, I undertake to owe him another five dollars on top of that, provided I never need to hear the unhappy word *la religion* again in this life.

Parbleu, Madame! my French is very good indeed! I can understand not only patois, but also the French of noble nursemaids. Not long ago, in an aristocratic gathering, I could understand almost half the conversation of two German countesses, each of whom numbered more than sixty-four years and as many ancestors. Indeed, I once heard Monsieur Hans Michel Martens[26] talking French in the Café Royal at Berlin, and understood every word, though he lacked an understanding. You have to know the spirit of the language, and that is best learnt from drumming. *Parbleu*! how much I owe to the French drummer who was quartered on us for so long, and looked like a devil, and yet was as kind-hearted as an angel, and drummed so admirably.

He was a small, nimble figure with a fearsome black moustache, under which his red lips were thrust out defiantly, while his fiery eyes darted to and fro.

As a little boy I followed him about continually, and helped him polish his buttons till they shone like mirrors, and whiten his waistcoat with chalk – for Monsieur Le Grand wanted to make a good impression – and I followed him to guard-duty, to roll-call, to parade – that consisted solely of shining weapons and merriment – *les jours de fête sont passés!* Monsieur Le Grand could speak only a little broken German, only the most important expressions, like 'bread', 'kiss', 'honour' – but he could make himself very well understood on the drum. For instance, if I did not know what the word *liberté* meant, he would drum the Marseillaise – and I understood. If I did not know the meaning of the word *égalité*, he would drum the march 'Ça ira, ça ira – les aristocrates à la lanterne!' – and I understood. If I did not know what *bêtise* was, he would drum the Dessau March, which we Germans drummed in Champagne, as Goethe[27] reports – and I understood. One day he wanted to explain to me the word *l'Allemagne*, and he drummed that simple, basic tune to which trained dogs sometimes dance on market-days, namely 'Dum – Dum – Dum' – I was annoyed, but I understood all right.

He taught me modern history in the same way. I did not understand the words he spoke, but since he drummed all the time he was speaking, I still knew what he meant. That is, after all, the best method of teaching. You cannot really understand the history of the storming of the Bastille, the Tuileries, and so on, until you know how the drum was beaten on these occasions. Our school textbooks merely say: 'Their Excellencies the Barons and Counts and their gracious spouses were beheaded – Their Graces the Dukes and Princes and their most gracious spouses were beheaded – His Majesty the King and his supremely gracious spouse were beheaded' – but when you hear the red Guillotine March being drummed, then you understand it properly, and learn the why and the wherefore. Madame, that is a very curious march! A shudder ran through my very marrow when I heard it for the first time, and I was glad to forget it – You forget something like that when you grow older, a young man nowadays has so much knowledge to keep in his head – whist, boston, genealogical tables, decrees of the Federal Diet, dramaturgy, liturgy, meat-carving – and really, however much I rubbed my forehead, it was a long time before I could recall that mighty march. But just think, Madame! not long ago I was sitting at table with a whole menagerie of Counts, Princes, Princesses, Lords of the Bedchamber, Lady Chamberlains, Lord High Cup-Bearers, High Governesses, Lord High Keepers of the Silver, Lady High Hunting-Mistresses, and whatever else these grand court servants may be called, and their inferior servants ran about behind their chairs and shoved the well-filled plates in front of their noses – but I, ignored and overlooked by all, was sitting idly, with nothing to keep my jaws occupied, and rolling pieces of bread into balls, and drumming with my fingers out of boredom, and to my horror I suddenly drummed the long-forgotten red Guillotine March.

'And what happened?' Madame, these people are not to be disturbed while eating, and do not know that other people, with nothing to eat, suddenly start drumming, and drum very curious marches that were thought to have been forgotten long ago.

Whether the talent for drumming is innate, or whether I developed it at an early age, never mind, I have it in my bones, in my hands and feet, and it sometimes announces itself without my volition. Without my volition. Once at Berlin I was at a lecture given by Privy Counsellor Schmalz,[28] a man who saved the state by his book on the danger from black-coats and red-coats – you remember, Madame, from Pausanias that an equally dangerous plot was once exposed by the braying of a donkey, and you know from Livy, or from Becker's[29] *History of the World*, that geese saved the Capitol, and you know very well from Sallust that it was through a talkative tart, Mrs Fulvia, that Catiline's frightful conspiracy came to light – but *revenons à nos moutons*: I was listening to Privy Counsellor Schmalz lecturing on international law, and it was a tedious summer afternoon, and I was sitting on the bench, listening less and less – my head went to sleep – but suddenly I was woken by the noise of my own feet, which had stayed awake, and had probably heard the lecturer expounding the exact opposite of international law and denouncing the constitutional mentality, and my feet, which know what is going on in the world better than the Privy Counsellor does with his head, these poor, mute feet, incapable of expressing their humble opinion in words, wanted to make themselves understood by drumming, and drummed so hard that I nearly got into serious trouble.

My confounded, thoughtless feet! they played a similar trick on me when I was attending one of Professor Saalfeld's[30] lectures in Göttin gen, and he was bounding to and fro on the platform with his stiff agility, and working himself into a lather so that he might denounce the Emperor Napoleon thoroughly – no, poor feet, I can't blame you for making me drum on that occasion, indeed I wouldn't even have blamed you if, with your mute naivety, you had conveyed your opinion with even clearer stamping. How can I, the pupil of Le Grand, hear the Emperor being insulted? The Emperor! the Emperor! the great Emperor!

Whenever I think of the great Emperor, my memory assumes the green and golden hues of summer, a long avenue of flowering lime-trees appears, nightingales are perching and singing on the leafy branches, the waterfall is murmuring, flowers are standing on round beds and moving their beautiful heads as though in a dream – I held a curious communion with them, the painted tulips greeted me with beggarly condescension, the hysterical lilies nodded with melancholy tenderness, the drunken red of the roses laughed to me from the distance, the violets sighed – I was not yet acquainted with the myrtles and laurels, for they did not lure me with shimmering blossoms, but I was especially intimate with the mignonettes, with which I am now on such bad terms – I am talking about the Hofgarten at Düsseldorf, where I often lay on the grass, listening devoutly, when Monsieur Le Grand talked about the warlike deeds of the great Emperor, and beat the marches that were drummed as those deeds were happening, so that I saw and heard everything with the utmost vividness. I saw the army crossing the Simplon – the Emperor ahead, with the brave grenadiers scrambling after him, while frightened birds squawk and the glaciers thunder in the distance – I saw the Emperor holding the flag on the bridge at Lodi – I saw the Emperor in his grey cloak at Marengo – I saw the Emperor on horseback in the Battle of the Pyramids – nothing but gun-smoke and Mamelukes – I saw the Emperor in the Battle of Austerlitz – hey! how the bullets whistled across the smooth icy surface! – I saw, I heard the Battle of Jena – dum, dum, dum – I saw, I heard the battles of Eylau, Wagram – – – – no, I could hardly stand it! Monsieur Le Grand drummed so hard that my own ear-drums almost split.

CHAPTER 8

But how did I feel when I actually saw him, with my own highly favoured eyes? – *him* – Hosanna! the Emperor.

It was in that very place, in the avenue of the Hofgarten at Düsseldorf. As I forced my way through the gaping populace, I thought of the deeds and battles that Monsieur Le Grand had drummed into me, my heart was beating the general march – and yet at the same time I was thinking of the police regulation that no one may ride down the middle of the avenue on pain of a five-dollar fine. And the Emperor with his train was riding down the middle of the avenue, the shuddering trees bent forwards as he passed, the sunbeams trembled with timorous curiosity through the green foliage, and in the blue sky above a golden star could be seen floating. The Emperor was wearing his modest green uniform and his small world-historical hat. He was riding on a white pony, and it was walking with such quiet pride, such assurance, such distinction – if I had been Crown Prince of Prussia, I would have envied that pony. The Emperor sat in a relaxed, almost slouching posture, holding the reins with one hand and good-humouredly patting the pony's neck with the other. It was a hand of sunny marble, a powerful hand, one of the two hands that had tamed the many-headed monster of anarchy and regulated the duel between the nations – and it was good-humouredly patting the pony's neck. His face, too, had the colour that we find on Greek and Roman marble busts, his features were noble and dignified, like those of ancient sculptures, and on his face were written the words: 'Thou shalt have no other gods beside me.' A smile that warmed and reassured every heart was hovering about his lips – and yet we knew that these lips had only to whistle, – *et la Prusse n'existait plus*[31] – these lips had only to whistle – and the whole of the clergy would sink into silence – these lips had only to whistle – and the entire Holy Roman Empire would dance. And these lips were smiling, and his eyes, too, were smiling. They were eyes as clear as the sky, they could read the heart of man, they could survey everything in the world at once, while the rest of us see things only in succession, and see only their coloured shadows. His brow was not so clear, it was haunted by the ghosts of future battles, and occasionally this brow would twitch, and that indicated the creative thoughts, the great thoughts in seven-league boots, with which the Emperor's mind invisibly bestrode the world – and I believe that any one of these thoughts would have supplied a German writer with ample material to write about for the whole of his life.

The Emperor rode calmly down the middle of the avenue, no policeman tried to stop him; behind him, proudly mounted on snorting steeds, and weighed down with gold and finery, rode his train, the drums rolled, the trumpets sounded; beside me mad Alouisius was spinning round and rattling off the names of his generals, and drunken Gumpertz was howling nearby, and the populace cried in a thousand voices: 'Long live the Emperor!'

CHAPTER 9

THE Emperor is dead. On a desolate island in the Indian Ocean[32] lies his lonely grave, and He, for whom the earth was too small, is lying quietly under the mound where five weeping willows hang down their green hair in grief and a pious streamlet trickles past with a melancholy lament. There is no inscription on his gravestone; but Clio, with her just chisel, wrote invisible words on it which will ring down the millennia like spiritual music.

Britannia! you own the sea. But the sea has not water enough to wash away the disgrace that this great man bequeathed to you as he died. It was not your sly Sir Hudson,[33] no, you yourself were the Sicilian assassin hired by a conspiracy of kings to take secret revenge on the man of the people for what the people had once done publicly to one of your own kind – and he was your guest, and was sitting by your fireside –

Throughout all future ages the boys of France will sing and speak about the terrible hospitality of the Bellerophon, and when these mournful and mocking songs shall sound across the Channel, the cheeks of all decent Britons will blush. One day, though, this song will sound across the Channel, and there will no longer be a Britain; the proud nation will be overthrown, Westminster's monuments will lie in ruins, and the royal dust they enclose will be forgotten – And St Helena will be the Holy Sepulchre to which the nations of the Orient and the Occident will make pilgrimages in ships gay with flags, and fortify their hearts by remembering the deeds of the secular Saviour, who suffered under Hudson Lowe, as it is written in the Gospels of Las Cases, O'Meara, and Antommarchi.

Strange! the Emperor's three greatest antagonists have all met a terrible fate: Londonderry[34] cut his throat, Louis XVIII rotted on his throne, and Professor Saalfeld is still a professor at Göttingen.

CHAPTER 10

It was a bright autumn day, with a touch of frost in the air, as a young man with a student-like appearance wandered slowly along the avenue of the Hofgarten in Düsseldorf, sometimes, as though with childish pleasure, kicking the rustling leaves that covered the ground, but sometimes casting melancholy glances up to the withered trees on which only a few golden leaves were still hanging. Whenever he looked up in this way, he remembered the words of Glaucus:

> Very like leaves
> upon this earth are the generations of men –
> old leaves, cast on the ground by wind, young leaves
> the greening forest bears when spring comes in.
> So mortals pass; one generation flowers
> even as another dies away.[35]

In former days the young man had looked up at these very trees with quite different feelings, and at that time he was a boy, looking for birds' nests or beetles, which greatly delighted him when they buzzed merrily and enjoyed the pretty world and were pleased with a juicy green leaf, with a droplet of dew, with a warm sunbeam, and with the sweet scent of herbs. At that time the boy's heart was as happy as the creatures fluttering around him. Now, however, his heart had grown older, the little sunbeams in it were extinguished, all its flowers were dead, even its beautiful dream of love had faded away, the poor heart contained only courage and grief, and so that I may tell you the worst: it was my heart.

On the same day I had returned to my old home-town, but I did not want to spend the night there and was longing to be in Godesberg, so that I could sit down at the feet of my friend there and tell her about little Veronika. I had been visiting the beloved graves. Of all my living friends and relatives I had found only an uncle and an aunt. If I met any other familiar figures in the street, nobody recognized me any longer, and the town itself looked at me with a stranger's eyes, many houses had been repainted in the meantime, strangers' faces peered out of the windows, aged sparrows were fluttering round the old chimneys, everything looked dead and yet fresh, like lettuce growing in a churchyard; where people had once spoken French, they now spoke Prussian, even a miniature Prussian court had migrated there in the interval, and people bore courtly titles, my mother's former hairdresser was now Hairdresser Royal, and there were Tailors Royal, Cobblers Royal, Bug-Exterminators Royal, Gin-Shops Royal, the whole town seemed to be an Asylum Royal for Lunatics Royal. Only the old Elector recognized me, he was still standing in his old place; but he seemed to have grown thinner. Since he had remained standing in the middle of the market-place, he had witnessed all the misery of the time, and such sights do not make you fat. I felt as though I were dreaming, and thought of the fairy-tale about the enchanted towns, and I hastened out of the gate so that I should not wake up too soon. In the Hofgarten I missed many trees, and many were stunted, and the four tall poplars which used to seem like green giants had shrunk. Some pretty girls were out strolling, smartly dressed in bright colours, like walking tulips. And I had known these tulips when they were little bulbs; for alas, they were the children of neighbours, with whom I used to play 'Princess in the Tower'. But the beautiful maidens whom I used to know as blooming roses now looked like faded roses, and in many lofty foreheads, whose pride used to delight my heart, Saturn had cut deep wrinkles with his scythe. Only now, but alas! far too late, did I discover the meaning of the glance they used to throw to the boy as he grew into a young man; for in the interval, while abroad, I had noticed many parallel passages in beautiful eyes. I was deeply moved by seeing a man humbly doff his hat whom I had formerly beheld in wealth and grandeur and who had since sunk into beggary; just as it may everywhere be seen that once people are sinking, as in Newton's law of gravity, they fall terrifyingly faster and faster into misery. However, someone who did not seem to have changed at all was the little Baron who was tripping through the Hofgarten as merrily as ever, holding up his left coat-tail with one hand and swinging his slender cane to and fro with the other; he still had the same friendly little face, with its rubicund hue concentrated around his nose, he still had the same old conical hat, he still had the same old pigtail, except that some white hairs were emerging from the latter instead of the former black hair. But however happy he might look, I nevertheless knew that the poor Baron had had to endure much sorrow in the meantime; his face was trying to hide it from me, but the white hairs in his pigtail betrayed it behind his back. And the pigtail itself would have liked to deny it, and wagged with melancholy merriment.

I was not tired, yet I took a fancy to sit once more on the wooden bench in which I had once carved the name of my sweetheart. I could hardly find it, so many new names had been carved over it. Alas! I once fell asleep on this bench and dreamed of happiness and love. 'Dreams go by contraries.' The games I played as a child came back into my mind as well, and the pretty old fairy-tales; but a new, cheating game and a new, nasty tale kept breaking in, and it was the story of two poor souls who were unfaithful to each other, and afterwards took unfaithfulness so far that they were even unfaithful to God. It is a bad story, and if you happen to have nothing better to do, it can make you cry. O God! the world used to be so pretty, and the birds sang your everlasting praises, and little Veronika looked at me with her quiet eyes, and the two of us sat in front of the marble statue on the Castle Square – on one side stands the old ruined castle, which is haunted, for at night a lady in black silk, without her head, walks about with a long, rustling train; on the other side stands a high white building in whose upper rooms bright pictures gleamed marvellously in their gold frames, and in whose ground-floor rooms were so many thousands of huge books, which I and little Veronika would often look at inquisitively, when pious Ursula lifted us up to the height of the big windows – Later, when I was a big boy, I climbed the highest rungs of the ladders there every day, and read until I was no longer afraid of anything, least of all headless ladies, and I became so clever that I forgot all the old games and fairy-tales and pictures and little Veronika and even her name.

But as I was musing on the past, seated on the old bench in the Hofgarten, I heard behind me a confused sound of human voices, lamenting the fate of the poor Frenchmen who had been transported to Siberia as prisoners during the Russian campaign, kept there for several years even though peace had been declared, and were only now returning home. Looking up, I saw these orphan children of glory; naked misery was peeping through the rents in their ragged uniforms, their weatherbeaten faces had deep, lamenting eyes, and although mutilated, weary and mostly limping, they retained a sort of military step, and, strange to say, a drummer with a drum was tottering at their head; and with inward horror I recollected the tale of the soldiers who are killed in battle by day and rise again from the battlefield at night and march to their home-town led by the drummer; as the old folk-song goes:

He beat the drum both up and down,
They are back in their native town,
And in the moonlit street,
Tra-la-lee, tra-la-lai, tra-la-la,
Where dwells a lover sweet.

At dawn, the bones of the brave
All stand in ranks, like graves,
The drummer's at their head,
Tra-la-lee, tra-la-lai, tra-la-la,
His sweetheart sees him stride.

Indeed, the poor French drummer seemed to have risen from his grave half decayed: he was only a little shadow in a dirty, ragged grey cloak, a deathly yellow face with a large moustache hanging sorrowfully down over his faded lips; his eyes were like burnt tinder in which only a few small sparks still glimmer, and yet a single one of these sparks was enough for me to recognize Monsieur Le Grand.

He recognized me as well, and drew me down on to the grass, and we sat there as before, when he used to give me lectures with his drum on the French language and modern history. It was still the old, familiar drum, and I never ceased to marvel that he saved it from Russian greed. He was again drumming as before, but without speaking. However, if his lips were pressed together in a sinister fashion, his eyes said all the more, shining victoriously as he drummed the old marches. The poplars near us trembled as he made the red Guillotine March thunder forth once more. He also drummed the old struggles for freedom, the old battles, the Emperor's deeds, as before, and the drum itself seemed to be a living being which was glad to utter its deep joy. I heard once more the cannons' thunder, the whistling of the bullets, the uproar of the battle, I saw once more the fluttering flags, I saw once more the Emperor on horseback – but gradually a gloomy note entered the joyful drum-roll, the drum uttered sounds in which the wildest rejoicing and the most terrible mourning were uncannily mingled, it seemed to be at once a victory march and a dead march. Le Grand's eyes opened wide as though haunted, and I saw in them nothing but a broad white field of ice covered with corpses – it was the Battle of Borodino.

I would never have thought that the tough old drum could utter such cries of agony as Monsieur Le Grand now managed to wring from it. They were a drum's tears, and they sounded softer and softer, and like a dismal echo deep groans broke forth from Le Grand's bosom. And he became paler and more ghost-like, his withered hands were trembling with frost, he sat there like a man in a dream, and moved only the air with his drum-sticks, and seemed to be listening to distant voices, and at last he looked at me with a deep, abysmal, imploring look – I understood him – and then his head sank down on to the drum.

Monsieur Le Grand never drummed again in this life. Nor did his drum ever utter another sound, it was not to beat a servile tattoo for any enemy of freedom: I had understood Le Grand's last imploring look very well, and I at once drew the blade from my sword-stick and punctured the drum.

CHAPTER II

Du sublime au ridicule il n'y a qu'un pas, Madame![36]

But life is really so dreadfully serious that it could not be endured without such a link between the pathetic and the comic. Our poets know this. Aristophanes shows us the most hideous images of human madness only in the laughing mirror of wit; Goethe ventures to utter the agony of the thinker who understands his own nullity only in the doggerel verses of a puppet-play; and Shakespeare places the most deadly lament about the misery of the world in the mouth of a fool, shaking his cap and bells in terror.

They have all modelled themselves on the great primal poet, whose world tragedy in a thousand acts carries humour to its highest pitch, as we see every day: after the death of the hero the clowns and buffoons come on stage with their custard pies, after the bloody revolution scenes and the imperial action the fat Bourbons come waddling along with their stale jokes and delicately legitimate *bons mots*, and the old *noblesse* come gracefully mincing with their half-starved smiles, and after them troop the pious monks in their cowls with candles, crosses and banners; – touches of comedy tend to creep even into the supreme pathos of the world tragedy, the despairing republican who plunges a dagger into his heart, like Brutus, may have smelt the dagger beforehand in case it had been used to cut up a herring, and the world's great stage is just like our small-town theatres in other respects: it too has drunken heroes, kings who forget their lines, backdrops that get stuck, prompters with voices everyone can hear, dancers who rely on the poetic effect of their thighs, costumes which are shiny and not much else – And up in heaven, in the front row of the stalls, sit the little angels, eyeing us earthly comedians through their opera-glasses, and God sits solemnly in his box, perhaps bored, or calculating that this theatre cannot stay in business much longer, since one actor is paid too much and another too little, and all of them act execrably.

Du sublime au ridicule il n'y a qu'un pas, Madame! As I was writing the end of the last chapter, and telling you about the death of Monsieur Le Grand, and how I faithfully executed the *testamentum militare* in his dying gaze, there was a knock at the door of my room, and in came a poor old woman who asked me kindly if I was a doctor? And when I said yes, she asked me very kindly to go home with her to cut her husband's corns.

CHAPTER 12

THE German censors — — — — — — — — — — — — — —
— — — — — — — — — — — — — — — — — — — —
— — — — — — — — — — — — — — — — — — — —
— — — — — — — — — — — — — — — — — — — —
— — — — — — — — — — — — — — — — — — — —
— — — — — — — — — — — — — — — — — — — —
— — — — — — — — — — — — — — — — — — — —
— — — — — — — — — — — — — — — — — — — —
— — — — — — — — — — — — — — — — — — — —
— — — — — — — — — — — — — — — — — — — —
— — — — — — — — — — — — — — — — — — — —

— — — — — — — — — — — — — — — — — — — —
— — — — — — — — — — — — idiots — — — — — — — —
— — — — — — — — — — — — — — — — — — — —
— — — — — — — — — — — — — — — — — — — —
— — — — — — — — — — — — — — — — — — — —
— — — — — — — — — — — — — — — — — — — —
— — — — — — — — — — — — — — — — — — — —
— — — — — — — — — — — — — — — — — — — —
— — — — — — — — — — — — — — — — — — — —
— — — — — — — — — — — — — — — — — — — —
— — — — — — — — — — — — — — — — — — — —
— — — — — — — — — — — — — — — — — — — —

CHAPTER 13

MADAME! the entire Trojan War already lay under Leda's brooding hemispheres,[37] and you cannot possibly understand the famous deeds of Priam unless I first tell you about the old swan's eggs. Therefore do not complain about my digressions. In all the preceding chapters there is not a single line that is not strictly relevant; I write concisely, avoiding everything superfluous, indeed I often miss out essential matters: for example, I have not yet done any proper quoting – not of prices, but of writers – and yet quoting from old and new books is a young author's chief pleasure, and a couple of profoundly learned quotations adorn the whole man. Do not think, Madame, that I lack acquaintance with the titles of books. I also have the knack of great spirits who know how to pluck the currants out of rolls and quotations out of lecture-notes; I know which side my bread is buttered on. In an emergency I could raise a loan of quotations from my learned friends. My friend G.[38] in Berlin is, as it were, a little Rothschild of quotations, and would be glad to lend me a few million, and if he doesn't have them ready to hand, he can easily get them from a few other cosmopolitan bankers of the mind. But I have no need to raise a loan at present, I am very comfortably off, I have 10,000 quotations a year to live on, and indeed I have even invented a way of passing off false quotations as genuine. If any great, rich scholar, like Michael Beer,[39] wants to buy this secret from me, I will readily part with it for 19,000 dollars in specie; and I would be prepared to negotiate. There is another invention which, for the good of literature, I shall not keep secret, but will communicate gratis:

I consider it advisable to quote all obscure authors by the numbers on their front doors.

These 'good folk and bad musicians', as the orchestra is called in *Ponce de Leon*[40] – these obscure authors always themselves possess a little copy of their long-forgotten slim volumes, and to obtain them, you have to know the numbers on their front doors. For example, if I were to quote Spitta's *Song-Book for Apprentice-Boys* – my dear Madame, where could you find it? But if I quote:

> 'see *Song-Book for Apprentice-Boys*, by P. Spitta, Lüneburg: number 2, Lüner Street, round the corner on your right' –

then, Madame, if you think it worth your while, you can obtain the book. However, it is not worth your while.

What is more, Madame, you have not the least idea how easily I can quote. I find opportunities everywhere to display my profound erudition. If I am talking about food, for instance, I observe in a footnote that the Romans, Greeks and Hebrews used likewise to eat, I quote all the delicious dishes prepared by Lucullus's[41] cook – alas that I was born a millennium and a half too late! – I also observe that communal meals were called such and such by the Greeks, and that the Spartans ate bad black soup – It is a good thing, after all, that I was not yet living in those days, I can imagine nothing more frightful than for a poor fellow like me to be a Spartan, soup is my favourite dish – Madame, I am planning to visit London soon, but if it is true that there is no soup there, yearning will drive me back to the soup-plates and flesh-pots of my fatherland. I could hold forth at some length about the food of the ancient Hebrews and go down to the Jewish cuisine of the most recent times – on this subject I quote the entire Steinweg[42] – I could also cite the humanity with which many Berlin scholars have spoken of the Jews' food, and that would bring me to the other admirable and excellent qualities of the Jews, the inventions we owe to them, such as bills of exchange and Christianity – but stop! we must not give them too much credit for the latter, since we have really made little use of it so far – I think the Jews themselves have found it of less account than the invention of bills of exchange. While on the subject of the Jews I could also quote Tacitus[43] – he says they worshipped donkeys in their temples – and on the subject of donkeys, what a vast array of quotations opens up before my eyes! How many noteworthy things could be said about ancient donkeys, in contrast to modern ones. How sensible the former were, and, alas, how stupid the latter are. How intelligently Balaam's ass[44] speaks:

see Pentat. *lib.* –

Madame, I haven't got the book to hand at the moment, and will leave this reference blank, to be filled in later. With regard to the idiocy of modern donkeys, however, I cite:

see —

no, I'll leave this reference blank as well, or else I shall be cited myself, for libel. Modern donkeys are great donkeys. The ancient donkeys, who were so cultivated,

see Gesneri *De antiqua honestate asinorum* (*In comment.*, Götting., Vol. II, p. 32)[45]

would turn in their graves if they heard how people talk about their descendants. At one time 'donkey' was an honourable title, meaning the same as 'Aulic Counsellor', 'Baron', 'Ph.D.' nowadays – Jacob[46] compares his son Issachar to a donkey, Homer compares his hero Ajax to one, and now this comparison is made with Herr von ....! Madame, on the subject of such donkeys I could go deeply into the history of literature, I could cite all the great men who have been in love, e.g. Abelardum, Picum Mirandulanum, Borbonium, Curtesium, Angelum Politianum, Raymundum Lullium, and Henricum Heineum. On the subject of love I could cite all the great men who did not smoke tobacco, e.g. Cicero, Justinian, Goethe, Hugo, Me – it so happens that all five of us are lawyers of a sort. Mabillon could not even stand the smoke of someone else's pipe, in his *Itinere germanico* he complains, referring to German inns, 'quod molestus ipsi fuerit tabaci grave olentis foetor'. Other great men, however, are said to have been fond of tobacco. Raphael Thorus composed a hymn to tobacco – you may not be aware, Madame, that it was published in quarto by Isaak Elseverius at Leyden in 1628 – and Ludovicus Kinschot wrote a verse preface for it. Graevius even wrote a sonnet about tobacco. The great Boxhornius also liked tobacco. Bayle, in his *Dict. hist. et critiq.*, claims to have heard that when smoking the great

Boxhornius wore a great hat with a hole in the front brim, in which he often placed his pipe, so that it should not disturb him in his studies – That reminds me, on mentioning Boxhornius I could cite all the great scholars who did not know how to box and therefore ran away from a fight. However, I shall refer merely to Johann Georg Martius, *De fuga literatorum*, etc. etc. etc. If we examine history, Madame, all great men have had to run away at some point in their lives: Lot,[47] Tarquin, Moses, Jupiter, Madame de Staël, Nebuchadnezzar, Benjowsky, Muhammad, the entire Prussian army, Gregory VII, Rabbi Yitskhok Abarbanel, Rousseau – I could cite many, many more names, including those written up on the blackboard at the Stock Exchange.

You see, Madame, I am not lacking in thoroughness and profundity; only I cannot as yet manage to be methodical. As a true German I should have begun this book with an explanation of its title, as is the use and wont in the Holy Roman Empire. It is true that Phidias did not write a preface to his Jupiter, any more than a quotation can be found on the Medici Venus – I have inspected her from all sides; – but the ancient Greeks were Greeks, and people like us are honest Germans and cannot quite deny our German character, and therefore I must say something retrospectively about the title of my book.

Madame, I shall accordingly speak:

- I. Of ideas.
  - A. Of ideas in general.
    - (a) Of sensible ideas.
    - (b) Of senseless ideas.
      - α. Of ordinary ideas.
      - β. Of ideas upholstered in green leather.

These in turn are subdivided into – but we shall come to that in due course.

CHAPTER 14

MADAME, have you any idea of an idea? What is an idea? 'There are some good ideas in this coat,' said my tailor, casting a gravely appreciative look at the surtout, dating back to my days of Berlin elegance, which was now to be made into a decent dressing-gown. My laundry-woman complains that 'Pastor S.[48] has put ideas into her daughter's head, and she's gone all silly and won't see reason'. Pattensen the coachman is always muttering: 'That's an idea! that's an idea!' Yesterday, however, he became quite cross when I asked him what he understood by an idea, and he muttered crossly: 'Well, well, an idea's an idea! an idea's all the nonsense people get into their heads.' The word is used in the same sense in the title of a book by Aulic Counsellor Heeren[49] in Göttingen.

Pattensen the coachman is a man who can find his way on the vast Lüneburg Heath in pitch darkness; Aulic Counsellor Heeren is a man who by a similar astute instinct discovers the old caravan routes of the East, and has been travelling along them for many a long year, as securely and patiently as any camel of antiquity; you can rely on such people, you can follow them with an easy mind, and that is why I have entitled this book *Ideas*.

Accordingly the book's title means just as little as its author's title: it was not chosen by him in a spirit of scholarly arrogance, and must not be interpreted as reflecting his vanity. Accept my most sorrowful assurance, Madame, that I am not vain. This observation is necessary, as you will notice from time to time. I am not vain – And even if a forest of laurels grew on my head, and a sea of incense flowed into my young heart – I should not become vain. My friends, and the other people who share my time and my space, have taken good care of that – You know, Madame, that old women whose foster-children are praised for their beauty spit on them, so that the praise may not harm the children – You know, Madame, that in Rome, when a general celebrating a triumph, crowned with glory and adorned in purple, drove from the Campo Martii in his gold chariot with white horses, standing out like a god from the solemn procession of lictors, musicians, dancers, priests, slaves, elephants, trophy-carriers, consuls, senators, soldiers, then the rabble following sang all manner of mocking songs – And you know, Madame, that in dear old Germany there are plenty of old women and rabble.

As I said, Madame, the ideas dealt with here are just as remote from the Platonic ones as Athens is from Göttingen, and you should not expect too much from the book, any more than from the author. Truly, it is as baffling to me as to my friends how he could ever have aroused such expectations. Trying to explain the matter, Countess Julie declares that if the aforesaid author does occasionally say something really witty and original, he is merely pretending, and at bottom he is just as stupid as everyone else. That is false, I am not pretending in the slightest, I speak plainly and bluntly, I write whatever comes into my head, in all innocence and simplicity, and I am not to blame if it is something clever. But I have better luck in writing than in the Altona lottery – I wish it were the other way round – and my pen produces many bull's-eyes, many quaternes, and that is God's doing; – for HE, who denies the most devout psalmists and the most edifying poets any good ideas or glory in literature, so that they may not be praised too much by their earthly fellow-creatures and thus forget about heaven, where angels are already preparing their rooms: – HE blesses us profane, sinful, heretical writers, for whom heaven is bolted and barred, all the more with excellent ideas and human glory, and this comes from his divine grace and compassion, so that the poor soul, once it has been created, shall not be left empty-handed and shall at least on earth feel something of the bliss which is denied to it up above.

See Goethe and the tract-writers.

Thus you see, Madame, that you may read my writings, they testify to the grace and compassion of God, I write trusting blindly in his omnipotence; in this regard I am a truly Christian writer, and, to speak with Gubitz,[50] in beginning the present period, I still do not know how to end it, or what I am to say, and I rely on God to help me. And how could I write without this pious certainty? The lad from Langhoff's printing-house is already standing in my room waiting for copy, the word is scarcely born before it travels, warm and moist, to the press, and what I think and feel at this moment may already be scrap paper by lunchtime tomorrow.

It is easy for you to talk, Madame, when you remind me of Horace's *nonum prematur in annum*.[51] This precept, like others of the kind, may well hold good in theory, but in practice it is worthless. When Horace gave authors the famous precept that they should keep their work in their desk for nine years, he should at the same time have given them the secret of spending nine years without eating. When Horace devised this rule, he was probably sitting at Maecenas's table and eating turkeys with truffles, pheasant pudding in game sauce, larks' ribs with Teltow beetroot, peacocks' tongues, Indian birds' nests, and heaven knows what else, and all without paying a penny. But we wretches were born too late: we live in a different epoch, our Maecenases have very different principles, they think that authors and medlars are best after lying on straw for a while, they think the dogs would be unable to hunt ideas and images if they were fed too fat, and alas! if they ever do feed a poor dog, it is the wrong one, who least deserves the crumbs, such as the dachshund who licks their hands, or the tiny Bolognese lap-dog who nestles in the fragrant lap of the lady of the house, or the patient poodle whose studies have been vocational and knows how to fetch, dance, and beat the drum – As I write these words, my little pug-dog is standing behind me and barking – Do be quiet, Ami, I didn't mean you, for you love me and accompany your master through hardship and danger and would die on his grave, as faithfully as many another German dog, who, cast into exile, lies outside the gates of Germany, starving and whimpering – Please excuse me, Madame, for digressing in order to give my poor dog an honourable explanation, I am returning to the Horatian precept and its inapplicability to the nineteenth century, in which poets must cling to the apron-strings and purse-strings of the Muse – *Ma foi*, Madame, I could not stand it for twenty-four hours, let alone nine years, my stomach does not care about immortality, I have changed my mind, I wish to be half immortal and completely well fed, and if Voltaire would have given three hundred years of his everlasting fame to be able to digest his food, I offer twice as much for food itself. Alas! what beautiful, blooming food there is in this world! The philosopher Pangloss[52] is right: it is the best of worlds! But you need money in this best of worlds, money in your pocket, not manuscripts in your desk. The landlord of the 'King of England', Mr Marr, is himself a writer and knows the Horatian precept, but I do not think that if I practised it he would feed me for nine years.

In any case, why should I practise it? I have so much good stuff to write that I have no need to make a fuss about it. So long as my heart is full of love and the heads of my fellow-men are full of folly, I shall never lack something to write about. And my heart will always love, so long as there are women; if it grows cold towards one, it will promptly burn for another; as in France the king never dies, so the queen in my heart will never die, and the word is: *la reine est morte, vive la reine!* Similarly, the folly of my fellow-men will never die out. For there is only one intelligence, and it has definite limits; but there are a thousand immeasurable follies. The learned casuist and writer Schupp[53] even says: 'There are more fools than people in the world –'

see the instructive writings of Schuppius, p. 1121.

If you consider that the great Schuppius lived in Hamburg, you will find this piece of statistical information far from exaggerated. I am in the same place, and I can say that I feel very pleased to think that all these fools I see here can be used in my writings, they are money in the bank, cash in hand. I'm in clover. The Lord has blessed me, there is a particularly fine crop of fools this year, and as a provident housekeeper I consume only a few, select the most fertile and store them up for the future. I am often seen on the promenade, cheerful and merry. Like a wealthy merchant, walking among the chests, bales and barrels in his warehouse and rubbing his hands with glee, so I walk among my people. You are all mine! You are all equally dear to me, and I love you as much as you love your money, and that is saying a lot. I could not help laughing heartily on hearing not long ago that one of my people had remarked anxiously that he could not tell how I would make my living in the long run – and yet he himself is such a capital fool that I could live on him alone, as though on capital. There are many fools, though, who are not merely cash in my hand; the cash I can extract from them by writing is already destined for some purpose. So, for example, there is a certain plump, well-padded millionair-head with whom I shall purchase a certain well-padded seat which French ladies call *chaise percée*. With his fat she-millionaire I shall buy a horse. Whenever I see the fat fellow – it is easier for a camel to enter the kingdom of heaven than for this man to pass through the eye of a needle – whenever I see him waddling along the promenade, I have a very odd feeling: although he does not know me from Adam, I cannot help bidding him good-day, and he returns my greeting so cordially, so invitingly, that I should like to make use of his kindness on the spot, and yet am embarrassed by the large numbers of smartly dressed people who happen to be passing. His lady wife is not too bad a lady – it is true that she has only one eye, but then it is all the greener; her nose is like the tower that looks towards Damascus;[54] her bosom is as vast as the sea, and on it are fluttering all manner of ribbons, like the flags of ships on these heaving billows – the very sight is enough to make you sea-sick – her neck is pretty with swelling curves like – the term of comparison is to be found further down – and the violet curtain that covers this term of comparison has undoubtedly taken the lives of thousands upon thousands of silkworms to spin. You see, Madame, what a steed I shall purchase! If the lady meets me on the promenade, my heart positively expands, I feel as though I could leap astride her, I brandish my riding-crop, I snap my fingers, I click my tongue, I make all kinds of equestrian movements with my legs – giddy-up! gee-up! – and the dear lady looks at me so soulfully, with such deep understanding, she whinnies with her eyes, she dilates her nostrils, she wiggles her crupper, she curvets, she suddenly goes into a short dog-trot – And I then stand with my arms folded, following her complacently with my eyes, and considering whether she should be ridden on a bit or a snaffle, whether I should give her an English or a Polish saddle – and so forth – People who see me standing still cannot make out what attracts me so much about the lady. Tale-bearing tongues have already tried to alarm her husband, hinting that I was watching his better half with the eyes of a roué. But my honest soft leather *chaise percée* is said to have replied that he considered me an innocent, indeed rather shy young man who watched him with some embarrassment as though anxious to become better acquainted but restrained by blushing bashfulness. My noble steed, however, opined that I had a free, unselfconscious, chivalrous manner, and my officious politeness merely signified my desire to be invited by them to lunch one day. –

You see, Madame, I can use everyone, and the directory of addresses is really the inventory of my belongings. And so I can never go bankrupt, for I would turn even my creditors into sources of revenue. Moreover, as I said, I really live very economically, damned economically. For instance, as I write this, I am sitting in a dark, dismal room on Düster Street – but I am happy to put up with it; after all, if I wanted to, I could sit in the most beautiful garden, like my friends and dear ones; I need only realize my schnapps-clients. These last, Madame, consist of depraved hairdressers, down-and-out procurers, restaurant-owners with nothing to eat, a parcel of rogues who know how to find my lodgings and tell me the *chronique scandaleuse* of their neighbourhood in return for a tip – Madame, you are surprised that I do not throw such gentry out of my house, once and for all? – What on earth are you thinking of, Madame! One day I shall describe them in a beautiful book, and with its proceeds I shall buy myself a garden, and with the red, yellow, blue and multi-coloured blotches on their faces they already seem like the flowers in this garden. What do I care if other people's noses maintain that these flowers only smell of brandy, cheese, tobacco and vice! my own nose, the chimney of my head, in which imagination climbs up and down as a chimney-sweep, maintains the contrary, and smells nothing in these people but the scent of roses, jasmine, violets, carnations, violas – Oh, how comfortably I shall sit in my garden of a morning, listening to the song of the birds, and warming my limbs in the dear sun, and inhaling the fresh breath of the greenery, and being reminded of those old rogues by the sight of the flowers!

For the moment, however, I am still sitting in my dark room on dark Düster Street, and contenting myself by hanging this country's obscurest man[55] in the middle of my room – *'Mais, est-ce que vous verrez plus clair alors?'* Self-evidently, Madame – but do not misunderstand me, I am not hanging the man himself, only the crystal chandelier which I shall buy with the fee I shall earn by writing about him. If people cannot be hanged, though, they must be branded. I am again speaking figuratively, I brand people in effigy. Certainly, Herr von Weiss – he is as free from vice as a lily – was persuaded that I told people in Berlin that he really had been branded; and so the fool asked the authorities to inspect him and testify that no coat of arms had been imprinted on his back, and he regarded this non-heraldic certificate as a diploma which must give him entrée into the best society, and was surprised to be thrown out despite it, and now calls down execrations on such a poor fellow as me, and intends to shoot me with a loaded pistol wherever he finds me – And what do you think, Madame, that I am doing about this? Madame, with this fool, that is, with the fee that I shall extract from him with my pen, I shall buy a good barrel of Rüdesheimer wine. I mention this in case you might think it is malice that makes me look so cheerful when I meet Herr von Weiss in the street. Truly, I see in him only my dear Rüdesheimer, no sooner do I catch sight of him than a blissful sensation steals over me, and I find myself lilting: 'On the Rhine, on the Rhine, there our vines are growing'[56] – 'This picture is divinely fair' – 'O white lady –' My

Rüdesheimer then looks extremely sour, as though it consisted only of gall and wormwood – But I assure you, Madame, it is a genuine vintage, and even if it is not branded with the stamp of authenticity, the connoisseur can appreciate it; I shall tap this barrel with the greatest of pleasure, and if it should bubble dangerously and threaten to burst asunder, it must be officially secured by a few iron hoops.

You see, Madame, you have no need to worry about me. I can look calmly at anything in the world. The Lord has blessed me with earthly goods, and even if he has not delivered the wine conveniently to my cellar, he still allows me to work in his vineyard, I have only to pick the grapes, to tread them, press them, and put them in vats, and I have God's own gift; and even if the fools do not fly into my mouth already roasted, but usually bump into me in a crude and tasteless manner, nevertheless I can turn them on the spit, baste them and pepper them, until they are tender and ready to eat. You will enjoy yourself, Madame, when I get round to giving my great *fête*. You will praise my cooking. You will confess that I can feast my satraps just as magnificently as the great Ahasveros, who was king over one hundred and twenty-seven provinces, from India to the blackamoors. I shall slaughter whole hecatombs of fools. The great schnapsophile who now woos Europe as ardently as Jupiter, in the shape of a bull, wooed Europa, will provide the roast; a sorrowful tragedian,[57] who showed us a sorrowful Alexander on a stage representing a sorrowful Persian kingdom, will provide my table with an excellent pig's head, smiling in the usual vinegary way, with a lemon segment in its mouth and a laurel wreath added by the talented cook; the singer of coral lips, swan-like necks, heaving snowy hillocks, thingummies, slender ankles, tender Mimilis, tender kisses and tender tax-assessors, none other than H. Clauren,[58] or, as the pious nuns of St Bernard on Friedrich Street call him, 'Father Clauren! our Clauren!' – this genuine specimen will provide all the dishes that he describes so divinely in his annual pocket-bordellos with the imagination of a sweet-guzzling kitchenmaid, and he will also give us a special little plate of celery 'that makes little hearts go pit-a-pat with love'; a wise and withered lady-in-waiting, whose head alone is edible, will provide an analogous dish, that is, asparagus; and there will be no shortage of Göttingen sausages, smoked meat from Hamburg, pigeon-breasts from Pomerania, ox-tongues, steamed calf's brains, cow's lips, dried fish, and all varieties of jelly, Berlin pancakes, Viennese tarts, jam –

Madame, the very thought is too much for my stomach! The devil take such gormandizing! I cannot take very much. I have a bad digestion. The pig's head has the same effect on me as on the rest of the German public – I must eat a Willibald Alexis[59] salad after it, to clean my mouth – O, the wretched pig's head with the still more wretched sauce, which tastes neither Greek nor Persian, but like tea with green soap; – Call my fat millionair-head!

CHAPTER 15

MADAME, I observe a slight cloud of displeasure on your lovely forehead, and you seem to be asking if it is not wrong of me to prepare fools thus, spitting them, chopping them up, larding them, not to mention the many whom I slaughter and must leave uneaten, and who fall prey to the sharp teeth of biting satirists, while their widows and orphans howl and lament –

Madame, *c'est la guerre*! I will now solve the entire riddle for you: I myself am not one of the reasonable people, but I have taken their side, and for the past 5,588 years[60] we have been at war with the fools. The fools think we have harmed them, for they maintain that the world contains only a limited quantity of reason, this entire quantity has been usurped, God knows how, by the reasonable people, and they add that it is a crying shame how often a single person has acquired so much reason that his fellow-citizens and all the country round him have become wholly obscure. This is the secret cause of the war, and it is a veritable war of annihilation. The reasonable people show themselves, as usual, to be the quietest, most moderate and most reasonable; they are well entrenched behind their old Aristotelian defences, with plenty of artillery and ample munitions, for after all it was they who invented gunpowder, and now and again they throw rationally proven bombs into their enemies' ranks. But unfortunately the latter are extremely numerous, and they make a great noise, and add daily to the horrors of war; just as all stupidity is a horror to the man of reason. Some chieftains in the great army take good care not to confess the secret cause of the war. They have heard that a well-known dishonest man, who took dishonesty so far that he ended up writing false memoirs, none other than Fouché,[61] once said: 'Les paroles sont faites pour cacher nos pensées'; and now they are very wordy in order to conceal their total lack of thoughts, and deliver long speeches and write fat books, and when you listen to them, they praise the sole redeeming source of thoughts, namely reason, and when you look at them, they are busy with mathematics, logic, statistics, mechanical improvements, civic responsibility, stable feeding, and so on – and as the ape becomes more ridiculous the more he resembles a man, so these fools become more ridiculous the more sensibly they carry on. Other chieftains in the great army are franker, and admit that their share of reason is very small, indeed that they may have missed out on it entirely; yet they cannot help declaring that reason is very sour and basically of little value. This may be true, but unfortunately they have not so much reason as is required to prove it. They therefore resort to all manner of expedients, they discover new powers within themselves which they allege to be just as effective as reason, indeed much more effective in certain emergencies; these powers include feeling, faith, inspiration, etc., and they console themselves with this substitute reason, this mangel-wurzel reason. But they have a particular hatred for poor me, maintaining that I am by nature one of themselves, that I am a renegade, a turncoat who has broken the most sacred ties; they even claim that I am now a spy, secretly watching the goings-on of the fools, in order to expose them afterwards to the laughter of my new associates; and that I am too stupid to realize that the latter at the same time laugh at me and will never consider me one of their own – And in this the fools are perfectly right.

It is quite true: they do not consider me one of their own, and they often snigger at me in secret. I am well aware of this, but I do not let it show. My heart bleeds inwardly, and when I am alone, my tears flow. I am well aware that my position is unnatural; everything I do is folly to the reasonable and a horror to the fools. They hate me, and I feel the truth of the proverb: 'A stone is heavy, and the sand weighty: but a fool's wrath is heavier than both.' Nor are they wrong to hate me. It is perfectly true, I have broken the most sacred ties, by all the laws of God and man I should have lived and died among the fools. And alas! I should have been so comfortable among these people! If I were willing to turn back, they would still receive me with open arms. They would read in my eyes whatever kindnesses they could render me. They would invite me to lunch every day and in the evenings they would take me to their tea-parties and clubs, and I could play whist, smoke tobacco, and talk politics with them, and whenever I yawned, they would say behind my back: 'What beautiful feelings! a soul full of faith!' – permit me, Madame, to dedicate a tear to my emotion – alas! and I would drink punch with them, until the right inspiration came, and then they would take me home in a sedan-chair, anxious lest I might catch cold, and one of them would hasten to hand me my slippers, another my silk dressing-gown, another my white night-cap, and they would then give me a personal professorship, or make me president of a society for converting the heathen, or chief calculating clerk, or director in charge of Roman excavations; – for I would be just the man to be useful in any field, not least because I can distinguish accurately between Latin declensions and conjugations, and am less liable than other people to mistake a Prussian postillion's boot for an Etruscan vase. My feelings, my faith, my inspiration could also accomplish much good at the hour of prayer – for me, that is; and as for my outstanding poetic talent, that would do me good service on the birthdays and wedding-days of important persons, and it would be no bad thing if in a great national epic I were to sing all the heroes whose rotting corpses are known to have produced worms that claim to be their descendants.

Because of these benefits, many people who are not born fools, and were once endowed with reason, have gone over to the fools and live like fighting-cocks; the nonsense that at first still cost them some effort has now become second nature; they should no longer be regarded as hypocrites, but as true believers. One of them, in whose head the sun is not yet completely eclipsed, is very fond of me, and recently, when I was alone with him, he locked the door and said to me in serious tones: 'O fool, who plays the wise man and yet has not so much intelligence as a recruit in his mother's womb! Don't you know that the great ones of this country raise only him who debases himself and praises their blood as better than his own? And now you are in bad odour with the country's pious ones! Is it so very difficult to turn up your eyes in blissful acknowledgement of divine grace, to clasp your hands devoutly and hide them in your sleeves, to hang down your head like a lamb of God, and to whisper Bible verses that you have learnt by heart? Believe me, none of the great and good will pay you for your godlessness, the men of love will hate you, slander you and persecute you, and you will make a career neither on earth nor in heaven!'

Alas! all this is true! But I simply have this unfortunate passion for reason! I love it, although it does not reward me by returning my love. I give it everything, and it allows me nothing. I cannot abandon it. And as the Jewish King Solomon, in the Song of Songs, once sang the Christian Church in the image of a dark girl burning with love, so that his Jews should not notice anything; so I, in innumerable poems, have sung the exact opposite, that is, reason, in the image of a pale, cold virgin who attracts and repels me, smiling at me one moment, angry with me the next, and finally turning her back on me. This secret of my unfortunate love, which I reveal to no one, gives you, Madame, a standard by which to appreciate my folly; it shows you that the latter is of an extraordinary sort, standing out magnificently from the usual foolish goings-on of mankind. Read my *Ratcliff*, my *Almansor*, my *Lyrical Intermezzo* – reason, reason, nothing but reason! – and you will be terrified by the lofty height of my folly. In the words of Agur,[62] the son of Jakeh, I can say: 'Surely I am more foolish than any man, and have not the understanding of a man.' The oak forest rises high into the air, the eagle soars high above the oaks, the clouds pass high above the eagle, the stars shine high above the clouds – Madame, aren't you getting high? – the angels float high above the stars, and high above the angels – no, Madame, my folly can ascend no higher. It ascends high enough! It is dizzy with its own sublimity. It makes me a giant with seven-league boots. At lunchtime I feel as though I could eat up all the elephants in Hindustan and pick my teeth with Strasbourg Cathedral; in the evening I become so sentimental that I should like to drink up the Milky Way, without considering that the little stars would remain very indigestibly in my stomach; and at night it is really fast and furious, a congress is held in my head by the nations of the present and the past, the Assyrians, Egyptians, Medes, Persians, Hebrews, Philistines, Frankfurters, Babylonians, Carthaginians, Berliners, Romans, Spartans, Arabs, Street-Arabs – Madame, it would take far too long if I were to describe all these nations, just read Herodotus, Livy, the *Haude and Spener Gazette*,[63] Curtius, Cornelius Nepos, the *Companion* – Meanwhile I will have breakfast, it is not very easy to write this morning, I see that God is letting me down – Madame, I fear you noticed it before I did – yes, I see that true divine assistance has not yet arrived today, – Madame, I shall begin a new chapter, and tell you how I arrived in Godesberg after the death of Le Grand.

CHAPTER 16

WHEN I arrived in Godesberg, I again sat at the feet of my beautiful friend, – and her brown dachshund lay down beside me, – and we both looked up into her eyes.

Merciful heavens! all the glory of the earth lay in her eyes, and an entire heaven into the bargain. I could have died of bliss while gazing into those eyes, and if I had died at such a moment, my soul would have flown directly into her eyes. Oh, I cannot describe those eyes! I shall fetch a poet from the madhouse, who has gone crazy with love, to bring up from the abyss of madness an image with which I can compare those eyes – Between ourselves, I would probably have been crazy enough to need no assistant in such a task. 'God d—n!' said an Englishman once, 'when she looks you up and down so calmly, the copper buttons on your tail-coat melt, and so does your heart.' 'F—e!'[64] said a Frenchman, 'she has eyes of the heaviest calibre, and when such a thirty-pounder of a look flashes out, crash! you're in love.' There was a red-headed advocate from Mainz who said: 'Her eyes look like two cups of black coffee' – He intended this to be a very sweet remark, for he always poured monstrous amounts of sugar into his coffee – Odious comparisons – I and the brown dachshund lay quietly at the feet of the beautiful woman, and gazed and listened. She was sitting beside an old, iron-grey soldier, a chivalrous figure with scars running diagonally across his lined forehead. They were talking about the seven hills lit by the beautiful rays of the setting sun, and about the blue Rhine that was flowing past nearby, great and calm – What did we care about the seven hills, and the setting sun and the blue Rhine, and the boats with white sails floating on it, and the music sounding from one of the boats, and the ninny of a student in it, who was singing so meltingly and delightfully – I and the brown dachshund gazed into our friend's eyes and contemplated her face, which shone forth in rosy pallor from her dark braids and curls, like the moon amid dark clouds – She had lofty Grecian features, boldly arched lips with happiness, melancholy, and childish whimsy playing round them, and when she spoke, she breathed forth her words in deep, almost sighing tones, yet uttered them rapidly and impatiently – and when she spoke, and her speech snowed down from her beautiful lips like a warm, cheerful rain of flowers – Oh, then the setting sun shone on my soul, childhood memories passed through it with faint music, but above all, like little bells, there sounded in me the voice of little Veronika – and I seized my friend's beautiful hand and pressed it to my eyes, till the music in my soul had ceased – and then I jumped up and laughed, and the dachshund barked, and more serious lines appeared on the old General's forehead, and I sat down again and again seized that beautiful hand and kissed it and talked and told the story of little Veronika.

CHAPTER 17

MADAME, you would like me to describe little Veronika's appearance. But I will not. You, Madame, cannot be forced to read any further than you want, and I in turn have the right only to write what I want. Now, however, I want to describe the appearance of the beautiful hand that I kissed in the previous chapter.

Before I start, I must confess that I was not worthy to kiss that hand. It was a beautiful hand, so delicate, translucent, shining, sweet, fragrant, gentle, delightful – truly, I must send to the chemist's for twelve pence worth of adjectives.

On her middle finger was a ring with a pearl – I never saw a pearl play a more lamentable part – on her third finger she wore a ring with a classical figure in blue – I spent hours studying archaeology from it – on her index finger she wore a diamond – it was a talisman, as long as I looked at it I was happy, for wherever it was, there was the finger with its four colleagues – and with all five fingers she often slapped me on the lips. Since being manipulated in such a manner, I have been a firm believer in magnetism. But she did not slap me hard, and whenever she slapped me, I had always earned it by uttering some godless expression, and whenever she had slapped me, she repented immediately and took a cake, broke it in two, and gave half to me and the other half to the brown dachshund, and then smiled and said: 'You two have no religion, and will not be saved, and you must be fed with cakes in this world, for there will be no table spread for you in heaven.' She was not far wrong; at that time I was very irreligious and read Thomas Paine,[65] the *Système de la Nature*, the *Westphalian Advertiser* and Schleiermacher, and let my beard and my reason grow, and wanted to join the rationalists. But whenever her beautiful hand stroked my brow, my reason stopped dead, and I was filled with sweet dreams, and I felt as though I were again hearing devout hymns to the Virgin, and I thought of little Veronika.

Madame, you can scarcely imagine how pretty little Veronika looked as she lay in her little coffin. The burning candles that stood all round it cast their light on the pale, smiling little face, and on the red silk rosettes and rustling scraps of tinsel with which her little head and her little white shroud were adorned – pious Ursula had taken me into the quiet room in the evening, and when I saw the little corpse laid out on the table, with the lights and flowers, I thought at first that it was a pretty little wax image of a saint; but I soon recognized the dear face, and asked, laughing, why little Veronika was so quiet; and Ursula said: 'It's because she's dead.'

And when she said: 'It's because she's dead' – But I do not want to tell the story today, it would take too long, and I should also have to speak first about the lame magpie that hobbled around the Castle Square and was three hundred years old, and I might become quite melancholy – I suddenly feel like telling a different story, and it is a cheerful one, and suitable at this point, for it is the real story that was meant to be recounted in this book.

CHAPTER 18

THE knight's bosom was filled with darkness and pain. Slander's dagger had wounded him deeply, and as he crossed St Mark's Square he felt as though his heart would break and he would bleed to death. His feet were unsteady with weariness – the noble stag had been harried all day, and it was a hot summer's day – there was perspiration on his brow, and as he climbed into the gondola he gave a deep sigh. He sat in the black gondola thinking of nothing, the soft waves thought of nothing as they rocked him, and bore him by the well-known way into the Brenta – and as he climbed out in front of the well-known palace, he heard that Signora Laura was in the garden.

She stood leaning on the statue of Laocoön beside the red rose-tree at the end of the terrace, not far from the weeping willows that bow their sorrowful heads over the passing river. She stood there smiling, a soft image of love, surrounded by the scent of the roses. But he awoke as though from a black dream, and seemed suddenly transformed into gentleness and yearning. 'Signora Laura!' – he said – 'I am wretched and oppressed by hatred and hardship and lies' – and then he stopped, and stammered: – 'but I love you' – and then a joyous tear darted into his eye, and with moist eyes and flaming lips he cried: – 'Be my sweetheart, and love me!'

A veil of dark mystery lies over this moment, no mortal knows what Signora Laura replied, and if her good angel in heaven is asked this question, he covers his face and sighs and is silent.

The knight remained alone for a long time beside the statue of Laocoön, his face was equally distorted and white, he unconsciously picked the petals off all the roses on the rose-tree, he even crushed the young buds – the tree never bore flowers again – far away a mad nightingale lamented, the weeping willows whispered in alarm, the cool waves of the Brenta murmured faintly, night arose with her moon and her stars – a beautiful star, the most beautiful of all, fell from the heavens.

CHAPTER 19

Vous pleurez, Madame?[66]

Oh, may the eyes that are now shedding such beautiful tears long continue to light the world with their beams, and may a dear, warm hand close them at last in the hour of death! A soft pillow, Madame, is also a good thing in the hour of death, and may you not lack one then; and when your beautiful, weary head sinks on to it and your black curls flow over your pale face: Oh, may God then repay you for the tears you shed for me – for I am myself the knight for whom you wept, I am myself the wandering knight of love, the knight of the fallen star.

Vous pleurez, Madame?

Oh, I know these tears! Why should I keep up the pretence? You yourself, Madame, are the beautiful woman who wept so charmingly in Godesberg when I recounted the dismal fairy-tale of my life – Like pearls on roses, the beautiful tears rolled over your beautiful cheeks – the dachshund was silent, the evening bells of Königswinter died away, the Rhine murmured more softly, night covered the earth with her dark cloak, and I sat at your feet, Madame, and looked up, into the starry heavens – At first I thought your eyes were two more stars – But how can anyone confuse such beautiful eyes with stars? Those cold lights in the sky cannot weep at the misery of a human being, who is so wretched that he can no longer weep.

And I had special reasons for recognizing these eyes – in these eyes dwelt the soul of little Veronika.

I have worked out, Madame, that you were born on the very same day that little Veronika died. Johanna in Andernacht foretold that I would find little Veronika again in Godesberg – And I recognized you at once – It was a bad idea, Madame, that you died at that time, when our pleasant games were just about to start. After pious Ursula had said to me: 'It's because she's dead', I walked alone and gravely in the great picture gallery, the pictures no longer gave me such pleasure as in the past, they suddenly seemed faded, only one retained its colour and gloss – You know, Madame, which painting I mean:

The Sultan and Sultaness of Delhi.

Remember, Madame, how we often stood for hours in front of this painting, and pious Ursula gave such odd chuckles when people noticed that the faces in the picture had so much similarity to ours? Madame, I think that the picture was an excellent likeness of you, and it is impossible to understand how the painter portrayed you even down to the clothes that you were wearing at that time. He is said to have been mad and to have dreamed of your image. Or was his soul lodged in the big sacred monkey which in those days attended you like a jockey? – in that case he must have remembered the silver-grey veil which he once ruined by spilling red wine on it – I was glad when you ceased to wear it, it did not suit you particularly, just as in general European costume is much more becoming for females than Indian clothes. Of course, beautiful women are beautiful in every costume. Do you remember, Madame, how a gallant Brahmin – he looked like Ganesha,[67] the god with the elephant's trunk, who rides on a mouse – once paid you the following compliment: 'When the divine Maneka descended from Indra's golden castle to the royal penitent Visvamitra, she cannot have been more beautiful than you, Madame!'

You don't remember? It is barely three thousand years since this was said to you, and beautiful women are not usually so quick to forget a piece of delicate flattery.

For men, however, Indian costume is much more becoming than European clothing. Oh, my pink Delhi trousers with lotus flowers! if I had worn you when I stood before Signora Laura and pleaded for love – the last chapter would have been different! But alas, I was then wearing straw-yellow trousers woven by a sober Chinaman in Nanking – my destruction was woven into them – and I was wretched.

It often happens that a young man sits in a little German coffee-house, quietly drinking his cup of coffee, while far away in distant China his destruction is growing and gathering strength, and is being spun and woven, and despite the lofty Chinese Wall it manages to find its way to the young man, who mistakes it for a pair of nankeen trousers and unsuspectingly puts them on and is wretched – And, Madame, a great deal of misery may be concealed in a person's narrow bosom, and concealed so well that the poor wretch himself does not feel it for days, and is full of good cheer, and dances merrily, and whistles and trills – tra-la-la-la, tra-la-la-la – tra-la – la – la – la.

CHAPTER 20

> She was lovable, and he loved her; but he was not lovable, and she did not love him.
>
> (Old Play)

'And you were going to shoot yourself because of this silly story?' Madame, when somebody is about to shoot himself, he always has sufficient reasons. You may be sure of that. But whether he himself knows these reasons is another matter. Right up to the last moment we play a comedy with ourselves. We even mask our misery, and while dying of a wound in the chest, we complain about toothache.

Madame, you must surely know a remedy for toothache?

But I had toothache in my heart. That is a grave illness, and best cured by a filling of lead and the tooth-powder invented by Barthold Schwarz.[68]

Like a worm, misery gnawed at my heart, and gnawed – It was not the poor Chinaman's fault, I brought this misery with me into the world. It lay beside me in my cradle, and when my mother rocked me, she rocked it too, and when she sang me to sleep, it fell asleep with me, and woke up again the moment I opened my eyes. When I grew up, my misery grew as well, until at last it became enormous, and burst my –

Let us talk about other things, about the maiden's wreath, about masked balls, about pleasure and merry weddings – tra-la-la-la, tra-la-la-la – tra-la – la – la – la.

THE TOWN OF LUCCA

I can never refrain from laughing at the English who pass such lamentably philistine judgements on this, their second poet (for after Shakespeare the palm belongs to Byron), because he mocked their pedantry, would not conform to their small-town manners, did not share their cold faith, loathed their sobriety, and complained of their arrogance and their hypocrisy. Many people make the sign of the cross when they so much as speak of him, and though women's cheeks glow with enthusiasm when they read him, even they are violently hostile in public to their secret darling . . .

Letters from a Dead Man:
A Fragmentary Journal from England (Munich, 1830)[1]

CHAPTER I

MAN is influenced by his natural surroundings – why should man not influence the nature which surrounds him? In Italy nature is as passionate as the people who live there; with us in Germany, nature is more serious, pensive, and patient. Did nature, like mankind, once possess more inner life? The emotional power of an Orpheus, it is said, could make trees and stones move to inspired rhythms. Could something of the sort happen even today? Man and nature have grown phlegmatic, and yawn in each other's faces. A poet by appointment to the King of Prussia will never be able to make Templow Hill or the lime-trees on Unter den Linden dance to the sound of his lyre.

Nature, too, has its history, and it is a different natural history from the one taught in schools. One of the grey lizards that have been living for millennia in the rocky crevices of the Apennines should be appointed as a very extraordinary professor at one of our universities, and we would hear very extraordinary things. But the pride of some gentlemen in the law faculty would revolt against such an appointment. After all, one of them already nurtures a secret jealousy of poor Fido,[2] the intelligent dog, fearing that Fido may one day take his place in the science of fetching and carrying.

The lizards, with their clever little tails and their sharp little eyes, told me wondrous things when I scrambled about on my own among the rocks of the Apennines. Truly, there are things between heaven and earth which not only our philosophers but even the most ordinary blockheads cannot understand.

The lizards told me that there was a legend among the stones that God would one day become stone, in order to redeem them from their fixity. An old lizard opined, however, that this divine petrifaction would occur only after God had transformed himself into every species of animal and plant and redeemed them all.

Only a few stones have feelings, and they breathe only by moonlight. But these few stones that feel their condition are terribly miserable. The trees are much better off, they can weep. Animals, however, are most highly favoured, for they can speak, each in his own way, and mankind best of all. One day, when the whole world is redeemed, all other created things will likewise be able to speak, as in those ancient times of which poets sing.

The lizards are an ironic race, and like to make fools of the other animals. But they were so humble towards me, they gave such honest sighs, they told me stories about Atlantis which I shall presently write down for the world's benefit. My heart warmed to these little creatures, who, as it were, preserve the secret annals of nature. Are they families of enchanted priests, like those of ancient Egypt, who likewise dwelt in labyrinthine rocky grottoes and listened to nature? On their little heads, bodies, and tails there are wondrous signs and images, like those on the Egyptians' hieroglyphic caps and hierophantic coats.

My little friends also taught me a sign-language by means of which I can speak with mute nature. It often brings peace to my soul, especially towards evening, when the mountains are shrouded in sweet and sinister shadows, and the waterfalls murmur, and all the plants emit fragrance, and sudden flashes of lightning dart to and fro.

O nature! you mute virgin! I understand your summer lightning, the futile attempt at speech that darts across your lovely face, and I feel so sorry for you that I weep. But immediately you understand me as well, and you brighten up, and laugh at me with golden eyes. Lovely virgin, I understand your stars and you understand my tears!

CHAPTER 2

'NOTHING in the world goes backwards,' an old lizard told me, 'everything strives forwards, and ultimately there will be a general promotion throughout nature. Stones will become plants, plants will become animals, animals will become human beings, and human beings will become gods.'

'But,' I exclaimed, 'whatever will become of those good people, the poor old gods?'

'Something will be worked out, my friend,' replied the lizard; 'I expect they will abdicate, or take early retirement in some honourable fashion.'

I learnt many other secrets from my natural philosopher with hieroglyphics on his skin; but I gave my word of honour not to reveal any. I now know more than Schelling and Hegel.

'What do you think of those two?' asked the old lizard with a scornful smile, when I happened to mention these names.

'When you consider,' I replied, 'that these people are only human, not lizards, you cannot but be astonished by their knowledge. At bottom they teach one and the same doctrine, the philosophy of identity, with which you are familiar; they differ only in the way they present it. When Hegel puts forward the principles of his philosophy, it is like seeing the pretty figures that a skilful schoolmaster can form by an artful arrangement of numbers, in such a way that an ordinary observer sees only the surface, only the little house or ship or absolute soldier formed from the numbers, while a thinking schoolboy can perceive in the figure itself the solution of a profound arithmetical sum. Schelling's presentation is more like those Indian animal pictures which are composed of all manner of other animals, snakes, birds, elephants, and suchlike living ingredients, fantastically intertwined. This manner of presentation is much pleasanter, more cheerful, with more pulsing warmth; everything in it is alive, whereas the abstract Hegelian ciphers appear so grey, cold and dead.'

'Very well,' replied the old he-lizard, 'I see what you are getting at; but tell me, have these philosophers much of an audience?'

I now described how in the learned caravanserai in Berlin the camels gather round the well of Hegelian wisdom, kneel down before it, are loaded with precious water-skins, and proceed on their way through the desert sands of Prussia. I also described how the modern Athenians crowd round the fountain of Schelling's intellectual liquor as though it were the best beer, the Breihahn[3] of life and the booze of immortality.

The little natural philosopher became green with envy on hearing that his colleagues were in such great demand, and he asked with irritation: 'Which of the two do you think the greater?'

'I cannot decide,' I replied, 'any more than I can decide whether Schechner[4] is greater than Sontag, and I think –'

'Think!' exclaimed the lizard in a piercing, well-bred tone of the deepest disdain, 'think! which of you thinks? My wise sir, I have been studying the intellectual functions of animals now for close on three thousand years, I have made humans, monkeys, and snakes the particular objects of my study, I have devoted as much industry to these strange creatures as Lyonnet[5] did to his caterpillars, and as the result of all my observations, experiments, and anatomical comparisons, I can assure you categorically that no human being thinks; people occasionally have an idea, they give these entirely involuntary ideas the name of thoughts, and arranging them in a series is called thinking. But you can repeat in my name that no human being thinks, no philosopher thinks, neither Schelling nor Hegel thinks, and as for their philosophy, it is nothing but air and water, like the clouds in the sky; I have seen innumerable such clouds pass over my head, proud and self-assured, and the next morning's sun has dissolved them into their original nothingness; – there is only one true philosophy, and that is written, in everlasting hieroglyphs, on my own tail.'

With these words, spoken with haughty eloquence, the old lizard turned his back on me, and as he paced slowly away, I saw on it the most curious letters, running in portentous colours right down to the tip of his tail.

CHAPTER 3

It was on the road between the baths of Lucca and the town of that name, not far from the big chestnut tree whose green branches overshadow the stream, and in the presence of an old white-bearded billy-goat, grazing there like a hermit, that the conversation took place which I reported in the preceding chapter. I was going to the town of Lucca to find Francesca and Matilda, whom, according to our arrangement, I should have met there a week earlier. At the appointed time, however, I had gone there in vain, and I had now set out for the second time. I walked past the beautiful hills and clumps of trees where the golden oranges, like daylight stars, gleamed from the dark green foliage, and garlands of vines stretched for miles in festive convolutions. The whole countryside in these parts has a decorative, garden-like appearance, like the rural scenes depicted on our theatre backdrops; and the country people themselves resemble the colourful figures whose singing, smiling and dancing delights us when we see them painted there. No philistine faces anywhere. And even if there are philistines here, at least they are Italian orange-philistines, not clumsy German potato-philistines. The people are just as picturesque and ideal as the country, and yet every man has such an individual expression on his face, and succeeds in asserting his personality by his posture, by the way he wears his cloak, and if necessary by using his knife. In our country, on the other hand, there are only people with average, uniform physiognomies; if twelve of them are together they make a dozen, and if anyone attacks them they call the police.

I was struck by the fact that in the Lucca region, as in most of Tuscany, the women wear large black felt hats with black ostrich-plumes hanging down; even the basket-makers wear this heavy head-gear. The men, on the other hand, mostly wear a light straw hat, and young lads receive these as presents from girls who make them themselves, weaving in their amorous thoughts and, perhaps, many sighs as well. Thus Francesca once sat among the girls and flowers of the Arno valley, weaving a hat for her *caro Cecco*, kissing every piece of straw she used for it, and trilling her charming *'Occhie, stelle mortali'*;[6] the curly head that afterwards wore the charming hat so charmingly now has a tonsure, and the hat itself, old and battered, is hanging in the corner of an Abbate's dismal little room in Bologna.

I am one of those people who always take a short cut rather than follow the main road, and who then may well lose their way on narrow paths among trees and rocks. That happened here as well, and my journey to Lucca must have taken me twice as long as ordinary people who stick to the main road. A sparrow whom I asked the way twittered and twittered, yet could not give me any definite information. Perhaps he did not know the way himself. I could not extract a single word from the butterflies and dragonflies that were perching on large bell-flowers; they fluttered off before they had heard my question, and the flowers shook the silent bells of their heads. At times I was aroused by the wild myrtles, giggling in the distance with their faint, clear voices. Then I would hastily scramble up to the summits of the highest rocks, and call: 'Clouds of the sky! Sailors of the air! Tell me, which road leads to Francesca? Is she in Lucca? Tell me, what is she doing? What is she dancing? Tell me everything, and when you have told me everything, tell me again!'

With such abundance of folly it could easily happen that a grave eagle, woken by my cries from his lonely dreams, looked at me with contemptuous displeasure. But I was willing to forgive him; for he had never seen Francesca, and that was why he could perch on his firm rock with such sublimity of mind, and stare up to heaven with such an untroubled soul, or goggle down at me with such insolent calm. Such an eagle has an insufferably proud gaze, and looks at you as though he were saying: 'What kind of bird are you? Do you know that I am still a king, just as in those heroic times when I carried Jupiter's lightning and adorned Napoleon's banners? Are you an educated parrot who has learnt the old songs by heart and repeats them pedantically? Or a sentimental turtle-dove, whose feelings are beautiful and whose cooing is wretched? Or a nightingale from a poetry magazine? Or a broken-down old gander whose ancestors saved the Capitol? Or perhaps a servile barnyard cock, round whose neck someone has ironically hung an emblem of bold flight, namely a miniature picture of myself, and who accordingly puts on such grand airs as though he were an eagle himself?' You know, dear reader, how little reason I have to feel insulted if an eagle thinks of me in this manner. I believe the gaze I returned was even prouder than his own, and if he inquired of the first laurel-tree he came to, he will now know who I am.

I had quite lost my way among the mountains by the time twilight fell, the bright songs of the forest gradually died away and the rustling of the trees became more serious. A sublime stillness and profound solemnity passed like the breath of God through the luminous silence. Here and there a beautiful dark eye looked up at me from the ground, vanishing in the same moment. Tender whispers played about my heart, and I felt the airy touch of invisible kisses on my cheeks. The red sky of evening enfolded the mountains as though in crimson cloaks, and the last rays of the sun illuminated their peaks, making them appear like kings with golden crowns on their heads. But I stood, like the emperor of the world, in the midst of these crowned vassals, who paid me silent homage.

CHAPTER 4

I DO not know whether the monk whom I met near Lucca is a pious man. But I know that his old body, poor and naked, is wrapped in a coarse habit, year in, year out; his torn sandals provide insufficient protection for his bare feet when he clambers up the rocks, through thorns and thickets, to comfort sick people or to teach children to pray; – and he is content if in return people put a crust of bread in his bag, and give him a little straw to sleep on.

'I shall not write against *that* man,' I said to myself. 'When I am back home in Germany, sitting in my armchair with a fire crackling in the stove, warm and well fed with a cosy cup of tea, and write against the Catholic priesthood – I shall not write against that man.'

In order to write against Catholic priests, one must also know their faces. The true original faces, however, are to be seen only in Italy. German Catholic priests and monks are merely bad imitations, often indeed parodies, of those in Italy; to compare the two would be like comparing the pictures of saints from Rome or Florence with those pious, locust-like physiognomies that owe their sorrowful existence to the philistine pencil of a municipal painter in Nuremberg, or indeed to the charming simplicity and heartfelt zeal of the long-haired Christian neo-German school.[7]

The priests in Italy have long since arrived at a compromise with public opinion; the populace there has long been used to distinguishing between the spiritual dignity and the undignified person, and to respecting the former even if the latter is contemptible. Indeed, it is the inevitable contrast between the ideal duties and claims of the clerical estate and the peremptory demands of sensual nature, that ancient and everlasting conflict between spirit and matter, that has made the Italian priests into established characters of popular humour, in satires, songs and novellas. Similar phenomena are manifest wherever a similar priestly caste exists, e.g. in Hindustan. In the comedies of that intensely pious land, as we already saw in *Sakontala*[8] and find confirmed in the newly translated *Vasantasena*, it is always a Brahmin who plays the comic part, the priestly buffoon as it were, without the slightest detriment to the respect due to his sacrificial ceremonies and his privileged sanctity – just as an Italian is no less devout in attending

Mass or confessing to a priest whom he has found the day before lying drunk in the muddy street. In Germany it is different: there the Catholic priest not only wants his dignity to be represented by his office, but also his office by his person; and since he may originally have taken his profession quite seriously, he does not wish to injure it publicly when his vows of chastity and humility later collide somewhat with the old Adam, especially as he does not wish to expose himself to attacks from our friend Krug[9] in Leipzig, and therefore he tries to maintain at least the semblance of a godly way of life. That is why German priests are so hypocritical, unctuous and sanctimonious; among the Italians, however, the mask is much more transparent, and they display a certain plump irony and a comfortably secular digestive system.

But what is the use of such general reflections! They can be of little service to you, dear reader, if you should take it into your head to write against the Catholic priesthood. For this purpose one must, as I said, see with one's own eyes the faces in question. Truly, it is not even sufficient to have seen them in the Royal Opera House at Berlin. The last director certainly did all he could to present the coronation parade in *The Maid of Orleans*[10] as faithfully and convincingly as possible, to display to his fellow-countrymen the idea of a procession, and to display to them priests of every stripe. But the most faithful costume cannot replace the original faces, and even if an additional 100,000 dollars were frittered away on golden mitres, trimmed surplices, embroidered vestments, and suchlike fripperies – even then the rational Protestant noses sticking out protestingly from under the mitres, the skinny legs of a thinking man's faith peeping from the white lace of the surplices, the enlightened bellies for which the vestments would be much too big, everything would remind people like ourselves that the figures on stage were not Catholic clergy but Berlin laity.

I have often wondered whether the director could not present the parade much better, and display the image of a procession much more faithfully, if he had the Catholic priests played not by the usual extras but by the Protestant clergymen who deliver the most orthodox sermons in the pulpit, the theological faculty, and the *Church Times*[11] against reason, worldliness, Gesenius and devilry. We should then see faces whose priestly stamp was much more convincing and suitable for such parts. After all, it is a familiar observation that priests all over the world, rabbis, muftis, Dominicans, consistory counsellors, Orthodox popes, Chinese bonzes, in short, God's entire diplomatic corps, have a certain family resemblance in their faces, such as is always found in people who practise the same trade. Tailors all over the world are distinguished by the delicacy of their limbs; butchers and soldiers everywhere have the same *farouche* manner; Jews have their distinctively honest appearance, not because they are descended from Abraham, Isaac, and Jacob, but because they are merchants, and the Christian Frankfurt merchant and the Jewish Frankfurt merchant are as like as two peas, or two bad eggs. Hence spiritual merchants, who make their living in the religion business, acquire a similarity of features. Admittedly, some nuances result from the manner in which they pursue their business. The Catholic priest pursues his like the clerk employed in a large company; the Church, the great commercial house whose chairman is the Pope, gives him a specified occupation and pays him a specified salary for it; he works sluggishly, as does anyone who is not working on his own account, has many colleagues, and can easily remain unobserved in the great hubbub of business – he cares only about the credit of the company, and still more about its survival, since he would lose his source of income if it were to go bankrupt. The Protestant priest, on the other hand, is everywhere himself the principal, and conducts the religion business on his own account. He does not do wholesale trade, like his Catholic counterpart, but only retail trade; and since he must be in sole charge of it, he cannot be idle, he must advertise his own articles of faith and cry down his competitors' articles, and he stands in his booth like a real retailer, full of commercial envy against all large companies, especially the great house in Rome which employs many thousands of book-keepers and dispatchers and has its trading-posts in all four continents.

All this, of course, has physiognomic effects, but they are not visible from the stalls; the family resemblance in the faces of Catholic and Protestant priests remains unchanged in its main features, and if the director pays the above-mentioned gentlemen properly, they will play their parts very convincingly, as always. Their gait, too, will add to the illusion; although a sharp and experienced eye will observe that it is likewise distinguished by fine nuances from the gait of Catholic priests and monks.

A Catholic priest strolls along as if heaven belonged to him; a Protestant priest, on the other hand, bustles about as though he had taken a lease of heaven.

CHAPTER 5

It was already dark when I reached the town of Lucca.

How very different it seemed the week before, when I strolled through the echoing, deserted streets in the daytime, and fancied myself transported to one of the enchanted towns about which my nurse used to tell me so many stories. The whole town was as silent as the grave, everything was so colourless and motionless, the sunlight played on the roofs like gilded tinsel on the head of a corpse, tendrils of ivy hung down here and there, like dried-up green tears, from the windows of a ruinous house, the gleam of mildew and the fearful mouldering of death could be sensed everywhere, the town seemed only the ghost of a town, a stone spectre in broad daylight. I searched for a long time in vain for the trace of a living being. All I remember is that a beggar was lying asleep, with his palm outstretched, outside an old palazzo. I also remember seeing a monk, at the upper window of a blackish, decaying little house, with his red neck and his fleshy bald head protruding far out of his brown habit, and beside him could be seen a naked female with a full bosom; down below I saw a little boy entering the half-open front door, dressed as an Abbate in black, and carrying in both hands a huge, fat-bellied wine-bottle. – At that moment a faint, ironic bell rang nearby, and the novellas of Boccaccio chuckled slyly in my memory. These sounds, however, could not quite dispel the strange horror that gripped my soul. Its power was perhaps strengthened by the warm, bright sunshine that lit the sinister building; and I perceived that ghosts are still more terrifying when they throw off the dark mantle of night and appear in the clear light of noonday.

Returning to Lucca now, a week later, how astonished I was by the changed appearance of the town! 'What is this?' I cried, as lights dazzled my eyes and crowds surged through the alleyways. 'Has an entire population risen from its grave as a nocturnal ghost, to mimic life in the maddest of masquerades? The lofty, gloomy houses are adorned with lamps, brightly coloured tapestries are hanging from all the windows, almost covering the grey, decaying walls, and lovely girls' faces are looking out above them, so fresh and blooming that I perceive it is life itself which has invited beauty and youth to help celebrate its marriage-feast with death.' Indeed, it was a living festival of the dead; I do not know what it is called in the calendar, but at any rate it must have been the day when some patient martyr was flayed, for I later saw a holy skull and a few additional bones, adorned with flowers and jewels, being carried about to nuptial music. It was a beautiful procession.

At its head walked the Capuchins, who were distinguished from the other monks by their long beards, and formed, as it were, the sappers in this army of faith. They were followed by Capuchins without beards, including many noble masculine faces, and even several handsome, youthful faces; the tonsure suited these, because it seemed to cast a dainty wreath of hair round their heads, which, together with their bare necks, rose pleasingly from their brown habits. These in turn were followed by habits of different colours, black, white, yellow, striped, and by three-cornered hats worn low over the eyes, in short, by all the monastic costumes with which we have long been familiar, thanks to the efforts of our theatre director. After the monastic orders came the priests proper, wearing white shirts over black trousers, and coloured birettas; after them came yet grander clerics, wrapped in blankets of coloured silk and wearing on their heads a kind of lofty cap, probably of Egyptian origin, which can be seen in Denon's[12] work, in *The Magic Flute* and in Belzoni; their faces indicated long service, and they seemed to be a kind of old guard. The general staff brought up the rear: a baldaquin and under it an old man with an even loftier cap, and wearing a still more sumptuous blanket, whose corners were carried by two old men, similarly dressed, in the manner of pages.

The monks at the front walked with their arms folded, in grave silence; but those in lofty caps uttered a most unfortunate nasal chant, which sounded both like someone noisily drinking soup and like a turkey gobbling; so that I am convinced that if the Jews formed the majority of the population, and theirs were the official religion, the above-mentioned chanting would be called 'Ikey-talk'. Fortunately it was only partly audible, since several companies of soldiers were marching just behind the procession, loudly drumming and playing the fife, and the procession was accompanied, along its whole length, by two grenadiers on either side. There were almost more soldiers than clerics; but nowadays religion needs the support of large numbers of bayonets, and when the blessing is given, distant cannon must thunder portentously.

Whenever I see such a procession, in which the clergy walk along so dolefully and dismally with a proud military escort, I am always painfully moved, and I feel as though I were seeing our Saviour himself being led to execution, surrounded by soldiers with lances. The stars of Lucca must have thought as I did, and as I looked up to them with a sigh, they gazed at me with such agreement in their pious eyes, so bright, so clear. But their light was not needed, many thousands of lamps and candles and girls' faces were flickering in all the windows, torches of burning pitch were planted at every street corner, and then every cleric had his own candle-bearer at his side. The Capuchins mostly had little boys to carry their candles, and the fresh, youthful little faces sometimes looked up happily and inquisitively at the grave old beards; such a poor Capuchin cannot pay a grown-up candle-bearer, and the boy to whom he teaches the Ave Maria, or whose granny confesses to him, must no doubt undertake this office gratis in processions, and it is assuredly not done with any less love. The monks following had boys who were not much bigger, some grander orders had practically grown-up scallywags, and the priests in lofty caps had genuine citizens as candle-bearers. Finally, however, the Archbishop himself – for he must have been the man walking with noble humility under the baldaquin, with elderly pages carrying the corners of his garment – he had a lackey on either side, both resplendent in blue liveries with yellow braiding, and carrying the white wax candles as ceremoniously as though they were serving at court.

In any case, this candle-carrying seemed to me a good institution, for it gave me a clearer view of the faces typical of Catholicism. And now I have seen them, in the best lighting. And what did I see? Well, the mark of the cleric was never missing. But that apart, the faces were as diverse as any other faces. One was pale, another red, this nose jutted out proudly, another hung down, here a sparkling black eye, there a shimmering grey one – but in all these faces there lay the signs of the same illness, a terrible, incurable illness, which will probably be the reason why my grandson, if he sees the procession in Lucca in a hundred years' time, will recognize none of these faces. I fear I am myself infected by this illness, and one consequence is the gentle emotion that wondrously steals over me whenever I contemplate such a sickly monastic face and see on it the symptoms of the sufferings concealed under the coarse habit: – injured love, gout, disappointed ambition, spinal paralysis, repentance, haemorrhoids, the wounds inflicted on our hearts by the ingratitude of our friends, the slanders of our enemies, and by our own sins, all this and much more that can find its place as easily beneath a coarse habit as beneath a fine fashionable swallow-tail coat. Oh! it is no exaggeration when the poet cries in his agony: 'Life is an illness, the whole world is a hospital!'

'And death is our doctor –' Alas! I do not want to speak ill of him, nor to shake the assurance of others; for as he is the only doctor, they may as well believe that he is the best, and that his sole remedy, the eternal earth-cure, is also the best. At least he can be praised for always being prompt; despite his large practice, he never keeps you waiting when you call him. Sometimes he even follows patients to the procession, and carries their candles. It was undoubtedly death himself whom I saw walking at the side of a pale, careworn priest; he was carrying the priest's flickering candle in his thin, trembling, bony hands, nodding good-humouredly and reassuringly with his fearful bare head, and however unsteady he was on his own legs, yet he sometimes supported the poor priest, who grew paler at every step and was ready to collapse. Death seemed to whisper encouragingly: 'Wait a few short hours, then we shall be home, and I shall extinguish the candle, and put you to bed, and your cold, tired legs can rest, and you will sleep so soundly that you will not hear the whimpering bells of St Michael's.'

'I shall not write against *that* man, either,' I thought, seeing the poor, pale priest whom death in bodily form was lighting to his bed.

Alas! one should not write against anybody in this world. Everyone is ill enough himself in this great hospital, and many polemical writings remind me involuntarily of a repulsive squabble in a small hospital at Cracow, of which I was an accidental spectator. It was terrible to hear the sick men taunting one another with their ailments, to hear desiccated consumptives mocking the swollen dropsy victim, to hear one man laughing at another's cancer of the nose, and the latter in turn laughing at his neighbours' lockjaw and wall-eyes, till finally the delirious fever patients leapt naked from their beds and tore the sheets and blankets from the other patients' aching bodies, and nothing was to be seen but hideous misery and mutilation.

CHAPTER 6

THEN, dipping from the winebowl, round he went
from left to right, serving the other gods
nectar of sweet delight. And quenchless laughter
broke out among the blissful gods
to see Hephaestus wheezing down the hall.
So all day long until the sun went down
they spent in feasting, and the measured feast
matched well their hearts' desire.
So did the flawless harp held by Apollo
and heavenly songs in choiring antiphon
that all the Muses sang.

(Vulgate)[13]

Then suddenly a pale, bloodstained Jew came panting in, with a crown of thorns on his head and a great wooden cross over his shoulder; and he threw the cross on to the gods' high table, so that the golden goblets trembled, and the gods fell silent and turned pale, and became paler and paler, till at last they entirely dissolved into mist.

Now there was a sorrowful time, and the world turned grey and dark. There were no longer any happy gods; Olympus became a hospital where gods who had been flayed, roasted and impaled crept tediously about, bandaged their wounds, and sang dismal songs. Religion no longer granted any joy, but only consolation; it was a doleful, bloodthirsty religion for delinquents.

May it have been necessary for sick and oppressed humanity? Anyone who sees his god suffering finds it easier to endure his own pain. The merry gods of the past, who felt no pain, did not know either how poor tortured human beings feel, and a poor tortured person in desperation could have no real confidence in them. They were holiday gods; people danced around them merrily, and could only thank them. For this reason they never received whole-hearted love. To receive whole-hearted love, one must suffer. Compassion is the last sacrament of love; it may be love itself. Therefore of all the gods who ever lived, Christ is the god who has been loved the most. Especially by women –

To escape the busy throng, I have strayed into a lonely church, and what you have just read, dear reader, is not so much my own thoughts but rather some words I involuntarily uttered while lying stretched out on one of the old benches and letting the sounds of the organ enter my breast. There I lie, my soul lost in fantasies, composing even stranger texts for the strange music; now and again my gaze roams through the twilit cloisters in search of the dark acoustic figures to match the organ's melodies. Who is the veiled woman kneeling before the picture of a Madonna? The lamp hanging in front of the picture casts an eerily sweet light on our beautiful Lady of Sorrows, mother of a crucified love, the Venus Dolorosa; but at times mysterious, pandering lights fall, as though surreptitiously, on the beautiful figure of the veiled supplicant. True, she is lying motionless on the stone steps of the altar, but her shadow is moving in the changing light, sometimes running towards me and then hastily withdrawing, like a mute blackamoor, timorously bearing a message of love in a harem – and I understand it. He is announcing the presence of his mistress, the sultaness of my heart.

However, it is growing gradually darker in the empty building; here and there a vague shape scurries along the pillars, now and again a soft murmur rises from a side-chapel, and the organ heaves its long, long-drawn-out groans, like sighs from a giant's heart –

But it seemed as though the organ's sounds would never cease, as though its dying groans, its living death, would last for ever; I felt such unspeakable apprehension, such nameless fear, as though I had been buried alive, indeed, as though, having died long ago, I had risen from my grave and entered the ghostly church with my sinister nocturnal associates to hear the prayers for the dead and confess the sins of a corpse. At moments I seemed really to see them sitting beside me in the spectral twilight, the departed congregation, in the old Florentine costumes of a vanished age, with long pale faces, gold-plated prayer-books in their thin hands, whispering in hushed tones and nodding mournfully to one another. The whimpering sound of a distant death-knell reminded me once more of the sick priest I had seen in the procession, and I said to myself: 'He is dead too now, and is coming here to read the first Mass of the night, and then the dismal nightmare will begin in earnest.' Suddenly, however, the lovely figure of the veiled supplicant rose from the steps of the altar –

Yes, it was she, her living shadow was enough to drive away the white ghosts, I had eyes only for her, I quickly followed her out of the church, and as she threw back her veil outside the door, I saw Francesca's tear-stained face. It was like a yearning white rose, touched by pearls of nocturnal dew and lit by the beams of the moon. 'Francesca, do you love me?' I asked many questions and received few answers. I accompanied her to the Croce di Malta Hotel, where she and Matilda were lodging. The streets had emptied, the houses were sleeping with their window-eyes closed, and only the occasional light flashed through their wooden lashes. In the sky above, however, a wide green space emerged from the clouds, and in it floated the crescent moon, like a silver gondola in a sea of emeralds. It was in vain that I asked Francesca to cast a single glance up to our dear confidant of yore; her little head remained dreamily bowed. Although she used to glide along so serenely, she now walked at a measured, ecclesiastical pace; her gait was gloomy and Catholic, as if she were moving to the beat of a solemn organ, and as in former nights she seemed to have sin in her bones, now she had religion. Every time she passed the image of a saint, she crossed her head and bosom; my attempts to help her were in vain. On the market-place, however, as we passed the church of San Michele, where our marble Lady of Sorrows shone from the dark niche with gilded swords piercing her heart and a lamp crowning her head, Francesca flung her arms round my neck, kissed me, and whispered: 'Cecco, Cecco, caro Cecco!'

I accepted the kisses calmly, though I was well aware that they were really intended for a Bolognese Abbate, a servant of the Roman Catholic Church. As a Protestant I had no scruples about appropriating the goods of the Catholic clergy, and I secularized Francesca's pious kisses on the spot. I know that this will infuriate the priests, they are sure to howl about robbing the Church, and would be glad to apply the French law of sacrilege against me. I must unfortunately admit that the aforesaid kisses were all I was able to obtain that night. Francesca had decided to use the night exclusively for her soul's salvation, kneeling and praying. In vain did I offer to share her devotions; – on reaching her room, she shut the door in my face. In vain did I stand outside for a whole hour, begging for admission, groaning all possible groans, affecting pious tears, and swearing the most sacred oaths –

with a mental reservation, of course; I felt myself gradually becoming a Jesuit, I was quite corrupted, and finally offered to become a Catholic just for this one night –

'Francesca!' I cried, 'star of my thoughts! Thought of my soul! *vita della mia vita!* my beautiful, much-kissed, slender, Catholic Francesca! for the single night you grant me I will become a Catholic myself – but only for this single night! Oh, the beautiful, blest, Catholic night! I will lie in your arms, with a strict Catholic faith in the heaven of your love; from our lips we shall kiss each other's lovely confessions, the word will become flesh, faith will become sensual, in shape and form – what a religion! You priests! chant your Kyrie Eleison[14] meanwhile, tinkle, ring the bells, swing the censer, let the organ boom, let Palestrina's Mass resound – "this is the body!" – I shall believe myself among the blest as I fall asleep – but as soon as I wake up next morning, I shall rub the sleep and the Catholicism from my eyes, and again see the sunshine and the Bible clearly, and be rational, sensible and Protestant, as before.'

CHAPTER 7

NEXT day, when the sun again laughed cordially down from the sky, I shed all the mournful thoughts and emotions which had been aroused in me by the previous evening's procession, and had caused me to regard life as an illness and the world as a hospital.

The whole town was swarming with cheerful crowds, smartly dressed in bright colours, with the odd black priestling skipping here and there among them. There was so much din, laughter, and chatter that you could hardly hear the jingling bells inviting everyone to a great Mass in the cathedral. The latter is a simple, handsome church, its coloured marble façade decorated with those short columns, built on top of one another, that look so comically dismal. Inside, the pillars and walls were draped in red cloth, and cheerful music flowed over the surging throng. I had Signora Francesca on my arm, and as I offered her holy water at the entrance, and our souls were electrified by the sweet, moist contact of our fingers, I simultaneously received an electric shock in my leg. In my alarm I almost fell headlong over the kneeling peasant women, dense groups of whom, clad all in white and weighed down by long ear-rings and yellow gold necklaces, covered the floor. Looking round, I caught sight of a female who was kneeling likewise and fanning herself, and behind the fan I spied the chuckling eyes of Milady. I bent down to her, and she breathed languishingly into my ear: 'Delightful!'[15]

'For heaven's sake!' I whispered to her, 'keep a straight face, don't laugh, or else we really shall be thrown out!'

But it was useless to beg and plead. Fortunately nobody understood our language. For when Milady rose and followed us through the throng to the high altar, she gave way to her wild whimsies without the least restraint, as though we were standing alone on the Apennines. She made fun of everything, even the poor painted images on the walls were not safe from her darts.

'Behold!' she cried, 'there's Lady Eve, one of the Ribs by extraction, chatting to the snake! It was a good idea of the painter to give the snake a human head with a human face; but it would have been much wittier to adorn this seducer's face with a military moustache. Do you see the angel there, Doctor, informing the blessed Virgin of her interesting condition, with such an ironic smile? I know what that scoundrel is thinking! And that Mary with the Holy Alliance of the East kneeling at her feet with gifts of gold and frankincense – doesn't she look like Catalani?'[16]

Signora Francesca, who, from her ignorance of English, had understood none of this prattle but the word Catalani, hastened to observe that the lady of whom our friend was speaking had now lost much of her reputation. Our friend, however, was not to be diverted, and commented on the pictures of the Passion, including the Crucifixion, an extremely fine painting which, among other things, showed three foolish, idle faces comfortably watching God's martyrdom. Milady insisted that these were the accredited representatives of Austria, Russia and France.

However, the old frescoes that were visible between the red draperies on the walls were able, by their inherent gravity, to offer some resistance to the British love of ridicule. They depicted faces from the heroic age of Lucca which is so much talked of in the history-books of Machiavelli, the Romantic Sallust; we encounter its passionate spirit also in the poetry of Dante, the Catholic Homer. Certainly these faces disclose the severe feelings and barbarous ideas of the Middle Ages; even though the mute lips of many a youth bear the smiling admission that not all the roses in those days were so stony and tear-dimmed, and though many a Madonna of that age has a mischievous love-signal flashing between her devoutly lowered eyelashes, as though she would happily present us with a second Christ child. At all events, however, it is a lofty spirit that speaks to us from these old Florentine paintings, it is the true heroic quality that we discern also in the marble statues of classical gods, consisting not, as our aestheticians maintain, in eternal quiet without passion, but in eternal passion without disquiet. This old Florentine spirit also survives, perhaps as a traditional echo, in some later oil paintings that hang in Lucca Cathedral. I was particularly struck by a Wedding at Cana, by a pupil of Andrea del Sarto, rather harshly painted with roughly drawn figures. The Saviour is sitting between the soft, beautiful bride and a Pharisee whose face, as stony as the tablets of the law, shows his surprise at the inspired prophet who cheerfully mingles with the ranks of cheerful people and regales the company with miracles that are yet greater than the miracles of Moses; for the latter, no matter how hard he struck the rock, could only bring forth water, whereas this prophet had only to utter a word for the jugs to be filled with the best wine. Much softer, almost Venetian in its colouring, is the painting by an unknown artist that hangs beside it, in which the colours' appealing glow is strangely muted by a shudder of pain. It shows Mary taking a pound of ointment of spikenard, very costly, and anointing Jesus's feet with it, and drying them with her hair. Christ sits surrounded by his disciples, a handsome, intelligent god; with human sorrow he feels an uncanny respect for his own body, which will soon have so much to endure, and already deserves and receives the ceremony of anointment which is bestowed on the dead; he smiles down with deep emotion at the kneeling woman, who is impelled by her loving and fearful forebodings to perform this compassionate act, an act which will never be forgotten so long as there are suffering people, and which sends its fragrance to soothe all suffering people down the millennia. Apart from the disciple who lay on Christ's bosom and who recorded this act, none of the apostles seems to feel its significance, and the one with the red beard seems to be making the peevish remark found in Scripture: 'Why was not this ointment sold for three hundred pence, and given to the poor?' This economical apostle is the very one who carries the purse, the habit of dealing with money has made him insensitive to all love's selfless fragrance of myrrh, he would like to change it into pennies for some useful purpose, and it was he, the penny-changer, who betrayed the Saviour – for thirty pieces of silver. Thus the Gospel reveals symbolically, in the story of the banker among the apostles, the sinister seductive power that lurks in the money-bag, and warns us against the treachery of business people. Every rich man is a Judas Iscariot.

'You're making a face like a stubborn believer, dear Doctor,' whispered Milady; 'I've been watching you, and I don't mean to insult you, but you looked like a good Christian.'

'Between ourselves, that's what I am; Christ, in fact –'

'You don't mean to tell me that you believe he's a god?'

'Of course, my dear Matilda. He is the god whom I love the most – not because he is a legitimate god, whose father was God before him and ruled the world since time immemorial; but because, although he was born the Dauphin of heaven, he has democratic tastes and dislikes courtly pomp and ceremony; because he is not the god of an aristocracy of tonsured scribes and braided spear-carriers, and because he is a modest god of the people, a citizen-god, a *bon dieu citoyen*. Truly, if Christ were not a god, I would vote for him to be one, and rather than an absolute god who had been imposed on us, I should obey him, the elected god, the god of my choice.'

CHAPTER 8

THE Archbishop, a grave, aged man, read Mass himself, and to tell the truth, not only I, but to some extent even Milady, was secretly moved by the spirit of this ceremony and by the sanctity of the old man who conducted it. Every old man, after all, is a priest in his own right, and the rites of the Catholic Mass are so ancient that they may be the only thing surviving from the world's childhood, and demand our piety as a memorial to the first forebears of all men. 'You see, Milady,' I said, 'every movement you observe here, the manner of clasping one's hands and extending one's arms, the curtsey, the washing of the hands, the scattering of incense, this cup, indeed the man's entire clothing, from his mitre to the hem of his surplice, all this comes from ancient Egypt and is the relic of a priesthood, something of whose wondrous character is reported only in the most ancient documents, a primeval priesthood, by whom the first wisdom was explored, the first gods invented, the first symbols chosen, and the young human race –'

'Was first deceived,' added Milady in a tone of bitterness, 'and I believe, Doctor, that nothing has survived from the world's earliest age but a few dismal formulae of deceit. And they are still effective. Do you see those pitch-dark faces? and especially that fellow on his stupid knees, looking so ultra-stupid with his gaping jaws?'

'For heaven's sake!' I soothed her gently, 'what does it matter that his head has received so little of the light of reason? What is that to us? What annoys you about it? Don't you see oxen, cows, dogs and donkeys every day that are just as stupid, without being upset by such a sight and provoked into ill-tempered remarks?'

'That's quite another matter,' interrupted Milady, 'these beasts have their tails behind them, and what annoys me is that a fellow of such bestial stupidity has his tail in front instead of behind.'

'Yes, that is quite another matter, Milady.'

CHAPTER 9

AFTER the Mass there was still plenty to look at and listen to, especially the sermon given by a big, burly monk whose ancient Roman face with its bold, commanding air was in remarkable contrast to his coarse habit, so that the man looked like an emperor of poverty. He preached about heaven and hell, and at times worked himself up into a frenzy of enthusiasm. His description of heaven was barbarously overdone, with plenty of gold, silver, jewels, delicious food, and wine of the best vintages; meanwhile he pulled faces as though he were licking his lips in ecstasy, and rolled blissfully to and fro in his habit, when among the little white-winged angels he imagined himself as a little white-winged angel. His description of hell was less delectable, indeed it was thoroughly practical and serious. Here the man was much more in his element. He inveighed especially against the sinners who no longer had a proper Christian belief in the old fires of hell and even fancied that they had grown cooler in recent years and would presently go out altogether. 'Even if hell were going out,' he cried, 'I would fan the last glimmering embers with my breath, that they might flare up into the glowing flames of yore.' When you heard the voice howling forth these words like the north wind, and saw the man's flaming face, his red neck like a buffalo's, and his mighty fists, you felt this infernal threat was no exaggeration.

'I like this man,' said Milady.[17]

'You are right,' I replied, 'I like him too, better than many of our mild, homoeopathic physicians of the soul, who pour a ten-thousandth of reason into a bucket of moral water, and preach us to sleep with it on Sundays.'

'Yes, Doctor, I have some respect for his hell; but I don't really trust his heaven. But then, as far as heaven is concerned, I got entangled in secret doubts very early on. When I was small, in Dublin, I would often lie on my back in the grass, and look up into the sky, and wonder if heaven really contained all the splendid things that people praised it for. "But how is it," I thought, "that none of these splendid things ever falls down, like a jewelled ear-ring, or a string of pearls, or at least a piece of pineapple tart, and all we ever get from on high is hail or snow or ordinary rain? That can't be right," I thought –'

'Why do you say that, Milady? Shouldn't you keep these doubts to yourself? Unbelievers who don't believe in heaven ought not to make proselytes; there is less to criticize, indeed much to praise, in the proselytism of those people who have a magnificent heaven and don't selfishly wish to enjoy it all by themselves, and therefore invite their fellow-men to share it, and will not be content until the latter have accepted the kindly invitation.'

'But I have always been surprised, Doctor, by many rich people of this kind. We see them, as presidents, vice-presidents, or secretaries of missionary societies, doing their utmost to make some mouldy old Jewish beggar capable of entering the kingdom of heaven and rejoining his former associates there. And yet it never occurs to them to let him share their pleasures here on earth, and they never, for example, invite him to spend the summer in their country houses, where there must be titbits that the poor rogue would savour as much as though he were enjoying them in heaven itself.'

'That can be explained, Milady; heavenly enjoyments cost them nothing, and it is a double pleasure to make our fellow-man happy at so little expense. But what pleasures does the unbeliever have that he can invite anyone to share?'

'Nothing, Doctor, but a long, peaceful sleep, which can sometimes be very desirable for an unbeliever, especially one who has previously been tormented by importunate invitations to heaven.'

The beautiful woman said this in a tone of acid bitterness, and I was not wholly unserious as I replied: 'Dear Matilda, in my actions in this world I am not even troubled about the existence of heaven and hell, I am too large-minded and too proud to be influenced by greed for heavenly rewards or fear of infernal punishments. I seek the good because it is beautiful and attracts me irresistibly, and I detest what is bad, because it is hideous and repellent. Even as a boy, when I read Plutarch[18] – and I still read him every evening in bed, and sometimes feel like jumping up, getting into the express coach, and becoming a great man – even then I liked the story about the woman who strode through the streets of Alexandria with a water-skin in one hand and a burning torch in the other, calling out that she was going to extinguish hell with the water and set fire to heaven with the torch, so that people would no longer refrain from evil for fear of punishment, nor do good in hope of a reward. All our actions should gush forth from selfless love, whether or not there is life after death.'

'So you don't believe in immortality, either?'

'Oh, you're cunning, Milady! I doubt of it? I, whose heart takes root ever more deeply in the remotest millennia of the past and the future, I who am myself one of the most eternal of people, every moment an eternal life, every thought an eternal star – how could I possibly not believe in immortality?'

'I think, Doctor, that after we have enjoyed so much that is good and beautiful on this earth, it takes a considerable share of vanity and presumption to ask God for immortality on top of all that! Man, the aristocrat among the animals, who thinks himself a cut above his fellow-creatures, also wants to obtain the privilege of eternity, by kneeling down as a supplicant at the throne of the king of this world and singing a courtier's hymns to his glory. – Oh, I know what that twitching of your lips means, immortal sir!'

CHAPTER 10

SIGNORA asked us to go with her to the monastery where the miracle-working cross, the most remarkable object in the whole of Tuscany, is kept. And it was fortunate that we left the cathedral, or else Milady's pranks would at last have got us into trouble. She was bubbling with wit and fancy, producing a torrent of charmingly extravagant ideas, as frolicsome as kittens cavorting in the May sunshine. At the cathedral door she dipped her forefinger three times into the holy water, sprinkled me each time, and murmured: 'Dem Zefardeyim Kinnim,'[19] which she claimed was the Arabic formula by which sorceresses turn a man into a donkey.

On the piazza outside the cathedral a crowd of troops were manoeuvring, almost all in Austrian uniforms and obeying commands in German. At least I made out the German words: 'Present arms! Lower arms! Shoulder arms! Righ. turn! Stop!' I believe that commands are uttered in German all over Italy, as among some other European nations. Ought we Germans to congratulate ourselves on this? Have we so many orders to give in the world that German has become the language of orders? Or are we ordered about so much that the spirit of obedience understands the German language best?

Milady seems no friend to parades and reviews. She pulled us away with ironic timidity. 'I don't like,' said she, 'being close to such people with sabres and guns, especially when they march along in serried ranks and in large numbers, as in extraordinary manoeuvres. What if one among all these thousands suddenly goes mad, and stabs me with the weapon in his hand? Or what if he suddenly regains his reason and thinks: "What are you risking? What have you to lose, even if they take your life? Even if the other world promised us after death is not as brilliant as it is cracked up to be, however bad it is, you can't get less there than they give you now, less than six ha'pence a day – so give yourself a treat and stab that little Englishwoman with the cheeky turned-up nose!" Am I not in danger of my life? If I were king, I should divide my soldiers into two classes. I would make some of them believe in immortality, so that they should be brave in battle and not fear death, and I would use them only in war. The others, however, would be kept for parades and reviews, and to prevent it occurring to them that they risked nothing by killing someone for a laugh, I would forbid them on pain of death to believe in immortality; in fact, I'd even give them some butter on their army bread, so that they should love life. But as for the first lot, those immortal heroes, I'd make their lives a misery, so that they should learn to despise them and regard the cannon's mouth as the entrance to a better world.'

'Milady,' I said, 'you would be a bad ruler. You know very little about governing, and you don't understand the first thing about politics. If you had read the political annals –'

'Perhaps I understand such matters better than you, my dear Doctor. I tried to find out about them at an early age. When I was small, in Dublin –'

'And lay on your back, in the grass, thinking – or not thinking, as in Ramsgate –'

Milady gave me a glance as though reproaching me gently for my ingratitude, but then she laughed once more and continued: 'When I was small, in Dublin, and could sit on a corner of the stool on which Mother's feet were resting, I always asked lots of questions about what the tailors, the cobblers, the bakers, in short, all the people in the world had to do. And my mother explained that the tailors make clothes, the cobblers make shoes, the bakers bake bread – and when I asked: "What do the kings do?" my mother replied: "They govern." "Do you know, Mother dear," said I, "if I were king, I'd stop governing for one whole day, just to see what the world would look like after that." "Dear child," answered my mother, "that's just what many kings do, as you can tell by looking at the world."'

'Indeed, Milady, your mother was right. Here in Italy, particularly, there are such kings, and you notice it in Piedmont and Naples –'

'But, dear Doctor, you can't blame an Italian king if there are many days when he does no governing, on account of the excessive heat. My only worry is that the Carbonari[20] might take advantage of one such day; for in recent times I've particularly noticed that revolutions have always broken out on days when there was no governing. If the Carbonari were to make a mistake, and think it was an ungoverned day, when there was some governing going on after all, they'd lose their heads. So the Carbonari can't be too careful, and must pick the right moment. On the other hand, however, it is the supreme policy of kings to keep secret the days on which they are not governing, and on such days to sit on the throne occasionally and sharpen their pens, or seal envelopes, or draw lines on blank paper, just for show, so that the populace outside, peeping inquisitively through the palace windows, will think some governing is going on.'

While such remarks flitted forth from Milady's dainty mouth, smiling contentment was floating on Francesca's full, rosy lips. She did not say much. Her gait, however, no longer displayed such a groaning frenzy of renunciation as on the previous evening; rather, she strode along with an air of victory, each step a trumpet-blast; yet it was more a clerical than a secular victory that revealed itself in her movements, she was almost the image of the Church Triumphant, and an invisible halo floated round her head. Her eyes, however, as though laughing through tears, were once again perfectly worldly, and in the colourful throng that flooded past us there was not a single item of clothing that escaped her scrutiny. '*Ecco!*' she would then exclaim, 'what a shawl! the Marchese must buy me cashmere like that for my turban, when I dance the part of Roxelane. Oh, he has also promised me a cross studded with diamonds!'

Poor Gumpelino! you will make no difficulties about the turban, but the cross will cost you many a pang; however, Signora will torment you, and stretch you on the rack, until you consent to that as well.

CHAPTER II

THE church where the miracle-working cross of Lucca is to be seen belongs to a monastery, the name of which escapes me for the moment.

As we entered the church, there were a dozen monks kneeling in silent prayer in front of the high altar. Only now and again, in a kind of chorus, did they utter a few broken words, which echoed through the lonely colonnades in a somewhat eerie manner. The church was dark, except that coloured light fell through small stained-glass windows on the bald heads and brown habits. Dull copper lamps shed meagre light on the blackened frescoes and altarpieces, the heads of wooden saints projected from the walls, painted in garish colours and grinning in the uncertain light as though they were alive – Milady gave a scream, and pointed to a gravestone at our feet, which had in relief the image of a bishop with mitre and crook, clasped hands, and the remains of a nose which had been trodden away. 'Oh dear!' she whispered, 'I trampled on his stone nose, and now he'll come poking his nose into my dreams tonight.'

The sacristan, a pallid young monk, showed us the miracle-working cross, and told us about the miracles it had performed. Whimsical as I am, I may have assumed the look of a believer; now and again I have fits of believing in miracles, especially when the time and place encourage such belief, as they did here. At such times I believe that everything in the world is miraculous, and the entire history of the world a sacred legend. Had I been infected by the devotion of Francesca, who was kissing the cross in a frenzy of enthusiasm? I was annoyed by the witty British woman with her equally frenzied compulsion to mock. It may have annoyed me all the more because I myself did not feel free from it, and regarded it as far from praiseworthy. There is no denying that the desire to ridicule, the enjoyment of absurdity, has something malicious about it, whereas seriousness is more allied with one's better feelings – virtue, passion for liberty, and love itself are very serious. And yet there are hearts in which seriousness and jest, evil and sanctity, heat and cold are so strangely combined that it is hard to judge them. Such a heart was in Matilda's bosom; at times it was a frozen lump of ice, from whose smooth, reflecting surface sprang blossoming forests of ardent, yearning palm-trees; at other times it was a volcano of fiery enthusiasm, suddenly extinguished by a laughing avalanche of snow. Despite her wildness, there was no harm in her, not even sensuality; indeed, I think she had picked up only the witty side of sensuality, and enjoyed it as one might a grotesque puppet-play. It was a humorous urge, a delicious curiosity, to see how some odd fellow or other would behave if he were in love. How completely different Francesca was! In her thoughts and feelings there was a Catholic unity. By day she was a pale, languishing moon, at night she was a burning sun – moon of my days! sun of my nights! I shall never see you again!

'You are right,' said Milady, 'I too believe in the miraculous powers of a cross. I'm certain that if the Marchese doesn't skimp on the jewels on the cross he has promised Signora, it will produce a brilliant miracle in her; she will end up by being so dazzled by it that she will fall in love with his nose. Besides, I have often heard of the miraculous powers of crosses and other decorations which can turn an honest man into a rogue.'

Thus the pretty woman poked fun at everything, she flirted with the poor sacristan, made droll apologies to the bishop whose nose had been trodden away, courteously requesting him not to return her visit, and as we reached the holy-water stoup, she insisted on making another attempt to turn me into a donkey.

Whether it was the mood induced by my surroundings, or whether I was irritated by this jest and wanted to condemn it as sharply as possible, I assumed the appropriate rhetorical tone and declared:

'Milady, I do not like women who despise religion. Beautiful women who have no religion are like flowers without scent; they resemble those cold, sober tulips that look so china-like in their Chinese porcelain pots, and, if they could speak, would undoubtedly explain to us how they developed naturally from a bulb, how it is sufficient in this world not to smell bad, and how, as far as scent is concerned, a rational flower has no need of any scent at all.'

The mere word 'tulip'[21] made Milady gesticulate violently, and while I was speaking, her personal antipathy to this flower had such a powerful effect on her that she stopped her ears in desperation. She was partly play-acting, but also seriously piqued, in giving me a bitter glance and asking in a tone of piercing, heartfelt mockery:

'And you, my dear flower, which of the available religions do you profess?'

'I profess them all, Milady! The fragrance of my soul ascends to heaven and intoxicates even the immortal gods!'

CHAPTER 12

WE had been conducting our conversation largely in English, and as Signora could not understand it, she took it into her head, God knows how, that we were disputing about the merits of our respective fellow-countrymen. She now praised the English and the Germans alike, though in her heart of hearts she thought that the former were not very bright and the latter were stupid. She had a very poor opinion of the Prussians, whose country, according to her geography, lay far beyond England and Germany, and she had a particularly low opinion of the King of Prussia, the great Federigo, whose part had been danced by her rival, Signora Seraphina, in a benefit performance the year before; for, strangely enough, this king, that is Frederick the Great, survives in the Italian theatre and in the memory of the Italian people.

'No,' said Milady, not listening to Signora's pleasant prattle, 'there's no need to turn this man into a donkey; not only does he change his mind every ten paces, and continually contradict himself, but he's now trying to make converts, would you believe, and I rather think he's a Jesuit in disguise. I had better pull devout faces for my own safety, or else he'll denounce me to his fellow-hypocrites in Christ, to the holy amateur inquisitors, who will burn me in effigy, since the police don't yet permit them to throw people themselves into the fire. Oh, reverend sir! you mustn't believe that I'm as clever as I look, I am not short of religion, I'm not a tulip, I do assure you, no, anything, anything but a tulip, I'll sooner believe everything! I do already believe the most important items in the Bible: I believe that Abraham begat Isaac, and Isaac begat Jacob, and Jacob begat Judah, and also that the latter knew his daughter-in-law Tamar[22] upon the highway. I also believe that Lot drank too much with his daughters. I believe that Potiphar's wife was left holding pious Joseph's coat in her hands. I believe that the two elders who surprised Susannah in her bath were very old. What's more, I also believe that the patriarch Jacob deceived first his brother and then his father-in-law, that King David gave Uriah a good position in the army, that Solomon acquired a thousand wives and then complained that all was vanity. I believe in the Ten Commandments, too, and even obey most of them; I take care not to covet my neighbour's ox, nor his maid, nor his cow, nor his ass. I do not work on the Sabbath, the seventh day, when God rested; in fact, since we are no longer sure which this seventh day of rest was, I often take the precaution of doing nothing the entire week. But as for the commandments of Christ, I have always obeyed the most important, the command to love one's enemies – for alas! although I never knew it at the time, the people I loved most were always my worst enemies.'

'For heaven's sake, Matilda, don't cry!' I exclaimed, as a note of agonized bitterness again darted forth from her merry mockery, like a snake from a flower-bed. I was familiar with this note, which shook the wonderful woman's witty crystal heart with a mighty but short-lived tremor, and I knew that it could be dispelled as easily as it had arisen, by the first humorous remark that came into one's head, or that flew into her mind. As she leaned against the gate of the monastery courtyard, pressing her burning cheeks against the cold stone and wiping the trace of tears from her eyes with her long hair, I tried to restore her good humour by pulling poor Francesca's leg in Matilda's own mocking fashion, and recounting the principal facts about the Seven Years War, which seemed greatly to interest her, and which she thought was not yet over. I told her many interesting things about the great Federigo, the witty, gaitered god of Sanssouci, who invented the Prussian monarchy, and played the flute very prettily as a young man, and also composed French verses. Francesca asked if the Prussians or the Germans would win. For, as was mentioned earlier, she thought the former were a quite distinct nation, and it is customary in Italy for the word 'Germans' to be taken to mean Austrians.[23] Signora was a good deal surprised when I told her that I myself had lived for a long time in the Capitale della Prussia, in Berelino, a city that lies near the top of the map, not far from the North Pole. She shuddered as I described the dangers to which you are sometimes exposed there, when you meet polar bears in the street.

'You see, dear Francesca,' I explained, 'in Spitzbergen there are a vast number of bears in the garrison, and they sometimes visit Berlin for the day, to see *The Bear and the Bassa*[24] out of patriotism, or to have a good meal and drink champagne in the Café Royal, kept by Beyerman; but they often drink more than is good for them, and go back to Spitzbergen feeling cross; whence the expression "like a bear with a sore head".[25] Many bears live in the city itself, and indeed some say that Berlin owes its origin to bears, and should really be called Bearlin. The city bears, though, are quite tame, and some of them are so cultivated that they write the finest tragedies and compose the most splendid music. Wolves are also numerous there, and since they wear sheep's clothing, imported from Warsaw, because of the cold, they are not very easy to recognize. Snow-geese flutter around singing bravura arias, and reindeer run about as art connoisseurs. For the rest, the people in Berlin lead very frugal, hard-working lives, and most of them sit with the snow up to their navels and write dogmatics, works of edification, religious histories for the daughters of the cultivated classes, catechisms, sermons for each day in the year, and hymns, and with all this they are very moral, for they sit with the snow up to their navels.'

'Do you mean people in Berlin are Christians?' cried Signora in amazement.

'Their Christianity is a curious business. Basically they haven't got any, and anyway they are far too rational to practise it seriously. But since they know that Christianity is necessary for the state, to keep their subjects properly humble and obedient, and to make sure that not too much robbery and murder goes on, they try with great eloquence at least to convert their fellow-men to Christianity; they look, as it were, for stand-ins, since they want their religion to survive but find it too laborious to practise it themselves. In this predicament they exploit the poor Jews' readiness to be of service; the latter must be Christians in their place, and since you can do anything with the Jews if you treat them right, they have drilled themselves into Christianity to such an extent that they already denounce unbelief, defend the Trinity to the death, believe in it even in the dog-days, rage against the rationalists, creep about the country as missionaries and God's spies, and in church are always the best at turning up their eyes and pulling sanctimonious faces; they play the creeping Jesus to such applause that professional envy is beginning to stir in some quarters, and the older masters of the trade are already complaining in secret that Christianity has become a Jewish monopoly.'

CHAPTER 13

IF Signora did not understand this, you, dear reader, will certainly understand it better. Milady also understood, and this understanding restored her good humour. But when I tried – I can't remember whether I had a straight face – to uphold the view that ordinary people need a definite religion, she again could not help opposing me in her own way.

'Ordinary people need a religion!' she cried. 'I've heard this doctrine zealously preached by a thousand stupid lips and many thousands of hypocritical ones –'

'It's true for all that, Milady. Just as a mother can't give truthful answers to all the questions a child asks, because the child's intellect doesn't permit it, so there must be a positive religion, a church, in existence to give definite, intelligible answers to all the questions ordinary people ask about supernatural matters beyond their intellectual grasp.'

'Oh dear! Doctor, this very comparison reminds me of a story that wouldn't provide much support for your view. When I was small, in Dublin –'

'And lay on your back –'

'But, Doctor, it's impossible to say a sensible word to you. Wipe that cheeky grin off your face, and listen. When I was small, in Dublin, and sat at my mother's feet, I asked her one day what happened to the old moons. "Dear child," said my mother, "God knocks the old moons into pieces with a sugar-hammer, and makes them into little stars." You can't blame my mother for giving me this obviously false explanation, for no matter how much she knew about astronomy, she still couldn't have described to me the whole system of sun, moon, and stars, and she gave definite, intelligible answers to questions about matters beyond my intellect. Still, it would have been better if she had kept the explanation until I was older, or at least had not invented a lie. For when I met little Lucy, and the full moon was in the sky, and I told her how it would soon be made into little stars, she laughed at me, and said her grandmother, old Mrs O'Meara, had told her that the moons were eaten in hell as fire-melons, and as there was no sugar there, people had to put pepper and salt on them. If Lucy had laughed at me for my rather naively Protestant view, I laughed still more at her gloomy Catholic opinion; our mockery turned into a serious quarrel, we hit each other, we scratched each other till the blood came, we spat polemically at each other, until little O'Donnell came out of the school and pulled us apart. This boy had received better instruction in astronomy, understood mathematics, and calmly corrected our respective errors and pointed out the folly of our quarrel. And what happened? We two girls put aside our dispute for the time being and promptly joined forces to give the calm little mathematician a good beating.'

'Milady, I'm annoyed, for you're right. But there is no changing it: people will always dispute about the merit of the religious notions taught them in childhood, and the rational person will always suffer twice over. At one time, of course, things were different: in those days it never occurred to anyone to make a special fuss about the doctrines and ceremonies of his religion, still less to force them on anyone else. Religion was a precious tradition, sacred narratives, ceremonies of commemoration, and mysteries, handed down from one's ancestors – a nation's family heirlooms, as it were – and a Greek would have been outraged if a stranger who was not of his kin had wanted to share his religion; he would have thought it still more inhuman to induce anyone, by compulsion or cunning, to abandon the religion he had been born with and adopt a strange one in its place. But then a nation came out of Egypt, the fatherland of crocodiles and priesthood, and along with its skin diseases and its stolen gold and silver vessels, it also brought what came to be called a positive religion, and what came to be called a church, a scaffolding of dogmas in which you had to believe, and of sacred ceremonies you had to perform, a model for subsequent state religions. And now that "fault-finding with humanity"[26] began, along with proselytizing, compulsion to believe, and all the holy horrors that have cost the human race so much blood and tears.'

'Goddam! what an evil nation!'

'Oh, Matilda, it has long since been damned, and it drags the torments of the damned through the millennia. Oh, that Egypt! its manufactures bid defiance to time, its pyramids are still standing immovably, its mummies are as indestructible as ever, and just as indestructible is that mummified nation that roams over the face of the earth, swaddled in its ancient letters, a fossilized lump of world history, a ghost that earns its keep by dealing in bills of exchange and cast-off trousers – Look, Milady, at that old man over there, with the white beard that seems to be turning black again at the tip, and with the haunted eyes –'

'Aren't the ruins of the old Roman graves over there?'

'Yes, that's where the old man is sitting, and perhaps, Matilda, he is even now saying his prayer, an eerie prayer in which he laments his sufferings and accuses nations which have long vanished from the earth and survive only in old wives' tales – but he in his pain scarcely notices that he is sitting on the graves of the very enemies whom he is beseeching heaven to destroy.'

CHAPTER 14

In the last chapter I spoke about positive religions only in so far as they receive special privileges from the state as churches, under the name of established religions. However, dear reader, there is a pious dialectic, which will prove conclusively to you that anyone opposed to the ecclesiastical apparatus of such an established religion is also an enemy of religion and the state, or, as the usual formula runs, an enemy of throne and altar. But I tell you that is a lie: I honour the inner sanctity of every religion, and submit myself to the interests of the state. Even though I have no particular respect for anthropomorphism, I still believe in the glory of God, and even if kings are foolish enough to resist the spirit of the people, or ignoble enough to injure the people's spokesmen by discrimination and persecution, yet I remain, in accordance with my deepest convictions, a supporter of kingship, of the monarchical principle. I do not hate the throne, but only the sly aristocratic vermin who have crawled into the cracks in the old throne, and whose character has been accurately described for us by Montesquieu[27] in these words:

> Ambition in league with idleness, baseness in league with arrogance, the desire to become rich without working, aversion to truth, flattery, treachery, faithlessness, perjury, contempt for civic duties, fear of virtuous princes, and an interest in supporting vicious ones!

I do not hate the altar, but I hate the snakes lurking beneath the old altars: the crafty snakes that can smile as innocently as flowers while secretly squirting their venom into the cup of life, and hissing slander into the pious worshipper's ear, the glittering worms with their soft words –

Mel in ore, verba lactis,
Fel in corde, fraus in factis.[28]

Precisely because I am a friend to the state and to religion, I hate that abortion that is called an established religion, that monster born of the coupling of secular and spiritual power, that mule sired by Antichrist's white horse on Christ's she-ass. If there were no such established religion, no preferential treatment for a dogma and a cult, Germany would be strong and united, and its sons would be glorious and free. As things stand, however, our poor fatherland is torn apart by confessional divisions, the populace is split into hostile religious parties, Protestant subjects are at odds with their Catholic princes or vice versa, everywhere there is suspicion about crypto-Catholicism or crypto-Protestantism, everywhere people are denounced as heretics, their very thoughts are spied on, there is pietism, mysticism, *Church Times* snooping, sectarian hatred, an obsession with making converts, and while we quarrel about heaven, we are perishing here on earth. A policy of impartial toleration in religious matters might well be the only thing that could save us, and by becoming weaker in the faith Germany could become stronger politically.

For religion itself, for its sacred essence, it is just as fatal to be granted privileges, to have its servants receive preferential endowments from the state, in return for which they are obliged to act as the state's representatives. Thus one hand washes the other, the spiritual hand washes the secular one and vice versa, and the wishy-washy effects are folly in the sight of God and an abomination to men. If the state has opponents, these become enemies of the religion which receives privileges from the state and is therefore its ally; and even the most inoffensive believer becomes suspicious when he scents political motives in religion. Most repulsive of all, however, is the arrogance of priests when in return for the services they think they render the state they also count on its support; when in return for the spiritual fetters they have lent the state to bind the people with, they can also employ the state's bayonets. Religion can never sink lower than when it is elevated into an established religion; it then loses, so to speak, its inner innocence, and becomes as haughty in public as an acknowledged mistress. Of course it receives more homage, more protestations of reverence; it celebrates new victories daily, in brilliant processions, and at such triumphs even Bonapartist generals carry its candles, the proudest spirits swear loyalty to its banner, unbelievers are converted and baptized daily – but pouring in all this much water does not thicken the soup, and the new recruits to an established religion resemble the soldiers gained by Falstaff[29] – they'll fill a church as well as better. Nothing more is heard about self-sacrifice: like commercial travellers with their books of samples, so missionaries travel about with their tracts and conversion manuals; this business is free from danger, and everything proceeds in mercantile and economical forms.

Only when religions have to compete with one another, and are persecuted rather than persecuting, are they magnificent and admirable; only then can there be inspiration, self-sacrifice, martyrdom, and palms. What beauty, what lovable sanctity, what hidden sweetness belonged to the Christianity of the first centuries, when it still resembled its divine founder in the sanctity of suffering. In those days it was still the beautiful legend of a hidden god who walked beneath Palestine's palms in the shape of a gentle youth, preaching love and charity, and revealing that doctrine of freedom and equality whose truth has since been acknowledged by the reason of the greatest thinkers, and which inspires our own age as the gospel of the French. Compare Christ's religion with the various Christianities that have been set up in various countries as established religions: for example, the Roman Apostolic Catholic Church, or even that Catholicism without poetry that we see ruling as the High Church of England, that miserable rotten skeleton of faith from which all blooming life has withered! A system of monopolies is as harmful to religions as to trade; they remain alive through free competition, and they will only return to their original splendour when political equality of worship is introduced – free trade in gods, as it were.

The noblest people in Europe have long since declared that this is the only way to save religion from disappearing entirely; yet its servants would sooner sacrifice the altar itself than lose the least part of the sacrifices performed thereon; just as the nobility would sooner abandon the throne itself, and His Majesty who sits on it, to certain perdition than deliberately give up the most unjust of its prerogatives. After all, their affected interest in throne and altar is merely a farce performed to bamboozle the populace! Anyone who has eavesdropped on the guild's secrets knows that priests have much less respect than laymen for the God whom they can knead from bread and words, just as they please, for their own advantage, and that the nobles have much less respect for the king than a *roturier*[30] could muster, and in their heart of hearts even mock and despise the monarchy for which they display so much reverence in public, and try to extort so much reverence from others. Truly, they resemble those people at fairgrounds who make money by showing the gaping public some Hercules, or giant, or midget, or wild man, or fire-eater, or some other freak, extolling his strength, sublimity, courage, invulnerability, or, if he is a midget, his wisdom, and blowing their trumpets, and wearing gaudy jackets. But under their jackets, in their hearts, they deride the credulity of the astounded populace and mock the poor object of this panegyric, in whom they have lost all interest, because they are used to seeing him every day, and are only too familiar with his weaknesses and the tricks that have been drummed into him.

I do not know whether God will put up much longer with the priests' practice of making money by displaying a bogey-man in his name; at least I should not be surprised to read in the *Hamburg Impartial Correspondent* that Jehovah senior warns the public not to extend credit to anybody, whoever it may be, not even his son, in his name. However, I am certain that in the course of time we shall see kings refusing to be marionettes displayed by their aristocratic despisers; they will break their placards, jump out of their marble booths, and angrily throw off the glittering trappings which were intended to impress the people – the red coat that was meant to inspire terror, like an executioner's; the circlet of diamonds that was pulled over their ears to shut out the voices of the people; the golden stick placed in their hands as an illusory symbol of rule – and the liberated kings will be free like other people, and walk among them freely, have free feelings and make free marriages, and state their opinion freely – and that is the emancipation of kings.

CHAPTER 15

BUT what will the aristocrats do when they are deprived of their crowned means of subsistence, when kings are the property of the people and govern honestly and securely, by the will of the people, the one and only source of all power? What will the priests do when kings realize that a little ointment cannot make any man's head proof against the guillotine, just as the people are realizing more clearly each day that you cannot grow fat on wafers? Well, of course, all the aristocracy and the clergy can do is to form an alliance, and mount cabals and intrigues against the new order of things.

Vain endeavours! A flaming giantess, the age marches calmly on, unconcerned about the priestlings and lordlings yelping and snapping at her ankles. How they howl whenever they burn their snouts on the giantess's foot, or when she accidentally steps on their heads, making the poison of obscurantism gush out! They then turn their fury all the more maliciously against single children of the age, and, impotent against the mass, they try to vent their cowardly petulance against individuals.

Alas! we must confess that many a poor child of the age is no less sensitive to the injuries that lurking priests and nobles manage to inflict on him under cover of darkness, and alas! even if a halo surrounds the victor's wounds, they still bleed, and still hurt! It is a strange martyrdom that such victors endure nowadays; it cannot be disposed of by a bold confession of one's faith, as in earlier times, when prisoners of conscience met a quick death on the scaffold or the jubilant pyre. The essence of martyrdom, sacrificing all earthly goods for heavenly pleasure, is still the same; but it has lost much of its former joyous faith, it has become more of a resigned tenacity, a persistent endurance, a life-long dying, and it may happen that in cold, grey hours even the holiest martyrs are assailed by doubt. There is nothing more terrible than the moment when a Marcus Brutus[31] began to doubt the reality of the virtue for which he had sacrificed everything! And alas! he was a Roman, who lived when the Stoa was flourishing; but we moderns are of softer material, and besides, we are witnessing the success of a philosophy which assigns only a relative meaning to enthusiasm, and thus annihilates it in itself, or at best neutralizes it into something consciously quixotic!

These cool, clever philosophers! With what compassion they smile down on the self-tormenting madness of a poor Don Quixote, and yet with all their school-wisdom they do not notice that such quixotic behaviour is still the most valuable thing in life, indeed it is life itself, and that such quixotic behaviour inspires the whole world, and all its philosophy, music, farming and yawning, to bolder flights! For the great mass of the people, including the philosophers, is, without knowing it, nothing but a colossal Sancho Panza, who, for all his sober fear of beatings and his homely common sense, follows the mad knight on all his crazy adventures, allured by the promised reward which he believes in because he desires it, but still more impelled by the mystical power which enthusiasm always exercises over the great mass – as we can see in all political and religious revolutions, and perhaps in the smallest events of daily life.

Thus, for instance, you, dear reader, are the involuntary Sancho Panza of the crazy poet whom you are following through the meanderings of this book; you may be shaking your head, but you are still following him.

CHAPTER 16

STRANGE! *Life and Adventures of the Ingenious Nobleman Don Quixote of La Mancha, recounted by Miguel de Cervantes Saavedra* was the first book I read, once I had attained the boyish age of reason and had some knowledge of the alphabet. I can still clearly remember the time when I stole away from home early in the morning and hastened to the Hofgarten to read *Don Quixote* there undisturbed. It was a beautiful May day; the blooming spring lay in the quiet light of morning, listening to the praises of the nightingale, its sweet flatterer, who sang her eulogy with such caressing gentleness, such melting enthusiasm, that the most bashful buds opened, and the lustful grasses and the fragrant sunbeams kissed each other more quickly, and trees and flowers shivered for very delight. But I sat down on an old mossy stone bench in the Avenue of Sighs, as it was called, near the waterfall, and delighted my little heart with the great adventures of the bold knight. In my childish honesty I took everything quite seriously: however ridiculous the blows might be that fate dealt to the poor hero, I assumed that it had to be so, that being laughed at was just as much part of heroism as receiving bodily wounds, and the former annoyed me as much as I sympathized with the latter in my soul. I was a child and did not know the irony which God put into the world as he created it, and which the great author had imitated in his printed microcosm – and I could shed the bitterest tears when the noble knight received only ingratitude and blows for all his nobility of soul; and since, being an inexperienced reader, I spoke every word aloud, the birds and the trees, the brook and the flowers were able to listen to it all, and since such innocent natural beings, like children, know nothing of the world's irony, they likewise took everything seriously and wept with me at the sufferings of the poor knight; even an old veteran oak uttered sobs, and the waterfall shook its white beard more vigorously, and seemed to be denouncing the wickedness of the world. We felt that the knight's heroic temper deserved no less admiration when the lion turned its back on him without showing any fighting spirit, and that his deeds were rendered all the more praiseworthy by the weakness and desiccation of his body, by the rottenness of the armour that protected him, and by the pitiful state of the broken-down nag that carried him. We despised the base rabble who treated the hero so brutally, but we despised still more the high-born rabble, adorned with cloaks of coloured silk, lofty phrases and ducal titles, who mocked a man who was so far superior to them in intelligence and nobility of spirit. The more I read this wondrous book, the higher Dulcinea's knight rose in my esteem, and the more my love for him grew; and this went on every day in the same garden, so that by autumn I had already reached the end of the story, – and never will I forget the day when I read about the lamentable duel in which the knight was so shamefully defeated!

It was an overcast day, ugly clouds were passing across the grey sky, the yellow leaves were falling sorrowfully from the trees, heavy teardrops were hanging on the last flowers, which were bowing their dying heads, sad and faded, the nightingales had long since vanished, the image of transience was staring at me from every side, – and my heart came close to breaking as I read how the noble knight lay on the ground, stunned and shattered, and without raising his visor, as though he were speaking from the grave, he spoke to the victor in a faint, feeble voice: 'Dulcinea is the most beautiful woman in the world and I am the most unfortunate knight on earth, but it would be wrong for my weakness to deny this truth – strike home with your lance, knight!'

Alas! the brilliant Knight of the Silver Moon,[32] who defeated the bravest and noblest man in the world, was a barber in disguise!

CHAPTER 17

THAT was long ago. Many new springs have blossomed in the meantime, yet they always lacked their most powerful charm, for alas! I no longer believe the sweet lies of the nightingale, springtime's flatterer, I know how soon spring's splendour fades, and when I catch sight of the youngest rosebud, I see it in my mind's eye blooming in the red colour of agony, turning pale and being blown away by the winds. Wherever I look, I see winter in disguise.

In my heart, however, there still blossoms the flaming love that rises yearningly above the earth, roams wildly through the vast, yawning expanses of the sky, is rejected by the cold stars, and sinks back homeward to the little earth, and must confess, sighing and rejoicing, that after all there is nothing in the whole of creation better or more beautiful than the heart of man. This love is enthusiasm, which is always divine, whether it performs foolish actions or wise ones – And so it was by no means a futile waste when the little boy shed tears over the sufferings of the eccentric knight, any more than when the youth later spent many nights in his cramped study weeping for the deaths of the sacred heroes of freedom, King Agis[33] of Sparta, Gaius and Tiberius Gracchus of Rome, Jesus of Jerusalem, and Robespierre and Saint-Just of Paris. Now that I have donned the *toga virilis*[34] and claim myself to be a man, the time for weeping is past, and my duty is to act like a man, imitating my great predecessors, and, please God, likewise to be mourned in future by boys and youths. Yes, it is they on whom one can still count in our cold times; for they can still catch fire from the ardent breath that emanates from the ancient books, and for this reason they also understand the flaming hearts of the present. Young people are selfless in thought and feeling, and therefore think and feel the truth most deeply, and are not sparing when called on to participate boldly in declarations and deeds. Old people are selfish and petty; they are more concerned about the interest on their capital than about the interests of humanity; they calmly let their toy boats float down the gutter of life, and care little about the sailor who is struggling with the waves on the high seas; or they crawl with glutinous persistence up the greasy pole to reach the dignity of mayor or the presidency of their club, and shrug their shoulders at the heroic statues thrown down by the gale from the column of fame. They may recount that they themselves, in their youth, likewise dashed their heads against a brick wall, but afterwards made their peace with the wall, for the wall is the absolute, the positive, that which exists in and for itself, that which, being real, is also rational, wherefore it is irrational to refuse to endure an absolutism imposed by high and mighty rationality, firmly established and incontrovertibly existing. Alas! the reprehensible people who try to reason us philosophically into a mild servitude at least deserve more respect than the reprobates who defend despotism without even appealing to rational grounds, but support it from their historical knowledge as a customary right, to which people have grown gradually accustomed in the course of time, and which is therefore legally valid and juridically unassailable.

Alas! I shall not, like Ham,[35] lift the blanket from the private and shameful parts of my fatherland, but it is appalling how slavery has been made loquacious among us, and how German philosophers and historians rack their brains to defend all despotism, however silly and cloddish, as rational or legally valid. Silence is the honour of slaves, says Tacitus; these philosophers and historians maintain the contrary view and point to the ribbon of honour in their buttonhole.

Perhaps you are right after all, and I am only a Don Quixote, and reading all sorts of wondrous books has addled my wits, as with the nobleman of La Mancha, and Jean-Jacques Rousseau was my Amadis of Gaul, Mirabeau was my Roland or Agramanth, and I have spent too much time studying the heroic deeds of the French paladins and the Round Table of the National Convention. Admittedly my madness and the *idées fixes* I drew from these books are of the opposite kind from the madness and the *idées fixes* of the La Manchan; he wanted to restore the vanished age of chivalry, whereas I want to annihilate completely whatever has survived from that age, and we are thus acting with entirely different opinions. My colleague mistook windmills for giants, whereas I can see in our present-day giants nothing but bragging windmills; he mistook leather wineskins for mighty magicians, but I see in our present magicians only the leather wineskin; he mistook beggars' dens for castles, donkey-drivers for cavaliers, stable-wenches for court ladies, whereas I consider our castles to be rogues' dens, our cavaliers to be donkey-drivers, our court ladies to be common stable-wenches; as he took a puppet-play to be a tragedy of state, so I take our tragedies of state to be wretched puppet-plays – but I strike the wooden villains as bravely as the brave La Manchan did. Alas! such a heroic deed often ends as badly for me as it did for him, and, like him, I must endure a great deal for my lady's honour. Were I to disavow her, from simple fear or vile cupidity, I could live comfortably in this rational, existing world, and I would lead a beautiful Maritorne[36] to the altar, and receive confirmation from plump magicians, and banquet with noble donkey-drivers, and sire harmless stories and other little slave-children! Instead, decorated with my lady's tricolour, I must engage in continual duels, and fight my way through unspeakable afflictions, and I never win a victory that does not cost me some of my heart's blood. Night and day I am hard beset; for these enemies are so malicious that many whom I wounded mortally still put on airs as though they were alive, and by transforming themselves into every shape they have soured my nights and my days. How many torments this vile wizardry has forced me to endure! Wherever a flower grew that was dear to me, they crept thither, the treacherous ghosts, and broke even the most innocent buds. Everywhere, and even where I least expect it, I discover their silvery trail of slime on the ground, and if I am not careful I can slip and injure myself, even in the house of my nearest and dearest. You may smile, and dismiss such worries as mere imaginings, like those of Don Quixote. But imaginary pains hurt no less for all that, and if you imagine that you have drunk hemlock, you may suffer a wasting disease; at any rate, you will not grow fat on it. And to say that I have grown fat is a slander; at least I have not yet obtained a fat sinecure, though I have the necessary talents. Nor has the fat of rich relatives rubbed off on me. I fancy that everything possible has been done to keep me thin; when I was hungry, I was fed with serpents, when I was thirsty, I was given bitter gall to drink, hell was poured into my heart so that I wept poison and sighed fire, they pursued me even by crawling into my dreams of the night – and there I see the hideous masks, the noble lackeys' faces gnashing their teeth, the bankers' menacing noses, the deadly eyes that dart and sting from under cowls, the Pale hands in shirt-cuffs with naked knives –

Even the old woman who lives next door, through the wall from me, thinks I am mad, and maintains that I talk the craziest nonsense in my dreams, and that last night she distinctly heard me exclaiming:

'Dulcinea is the most beautiful woman in the world and I am the most unfortunate knight on earth, but it would be wrong for my weakness to deny this truth – strike home with your lance, knight!'

Postscript

(November 1830)

I do not know what strange piety prevented me from making the slightest change to some remarks which, when I later re-read the above pages, struck me as rather too bitter. The manuscript was already as yellow and faded as a dead man, and I was reluctant to mutilate it. All writing that has been invalidated by the passage of time has such an inherent right to escape injury, especially these pages, which belong in a manner of speaking to the obscure past. For they were written almost a year before the third Hegira of the Bourbons,[37] at a time that was far more bitter than the bitterest remarks, at a time when it looked as though the victory of freedom might be delayed by another century. It was worrying, to say the least, that our knights assumed such confident expressions, that they had their faded armorial bearings repainted in bright new colours, that they held tournaments with shields and spears at Munich and Potsdam, that they sat so proudly astride their lofty steeds as though about to ride to Quedlinburg to be republished by Gottfried Bassen.[38] Still more unendurable was the malicious glint of triumph in the little eyes of our priestlings, who managed to conceal their long ears so craftily beneath their cowls that we expected the direst injuries. There was no way of knowing in advance that the noble knights would shoot their arrows with such lamentable ineptitude, anonymously for the most part, or at least as they were galloping away, with averted faces, like fleeing Bashkirs. Nor could we know in advance that the serpent-like cunning of our priestlings would fail so miserably – oh, it almost makes one feel sorry for them to see how little they know what to do with their best poison, since their rage makes them throw it at our heads in great lumps instead of pouring it lovingly into our soup, an ounce at a time; to see them unearthing their enemies' discarded swaddling-clothes from among the baby-linen in order to sniff out foul play, and even digging up their enemies' fathers from the grave, to see whether they were circumcised – Oh, what fools, who think they have discovered that the lion is a species of cat, and will hiss about this scientific discovery until the great cat demonstrates the maxim *ex ungue leonem*[39] on their own flesh! Oh, what obscurantist villains, who will not see the light until they themselves are hanging from the lamp-posts! I should like to string my lyre with a donkey's entrails, to sing them as they deserve, the tonsured blockheads!

A mighty pleasure grips me! As I sit writing, music sounds beneath my window, and from the elegiac anger of the long-drawn-out melody I recognize the Marseillaise with which the handsome Barbaroux[40] and his companions greeted the city of Paris, the cow-bells of freedom, whose notes made the Swiss Guards in the Tuileries feel homesick, the triumphal death-song of the Gironde, the sweet old lullaby –

What a song! It runs through my veins with fiery joy, and kindles in me the glowing stars of enthusiasm and the rockets of ridicule. No, these shall not be lacking in the age's great firework display. Musical streams of fiery song shall fall in bold cascades from the summit of freedom's delight, as the Ganges dashes from the Himalayas! And you, lovely Satyra, daughter of just Themis and goat-footed Pan, lend me your aid, for you are sprung from the race of Titans on your mother's side, and you hate, as I do, the enemies of your kindred, the feeble usurpers of Olympus. Lend me your mother's sword that I may judge the hateful brood, and give me your father's pipes, that I may pipe them to death –

They already hear the fatal piping, and are seized by panic terror, and they again flee, in bestial shapes, as in the days when we piled Pelion upon Ossa –

Aux armes, citoyens!

It is a great injustice to us poor Titans to criticize the gloomy ferocity with which we came storming aloft when we attacked heaven – alas, down in Tartaros it was hideous and dark, and we heard only the howling of Cerberus and the rattling of chains, and it is pardonable if we seemed somewhat uncouth in comparison with those gods *comme il faut* who, with their fine manners, had enjoyed so much delightful nectar and so many sweet concerts of the Muses in the pleasant drawing-rooms of Olympus.

I can write no more, for the music beneath my window is turning my head, and the refrain rises with ever-increasing power:

Aux armes, citoyens!

DIFFERING CONCEPTIONS OF HISTORY

THE book of history is interpreted in diverse ways. Two mutually opposed views are particularly notable.

Some people see in all earthly things only a dreary cyclical movement: in the lives of nations as in the lives of individuals, and throughout organic nature, they see growth, flourishing, fading, and death; spring, summer, autumn, and winter. 'There is no new thing under the sun!'[1] is their watchword; and even this is nothing new, for the king of the Orient groaned it out two thousand years ago. They shrug their shoulders at our civilization, which they say will eventually yield once more to barbarism; they shake their heads at our struggles for liberation, which they say will only assist the emergence of new tyrants; they smile at all the efforts of a political enthusiasm which wants to make the world better and happier, and which they say will finally die down without accomplishing anything. In the little chronicle of hopes, hardships, misfortunes, sorrows and joys, errors and disappointments, on which the individual spends his life – in the story of each man they see also the history of mankind. In Germany it is the sages of the Historical School and the poets of Wolfgang Goethe's artistic period who are especially devoted to this opinion, and the latter often use it as a sugar-coating to disguise their sentimental indifference to all the political affairs of their native land. A sufficiently well-known government[2] in North Germany sets particular store by this view, and promotes it by encouraging people to travel, so that amidst the elegiac ruins of Italy they may develop the cheerful and consoling notion of fatalism, and may subsequently co-operate with preachers of Christian submission to damp down the people's tertian fever of liberty[3] by applying cold compresses of newsprint. Still, if anyone cannot shoot up by free intellectual power, let him twist his tendrils on the ground; the future will teach this government just how far it can get by twisting and turning.

In contrast to the fatalistic and indeed fatal view discussed above, there is a brighter view, more closely related to the idea of providence. According to this view, all earthly things are maturing towards a beautiful state of perfection, and the great heroes and heroic epochs are merely stages on the way to a higher, god-like condition of the human race, whose moral and political struggles will at last lead to the holiest peace, the purest brotherhood, and the most everlasting happiness. The Golden Age, it is said, does not lie behind us, but ahead of us; we were not driven out of paradise by a flaming sword, rather we must conquer it by a flaming heart, by love; the apple of knowledge will not give us death, but rather eternal life. For a long time 'civilization' was the watchword among the disciples of this doctrine. In Germany the philosophers of humanity[4] were its principal adherents. It is well known how firmly the Philosophical School, as it is called, was devoted to this view. It particularly encouraged the investigation of political questions, and as the finest flower of this doctrine people preach an ideal political form, based entirely on rational foundations, which will ultimately ennoble mankind and render them happy. I scarcely need to name the inspired champions of this view. Their ardent endeavours are at any rate more pleasing than the petty twisting and turning of base machinations; if we ever oppose them, let it be done with the most precious sword of honour, while we shall dispatch a malicious serf only with the knout that suits his station.

Neither of the views I have outlined accords fully with the most vital emotions of our lives: on the one hand, we do not wish our enthusiasm to have been futile, nor to regard what is dead and gone as the supreme achievement; on the other hand, we want the present to retain its value, not to count simply as the means while the future is its end. And indeed we take ourselves too seriously to consider ourselves only as means to an end; we are inclined to regard end and means only as conventional notions, which human speculation has introduced into nature and history, but which were unknown to the Creator. Every created thing is its own purpose, every event is self-determined, and everything, like the world itself, exists and occurs for its own sake. Life is neither end nor means; life is a right. Life wants to enforce its right against the cold hand of death, against the past, and this enforcement is revolution. The elegiac indifference of historians and poets shall not paralyse our energies as we go about this business; and the rhapsodies of starry-eyed prophets shall not seduce us into jeopardizing the interests of the present and of the first human right that needs to be defended – the right to live. 'Le pain est le droit du peuple,' said Saint-Just,[5] and that is the greatest declaration made in the entire French Revolution.

ON THE HISTORY OF RELIGION AND PHILOSOPHY IN GERMANY

PREFACE TO THE FIRST EDITION

I MUST draw the particular attention of the German reader to the fact that these pages were originally composed for a French periodical, the *Revue des deux mondes*, and for a specific purpose. They form part of a survey of German intellectual life, parts of which I had earlier presented to the French public, and which have also appeared in German as essays 'on the history of recent belles-lettres in Germany'. Owing to the demands of the periodical press, its defective economy, my lack of scholarly reference works, French inadequacies, a law[1] recently promulgated in Germany concerning publication abroad which was applied only to me, and other such obstacles, I was unable to impart the various sections of this survey in chronological sequence and under an overall title. Hence the present book, despite its internal unity and its external coherence, is only the fragment of a larger whole.

I send my warmest regards to my native land.

Written at Paris, in December 1834.
HEINRICH HEINE.

PREFACE TO THE SECOND EDITION

WHEN the first edition of this book left the press and I inspected a copy, I was not a little alarmed by the mutilations whose traces were everywhere apparent. Here an adjective was missing, there a clause; whole passages were omitted without any concern for continuity, so that not only the sense but sometimes even the sentiments disappeared. It was more the fear of Caesar than the fear of God that guided the hand in these mutilations, and while it timorously elided anything that might cause political offence, it spared even the most questionable references to religion. Thus the true message of this book, which was patriotic and democratic, was lost, and a wholly alien spirit glared at me from it, recalling the polemical wranglings of scholastic theologians, and deeply repugnant to my humanistic and tolerant nature.

At first I flattered myself with the hope that in a second impression I would be able to supply the book's lacunae; but no such restoration is now possible, since the original manuscript was lost in my publisher's house in the great fire of Hamburg. My memory is too weak for my recollection to be of any help, and moreover the state of my eyes would scarcely permit me to examine the book closely. I have contented myself with using the French version, which was printed before the German, to translate some of the longer omitted passages back from French and to intercalate them. One of these passages, which has been reprinted and discussed in innumerable French papers and even commented on in last year's Chamber of Deputies by one of the greatest French statesmen, Count Molé,[2] can be found at the end of this new edition and may show how much truth there is in the charge of belittling and disparaging Germany in the eyes of foreigners, which, as I am assured by certain honest people, has been levelled against me. If I spoke with irritation about the old official Germany, the mouldy land of philistines – which, however, has produced no Goliath, not a single great man – what I said has been misrepresented as though I were talking about the real Germany, the great, mysterious, and as it were anonymous Germany of the German people, the sleeping sovereign, whose sceptre and crown are playthings for monkeys.[3] It was all the easier for the honest people to make this insinuation, because for a long period it was wellnigh impossible for me to proclaim my true sentiments, especially when the Federal Diet issued its decrees against 'Young Germany', which were directed principally against me and brought me into a situation of captivity without precedent in the annals of press servitude. Later, when I was able to loosen the muzzle somewhat, my thoughts remained gagged.

The present book is a fragment, and shall remain a fragment. Quite honestly, I should have preferred the book to remain unpublished. Since its appearance my views on many matters, especially divine matters, have undergone a considerable change, and many of my earlier assertions now run contrary to my better convictions. But the arrow no longer belongs to the archer once it flies from the bowstring, and the word no longer belongs to its speaker once it has passed his lips, let alone when it has been multiplied by the press. Besides, external authorities would confront me with compelling objections if I were to leave this book unpublished and withdraw it from my collected works. I could indeed take refuge, as many writers do in such cases, in toning down my language and concealing my opinions under conventional phrases; but I hate ambiguous words, hypocritical flowers, cowardly fig-leaves, from the depths of my soul. Under all circumstances, however, an honest man retains the inalienable right to admit his mistakes openly, and I will exercise it here unflinchingly. I therefore frankly confess that everything in this book bearing on the great problem of God is as false as it is ill-considered. Both ill-considered and false is the claim which I made, mindlessly following the philosophers, that deism is theoretically exploded and is merely dragging out its existence in the phenomenal world. No, it is not true that the rational criticism that has annihilated the proofs of God's existence worked out by St Anselm has also put an end to God's existence itself. Deism is alive, living its most lively life; it is not dead, and least of all has it been killed by the most recent German philosophy. The cobwebbed dialectic of Berlin cannot tempt a dog from behind the stove; it cannot kill a cat, far less a God. I know from my own experience how little dangerous its destructive powers are; it is constantly destroying, yet people remain alive. The door-keeper of the Hegelian school, the fierce Ruge,[4] once declared flatly (but all his declarations fall flat) that he had killed me with his porter's stick in the *Halle Yearbooks*, and yet at that very time I was walking about on the Paris boulevards, fresh and healthy and more immortal than ever. Poor, worthy Ruge! later he himself could not withhold an honest smile when I confessed to him here in Paris that I had never set eyes on his frightful murderous periodical, the *Halle Yearbooks*, and my plump red cheeks, as well as the good appetite with which I was consuming oysters, convinced him how little I deserved to be called a corpse. Indeed, I was still healthy and stout at that time, I was at the zenith of my fat, and as insolent as King Nebuchadnezzar before his fall.

Alas! a few years later a physical and spiritual change occurred. How often have I thought since about the story of that King of Babylon who believed himself to be God but plunged down lamentably from the pinnacle of his pride, crawled on the ground like an animal, and ate grass (I expect it was lettuce). This legend is in the grandiose and magnificent Book of Daniel, and I recommend it not only to the good Ruge, but also to my much more obstinate friend Marx,[5] not to mention Messrs Feuerbach, Daumer, Bruno Bauer, Hengstenberg, and whatever their names may be, these godless self-gods, as an edifying tale which they should take to heart. There are, indeed, many other fine and curious stories in the Bible which deserve their attention; right at the start, for example, you have the story of the forbidden tree in Paradise and the snake, the little lecturer, who expounded the entire Hegelian philosophy six thousand years before Hegel's birth. This blue-stocking without legs demonstrates very acutely how the absolute consists in the identity of being and knowing, how man becomes God through knowledge, or, what is the same thing, how God becomes conscious of himself in man. This formula is less clear than the original words: 'If ye eat of the tree of knowledge, ye shall be as God!'[6] Madame Eve understood only one thing in the whole demonstration, that the fruit was forbidden, and because it was forbidden she ate some, the good woman. But scarcely had she tasted the tempting apple than she lost her innocence, her naive immediacy; she discovered that she was much too naked for a person of her standing, the ancestress of so many future emperors and kings, and she demanded a dress. Only a dress of fig-leaves, of course, since at that time no Lyons silk-manufacturers had yet been born, and even in Paradise there were still no milliners or fashion-dealers – O Paradise! It is strange, as soon as woman attains intellectual self-awareness, her first thought is a new dress! This Bible story too, especially the speech of the snake, haunts my mind, and I should like to prefix it to this book as a motto, just as you often see outside princes' estates a board with the warning: 'Man-traps and spring-guns in operation'.

In my most recent book, *Romanzero*, I have already spoken of the transformation which has occurred in my mind with respect to divine things. Since then, with true Christian impertinence, many inquiries have reached me, asking how this illumination came upon me. Pious souls seem to thirst for me to invent some miracle for them, and they are anxious to know if, like Saul, I saw a light on the road to Damascus, or if, like Balaam the son of Beor, I was riding on a donkey which suddenly stood still, opened its mouth, and began to talk like a human being. No, you credulous hearts, I have never been to Damascus; all I know about Damascus is that recently the Jews there were accused of devouring old Capuchins,[7] and the city's name might have been entirely unknown to me if I had not read the Song of Songs, where King Solomon compares his beloved's nose to a tower that looks towards Damascus. Nor have I ever seen a donkey, at least not a four-legged one, that talked like a human being, while I have met plenty of human beings who talked like donkeys whenever they opened their mouths. In fact, it was neither a vision, nor a seraphic ecstasy, nor a voice from heaven, nor a strange dream nor any other miraculous apparition, that set me on the path to salvation, and I owe my illumination quite simply to reading a book. A book? Yes, and it is an old, simple book, as modest as nature, and just as natural; a book with an unassuming, workaday appearance, like the sun that warms us, like the bread that feeds us; a book that gazes at us with such homeliness, such kindly benevolence, like an old grandmother, who reads this book every day, with her dear lips moving, and with her spectacles on her nose – and this book is known simply as *the* book, the Bible. It is rightly called the Holy Scriptures; anyone who has lost his God can find him again in this book, and anyone who has never known him will find here the breath of the divine word. The Jews, who are experts on precious objects, knew very well what they were doing when, at the burning of the Second Temple,[8] they abandoned the gold and silver sacrificial vessels, the candelabra and lamps, even the High Priest's breastplate with its great jewels, and saved only the Bible. This was the true treasure of the Temple, and, thank God, it did not fall prey to the flames or to Titus Vespasian, the villain, who came to such a bad end, as the rabbis relate. A Jewish priest named Joshua ben Sirach ben Eliezer, who lived at Jerusalem two hundred years before the burning of the Second Temple, during the heyday of the Ptolemaic ruler Philadelphus, uttered his age's ideas about the Bible in a collection of gnomic sayings, *Meshalim*, and I will pass on his fine words here. Despite their sacerdotal solemnity, they are as heart-warmingly fresh as though they had sprung only yesterday from a human breast, and they run as follows:

> All these things are the book of the covenant of the Most High God, even the law which Moses commanded us for a heritage unto the assemblies of Jacob. It is he that maketh wisdom abundant, as Pishon, and as Tigris in the days of new fruits; that maketh understanding full as Euphrates, and as Jordan in the days of harvest; that maketh instruction to shine forth as the light, as Gihon in the days of

vintage. The first man knew her not perfectly; and in like manner the last hath not traced her out. For her thoughts are filled from the sea, and her counsels from the great deep.[9]

Written at Paris, in May 1852.
HEINRICH HEINE.

BOOK ONE

In recent years the French have supposed that they could understand Germany by becoming acquainted with the works of our literature. This, however, has merely raised them from a state of complete ignorance to one of superficial knowledge. For our literary works are to them only mute flowers, the entire German idea is to them an unwelcoming enigma, as long as they remain unaware of the significance of religion and philosophy in Germany.

In trying to provide some explanatory information about these two subjects, I believe that I am doing a useful piece of work. This is no easy task for me. It is necessary, first of all, to avoid terms belonging to a professional jargon that is entirely unknown to the French. And yet I have not penetrated far enough into the subtleties of theology or metaphysics to be able to formulate them simply and concisely, as befits the needs of the French public. I shall therefore deal only with the great questions that have been debated in German divinity and philosophy, I shall explain only their importance for society, and I shall always bear in mind my limited ability to clarify these matters, and the French reader's powers of comprehension.

Any great German philosophers who may happen to glance into these pages will shrug their shoulders loftily at the paltriness of my observations. But they might be good enough to consider that the little I say is clearly and distinctly expressed, while their own works are certainly very thorough, immeasurably thorough, very profound, stupendously profound, but just as unintelligible. What good to the people are locked granaries to which they have no key? The people are hungry for knowledge, and will thank me for the crust of intellectual bread that I honestly share with them.

I do not think it is lack of talent that prevents most German scholars from putting their views on religion and philosophy in popular form. I think it is nervousness about the results of their own thinking, which they dare not convey to the people. As for me, I lack this nervousness, for I am no scholar, I myself belong to the people. I am no scholar, I am not one of Germany's seven hundred sages. I stand with the great crowd before the gates of their wisdom, and if some truth has slipped out, and if this truth has found its way to me, then it has come far enough: I write it on paper in good handwriting and give it to the typesetter; he sets it up in lead type and gives it to the printer; he prints it, and then it belongs to the whole world.

The religion that we in Germany rejoice in is Christianity. I shall therefore have to recount what Christianity is, how it turned into Roman Catholicism, how the latter gave rise to Protestantism, and how Protestantism gave rise to German philosophy.

Since I am beginning with a discussion of religion, I entreat all pious souls in advance on no account to be alarmed. Fear nothing, pious souls! No profane jests shall offend your ears. The latter do indeed still have their uses in Germany, where at present the power of religion needs to be neutralized. For there we are in the same position as you were before the Revolution, when Christianity was indissolubly allied with the *ancien régime*. The latter could not be destroyed so long as the former still held sway over the masses. Voltaire's shrill laughter had to rise before Sanson's[1] axe could fall. At bottom, however, the laughter, like the axe, proved nothing; it only achieved something. Voltaire could wound only the body of Christianity. All the jests he drew from Church history, all his jokes about dogma and worship, about the Bible, mankind's holiest book, about the Virgin Mary, poetry's finest flower, the entire *Dictionnaire*[2] of philosophical arrows that he fired at the clergy and the priesthood, wounded only the mortal body of Christianity, not its inner essence, not its deeper spirit, not its eternal soul.

For Christianity is an idea, and as such indestructible and immortal, like every idea. But what is this idea?

Precisely because this idea has not yet been clearly understood, and external trivia have been mistaken for the central issue, there is still no history of Christianity. Two opposed parties write Church history, continually contradicting each other, yet neither the one nor the other will ever state definitely what the idea is that forms the inner core of Christianity, that strives towards revelation in its symbolism, in dogma as in worship, and in its whole history, and has been manifested in the real life of the Christian nations. Neither Baronius,[3] the Catholic cardinal, nor the Protestant Aulic Counsellor Schröckh discloses to us what this idea actually was. Even if you turn over all the folios in Mansi's *Proceedings of the Sacred Councils*, Assemani's *Liturgical Codex*, and Saccarelli's entire *Ecclesiastical History*, you still will not understand what the idea of Christianity really was. After all, what do you see in the history of the Eastern and Western Churches? In the former, in the history of the Eastern Church, you see nothing but dogmatic hair-splitting, in which the art of the ancient Greek Sophists is again discernible; in the latter, in the history of the Western Church, you see nothing but disciplinary disputes concerning the Church's interests, in which ancient Roman legal casuistry and political science again come to the fore, in new guises and with new means of enforcement. Indeed, just as people in Constantinople argued about the Logos, so did people in Rome argue about the relation of the secular to the spiritual power; and just as the former quarrelled about *homousios*,[4] so the latter quarrelled about investiture. But the Byzantine questions – was the Logos *homousios* to God the Father? should Mary be called the Mother of God or the Mother of Man? was Christ obliged to be hungry for lack of food, or was he hungry only because he wanted to be? – all these questions are based merely on court intrigues, the upshot of which depends on whispering and tittering in the chambers of the Sacrum Palatium, for example, on the fall of either Pulcheria or Eudoxia;[5] for one of these ladies hates Nestorius for giving away her amorous dalliance, and the other hates Cyrillus, whom Pulcheria protects; everything refers ultimately to mere gossip among women and eunuchs, and in the dogma it is really a man, and in the man a party, that is persecuted or promoted. It is just the same in the West: Rome wanted to rule; 'after the downfall of its legions, it sent dogmas into its provinces';[6] all credal disputes went back to Roman usurpations; the main thing was to consolidate the supreme power of the Bishop of Rome. The latter was always very indulgent about actual points of faith, but breathed fire the moment the Church's rights were attacked; he disputed less about the Persons in Christ than about the consequences of Isidore's Decretals;[7] he centralized his power by means of canon law, installing bishops, reducing princely power, monastic orders, celibacy, and so forth. But was this Christianity? Does reading these histories reveal to us the idea of Christianity? What is this idea?

How this idea developed historically and manifested itself in the phenomenal world could doubtless be discovered by studying the first centuries A.D., and especially by unprejudiced research into the history of the Manicheans and Gnostics. Although the former were declared heretics, the latter were denounced, and both were condemned by the Church, their influence remained powerful within Christian dogma, their symbolism formed the basis of Catholic art, and their manner of thinking permeated the entire life of the Christian nations. Ultimately the Manicheans do not differ much from the Gnostics. The doctrine of the two conflicting principles, the good one and the evil one, is characteristic of both. Some, the Manicheans, acquired this doctrine from the ancient Persian religion, in which Ormuz, the light, is opposed to his enemy Ariman, the darkness. The others, the true Gnostics, believed rather in the pre-existence of the good principle, and explained the origin of the evil principle by emanation, by generations of Aeons, which become darker and more corrupt as they move further from their source. According to Cerinthus,[8] the creator of our world was far from being the supreme God, but only an emanation of him, one of the Aeons, the true Demiurge, who gradually degenerated and now, as the evil principle, is in hostile opposition to the good principle, the Logos, which sprang directly from the supreme God. This Gnostic world-view originated in ancient India and was accompanied by the doctrines of God's incarnation, the mortification of the flesh, and spiritual self-absorption; it produced the ascetic and contemplative monastic life, which is the finest flower of the Christian idea. This idea is expressed only obscurely in dogmatics and dimly in worship. Nevertheless, we can see the doctrine of the two principles emerging everywhere: the good Christ is opposed to the evil Satan; the spiritual world is represented by Christ, the material world by Satan; our souls belong to the former, our bodies to the latter; and hence the entire phenomenal world – nature – is originally evil, and Satan, the Prince of Darkness, wants to use it to lure us to our destruction, and we must renounce all life's sensual pleasures and torture our bodies, the fiefdom of Satan, that our souls may soar all the more magnificently into the luminous heaven, the radiant kingdom of Christ.

This world-view, the true idea of Christianity, spread with unbelievable rapidity through the entire Roman Empire, like an infectious disease; the sufferings it induced, however, lasted throughout the

Middle Ages, sometimes as raging fever, sometimes as exhaustion, and we moderns are still afflicted by cramps and paralysis in our limbs. Even though a few of us are cured, we still cannot escape from the general hospital atmosphere, and feel unhappy as the only healthy people among invalids. In a future era, when mankind regains its perfect health, when peace is restored between body and soul, and they again interpenetrate in their original harmony, it will scarcely be possible to understand the artificial strife introduced between them by Christianity. The happier and more beautiful generations, conceived in freely chosen embraces and flourishing in a religion of joy, will smile sadly at their poor ancestors, who remained dismally aloof from all the pleasures of this beautiful earth, and by mortifying their warm, colourful sensuality, almost faded into cold ghosts! Yes, I say it with certainty, our descendants will be happier and more beautiful than ourselves. For I believe in progress, I believe that mankind is destined to be happy, and thus I have a higher opinion of the Divinity than the pious people who fancy that he created mankind only to suffer. Here on earth, by the blessings of free political and industrial institutions, I should like to establish the bliss which, in the opinion of the pious, is to begin only on the Day of Judgement, in heaven. Perhaps mine is as foolish a hope as theirs, and there will be no resurrection of mankind, whether in the political and moral or in the apostolic and Catholic sense. Perhaps mankind is destined to everlasting misery, perhaps the nations are condemned eternally to be trampled upon by despots, exploited by their henchmen, and derided by their lackeys.

Alas! if that were so, one should try to support Christianity, even if it were recognized as an error; one should run barefoot through Europe, wearing a monk's habit, preaching renunciation and the nullity of all earthly goods, holding up the crucifix to console the victims of scorn and scourging, and promising them all seven heavens on high after their deaths. Perhaps it is just because the great ones of the earth are assured of their power, and have resolved in their hearts to use it eternally to make us wretched, that they are convinced of the necessity of Christianity for their subjects, and at bottom it is a tender feeling of humanity that makes them expend so much effort on supporting religion!

The ultimate fate of Christianity therefore depends on whether or not we need it. For eighteen centuries this religion was a boon to suffering mankind; it was providential, divine, sacred. All the benefits it brought to civilization, by taming the strong and strengthening the tame, by uniting the nations through common feelings and a common language, and whatever else its apologists may laud it for, are trivial by comparison with the great consolation that it brought to mankind. Everlasting glory is due to the symbol of the suffering God, the Saviour crowned with thorns, Christ crucified, whose blood, so to speak, was the soothing balm that flowed into humanity's wounds. The poet, in particular, will acknowledge with reverence the horrific sublimity of this symbol. The entire system of symbols expressed in the art and life of the Middle Ages will always arouse the admiration of poets. Indeed, what colossal consistency can be seen in Christian art, especially in architecture! These Gothic cathedrals, how well they harmonize with worship, and how clearly they reveal the idea of the Church itself! Everything strives aloft, everything is transubstantiated: the stone sprouts branches and foliage and becomes a tree; the fruits of the vine and the ear become blood and flesh; man becomes God; God becomes pure spirit! Christian life in the Middle Ages provides rewarding, precious, and inexhaustible material for the poet. Only through Christianity could there develop on earth a state of affairs containing such glaring contrasts, such motley agonies, and such fantastic beauties, so that one almost thinks that such things never existed in reality, and that it was all a colossal delirium, the delirium of an insane God. Nature herself seemed in those days to adopt a fantastic guise; for though man, engrossed in abstract meditations, sullenly turned his back on her, yet at times she addressed him in a voice that was so hideously sweet, so appallingly loving, so magically potent, that man could not help listening, and smiling, and being terrified, and falling deadly sick. Here the story of the nightingale of Basle comes into my head, and since you probably do not know it, I will tell it.

In May 1433, at the time of the Council,[9] a group of clerics went for a walk in a wood near Basle, including prelates, doctors, and monks of every colour, and they disputed about theological controversies, differentiating and reasoning, or argued about annates,[10] expectatives, and reservations, or inquired whether Thomas Aquinas was a greater philosopher than Bonaventura[11] – how can I tell! But suddenly they paused in the midst of their dogmatic and abstract discussions, and stopped, as though rooted to the spot, beside a flowering linden-tree. On the tree perched a nightingale, which was rejoicing and sobbing in the tenderest and most melting melodies. As they listened, the learned doctors felt wondrously happy; the warm, spring-like notes pierced the scholastic defences of their hearts, their feelings woke from their dull hibernation, they looked at one another with astonishment and delight. At last one of them made the astute observation that something peculiar was happening, that the nightingale might well be a devil, which was trying to distract them with its lovely sounds from their Christian conversations, and seduce them into sensual enjoyment and other sweet sins; and he began an exorcism, probably with what was then the customary formula: 'adjuro te per eum qui venturus est judicare vivos et mortuos',[12] etc. etc. To this conjuration, it is said, the bird replied: 'Yes, I am an evil spirit!' and flew away laughing. Those who had heard its song, however, are said to have fallen ill that very day, and to have died soon afterwards.

This story scarcely needs any comment. It bears the hideous stamp of an age that denounces everything sweet and charming as the work of the devil. Even the nightingale was slandered, and people made the sign of the cross when it sang. The true Christian walked about in blossoming nature with his senses timidly closed, like an abstract ghost. I may discuss the Christian's relation to nature more fully in a later book, when I have to give a detailed account of German popular beliefs in order to explain modern Romantic literature. For the moment I can only observe that French writers, misled by German authorities, are greatly in error when they assume that popular beliefs in the Middle Ages were the same throughout Europe. It was only about the good principle, the kingdom of Christ, that the same opinions were held in the whole of Europe; the Roman Church made sure of that, and anyone who deviated from the prescribed opinion was a heretic. But the evil principle, the kingdom of Satan, was the subject of varying opinions in various countries, and in the Germanic North quite different notions were held than in the Latin South. This came about because the Christian priesthood did not reject the ancient indigenous gods as mere fantasies, but conceded that they really existed, maintaining, however, that all these gods were nothing but devils and she-devils, who had been deprived by Christ's victory of their power over mankind and now sought to seduce us into sin by pleasure and cunning. The whole of Mount Olympus became an airy hell, and however beautifully a medieval poet might sing the Greek tales of the gods, the pious Christian saw in them mere ghosts and devils. The monks' dismal delusion bore hardest on poor Venus; she in particular was considered a daughter of Beelzebub, and the good knight Tanhüser tells her to her face:

'O Venus, my lady fair,
A she-devil thou art!'[13]

Tanhüser, you see, had been lured into the wondrous cavern known as Venusberg, where, according to legend, the beautiful goddess, with her ladies and her boyfriends, played, danced, and led the most dissipated life. Even poor Diana, despite her chastity, was not safe from a similar fate, and she was said to ride through the forests every night with her nymphs, whence arose the legend of the raging army, the Wild Hunt. This displays the Gnostic view that what had once been divine could become corrupt, and it is in this transformation of an older indigenous belief that the idea of Christianity is most profoundly manifested.

Indigenous beliefs in Europe, in the North much more than in the South, were pantheistic. Their mysteries and symbols referred to the worship of nature. Wondrous beings were revered in each of the elements, a god breathed in every tree, the entire phenomenal world was infused with divinity. Christianity turned this belief on its head, regarding nature not as divine but as devilish. However, the serene figures of Greek mythology, their beauty enhanced by art, who ruled in the South along with Roman civilization, were more difficult to transform into hideous satanic spectres than were the Germanic gods; the latter had not been shaped by any marked aesthetic sense, and were already as morose and dismal as the North itself. That is why you in France could not develop any such dark and terrifying devilry as we did, and why, in your hands, even the world of spirits and magic acquired a serene guise. How beautiful, clear, and colourful your popular legends are by comparison with ours – those abortions of blood and fog that grin at us so greyly and gruesomely. By choosing materials that you in Brittany and Normandy had either invented or had been the first to adapt, our medieval poets endowed their works, perhaps intentionally, with as much as possible of the cheerful old French spirit. But the gloomy Northern spirit, of which you have scarcely a notion, survived in our indigenous poems and in our orally transmitted popular legends. You have, as we do, several kinds of elemental spirit, but ours are as different from yours as a German from a Frenchman. How brightly coloured and, above all, how pure are the demons in your *fabliaux* and magical romances, by comparison with our grey and often obscene rabble of spirits. Wherever you got them from, whether from Cornwall or Arabia, your fairies and elemental spirits are completely naturalized, and a French spirit differs from a German one rather as a dandy, strolling down the Boulevard Coblence in yellow kid gloves, differs from a heavy German porter. Your nixies, such as Melusine,[14] are just as different from ours as a princess from a washerwoman. How alarmed Morgan Le Fay would be to meet a German witch, naked and smeared with ointments, riding to the Brocken on a broomstick. Instead of a cheerful Avalon, this mountain is a rendezvous for everything ugly and dreadful. On the mountain's summit sits Satan in the shape of a black goat. Each of the witches approaches him with a candle in her hand and kisses him behind, at the end of his back. Afterwards the abominable sisterhood dances round him singing 'Donderemus, donderemus!' The goat bleats, and the infernal cancan rejoices loudly. It is a bad omen for the witch if she loses a shoe during the dance, for that means that she will be burnt that same year. But all fears and forebodings are drowned by the sabbat's wild music, truly worthy of Berlioz;[15] and in the morning, when the poor witch awakes from her intoxication, she is lying naked and exhausted in the ashes beside the dying embers on the hearth.

The best information about these witches is to be found in the *Demonology* of the honourable and erudite Dr Nicholas Remigius,[16] criminal judge to his Grace the Duke of Lorraine. This astute man was, indeed, ideally placed to learn about the witches' goings-on, since he prepared the cases against them, and in his day 800 women mounted the pyre in Lorraine alone after they had been proved guilty of witchcraft. The proof normally consisted in binding them hand and foot and throwing them into the water. If they sank and were drowned, then they were innocent, but if they remained floating on the surface, they were seen to be guilty, and they were burnt. That was the logic of those days.

We may see it as a basic trait in the character of German demons that they are stripped of any idealization, and that they are a mixture of the vulgar and the horrible. The more crude familiarity they show in approaching us, the more hideous is their effect. There is nothing more uncanny than our poltergeists, goblins, and brownies. On this subject Praetorius[17] has a passage in his *Anthropodemus* which I will impart, quoting it from Dobeneck:

> Our ancestors could not believe other than that poltergeists were true human beings, resembling small children, with little coats or dresses of many colours. Certain writers add that some of them are said to have knives in their backs, while others are hideously deformed, depending on how, and by what instrument, they were formerly slain. For the superstitious consider them to be the souls of people formerly murdered in the house. And they report many tales: how, when the maids and cooks in the house have long been well served by the goblins, and have grown fond of them, some people take such a liking to them that they ardently long to behold these little servants, and beg for this favour; yet the poltergeists are always loth to agree, maintaining that people cannot behold them without being terrified. Yet, if the lustful maids persist in their desire, it is said that the goblins name a place in the house where they will display themselves in bodily form; but they say that a bucket of cold water must be brought also. Then it happens that such a goblin lies naked on a cushion on the floor, with a great butcher's knife sticking in his back; at which many maids are so frightened that they fall in a faint. Then the thing straightway leaps up, takes the water, and pours it over the wench, so that she may come to her senses. Whereupon the maids lose their desire, and never again wish to behold dear Chimgen. For though the goblins all bear particular names, they are said in general to be called Chim. They do all the housework for the servants and maids to whom they are devoted: they curry and feed the horses, clean out the stables, scrub the floor, keep the kitchen clean, and take good care of whatever else must be done in the house, and the cattle increase and thrive under their care. In return, the goblins must be looked after tenderly by the servants, who may not harm them in the slightest, either by laughing at them or by neglecting to feed them. For if a cook has taken the thing as her secret helper in the house, she must put a dish full of good food daily, at a certain time, in an agreed place in the house, and then go her ways; after this she may take her ease, and go early to bed at night, nevertheless she will find early next morning that her work has been done. But if she once forgets her duty, by neglecting the food, then she must do all her work by herself, and she suffers all manner of misfortunes: either she

> scalds herself in the hot water, breaks the pots and the crockery, spills her food or falls down, etc., so that she must unavoidably be severely scolded by her mistress or her master; at which it is said the goblin may often be heard laughing. And such a goblin is said always to remain in a house, even when the servants change. Indeed, a maid who takes her leave must advise her successor to take good care of the goblin, so that it may help her as well. If the new maid does not want the goblin's services, she has no lack of continual misfortune, and must leave the house again as soon as she can.

The following little narrative may be among the most horrible of these stories. A maid had an invisible spirit for many years; he sat at her hearth, where she had given him a place of his own, and where she conversed with him through the long winter evenings. One day the maid asked Heinzchen, as she called the spirit, to let her see him in his natural shape. But Heinzchen refused. Finally, however, he agreed, telling her to go down into the cellar, where she would see him. The maid took a candle, descended into the cellar, and there, in an open barrel, she saw a dead child weltering in its blood. Many years before, the maid had given birth to an illegitimate child, secretly murdered it, and hidden it in a barrel.

All the same, given the Germans' character, they often enjoy themselves most when terrified, and the popular legends about goblins are full of humorous features. Particularly amusing are the stories about Hüdeken, a goblin who played his tricks at Hildesheim in the twelfth century, and who is much talked of in our spinning-rooms and supernatural tales. An oft-reprinted passage from an old chronicle gives the following account of him:

> About the year 1132 an evil spirit appeared, for a long time, to many people in the bishopric of Hildesheim, in the shape of a farmer with a hat on his head: wherefore the farmers called him Hüdeken in the Saxon speech. This spirit took pleasure in people's company, revealing himself to them, sometimes visibly and sometimes invisibly, and asking and answering questions. He never offended anyone without cause. But if anyone laughed at him, or insulted him in other ways, he avenged the wrong he had suffered in full measure. When Count Burchard de Luka was slain by Count Hermann von Wiesenburg, and the latter's land was in danger of falling into the hands of the avengers, Hüdeken woke Bishop Bernhard of Hildesheim from his sleep and spoke to him in the following words: 'Get up, baldhead!

the county of Wiesenburg is abandoned and vacant because of murder, and will be easy for you to occupy.' The Bishop hastily assembled his warriors, invaded the territory of the guilty Count, and annexed it, with the Emperor's permission, to his own lands.

The spirit, without being asked, often warned the Bishop of approaching dangers, and showed himself especially often in the palace kitchen, where he talked to the cooks and performed all manner of services for them. Since people had gradually become familiar with Hüdeken, a kitchen-boy ventured to tease him whenever he appeared, and even poured dirty water over him. The spirit asked the head cook, or kitchener, to forbid the ill-mannered boy to do such mischief. The head cook answered: 'You are a spirit, and you are afraid of a young lad!' to which Hüdeken replied threateningly: 'As you will not punish the boy, I shall soon show you how little I am afraid of him.' Soon afterwards the boy who had offended the spirit was sitting all by himself, asleep in the kitchen. In this state he was seized by the spirit, who throttled him, tore him to pieces, and put the pieces in a pot on the fire. When the cook discovered this trick, he cursed the spirit, and on the following day Hüdeken spoiled all the roast meat on the spit by pouring over it the poison and blood of toads. This revenge made the cook curse him yet more, after which the spirit finally made him plunge into a deep trench by conjuring up the illusion of a bridge. At the same time he was assiduous in making the rounds of the city's walls and towers by night and compelling the watchmen to be constantly alert.

A man with an unfaithful wife once said jokingly to Hüdeken, as he was about to set out on a journey: 'Good friend, I put my wife in your charge; look after her carefully.' As soon as the man had gone, his adulterous wife invited one lover after another. But Hüdeken allowed none of them to come close to her, but threw them all out of bed and on to the floor. When the man returned from his journey, the spirit came some distance to meet him and said: 'I am very glad you have come back, so that I shall be free from the laborious service you imposed on me. I have, with unspeakable effort, prevented your wife from actually being unfaithful to you. But I beg you never again to entrust her to me. I would rather take care of all the pigs in Saxony than of a woman who tries to get into her lovers' arms by means of cunning tricks.'

For the sake of exactitude I must remark that Hüdeken's headgear differs from the goblins' usual costume. They are generally dressed in grey and wear red caps. At least, that is how people see them in Denmark, where they are said to be most numerous at the present day. I used to think that the reason goblins liked living in Denmark was that their favourite food was gruel made with redcurrant jelly. But a young Danish poet, Hans Andersen,[18] whom I had the pleasure of seeing here in Paris this summer, assures me categorically that *nissen*, as goblins are called in Denmark, are fondest of buttered porridge. Once these goblins have settled in a house, they are in no hurry to leave it. They never turn up unannounced, however, and when they want to live somewhere, they inform the master of the house in the following way: they carry all manner of wood-shavings into the house during the night, and strew cattle-dung in the milking-pails. If the master of the house does not throw away the wood-shavings, or if he and his family drink the polluted milk, then the goblins stay with him for ever. For many people this becomes extremely disagreeable. A poor man in Jutland became in the end so irritated by the company of such a goblin that he decided to abandon his house, and loaded his goods and chattels on to a cart and rode on it to the next village in order to settle there. When he happened to turn round during the journey, however, he caught sight of the goblin's red-capped head, peeping out of one of the empty tubs, and the goblin called out to him cheerfully: 'We're flitting!' (i.e. 'we're moving house').[19]

Perhaps I have dwelt too long on these little demons, and it is time for me to return to the big ones. But all these stories illustrate the beliefs and the character of the German people. In past centuries these beliefs were every bit as powerful as the faith taught by the Church. When the learned Doctor Remigius had finished his great book on witchcraft, he thought that he knew enough about the subject to be able to perform witchcraft himself; and, being a conscientious man, he did not fail to report himself to the courts as a wizard, and in consequence of this report he was burnt as a wizard.

These atrocities are not directly due to the Christian Church, but indirectly, owing to its malicious reversal of the indigenous Germanic religion by transforming the Germans' pantheistic world-view into a pandemonic one and turning the people's former objects of worship into hideous devilry. However, man is slow to abandon things that were dear to him and his ancestors, and his emotions secretly cling to such objects, even when they have been ruined and disfigured. Hence this reversed popular religion may survive in Germany longer than Christianity, which is not rooted in the national character. At the Reformation, the belief in Catholic legends vanished very rapidly, but not the belief in magic and witches.

Luther no longer believes in Catholic miracles, but he still believes in the Devil and his imps. His *Table-Talk* is full of curious tales about satanic arts, goblins, and witches. He himself, when in dire straits, believed that he was struggling with Old Nick in person. In the Wartburg, where he translated the New Testament, he was disturbed so much by the Devil that he threw an ink-well at his head. Ever since then the Devil has been afraid of ink, especially of printer's ink. The above-mentioned *Table-Talk* includes many humorous anecdotes about the Devil's cunning, and I cannot refrain from recounting one of them.

> Dr Martin Luther told how boon companions were once sitting together in a tavern. Among them was a wild, desperate fellow, who said: 'If any man will give me a good measure of wine, I will sell that man my soul in return.' Not long after, one came into the inn parlour, sat down beside him and drank with him, and said among other things to the man who had spoken so boldly: 'Hark ye, didst thou not say even now that if anyone would give thee a good measure of wine, thou wouldst sell him thy soul in return?' Then he said once more: 'Yea, I will do it, if today I may eat and drink my fill, and be merry.' The man, who was really the Devil, agreed, and soon afterwards he again slunk away. The reveller was merry the whole day, and when at last he was drunk, the same man as before, the Devil, returned, and sat down beside him, and asked the other drinkers: 'Masters, what think ye? When a man buys a horse, do not the saddle and bridle belong to him as well?' All the drinkers were alarmed at this. But at last the man said: 'Answer me straightway.' Then they confessed, saying: 'Yea, the saddle and bridle belong to him as well.' Then the Devil took that same wild, brutish fellow and bore him aloft through the ceiling, and no man could tell whither he had gone.

Although I have the greatest respect for our great master Martin Luther, I have a feeling that he entirely misunderstood Satan's character. Satan certainly holds no such low opinion of the body as is mentioned here. Whatever bad things may be said of the Devil, nobody could ever call him a Spiritualist.

More than the disposition of the Devil, however, Martin Luther misunderstood the disposition of the Pope and the Catholic Church. Being strictly impartial, I must defend them both, like the Devil, against Luther's excessive zeal. Indeed, if you appealed to my conscience, I would admit that the Pope, Leo X, was really much more reasonable than Luther, and that the latter did not grasp the basic principles of the Catholic Church. For Luther had not grasped that the idea of Christianity, the annihilation of sensuality, was too much in conflict with human nature ever to be realized in life; he had not grasped that Catholicism was a sort of concordat between God and the Devil, that is, between spirit and matter, whereby God's sole rule was proclaimed in theory, but matter was enabled in practice to exercise all the rights that had been declared void. Hence arose a crafty system of concessions made by the Church to sensuality, though always in forms that stigmatized every act of sensuality and maintained the spirit in its mocking usurpations. Thus, you could listen to the tender prompting of your heart and embrace a beautiful girl, but you had to confess that it was a shameful sin, and for the sin you had to do penance. Penance could be done with money, which was as beneficial for mankind as it was useful for the Church. The Church demanded wergild, so to speak, for all carnal pleasures, and a scale of charges was drawn up for all varieties of sin, and there were holy commercial travellers who went around in the name of the Roman Church hawking indulgences for every sin that was charged; one of these was Tetzel, against whom Luther first entered the lists. Our historians claim that this protest against the trade in indulgences was a trifling event, and that Luther, having originally denounced only one Church abuse, was driven by Rome's stubbornness to attack the entire authority of the Church at its supreme pinnacle. But this is a mistake: the trade in indulgences was not an abuse, but a logical consequence of the entire ecclesiastical system, and by attacking it, Luther was attacking the Church itself, which was obliged to condemn him as a heretic. Leo X, the refined Florentine, the pupil of Politian,[20] the friend of Raphael, the Greek philosopher with the triple crown, which the Conclave may have given him because he suffered from an ailment which by no means arises from Christian abstinence and was in those days still very dangerous . . . Leo de Medici could not help smiling at the poor, chaste, simple-minded monk who fancied that the Gospel was the charter of Christianity, and that this charter must be true! He may not have seen what Luther was after, since he was too preoccupied at the time with the building of St Peter's, which was to be paid for with money raised by selling indulgences, so that sin really did provide the money for building this church, which thus became, as it were, a monument to sensual pleasure, like the pyramid an Egyptian courtesan built with the money she had earned by prostitution. Although legend says Cologne Cathedral was built by the Devil, that could more easily be said of this house of God. The triumph of Spiritualism lay in compelling Sensualism to build its finest temple, and in gaining, in return for the mass of concessions made to the flesh, the means to glorify the spirit; but they did not understand this in the German North. For it was much easier here than it was under the glowing skies of Italy to practise a Christianity that made the fewest possible concessions to sensuality. We Northerners are cold-blooded, and we did not need so many certificates of indulgence for carnal sins as Leo sent us in his paternal anxiety. The climate helps us to practise Christian virtues, and on 31 October 1517, when Luther nailed his theses against indulgences to the door of the Augustinian Church in Wittenberg, the moat surrounding Wittenberg may already have been frozen over, so that people could skate on it, which is a very cold pleasure and hence not a sin.

I may already have used the words 'Spiritualism' and 'Sensualism' several times. Here, however, these words do not refer, as they do in French philosophy, to the two different sources of our knowledge. I use them rather, as is apparent from the drift of my account, as labels for two different ways of thinking. One of them seeks to glorify the spirit by striving to destroy matter, while the other tries to assert the natural rights of matter against the usurpations of the spirit.

I must draw your attention particularly to the beginnings of the Lutheran Reformation, described above, which already disclose its entire spirit, since here in France people retain the old misconceptions about the Reformation which were spread by Bossuet's *Histoire des variations*[21] and influence even writers of the present day. The French understood only the negative side of the Reformation, seeing in it simply a struggle against Catholicism, and often supposing that this struggle had always been waged beyond the Rhine for the same reasons as here in France. But the reasons there were quite different from here, and quite antithetical. The struggle against Catholicism in Germany was a war begun by Spiritualism when it perceived that its rule was only titular and *de jure*, while Sensualism, thanks to a long-established fiction, ruled in reality and *de facto*. The pedlars of indulgences were chased away, the priests' pretty concubines were exchanged for chilly wives, the charming images of the Madonna were broken to pieces, and here and there a Puritanism emerged which was bitterly hostile to the senses. The struggle against Catholicism in France in the seventeenth and eighteenth centuries, on the other hand, was a war begun by Sensualism when it perceived that, although it ruled *de facto*, every act of its rule was derided as illegitimate and insulted in the most painful manner by Spiritualism, which claimed to rule *de jure*. While in Germany the struggle was waged with chaste gravity, in France it was waged with lascivious jokes; and while the Germans conducted a theological disputation, the French composed some merry satire. Such satires usually took as their subject the contradiction in which man becomes ensnared when he tries to be nothing but spirit; and they produced the most delightful tales about pious men who succumb involuntarily to their animal nature, or, having done so, want to retain the appearance of sanctity and take refuge in hypocrisy. The Queen of Navarre[22] described such improper behaviour in her *nouvelles*: her usual theme is monks' relations with women, and she aims to shake not only our diaphragms but also our monasticism. The most malicious flower of this comic polemic is unquestionably Molière's *Tartuffe*; for this play is directed not only against the Jesuitism of its day, but against Christianity itself, indeed, against the idea of Christianity, against Spiritualism. Tartuffe's affected terror of Dorine's naked bosom, his words

> Le ciel défend, de vrai, certains contentements,
> Mais on trouve avec lui des accommodements –[23]

these poked fun, not only at ordinary hypocritical cant, but at the universal lie that necessarily arises from the impracticability of the Christian idea; they poked fun at the whole system of concessions that Spiritualism was obliged to make to Sensualism. Truly, Jansenism[24] had far more reason than Jesuitism to feel offended by the performance of *Tartuffe*, and Molière would doubtless cause as much discomfort to today's Methodists as he did to the devout Catholics of his day. That is why Molière is so great – because, like Aristophanes and Cervantes, he pokes fun not merely at temporal contingencies but at the everlastingly ridiculous, the primal foibles of mankind. Voltaire, who attacked only superficial and time-bound targets, is his inferior in this respect.

However, this kind of mockery, especially Voltaire's, has fulfilled its mission in France, and anyone who tried to continue it would be acting foolishly, and contrary to the spirit of the age. For, if the last visible remnants of Catholicism were annihilated, its idea might well take refuge in a new form, adopting, as it were, a new body, abandoning even the name of Christianity; and in this guise it might be a much sorer trial to us than it is in its present broken, ruined, and universally discredited shape. Indeed, it is no bad thing for Spiritualism to be represented by a religion which has already lost the best of its vigour and a priesthood which is directly and totally opposed to our age's enthusiasm for liberty.

But why do we find Spiritualism so repugnant? Is it such a bad thing? By no means. Attar of roses is something precious, and a bottle of it is refreshing if one is obliged to spend one's days mourning in the locked chambers of a harem. But that does not mean that we want all life's roses to be trodden and trampled to pieces to obtain a few drops of attar of roses, however consoling its effects may be. Rather, we are like the nightingales, which gladly enjoy the rose itself, and take as much delight in its blushing, blooming appearance as in its invisible scent.

I said earlier that among us it was really Spiritualism that attacked Catholicism. But this is true only of the beginning of the Reformation; as soon as Spiritualism had breached the ancient church walls, Sensualism plunged forward with all the ardour that had so long been held in check, and Germany became the scene of frantic orgies where the intoxication of freedom vied with the joys of the senses. The oppressed peasants found in the new doctrine spiritual weapons which enabled them to wage war against the aristocracy; the desire for such a war had existed for a good hundred and fifty years. At Münster, Sensualism ran naked through the streets in the shape of John of Leyden,[25] and lay with his twelve wives in the great bed that is still to be seen in the town-hall there. Everywhere the gates of the monasteries and convents were flung open, and monks and nuns rushed into each other's arms and began billing and cooing. Indeed, the external history of that age consists of virtually nothing but sensual insurrections; we shall see later how scanty the results were, how Spiritualism once more suppressed these disturbers of the peace, how it gradually established its rule in the North, but suffered a fatal wound at the hands of an enemy whom it had nourished in its bosom – philosophy. This is a very complicated story, difficult to disentangle. It is easy for the Catholic party to emphasize whatever evil motives it pleases, and to hear it talk, you would think that people wanted only to legitimize the most impudent sensuality and to plunder the possessions of the Church. Of course the interests of the spirit must always form an alliance with material interests if they are to be victorious. But the Devil had shuffled the cards in such a strange way that nothing can be stated with certainty about the players' intentions.

The august persons assembled in the Imperial Hall at Worms in 1521 probably had all manner of thoughts in their hearts that contradicted the words of their mouths. A young Emperor was seated there, wrapping himself in his new purple robe with youthful delight in his power, and secretly pleased that the proud Roman, who had maltreated so many imperial predecessors and had still not abandoned his overweening claims, had been so effectively taken to task. The Roman's representatives, for their part, were secretly glad that a division had occurred among the Germans, who, like drunken barbarians, had so often invaded and plundered beautiful Italy, and were still threatening to invade and plunder it anew. The secular princes were glad that along with the new doctrine they could also take the old Church property to their hearts. The high prelates were already wondering whether to marry their cooks and bequeath their electoral states, bishoprics and abbeys to their male progeny. The delegates of the towns were glad of a new extension of their independence. Each had something to gain and was secretly thinking about earthly profit.

But there was one man present who, I am convinced, was not thinking about himself, but about the divine interests that he was to represent. That man was Martin Luther, the poor monk chosen by Providence to break the worldly power of Rome, against which the strongest emperors and the boldest sages had struggled in vain. But Providence knows very well on whose shoulders to place its burdens; here not only spiritual but also physical strength was required. A body steeled by monastic severity and chastity ever since its youth was needed to endure the hardships of such an office. At that time our dear Master was still lean and looked very pale, so that the well-fed, rubicund gentlemen of the Imperial Diet looked down almost compassionately at the wretched man in his black habit. But he was in perfect health, and his nerves were so firm that the brilliant tumult did not intimidate him in the slightest, and his lungs, in particular, must have been strong. For after he had uttered his long defence, he had to repeat it all in Latin, because the Emperor did not understand German. It annoys me whenever I think of it; for our dear Master was standing by an open window, exposed to a draught, while the sweat was dripping from his brow. The long speech no doubt tired him, and his mouth no doubt became rather dry. The Duke of Brunswick must have thought: 'He is surely very thirsty'; at least we read that he sent three jugs of the best Eimbeck beer to Martin Luther in his lodgings. I shall always remember the house of Brunswick for this noble deed.

People in France have very mistaken ideas, not only about the Reformation, but about its heroes. The most obvious reason for their incomprehension is no doubt that Luther is not just the greatest, but also the most German man in our history; that in his character all the Germans' virtues and faults are magnificently united; that he represents in his own person the wonderful German character. Besides, he had qualities that we seldom find united and usually encounter as hostile antitheses. He was at once a dreamy mystic and a practical man of action. His thoughts had not merely wings, but also hands; he spoke and acted. He was not merely the tongue of his age, but also its sword. Moreover, he was at once a cold, scholastic quibbler and an inspired, God-intoxicated prophet. After spending the day tiring himself out with his dogmatic distinctions, in the evening he would reach for his flute, contemplate the stars, and melt in melody and devotion. The same man who could curse like a fishwife could be as mild as a tender maiden. Sometimes he was as furious as the gale that uproots the oak, and again he could be as gentle as the zephyr that caresses the violet. He was filled with awe-struck fear of God, ready to sacrifice himself to the Holy Ghost, capable of absorption in pure spirituality; and yet he was familiar with the splendours of the earth, and appreciated them, and it was from his lips that the famous slogan came: 'Who loves not women, wine, and song, / Remains a fool his whole life long.' He was a complete man, one might even say an absolute man, in whom spirit and matter were not separate. To call him a Spiritualist would be as mistaken as to call him a Sensualist. What am I to say? There was something primeval, incomprehensible, miraculous about him, such as we find in all men chosen by Providence. He was naive and terrifying, clumsy and astute, sublime and provincial, invincible and demonic.

Luther's father was a miner at Mansfeld, and the boy was often with him in the subterranean workshop, where the mighty metals grow and the strong wellsprings trickle, and it may be that his young heart unwittingly absorbed the secret powers of nature, or was rendered immune by the mountain spirits. This may also explain why so much earthy matter, so much of the dross of passion still clung to him, as his critics have often enough remarked. But they are wrong: without this admixture of earthiness he could not have been a man of action. Pure spirits cannot act. We learn, after all, from Jung-Stilling's treatise on ghosts[26] that spirits can make themselves visible with ample colour and distinctness, that they can walk, run, and dance like living people and make every kind of gesture, but that they cannot move any material object, not even the smallest bedside table, from its place.

Glory to Luther! Everlasting glory to the beloved man, to whom we owe the preservation of our noblest possessions, and whose great deeds still sustain us! It is not for us to complain about the limitations of his outlook. The dwarf standing on the giant's shoulders can of course see further than the giant, especially if he wears spectacles; but his lofty view is not matched by lofty feelings, by the giant heart, which we cannot acquire for ourselves. Still less does it befit us to pass a harsh judgement on Luther's faults; these faults have benefited us more than the virtues of a thousand other people. Erasmus's[27] refinement and Melanchthon's mildness would never have achieved as much as Brother Martin's divine brutality. Indeed, the initial error that I indicated above bore the most precious fruit, fruit that has refreshed the whole of mankind. The Imperial Diet at which Luther rejects the Pope's authority and declares publicly that 'his teaching can only be refuted by statements from the Bible itself or by rational arguments!' marks the beginning of a new age in Germany. The chain by which St Boniface[28] fettered the German Church to Rome is sliced asunder. This Church, previously an integral part of the great hierarchy, collapses into religious democracies. The religion itself changes; its Indian, Gnostic element disappears, and we see its Judaic and deistic element reasserting itself. Lutheran or Evangelical Christianity comes into being. By not just acknowledging but also legitimizing the most necessary claims of matter, religion again becomes truth. The priest becomes a human being, and takes a wife and fathers children, as God demands. God himself, on the other hand, again becomes a heavenly bachelor without a family; his son's legitimacy is disputed; the saints are forced to abdicate; the angels have their wings clipped; the Mother of God loses all her claims to the heavenly crown and is forbidden to perform miracles. Miracles in general cease henceforth, especially as the natural sciences are making such great strides. Perhaps God dislikes physicists looking suspiciously over his shoulder, or perhaps he is reluctant to compete with Bosco:[29] in recent times, when religion has been so gravely threatened, God has not deigned to support it by any spectacular miracle. It may be that henceforth, when introducing new religions on this earth, he will no longer go in for holy conjuring tricks, but will demonstrate the truth of the new doctrines by reason: which would be the most reasonable way to proceed. At any rate, the newest religion, Saint-Simonianism, has produced no miracles whatever, unless you count the fact that an old tailor's account which Saint-Simon left unpaid on earth was paid in cash by his disciples ten years after his death. I can still see the excellent Père Olinde,[30] filled with inspiration, rising to his feet in the Salle Taitbout and holding up the account and its receipt to the astonished congregation. Young grocers were incredulous at such supernatural testimony, but the tailors began to believe!

However, even if Protestantism deprived us in Germany of much poetry along with the old miracles, we gained a great deal in return. People became nobler and more virtuous. Protestantism had the most beneficial influence on the purity of manners and that rigour in the fulfilment of one's duties which we normally call morality; indeed, in many communities Protestantism took a course that finally converges with such morality, retaining the Gospel only as a beautiful parable. In particular, we now see a pleasing change in the life of the clergy. When celibacy vanished, so did pious perversions and monastic vices. Among the Protestant clergy we often find the most virtuous people, whom even an ancient Stoic would have respected. You have to be a poor student travelling on foot through North Germany to learn how much virtue – and, to give virtue an attractive adjective, evangelical virtue – may sometimes be found in the unassuming home of such a clergyman. How often I was hospitably received there on winter evenings – I, a stranger, with nothing to recommend me save that I was hungry and tired. After I had eaten well and slept well, and was about to continue my journey the next morning, the old pastor would come in his dressing-gown and give me a blessing on the way, which never brought me misfortune; and his good-natured, garrulous wife would put some bread and butter in my pocket, which refreshed me no less; and the pastor's beautiful daughters would stand silently at a distance, with their blushing cheeks and modest, violet-like eyes, whose shy fire would warm my heart, even in recollection, for a whole winter's day.

By stating the principle that his teaching could be refuted only by the Bible itself or by rational arguments, Luther granted human reason the right to interpret the Bible, and acknowledged reason as the supreme judge in all religious controversies. Thus arose in Germany what is variously called intellectual freedom or freedom of thought. Thought was recognized as a right, and the authority of reason became legitimate. For some centuries, of course, people had been able to think and speak with some degree of freedom, and the schoolmen disputed about things which to us seem scarcely possible even to utter in the Middle Ages. But this was accomplished by means of the distinction drawn between theological and philosophical truth, a distinction by which people expressly secured themselves against the charge of heresy; and it only happened in university lecture-rooms, and in a Latin of Gothic abstruseness which the people could not understand, so that little harm was to be apprehended for the Church. None the less, the Church never really permitted such conduct, and now and again it actually burnt a poor schoolman. After Luther, however, no distinction was any longer drawn between theological and philosophical truth, and disputations were held in the market-place, in the German vernacular, without fear or unease. The princes who accepted the Reformation legitimized this freedom of thought, and one of its most important products, important for the whole world, is German philosophy.

Indeed, not even in Greece was the human spirit able to express itself so freely as in Germany from the middle of the last century until the French invasion. In Prussia, especially, there was limitless freedom of thought. The Marquis of Brandenburg[31] had realized that as he could only be a legitimate King of Prussia by the Protestant principle, he must also preserve Protestant freedom of thought. Since then, of course, things have changed, and the natural guardian of our Protestant freedom of thought has joined forces with the Ultramontane party in order to suppress it, and for this he frequently employs the weapon that the Papacy first devised and used against us: censorship.

Strange! We Germans are the strongest and most intelligent nation. Our princely dynasties sit on all Europe's thrones, our Rothschilds control all the world's stock-markets, our scholars rule in all the sciences, we invented gunpowder and printing; and yet anyone among us who fires a pistol pays a fine of three dollars, and if we want the *Hamburg Correspondent* to print the news that 'my dear wife has been brought to bed of a baby daughter, as lovely as liberty!', then Dr Hoffmann[32] will reach for his red pencil and strike out 'liberty'.

Can this go on much longer? I do not know. But I know that the problem of press freedom, which is now being so vigorously discussed in Germany, is significantly linked to the above considerations, and I do not think it is difficult to solve if you bear in mind that the freedom of the press is simply the logical consequence of freedom of thought, and hence a Protestant right. For such rights the German has already shed his best blood, and he might well be induced to enter the lists once more.

The same argument can be applied to the problem of academic freedom, which now stirs up such passion in German hearts. Ever since the supposed discovery was made that political activity, that is, the love of liberty, is most vigorous in the universities, sovereigns have been assailed from all sides with hints that these institutions should be suppressed, or at least transformed into ordinary training centres. Plans are now being devised and the pros and cons discussed. However, neither the public opponents of the universities, nor their public defenders whom we have heard so far, seem to understand the ultimate principles behind the problem. Their opponents do not grasp that young people everywhere, in all disciplines, will be enthusiastic for the interests of freedom, and that if the universities are suppressed, these enthusiastic young people will speak their mind elsewhere, and may join forces with young businessmen and craftsmen to do so in a more forcible fashion. Their defenders seek to prove that the flower of German erudition would perish along with the universities, that academic freedom is beneficial to study, that it gives young people such a good opportunity to cultivate their minds in diverse ways, and so on. As if a few Greek words or a few loutish pranks were what mattered! And what would the princes care about learning, study, or education, if the sacred security of their crowns were threatened! They are heroic enough to sacrifice all these relative goods for the one absolute good – their absolute rule. For this has been entrusted to them by God, and when heaven commands, all earthly considerations must yield.

These matters are misunderstood both by the poor professors who represent the universities and by the government officials who oppose them. It is only the Catholic propaganda in Germany that understands the universities' importance. These pious obscurantists are the most dangerous opponents of our university system; they use lies and deceit in order secretly to undermine and destroy it; and if one of them assumes a winning air and appears to take the universities' side, that reveals the Jesuitical intrigue. These cowardly hypocrites know full well what they stand to gain. For if the universities fail, so will the Protestant Church, which has been rooted in the universities ever since the Reformation, so that the entire history of the Protestant Church over the last few centuries consists in virtually nothing but theological controversies among academics from Wittenberg, Leipzig, Tübingen and Halle. The consistories are only a pale reflection of the theological faculties; if the latter vanished, the consistories would lose their basis and their character, and would sink into dreary dependence on the ministries, or even on the police.

But let us not give too much space to such melancholy reflections, especially as we have more to say about the providential man who did such great things for the German people. I have indicated above how, thanks to him, we attained the highest degree of freedom of thought. But Martin Luther gave us not only freedom of movement, but also the means of movement: he gave the spirit a body. He provided thought with the word. He created the German language.

This he did by translating the Bible.

In fact, the divine author of this book seems to have known as well as the rest of us that it is not a matter of indifference by whom one is translated, and he chose his translator himself, and endowed him with the wondrous power of translating from a dead language, which was, so to speak, already buried, into another which was not yet alive.

It is true that people had the Vulgate, which they understood, as well as the Septuagint,[33] which they were capable of understanding. But the knowledge of Hebrew had vanished from the Christian world. Only the Jews, who kept themselves hidden here and there in odd corners of this world, still maintained the traditions of the language. Like a ghost guarding a treasure that was entrusted to him during his life, this murdered nation, this ghost-nation, sat in its dark ghettos and preserved the Hebrew Bible; and German scholars could be seen secretly descending into these disreputable dens in order to uncover the treasure, to acquire knowledge of the Hebrew language. When the Catholic clergy noticed that they were being threatened from this quarter, and that this by-way might lead the people to the true Word of God and reveal the Roman forgeries, then they would have liked to suppress the Jewish tradition, and they set about destroying all Hebrew books, and on the Rhine there began the persecution of books against which our excellent Dr Reuchlin[34] fought so gloriously. The Cologne theologians who were then active, especially Hoogstraeten, were not of such limited intellect as Reuchlin's brave comrade-in-arms, the knight Ulrich von Hutten, represents them in his *Litterae obscurorum virorum*. They wanted to suppress the Hebrew language. When Reuchlin had won, Luther could begin his work. In a letter he wrote to Reuchlin at that time, he seems already conscious of the importance of the victory that the latter had gained, and had gained while in a difficult and subordinate position, whereas Luther, as an Augustinian monk, was wholly independent. He says naively in this letter: 'Ego nihil timeo, quia nihil habeo' ('I fear nothing, because I have nothing').

To this day, however, I cannot understand how Luther acquired the language into which he translated his Bible. The old Swabian dialect had completely vanished, along with the chivalric poetry of the age of the Hohenstaufen emperors. The old Saxon dialect, known as Plattdeutsch, was dominant only in part of northern Germany, and despite all the attempts that have been made, it has never proved suitable for literary purposes. If Luther used the language spoken in present-day Saxony for his Bible translation, then Adelung would be right in maintaining that the Saxon dialect, particularly that of Meissen, was our true High German, that is, our written language. But this view has long since been refuted, and I must mention it here with all the more severity, since such an error is still current in France. Modern Saxon was never a dialect of the German people, any more than, say, Silesian; for both owe their existence to a Slavonic tinge. I therefore frankly confess that I do not know the origin of the language we find in Luther's Bible. But I do know that thanks to this Bible, of which thousands of copies were tossed among the people by the new-born press, the black art of printing, it took only a few years for Luther's language to be diffused throughout Germany and elevated to the language universally used in writing. This written language is still dominant in Germany, and gives literary unity to a country fragmented by politics and religion. Such a priceless service may compensate for the fact that in its present form this language lacks that warmth of feeling that we tend to find in languages that have been formed from a single dialect. The language in Luther's Bible is by no means lacking in such warmth, and this old book is an everlasting well of rejuvenation for our language. All the idioms and turns of phrase in Luther's Bible are German, the writer can still use them; and since this book is in the hands of the poorest people, they need no special learned instruction in order to express themselves in literary German. When the political revolution breaks out among us, this fact will have remarkable consequences. Freedom everywhere will be able to speak, and its language will be biblical.

Luther's own writings have likewise helped to fix the German language. Thanks to their polemical passion, they entered deep into the heart of the age. Their tone is not always decent. But religious revolutions are not made with orange-blossom, either. A rough word sometimes deserves a rough answer. Luther's awe in the presence of the spirit of God ensures that in the Bible his language always maintains a certain dignity. In his polemical writings, however, he yields to a plebeian crudity which is often repulsive as well as grandiose. His idioms and images resemble those gigantic stone figures that we find in Indian or Egyptian temples, and whose garish colouring and grotesque ugliness repel and attract us simultaneously. Thanks to the baroque violence of his style, the bold monk sometimes appears like a religious Danton, a preacher on the Mountain,[35] who from its summit hurls blocks of motley words down on to his adversaries' heads.

More curious and more significant than these prose writings are Luther's poems, the hymns which sprang from his heart in trouble and conflict. Sometimes they resemble a flower growing on a rock, sometimes a moonbeam trembling across a surging sea. Luther loved music, he even wrote a treatise about it, and therefore his hymns are extraordinarily melodious. In this respect, too, he was fittingly called the Swan of Eisleben. But he was anything but a gentle swan in many songs, in which he fires the courage of his followers and becomes inspired with the furious joy of combat. The defiant song with which he and his companions entered Worms was a battle hymn: 'A sure stronghold our God is still, / A trusty shield and weapon . . .'[36] The old cathedral trembled at these new sounds, and the ravens took fright in their obscure nests in the towers. That hymn, the Marseillaise of the Reformation, retains its inspiring power in our own times, and perhaps we shall soon need the fierce old words for similar struggles.

I have shown how we owe to our beloved Dr Martin Luther the intellectual freedom which modern literature required for its development. I have shown how he also created the word, the language, in which this literature could express itself. I have now only to add that he himself initiated this literature; that it begins with Luther, *belles-lettres* in particular; that his hymns are the first important examples of it, and already disclose its distinctive character. Anyone who wants to talk about modern German literature must therefore begin with Luther, not with a Nuremberg philistine by the name of Hans Sachs,[37] as some Romantic *littérateurs* have done in their dishonest efforts. Hans Sachs, that troubadour of the honourable cobbling trade, whose *Meistergesang* is only a childish parody of medieval love-lyrics and whose dramas are only a cloddish travesty of the old mystery-plays, that pedantic buffoon, may be seen as the last poet of old times, but certainly not as the first poet of modern times. I need supply no further proof of this than a clear account of the contrast between our modern literature and older literature.

If we examine the German literature that flourished before Luther, we find:

1. Its material, its subject-matter, like medieval life itself, is a mixture of two heterogeneous elements, which in the course of a long duel embraced each other so firmly that they finally became combined: the Germanic national spirit and the Indian, Gnostic Christianity which called itself Catholic.

2. The treatment, or rather the spirit of the treatment, in this older literature, is Romantic. This word is also applied, incorrectly, to the subject-matter of this literature and to all the medieval phenomena arising from the combination of the two above-mentioned elements, the Germanic national spirit and Catholic Christianity. For, just as some medieval poets treated Greek history and mythology in a wholly Romantic manner, so one can also represent medieval manners and legends in Classical form. The expressions 'Romantic' and 'Classical' therefore refer only to the spirit of the treatment. The treatment is Classical when the form of that which is represented is identical with the idea of that which is to be represented, as is the case in Greek art, where, because of this identity, the greatest harmony is also to be found between the form and the idea. The treatment is Romantic when the form does not reveal the idea through their identity, but suggests the idea parabolically. I am here using the word 'parabolic' in preference to the word 'symbolic'. Greek mythology had a series of divine figures, each of whom, despite the identity of form and idea, could acquire a symbolic meaning. But in Greek religion only the outward shape of the gods was fixed; all other aspects, their lives and activities, were left to be treated according to the poet's whim. In the Christian religion, however, there are no fixed external shapes, but definite facts, sacred events, and deeds, in which man's poetic heart could place a parabolic significance. It is said that Homer invented the Greek gods; that is not true, they already existed in definite outlines, but he invented their stories. Medieval artists, on the other hand, never dared to invent the slightest detail in the historical part of their religion; the Fall, the Incarnation, the baptism and crucifixion of Christ, and so forth, were inviolable facts, which could not be modified, but in which man's poetic heart could place a parabolic significance. In the Middle Ages all the arts were treated in this parabolic spirit, and this treatment is Romantic. Hence the mystical generality which distinguishes the poetry of the Middle Ages: the figures are so shadowy, what they do is so indefinite, everything is obscure, as though lit by the changing light of the moon; the idea is only hinted at in the form, like an enigma, and we see here a vague form, such as was appropriate for a Spiritualist literature. There is no luminous, sunny harmony between form and idea, as there was among the Greeks; instead, the idea sometimes surpasses the given form, and the latter strives desperately to attain the

idea, and we then see bizarre and extravagant sublimity; sometimes the form massively outgrows the idea, a ridiculous puny thought drags itself along in a colossal form, and we see grotesque farce; in almost every instance we see deformity.

3. The general character of this literature was that all its products manifested the firm, secure faith which then prevailed in all worldly as well as spiritual matters. All views held in that age were based on authorities; the poet walked as sure-footedly as a mule along the precipices of doubt, and his works were dominated by a bold calm, a blissful assurance, that later became impossible once the chief of all those authorities, namely the authority of the Pope, was broken and all the others came tumbling after. Hence the poems of the Middle Ages all have the same character: it is as though they had been composed not by individuals but by the entire people; they are objective, epic and naive.

In the literature that springs up along with Luther, on the other hand, we find precisely the opposite:

1. Its material, the subject-matter that is to be treated, is the conflict of Reforming interests and opinions with the old order of things. The spirit of the new age has no sympathy for the mixed faith arising from the two above-mentioned elements, the German national spirit and Indian, Gnostic Christianity; the latter seems like pagan idolatry which must be replaced by the true religion of the Judaic and deistic Gospel. A new order of things takes shape; the mind makes discoveries which promote the well-being of matter; thanks to thriving industry and to philosophy, Spiritualism is discredited in public opinion; the third estate arises; revolution is already seething in people's hearts and heads; and what the age feels and thinks and needs and wants is put into words, and that is the subject-matter of modern literature.

2. The spirit of the treatment is no longer Romantic but Classical. The revival of ancient literature caused a joyous enthusiasm for Greek and Roman writers to spread throughout Europe, and the scholars, the only people who wrote in those days, sought to acquire the spirit of classical antiquity, or at least to imitate the classical genres in their writings. If they could not attain a harmony of form and idea, like the Greeks, they adhered all the more strictly to the external features of Greek treatment: they distinguished the genres according to Greek precepts, abstained from all Romantic extravagance, and in this respect we call them Classical.

3. The general character of modern literature consists in the predominance of individuality and scepticism. The authorities are overthrown; reason alone is now man's sole lamp, and his conscience is his sole staff in the dark labyrinths of this life. Man now stands alone facing his Creator, and sings his song to him. Hence this literature begins with hymns. But even later, when it becomes secular, it is dominated by the most intimate awareness of the self, the feeling of personality. Poetry is now no longer objective, epic, and naive, but subjective, lyrical, and reflective.

BOOK TWO

IN the previous Book we dealt with the great religious revolution that was represented in Germany by Martin Luther. We have now to speak of the philosophical revolution which emerged from it and which is, indeed, no more than the ultimate logical consequence of Protestantism.

Before we recount how this revolution broke out thanks to Immanuel Kant, however, it is necessary to mention philosophical events outside Germany, the importance of Spinoza, the fortunes of Leibniz's philosophy, the interrelations of this philosophy with religion, the friction and eventual rupture between the two, and so forth. We shall, however, always keep our eye on those philosophical questions to which we can attribute a social significance, and in which philosophy competes with religion to find a solution.

One such question is that concerning the nature of God. 'God is the beginning and end of all wisdom!' say the faithful in their humility, and the philosopher, in all the pride of his knowledge, must concur with this pious utterance.

It is not Bacon,[1] as is commonly taught, but René Descartes who is the father of modern philosophy, and we shall show clearly to what extent German philosophy is descended from him.

René Descartes is a Frenchman, and here, too, the great land of France deserves credit for initiative. But the great land of France, the noisy, agitated, garrulous country of the French, has never been suitable soil for philosophy; it may be that philosophy will never thrive there; and René Descartes realized this, and went to Holland, the quiet, taciturn land of canal-barges and Dutchmen, and there he wrote his philosophical works. Only there could he free his mind from traditional formalism and construct an entire philosophy from pure ideas that were derived neither from faith nor from empirical observation, as has since been expected of any true philosophy. Only there could he immerse himself so deeply in the abysses of thought that he caught it in the very beginnings of self-consciousness, and was able through thought to establish self-consciousness in the world-famous sentence 'Cogito ergo sum' – 'I think, therefore I am.'

But it was perhaps only in Holland that Descartes could venture to teach a philosophy that came into open conflict with all the traditions of the past. He deserves the honour of having founded the autonomy of philosophy; philosophy no longer had to beg theology for permission to think, and could now take its stand alongside it as an independent science. I do not say 'oppose it', for at that time everyone accepted the principle that the truths attained by philosophy are ultimately the same as those handed down by religion. The schoolmen, on the other hand, as I mentioned earlier, had not only conceded religion the supremacy over philosophy, but also declared the latter to be a trifling game, a mere idle quibbling, as soon as it contradicted religious dogma. The schoolmen were concerned only to express their thoughts under no matter what conditions. They said, 'One times one is one,' and proved it; but they added with a smile, 'That is another error made by human reason, which always errs when it contradicts the decisions of Ecumenical Councils; one times one is three, and that is the true truth, long since revealed to us, in the name of the Father, the Son, and the Holy Spirit!' The schoolmen secretly formed a philosophical opposition against the Church. But in public they affected the utmost subservience; in many instances they even fought for the Church, and in processions they paraded in its train, rather like deputies of the French opposition during the solemnities of the Restoration. The schoolmen's comedy lasted more than six centuries, and became more and more trivial. By destroying scholasticism, Descartes also destroyed the outworn opposition of the Middle Ages. The old brooms had been blunted by long sweeping, there was too much rubbish sticking to them, and the new age called for new brooms. After every revolution the previous opposition must abdicate; otherwise great absurdities occur. We have seen this happen. It was not so much the Catholic Church but rather its old opponents, the rearguard of the schoolmen, that first attacked the Cartesian philosophy. Not until 1663 was it prohibited by the Pope.

I can assume that French readers have a sufficient and complacent acquaintance with the philosophy of their great compatriot, and I need not demonstrate here how the most antithetical doctrines could find in it the material they required. I am speaking of idealism and materialism.

Since these two doctrines, especially in France, are known as Spiritualism and Sensualism, and since I am using these two terms in different senses, I must forestall confusion by discussing the above expressions in more detail.

Ever since the earliest times there have been two contrary views about the nature of human thought, that is, about the ultimate grounds of intellectual cognition, about the origin of ideas. Some say that we obtain our ideas only from outside, and that our minds are only empty containers in which the perceptions swallowed by the senses undergo transmutation, rather as the food we have eaten does in our stomachs. To use a better image, these people regard the mind as a *tabula rasa* or clean slate on which experience later writes something new every day, according to fixed rules.

The others, those who take the contrary view, say that ideas are innate in people, that the human mind is the ideas' original residence, and that the external world, experience, and the mediation of the senses only enable us to realize what was already in our minds; they only arouse the ideas that are sleeping there.

The first of these views has been called sensualism, or sometimes empiricism; the other has been called spiritualism, or sometimes rationalism. This, however, can easily give rise to misunderstandings, since for some time, as I mentioned in the previous Book, we have used these names to refer to the two social systems that make themselves apparent in all life's manifestations. We shall therefore apply the term Spiritualism only to that iniquitous presumption of the spirit which, seeking to glorify itself alone, tries to crush matter, or at least to defame it; and we shall apply the term Sensualism to the energetic opposition which aims to rehabilitate matter and vindicate the rights of the senses, without denying the rights, indeed the supremacy, of the spirit. As for philosophical opinions about the nature of knowledge, I shall call them idealism and materialism; and by the former term I mean the doctrine of innate ideas, of ideas *a priori*, and by the latter term I mean the doctrine that the mind acquires its knowledge through experience and the senses, the doctrine of ideas *a posteriori*.

It is highly significant that the idealistic side of the Cartesian philosophy was never successful in France. Some famous Jansenists followed this line for a while, but they were soon absorbed into Christian Spiritualism. Perhaps this is what discredited idealism in

France. Nations have an instinctive sense of what they need to fulfil their missions. The French were already heading for the political revolution that broke out at the end of the eighteenth century, and for it they needed an axe and a materialistic philosophy that was equally cold and sharp. Christian Spiritualism was among the combatants in the ranks of their enemies, and so Sensualism became their natural ally. As the French Sensualists were usually materialists, the mistaken view arose that Sensualism proceeded only from materialism. Not at all: the latter can just as easily assert itself as a result of pantheism, and then its appearance is beautiful and magnificent. However, we do not wish to deny the achievements of French materialism. French materialism was a good antidote against the evils of the past, a desperate remedy for a desperate disease, mercury for an infected nation. The French philosophers chose John Locke as their master. He was the saviour they needed. His *Essay on Human Understanding* was their gospel, on which they swore. John Locke had taken Descartes as his master and had learnt from him all that an Englishman can learn: mechanics, analysis, deduction, construction, calculation. The only thing he could not grasp was the innate ideas. He therefore perfected the doctrine that we acquire our knowledge from outside, from experience. He made the human mind into a kind of counting-frame; the whole man became an English machine. This applies also to man as constructed by Locke's pupils, although they tried to distinguish themselves from one another by various labels. They are all afraid of the ultimate conclusions to be drawn from their supreme principle, and the disciple of Condillac[2] is alarmed to be classed together with a Helvétius, let alone with a Holbach, or, horror of horrors, with a La Mettrie. Yet this is unavoidable, and therefore I can describe the French philosophers of the eighteenth century and their present-day successors, one and all, as materialists. *L'homme-machine* is the most logical book in French philosophy, and its very title epitomises their entire outlook.

These materialists were for the most part also adherents of deism, for a machine presupposes a mechanic, and its highest perfection includes recognizing and appreciating the technical expertise displayed by such an artist both in its own construction and in his other works.

Materialism in France has fulfilled its mission. It may now be accomplishing the same work in England, where Locke provides the basis for the revolutionary parties, especially the Benthamites,[3] the preachers of utility. These mighty spirits have grasped the right lever with which to set John Bull in motion. John Bull is a born materialist, and his Christian Spiritualism is for the most part traditional hypocrisy or mere material slow-wittedness – his flesh resigns itself because his mind does not come to its aid. Things are different in Germany, and the German revolutionaries are mistaken in fancying that a materialist philosophy would assist their purposes.

From time immemorial Germany has manifested a distaste for materialism. It therefore became, for a century and a half, the true arena of idealism. The Germans too went to Descartes's school, and his greatest pupil was called Gottfried Wilhelm Leibniz. Just as Locke pursued the master's materialist line, so Leibniz followed his idealist line. Here we find the doctrine of innate ideas in its most definite form. He attacked Locke in his *Nouveaux essais sur l'entendement humain*. With Leibniz, a great enthusiasm for philosophical study began to flourish among the Germans. He aroused people's minds and guided them into new paths. Thanks to the indwelling mildness and the religious sensibility that animated his writings, even refractory minds were reconciled to their boldness, and their effect was immense. This thinker's boldness is shown especially in his doctrine of monads, one of the most curious hypotheses ever to have proceeded from a philosopher's head. It is at the same time the best of his achievements; for it contains a dim perception of the most important laws discovered by our present-day philosophy. The doctrine of monads may have been only a clumsy attempt to formulate the laws which have now been expressed in better formulae by the philosophers of nature. I ought really to say 'formula' instead of 'law'; for Newton rightly remarks that what we call laws of nature do not really exist, and are only formulae which assist our intellectual powers to explain a series of natural phenomena. Of all Leibniz's writings, the one most discussed in Germany has been his *Theodicy*. However, it is his weakest work. Along with some other writings that express Leibniz's religious spirit, this book caused him to be maliciously slandered and cruelly misunderstood. His enemies charged him with complacent feeble-mindedness; his friends, in defending him, represented him as a sly hypocrite. Leibniz's character was for a long time a subject of controversy among us. The fairest judges could not acquit him of the charge of ambiguity. He was reviled most of all by free-thinkers and proponents of the Enlightenment. How could they forgive a philosopher for defending the Trinity, eternal punishment in hell, and even the divinity of Christ! Their tolerance did not extend that far. But Leibniz was neither a fool nor a rogue, and from his harmonious eminence he could easily defend the whole of Christianity. I say 'the whole of Christianity', because he was defending it against partial Christianity. He pointed out the logical conclusions of the orthodox in contrast to the half-heartedness of their opponents, and never sought to do more than that. And then he stood at the point of indifference from which the most diverse systems can be seen as only diverse facets of the same truth. This point of indifference has since been recognized by Herr Schelling, and Hegel has given it a scientific basis as a system of systems. Similarly, Leibniz was occupied in harmonizing Plato with Aristotle. More recently, too, this problem has often been tackled among us. Has it been solved?

No, most certainly not! For this problem consists precisely in settling the conflict between idealism and materialism. Plato is an ingrained idealist, concerned only with innate ideas, or rather, with ideas born along with man: man brings ideas into the world, and when he becomes conscious of them, they seem like memories of an earlier existence. This accounts also for Plato's vague, mystical quality: his memories may be more or less clear. In Aristotle, on the other hand, everything is clear, everything is distinct, everything is certain; for his insights have no reference to an earlier existence, but are all drawn from experience, and can be classified in the most definite manner. He is therefore still a model for all empiricists, and the latter cannot praise God enough for making him the teacher of Alexander, because the latter's conquests provided so many opportunities for advancing science, and because Aristotle's victorious pupil gave him so many thousand talents for zoological purposes. The old schoolmaster spent this money prudently, and it enabled him to dissect plenty of mammals and stuff plenty of birds, making important observations in the process; unfortunately, however, he overlooked and failed to study the great beast in front of his nose, whom he had himself educated, and who was far more curious than all the rest of the world's menagerie. In fact, he left us completely uninformed about the nature of the youthful king whose astounding life and deeds still appear wondrous and enigmatic. Who was Alexander? What did he want? Was he a madman or a god? We still do not know. However, Aristotle is a sure guide to Babylonian monkeys, Indian parrots, and Greek tragedies, which he likewise dissected.

Plato and Aristotle! These not only represent two systems, but also typify two different human dispositions which from time immemorial, in a variety of guises, have confronted each other with more or less hostility. In particular, such a conflict went on throughout the Middle Ages and has continued to the present day; it forms the essential content of the history of the Christian Church. Plato and Aristotle are at issue, albeit under different names. Enthusiastic, mystical, Platonic dispositions reveal Christian ideas, together with the appropriate symbols, from the abysses of their hearts. Practical, orderly, Aristotelian dispositions build these ideas and symbols into a definite system, a dogmatics and a cult. The Church comprehends both dispositions: the former are mostly entrenched among the clergy and the latter in monastic orders, but both are perpetually at loggerheads. The same conflict is apparent in the Protestant Church as the division between Pietists and the orthodox, corresponding after a fashion to Catholic mystics and dogmatists. The Protestant Pietists are unimaginative mystics, and the orthodox Protestants are mindless dogmatists.

In Leibniz's day we find these two Protestant parties engaged in a furious conflict, and Leibniz's philosophy was later to intervene, once Christian Wolff had laid hold of it, adapted it to the needs of his age, and, most importantly, presented it in the German language. However, before we describe this pupil of Leibniz, the effects of his activity, and the later fortunes of Lutheranism, we must mention the providential man who was trained in Descartes's school at the same time as Locke and Leibniz, was long regarded only with scorn and hatred, and yet nowadays is attaining the sole supremacy over people's minds.

I am speaking of Benedict Spinoza.

A great genius is formed by another great genius, not so much by assimilation as by friction. One diamond sharpens the other. Hence Descartes's philosophy did not produce Spinoza's; it only encouraged it. In the pupil, therefore, we find initially the method of the master; that is a great gain. Next, we find in Spinoza, as in Descartes, a mode of argument borrowed from mathematics. That is a great defect. His mathematical form gives Spinoza a dry, uninviting appearance. But this is like the sour exterior of the almond: the core is all the more pleasing. Reading Spinoza, we feel as though we were contemplating great nature in her most vital repose. A forest of sky-high thoughts, whose blooming crowns are in surging motion, while their immovable trunks are firmly rooted in the eternal earth. There is in Spinoza's writings a certain inexplicable atmosphere, as though one could feel the breeze of the future. Perhaps the spirit of the Hebrew prophets still rested on their late descendant. At the same time, he has a gravity, a confident pride, an intellectual *grandezza*, that likewise seems hereditary; for Spinoza belonged to one of those families of martyrs that were expelled from Spain by the Most Catholic Kings. He also had the patience of the Dutchman, and this quality was never absent from either his writings or his life.

It has been established that Spinoza's life was wholly blameless, as pure and spotless as the life of his divine cousin Jesus Christ. Like him, Spinoza suffered for his teaching; like him, he wore a crown of thorns. Wherever a great mind utters its thoughts, there is Golgotha.

Beloved reader, if you should visit Amsterdam, let the paid attendants show you the Spanish synagogue. It is a handsome building, and its roof rests on four colossal pillars, and in the middle stands the pulpit where once the anathema was pronounced upon the despiser of the Mosaic law, the Hidalgo Don Benedict de Spinoza. On this occasion a blast was blown upon a goat's horn called the *shofar*. There must be something terrible about this horn. For as I have read in the life of Salomon Maimon,[4] the Rabbi of Altona once sought to guide Maimon, the pupil of Kant, back to the old faith, and when Maimon stubbornly persisted in his philosophical heresies, the Rabbi, assuming a threatening manner, showed him the *shofar* and said darkly: 'Do you know what this is?' When, however, the pupil of Kant calmly replied: 'It is the horn of a goat!', the Rabbi fell flat on his back in horror.

This horn provided the accompaniment to Spinoza's excommunication; he was solemnly expelled from the community of Israel and declared unworthy henceforth to call himself a Jew. His Christian enemies were magnanimous enough to let him keep this name. But the Jews, the Swiss Guards of deism, were implacable, and you can still see the place outside the Spanish synagogue at Amsterdam where they once stabbed at Spinoza with their long daggers.

I could not help drawing particular attention to this man's personal misfortunes. He was educated not only by a school, but also by life. This distinguishes him from most philosophers, and in his writings we perceive the direct effects of his life. For him theology was no mere academic subject, any more than politics. The latter, too, he learnt from practice. The father of his sweetheart was hanged in the Netherlands for political crimes.[5] And there is nowhere in the world where people are hanged worse than in the Netherlands. You have no notion of the endless preparations and ceremonies that take place there. The criminal dies of boredom, and the spectator has ample leisure for reflection. I am therefore convinced that Benedict Spinoza reflected a great deal on the execution of old van der Ende, and just as he had earlier come to understand religion with its daggers, so he now came to understand politics with its ropes. This is clear from his *Tractatus politicus*.

I wish only to emphasize how philosophers are more or less related to one another, and to show the degrees of relationship and the line of descent. The philosophy that Spinoza, the third son of René Descartes, teaches in his principal work, the *Ethics*, is as remote from the materialism of his brother Locke as from the idealism of his brother Leibniz. Spinoza does not rack his brains analytically over the question concerning the ultimate basis of our knowledge. He gives us his great synthesis, his explanation of the godhead.

Benedict Spinoza teaches that there is only one substance, and that is God. This single substance is infinite and absolute. All finite substances derive from it, are contained in it, appear in it, disappear in it; they have only relative, temporary, accidental existence. Absolute substance reveals itself to us both in the form of infinite thought and in the form of infinite extension. These two, infinite thought and infinite extension, are the two attributes of absolute substance. We perceive only these attributes, but God, absolute substance, may have more attributes that are unknown to us. 'Non dico, me deum omnino cognoscere, sed me quaedam eius attributa, non autem omnia, neque maximam intelligere partem.' 'I do not claim to know God entirely, but to perceive certain of his attributes, though not all or even most of them.'

Only stupidity and malice could label this doctrine with the adjective 'atheistic'. Nobody has ever spoken of the godhead with more sublimity than Spinoza. Instead of saying that he denies God, one could say that he denies man. For him all finite things are only modes of infinite substance. All finite things are contained in God, the human mind is only a ray of infinite thought, the human body is only an atom of infinite extension; God is the infinite cause of both, minds and bodies, *natura naturans*.[6]

In a letter to Madame du Deffand,[7] Voltaire shows himself delighted by an idea that had occurred to this lady: she had remarked that all the things man cannot know are doubtless of such a kind that it would be useless for him to know them. I should like to apply this remark to the statement by Spinoza that I have just given in his own words, to the effect that the godhead may possess not only the two knowable attributes of thought and extension, but also other attributes that we cannot perceive. What we cannot perceive has no value for us, at least no value from the social standpoint, where the crucial task is to give bodily existence to what the mind has perceived. In explaining the nature of God we shall therefore refer only to these two perceptible attributes. And then, in the last resort, what we call attributes of God are only various forms of our intuition, and these various forms are identical in absolute substance. In the last resort, thought is only invisible extension, and extension is only visible thought. Here we find ourselves in the principal doctrine of the German philosophy of identity, which is in essence not much different from Spinoza's doctrine. Herr Schelling is welcome to assert vociferously that his philosophy differs from Spinozism, that it is rather a 'living interpenetration of the ideal and the real', and that it differs from Spinozism 'as the masterpieces of Greek statuary do from their rigid Egyptian models';[8] none the less I must declare categorically that in his earlier period, when he was still a philosopher, Herr Schelling did not differ from Spinoza in the slightest. He simply reached the same philosophy by another route, and I must explain this later when I recount how Kant enters upon a new path, Fichte follows him, Herr Schelling marches along in Fichte's footsteps and, wandering about in the dark forest of the philosophy of nature, finally stands face to face with the great statue of Spinoza.

The sole achievement of the modern philosophy of nature is to have demonstrated, with great acuity, the eternal parallelism between mind and matter. I say 'mind and matter', and I shall use these terms as synonymous with what Spinoza calls thought and extension. These are much the same as what our philosophers of nature call mind and nature, or the ideal and the real.

In what follows, I shall apply the term pantheism not so much to

Spinoza's system as to his manner of apprehending things. Pantheism, like deism, assumes the unity of God. The God of the pantheists is in the world itself, but not in the sense that he pervades it with his divinity, as St Augustine[9] once tried to describe by comparing God to a great lake and the world to a great sponge lying in the middle of the lake and absorbing divinity: no, the world is not merely steeped in God, impregnated by God, but is identical with God. 'God', called the sole substance by Spinoza and the Absolute by the German philosophers, 'is everything there is';[10] he is both matter and spirit, everything is equally holy, and anyone who insults holy matter is just as sinful as he who commits the sin against the Holy Spirit.

The God of the pantheists, then, differs from the God of the deists by being in the world itself, while the latter is entirely outside or, what comes to the same thing, above the world. The God of the deists rules the world from above, as though it were a separate set of business premises. It is only about the manner of his rule that the deists disagree among themselves. The Hebrews imagine God as a thundering tyrant, the Christians as a loving father, while the pupils of Rousseau, the entire Geneva school, imagine him as an expert craftsman who made the world, rather as their daddy makes his watches, and, being connoisseurs of this craft, they admire the work and praise the master on high.

To the deist, who assumes that God is outside or above the world, nothing is holy save the spirit, and he regards this, so to speak, as the divine breath which the creator of the world breathed into the human body, the work which his hands had kneaded from clay. For this reason the Jews thought poorly of the body, considering it as a miserable covering for the *ruakh ha-kodesh*, the breath of the divine, the spirit, and it was to the latter alone that they devoted their care, their awe, their religious ceremonies. Hence they became the people of the spirit *par excellence*: chaste, abstemious, serious, abstract, stiff-necked, suited for martyrdom, and their most sublime flower is Jesus Christ. He is incarnate spirit in the true sense of the word, and a profound significance lies in the beautiful legend that he was born of an untouched, immaculate virgin and conceived only by spiritual agency.

If the Jews regarded the body with contempt, the Christians went much further along this path and regarded it as something foul and abominable, as evil itself. A few centuries after the birth of Christ we see a religion arising which will astonish mankind for ever and compel the latest generations to yield shuddering admiration. Yes, it is a great and holy religion, filled with infinite sweetness, one that wanted to attain absolute mastery for the spirit on this earth – but this religion was too sublime, too pure, too good for this earth, where its idea could only be proclaimed in theory but never put into practice. The attempt to realize this idea in the course of history has produced an infinite number of splendid phenomena, and the poets of all ages will sing of them for a long time to come. However, we can at last see that the attempt to put Christianity into practice has failed lamentably, and this unsuccessful attempt has cost mankind incalculable sacrifices, and one of its dismal consequences is the present unhappy state of society throughout Europe. If, as many believe, we are still living in the youth of mankind, then Christianity was one of its half-baked undergraduate notions, which do much more credit to its heart than to its intellect. Having abandoned matter, and all worldly things, to Caesar and his Jewish courtiers, Christianity was content to deny the supremacy of the former and defame the reputation of the latter – but behold! in the end, the sword it hated and the money it despised have none the less gained the upper hand, and the representatives of the spirit have had to come to terms with them. The result, indeed, has been a firm alliance. Not only the Roman priests, but the English, the Prussian, all privileged priests have joined forces with Caesar and Co. to oppress the nations. Thanks to this alliance, however, the religion of Spiritualism will perish all the more rapidly. Some priests[11] have already perceived as much, and in order to save religion they pretend to disavow that pernicious alliance and cross over into our ranks; they put on red caps of liberty, they swear death and hatred to all kings, to the seven blood-drinkers, they demand an equality of earthly goods, and they curse in spite of Marat and Robespierre. – Between ourselves, if you examine them closely, you will find that they read Mass in the language of Jacobinism, and just as once they brought Caesar poison concealed in the Host, so now they seek to bring the people their Hosts soaked in revolutionary poison; for they know we like this poison.

In vain, however, are all your exertions! Mankind has had enough of Hosts, and is longing for more nourishing food, for real bread and beautiful flesh. Mankind is smiling compassionately at the youthful ideals which could not be realized despite all its efforts, and it is becoming practical, as befits a grown man. Mankind now does homage to the earthly system of utility: it is thinking seriously about settling down in middle-class prosperity, managing its budget sensibly, and planning for a comfortable old age. Our immediate task is to become healthy; for we still feel very weak and faint. The holy vampires of the Middle Ages have sucked out so much of our life-blood. And then great expiatory sacrifices must be performed in deference to matter, so that it may forgive the old insults. It would even be advisable to organize festivals and pay extraordinary honours to matter as compensation for the past. For Christianity, unable to destroy matter, defamed it at every turn, degrading the noblest sensual enjoyments, and the senses were obliged to assume a hypocritical mask, creating lies and sin. We must give our women new blouses and new ideas, and we must disinfect all our feelings, like survivors of a plague.

Thus the immediate purpose of all our new institutions is the rehabilitation of matter, the restoration of its dignity, its moral recognition, its religious sanctification, its reconciliation with the spirit. Purusa[12] is once more married to Prakriti. As the Indian myth shows with such profundity, it was their separation through violence that produced the great division in the world – namely, evil.

Do you know what is evil in the world? The Spiritualists have always charged that the pantheist view removes the difference between good and bad. The bad, however, is on the one hand only an illusion generated by their own outlook on the world; on the other, it is a concrete result of the way they run the world. According to their outlook, matter is bad in itself; this view is truly a slander, a frightful blasphemy against God. Matter only becomes bad if it must conspire secretly against the authority usurped by the spirit, if the spirit has defamed it and it prostitutes itself in self-contempt, or if it avenges itself upon the spirit in hatred born of despair; and thus evil is only a result of the way Spiritualists run the world.

God is identical with the world. He manifests himself in plants, which lead a cosmic and magnetic life without consciousness. He manifests himself in animals, which lead a sensual dream-life and are more or less dimly conscious of their existence. But he manifests himself most splendidly in man, who simultaneously feels and thinks, who can distinguish himself as an individual from objective nature, and whose reason already contains the ideas that display themselves to him in the phenomenal world. In man the godhead attains self-consciousness, and this self-consciousness is again revealed through man. But this does not happen in and through a single individual, but in and through the whole of mankind: so that each person only grasps and represents a part of the divine universe, but all mankind together will grasp and represent the divine universe as an idea and as reality. It may be that each nation has the mission of perceiving and manifesting a distinct part of the divine universe, of understanding a series of phenomena and giving phenomenal existence to a series of ideas, and of handing down the result to the nations who succeed it, and who have a similar mission. Hence God is the true hero of world history, the latter consists of his continued thought and action, his word, his deed; and the whole of mankind can rightly be called an incarnation of God!

It is quite wrong to suppose that this religion, pantheism, makes people indifferent to morality. On the contrary, the awareness of his divinity will inspire man to manifest it, and only now will true feats of true heroism confer splendour on this earth. The political revolution based on the principles of French materialism will find supporters, not opponents, in the pantheists; but supporters who have drawn their convictions from a deeper source, from a religious synthesis. We promote the well-being of matter, people's material happiness, not because we despise the spirit, as the materialists do, but because we know that the divinity of man is manifest also in his bodily shape, and misery destroys or degrades the body, the image of God, and thus the spirit perishes likewise. The great watchword of the Revolution, uttered by Saint-Just: 'Le pain est le droit du peuple', runs in our version: 'Le pain est le droit divin de l'homme.' We are not fighting for the human rights of the people, but for the divine rights of man. In this, and in many other things, we differ from the men of the Revolution. We do not wish to be sans-culottes, thrifty citizens, bargain-basement presidents: we are founding a democracy of gods who are all equally magnificent, equally holy, and equally happy. You demand simple costumes, abstemious manners, and pleasures without spice; we, on the other hand, demand nectar and ambrosia, purple robes, delicious scents, sensual pleasures, splendour, dances of laughing nymphs, music and comedies – Do not let this annoy you, you virtuous Republicans! To your censorious reproaches we reply in the words of a

Shakespearean fool: 'Dost thou think, because thou art virtuous, there shall be no more cakes and ale?'[13]

The Saint-Simonians had some such ideas and plans. But they were on unfavourable soil, and they were suppressed, at least for some time, by the materialism all around them. They were appreciated better in Germany. For Germany is the most fruitful soil for pantheism; this is the religion of our greatest thinkers, our best artists, and deism, as I shall later recount, has long since been theoretically overthrown there. No one says so, but everyone knows this; pantheism is the open secret in Germany. In fact, we have outgrown deism. We are free, and do not want a thundering tyrant. We have come of age and do not need a father's care. Nor were we cobbled together by a great mechanic. Deism is a religion for serfs, for children, for Genevans, for watchmakers.

Pantheism is Germany's hidden religion, and its emergence was foreseen by the German writers who, fifty years ago, inveighed so much against Spinoza. The most furious among these opponents of Spinoza was F. H. Jacobi,[14] who is sometimes granted the honour of being mentioned among the German philosophers. He was nothing but a quarrelsome sneak who wrapped himself in the cloak of philosophy and wormed his way in among the philosophers, first whining to them about his love and his soft heart, and then denouncing reason for all he was worth. His constant refrain was that philosophy, rational knowledge, was an idle delusion, that reason itself did not know where it led, that it brought man into a dark labyrinth of error and contradiction, and only faith could be his sure guide. The mole! he did not see that reason is like the eternal sun, which travels securely onwards, illuminating its path with its own light. I know nothing to compare with the pious, warm-hearted hatred that little Jacobi showed for the great Spinoza.

It is curious how the most diverse parties have struggled against Spinoza. They form an army whose motley composition provides a very amusing sight. Alongside a swarm of black and white cowls, with crosses and smoking censers, there marches the phalanx of Encyclopaedists, likewise inveighing against this *penseur téméraire*.[15] Alongside the rabbi of the Amsterdam synagogue, sounding the attack with his goat's horn of faith, walks Arouet de Voltaire, playing his satirical flute for the benefit of deism. Amidst this tumult can be heard the wailing of the old woman Jacobi, the camp-follower of this army of faith.

Let us lose no time in escaping from this charivari. Returning from our excursion into pantheism, we find ourselves back at Leibniz's philosophy, and have to recount its further fortunes.

Leibniz wrote his works, which you know, partly in Latin and partly in French. The excellent man who not only systematized Leibniz's ideas but also presented them in German was called Christian Wolff. His real achievement does not consist in shutting Leibniz's ideas inside the walls of a system, nor in making them accessible to a larger public by means of the German language; his achievement consists in encouraging us to philosophize in our mother tongue. Just as we could do theology only in Latin until Luther came on the scene, so we could do philosophy only in Latin until Wolff appeared. The example of a few people who had already presented something similar in German remained ineffectual, but the literary historian has to commemorate them with special praise. So we shall here give particular mention to Johannes Tauler,[16] a Dominican monk, who was born on the Rhine at the beginning of the fourteenth century and died there, I think in Strasbourg, in 1361. He was a pious man and was one of the mystics whom I have described as the Platonic party of the Middle Ages. In the last years of his life this man renounced all the arrogance of learning, was not ashamed to preach in the humble language of the people, and the sermons he wrote down, as well as the German translations he made of some of his earlier Latin sermons, are among the most curious monuments of the German language. For here, too, it shows itself not just adequate for metaphysical inquiries, but much better suited to them than Latin. The latter, the language of the Romans, can never deny its origins. It is a language of command for military officers, a language of decrees for administrators, a legal language for usurers, a lapidary language for the stony Roman people. It became the appropriate language for materialism. Although Christianity, with truly Christian patience, had toiled for over a millennium to spiritualize this language, it never succeeded; and when Johannes Tauler wished to immerse himself in the most awesome abysses of thought, and his heart swelled with the holiest feelings, he had to speak German. His language is like a mountain spring bursting forth from hard rocks, wondrously carrying the scent of unknown herbs and the mysterious powers of stones. But it was only in more recent times that the usefulness of the German language for philosophy became truly apparent. There is no other language in which nature could have revealed its most secret utterances as in our dear German mother tongue. Only on the mighty oak could the sacred mistletoe flourish.

This would have been the right place to discuss Paracelsus, or, as he called himself, Theophrastus Paracelsus Bombastus von Hohenheim.[17] For he also wrote mostly in German. But I have to speak of him later in a yet more significant context. His philosophy, you see, was what we nowadays call the philosophy of nature, and such a doctrine of nature as animated by ideas, which has so mysterious an appeal for the German mind, would have developed even then, if accidental influence had not raised the lifeless, mechanistic physics of the Cartesians to universal dominance. Paracelsus was a great mountebank, and always wore a scarlet coat, scarlet trousers, red stockings, and a red hat, and claimed to be able to make *homunculi*, little men; at any rate he was on familiar terms with hidden beings that dwell in the various elements – but at the same time he was one of the most profound students of nature who with the heart of a German scholar have grasped the pre-Christian popular belief, German pantheism, and, without realizing this, understood it quite correctly.

I ought also to speak here of Jakob Böhme.[18] For he too used the German language for philosophical treatises, and has gained high praise in this regard. But I have never yet been able to sit down and read him. I do not like being made a fool of. You see, I suspect this mystic's eulogists of wishing to mystify the public. As for the content of his works, Saint-Martin has conveyed some of it to you in French. The English have also translated him. Charles I was so impressed by this theosophical cobbler that he sent a scholar specially to Görlitz to study him. This scholar was more fortunate than his royal master. For while the latter lost his head at Whitehall by Cromwell's axe, at Görlitz the former, thanks to Jakob Böhme's theosophy, only lost his wits.

As I have already said, it was Christian Wolff who first succeeded in introducing the German language into philosophy. His minor achievement was systematizing and popularizing Leibniz's ideas. Both these activities have received harsh criticism, which we must mention in passing. His systematizing was a mere illusion, and the most important elements of Leibniz's philosophy were sacrificed to this illusion, for example, the best part of the doctrine of monads. Leibniz, of course, had not left any systematic doctrinal edifice behind, only the ideas necessary to construct one. A giant was needed to pile up the colossal ashlars and pillars which had been fetched from the deepest marble quarries and neatly chiselled by another giant. It would have made a beautiful temple. Christian Wolff, however, being of very small stature, could only cope with a few of these building materials, and he made them into a wretched deist tabernacle. Wolff had an encyclopaedic mind rather than a systematic one, and could understand the unity of a doctrine only in the form of completeness. He was content to classify things in pigeon-holes which were beautifully ordered, well filled, and clearly labelled. Thus he gave us an *Encyclopaedia of the Philosophical Sciences*. It goes without saying that, as Descartes's grandson, he inherited the mathematical form in which his grandfather had conducted demonstrations. I have already censured this mathematical form in the case of Spinoza. In Wolff's hands it did great mischief. Among his pupils it degenerated into the most insufferable schematism, and into a ridiculous mania for demonstrating everything mathematically. There arose what is known as Wolffian dogmatism. Any profounder inquiries were brought to a halt, and were replaced by a tedious insistence on clarity. Wolffian philosophy kept being watered down, till at last it flooded the whole of Germany. The traces of this deluge are visible even nowadays, and old fossils from the Wolffian school may still be found here and there at our principal seats of the Muses.

Christian Wolff was born in 1679 at Breslau and died in 1754 at Halle. His intellectual dominance in Germany lasted for half a century. We must make particular mention of his relations with the theologians of the time, thus extending our account of the fortunes of Lutheranism.

In the entire history of the Church there is no more complicated episode than the disputes among Protestant theologians since the Thirty Years War. It can be compared only with the hair-splitting squabbles of the Byzantines; these, however, were less tedious, since behind them lay great court intrigues affecting the interests of the state, whereas the Protestants' wrangling was largely based on the pedantry of narrow-minded dominies and ineffectual dons. The scenes of these theological combats are the universities, especially Tübingen, Wittenberg, Leipzig, and Halle. The two parties that we saw fighting throughout the Middle Ages in Catholic garb, the Platonic and the Aristotelian parties, have only changed their costumes and continued their feud. These are the Pietists and the orthodox whom I mentioned earlier, describing them as unimaginative mystics and mindless dogmatists. Johannes Spener was the Scotus Eriugena[19] of Protestantism, and just as Eriugena founded Catholic mysticism by his translation of the fabulous Dionysus the Areopagite, so Spener founded Protestant Pietism by his edifying meetings (*colloquia pietatis*), which may explain why the name 'Pietists' has stuck to his followers. He was a pious man; honour to his memory! A good biography of him has been provided by a Berlin Pietist, Herr Franz Horn. Spener's life was a continual martyrdom for the Christian idea. In this regard he was superior to his contemporaries. He insisted on piety and good works, and was a preacher of the Spirit rather than of the Word. His mode of preaching was praiseworthy at that time, for the whole of the theology taught at the universities just mentioned consisted only in petty dogmatics and nit-picking polemics. No attention was given to biblical exegesis or Church history.

One of Spener's pupils, Hermann Francke, began giving lectures in Leipzig in the manner and spirit of his teacher. He gave them in German, a service we are always glad to acknowledge. The applause he received for them aroused the envy of his colleagues, who accordingly gave our poor Pietist a very hard time. He was obliged to quit the field, and he moved to Halle, where he taught Christianity through words and deeds. His memory there will never fade, for he is the founder of the Halle Orphanage. The University of Halle was now populated by Pietists, who were called the 'Orphanage Party'. This party, incidentally, has survived there until the present day; Halle is still the main refuge of Pietism, and only a few years ago their disputes with Protestant rationalists started a scandal whose stench penetrated the whole of Germany. Happy French, who have heard nothing of it! You are unaware even of the existence of Evangelical scandal-sheets in which the pious fishwives of the Protestant Church curse to their hearts' content.

Happy French, who have no idea of the petty, revolting malice with which our Lutheran priests vituperate against one another. You know that I am not an adherent of Catholicism. My present religious convictions no longer contain the dogma of Protestantism, but they still contain its spirit. So I am still a partisan of the Protestant Church. And yet, for the sake of truth, I must confess that in the annals of popery I have never found such wretched rubbish as was printed in the *Evangelical Church Times* of Berlin during the above-mentioned scandal. Even the most cowardly monastic tricks, the pettiest convent intrigues, are noble and generous actions in comparison to the deeds of Christian heroism performed by our orthodox and Pietist Protestants against the detested rationalists. You French have no idea of the hatred that comes to light on such occasions. The Germans, however, are in general more vindictive than the Latin nations.

The reason is that they are idealists even in their hatred. We do not hate one another, as you do, because of externals, such as wounded vanity, an epigram, a visiting card that is not returned: no, in our enemies we hate what is deepest and most essential in them – we hate the idea. You French are frivolous and superficial, both in love and in hatred. We Germans are thorough and persevering in our hatred; since we are too honest, and also too clumsy, to avenge ourselves with swift treachery, we go on hating until our dying breath.[20]

If I am not mistaken, it was the orthodox of Halle who called on Wolffian philosophy for aid in their fight with the Pietist hermits. For now that religion can no longer burn us, it comes to beg from us. But all our gifts bring religion little profit. The garb of mathematical demonstration in which poor religion had lovingly been clad by Wolff fitted it so badly that it felt still more tightly constrained, and made itself most ridiculous. The garment kept bursting at the seams. In particular, the pudendum, original sin, was exposed in all its hideousness. No logical fig-leaf was of any use. The Christian and Lutheran conception of original sin is incompatible with the optimism of Leibniz and Wolff. Our theologians therefore did not mind French satire on optimism. The nakedness of original sin benefited from Voltaire's wit. The destruction of optimism, however, did great harm to the German Pangloss, who spent a long time searching for an equally comforting doctrine, until he found a partial substitute in Hegel's saying that 'whatever is, is rational!'[21]

As soon as a religion seeks help from philosophy, its doom is inevitable. Trying to defend itself, it talks its way further and further into its perdition. Like any other absolutism, religion must not justify itself. It is a silent power that chains Prometheus to the rock. Indeed,

Aeschylus[22] does not let the personification of power utter a single word. It must be mute. The moment religion publishes a reasoned catechism, the moment political absolutism issues an official newspaper, both are at an end. But this is precisely our triumph: we have made our adversaries speak, and they must abide our question.

Since religion, as I have just described, sought help from philosophy, German scholars have not only given religion a new garb but tried innumerable experiments upon it. They wanted to restore its youth, and they behaved more or less as Medea did in trying to rejuvenate King Aeson. First of all they opened a vein and drew off all its superstitious blood: they tried to extract all the historical content from Christianity, preserving only the moral part. Christianity thus became pure deism. Christ ceased to be a joint ruler alongside God; he was, so to speak, mediatized, stripped of his princedom, and enjoyed recognition and respect only as a private individual. His moral character was praised to the skies. People could not say warmly enough what a decent fellow he was. As for the miracles he had performed, they were explained away in physical terms, or else people tried to make as little fuss about them as possible. Miracles, said some, were necessary in those ages of superstition, and a rational man who had any truth to proclaim made use of them as a kind of advertisement. Those theologians who removed all the historical content from Christianity are called rationalists, and they felt the fury of both the Pietists and the orthodox, who thereafter fought each other less violently and not infrequently joined forces. What love could not accomplish was accomplished by common hatred – hatred of the rationalists.

This tendency in Protestant theology begins with the quiet Semler,[23] whom you do not know, reached an alarming height with the lucid Teller, whom you do not know either, and attained its peak with the shallow Bahrdt, whom you miss nothing by not knowing. The most powerful impulse came from Berlin, where Frederick the Great and Nicolai the bookseller[24] held sway.

About the first of these, materialism wearing a crown, you are adequately informed. You know that he made French verses, played the flute very well, won the Battle of Rossbach, took plenty of snuff, and believed only in cannons. Some of you must also have visited Sanssouci, where the old ex-soldier who looks after the palace took you into the library and showed you the French novels that Frederick used to read in church and had bound in black morocco, so that his severe father should think he was reading a Lutheran hymn-book. You know him, the royal sage, whom you called the Solomon of the North. The Ophir of this northern Solomon was France, whence he imported his poets and philosophers, of whom he was extremely fond, just like the Solomon of the South, who, as you may read in Chapter 10 of the Book of Kings, made his friend Hiram fetch whole ship-loads of gold, ivory, poets and philosophers from Ophir. Such a fondness for foreign talents meant of course that Frederick the Great could not exert any very great influence on the German spirit. Instead, he insulted and wounded the German national sentiment. Even we, two generations on, cannot but be annoyed by the contempt that Frederick the Great showed for our literature. Except for old Gellert,[25] no German writer enjoyed his most gracious favour. The conversation between him and Gellert is curious.

If Frederick the Great mocked us without supporting us, we received all the more support from the bookseller Nicolai, without having any scruples about mocking him. This man spent his entire life in unremitting activity on behalf of his country; he spared neither effort nor money where he hoped to encourage something good; and yet never has any man in Germany been the object of such cruel, relentless, and destructive jeering as this man. Although we, the later generation, are well aware that old Nicolai, the friend of the Enlightenment, was right in the essential point, and although we know that it was mainly our own enemies, the obscurantists, who ruined him by their satire, we still cannot keep a straight face when thinking of him. Old Nicolai wanted to do in Germany what the French philosophers had done in France: he tried to annihilate the past in the mind of the nation; a praiseworthy piece of spade-work without which no radical revolution can ever take place. But it was in vain: he was not equal to such work. The old ruins were still standing too firmly, and the ghosts arose from them and mocked him; and then he became very cross, and hit out blindly, and the onlookers laughed to see the bats squeaking about his ears and getting caught in his well-powdered wig. It also happened from time to time that he mistook windmills for giants and fought against them. He came off still worse, however, when he mistook real giants for mere windmills, as he did with Wolfgang Goethe. He wrote a satire against the latter's *Werther*, in which he misunderstood the author's intentions in the clumsiest way possible. And yet he was always right about the essential point: even if he did not understand what Goethe was getting at in *Werther*, he perfectly understood its influence – the emotional wallowing, the sterile sentimentality, that were encouraged by this novel and were completely at odds with the sensible state of mind that we needed. Here Nicolai was in entire agreement with Lessing, who delivered the following verdict on *Werther* in a letter to a friend:[26]

> If such an unwholesome product is not to do more harm than good, do you not think that it should have a short, cold closing address? A few hints at the end of the story about how Werther acquired such an extravagant character, and how another youth, similarly endowed by nature, could safeguard himself. Do you suppose that any Roman or Greek youth would have taken his own life in such a way and for such a reason? Certainly not. They were well able to secure themselves against the emotional excesses of love; and in Socrates' day such ἐξ ἐρωτος χατοχη [a seizure resulting from sexual love], urging one to τι τολμαν παραφυσιν [dare something unnatural], would scarcely have been pardoned in a young girl. The creation of such petty-great, contemptibly estimable eccentrics was an achievement reserved for Christian education, which is so adept at transforming a physical need into a spiritual excellence. So, dear Goethe, let us have one last little chapter; and the more cynical the better!

Our friend Nicolai did indeed produce a revised *Werther*[27] along these lines. In this version the hero turns out not to have shot himself, but only to have smeared himself with chicken blood; for the pistol was loaded with this, not with lead. Werther makes a fool of himself, remains alive, marries Charlotte – in short, he comes to an even more tragic end than in Goethe's original.

The periodical founded by Nicolai, in which he and his friends fought against superstition, Jesuits, court lackeys, and the like, was called *The Universal German Library*. There is no denying that many a blow aimed at superstition unfortunately struck poetry itself. Thus Nicolai opposed, for example, the burgeoning taste for old German folk-songs. But, once again, he was basically right: whatever their merits, these poems did contain many recollections that were out of keeping with the times; the sound of the old cow-bells of the Middle Ages could lead the nation's hearts back to the pious farmyard of the past. He sought, like Odysseus, to stop up his companions' ears to prevent them from hearing the Sirens' song, not worrying that they would also become deaf to the innocent notes of the nightingale. In order to eradicate the weeds of the past from the field of the present, this practical man did not hesitate to root up the flowers as well. This brought the party of flowers and nightingales into battle against him, along with all this party's allies – beauty, grace, wit, and humour – and poor Nicolai was defeated.

Circumstances in Germany have now changed, and the party of flowers and nightingales is closely allied to revolution. The future is ours, and the day of victory is already breaking. When at last this beautiful day illuminates the whole of our country, we shall also commemorate the dead; and we shall certainly commemorate you, old Nicolai, you poor martyr of reason! We shall bear your ashes to the German pantheon, your sarcophagus surrounded by the jubilation of a triumphal procession and accompanied by a chorus of musicians, whose instruments may on no account include the flute; we shall lay your own laurel wreath on your coffin, and we shall refrain from laughing.

Since I should like to convey some idea of the philosophical and religious situation at that time, I must here also mention those thinkers who were active in Berlin, more or less co-operating with Nicolai, and forming, as it were, a *juste milieu* between philosophy and *belles-lettres*. They had no distinct system, only a distinct tendency. In their style, and in the basis of their convictions, they resemble the English moral essayists. They write without the strict form of scholarship, and their knowledge comes solely from their moral awareness. Their tendency is exactly the same as that found among the French Philanthropists. In religion they are rationalists. Politically they are cosmopolitans. In morals they are human, nobly and virtuously human, strict with themselves and lenient with others. As for talent, their outstanding representatives are Mendelssohn,[28] Sulzer, Abbt, Moritz, Garve, Engel, and Biester. Moritz is my favourite. He contributed a great deal to experimental psychology. He was delightfully naive, and his friends barely understood him. His autobiography is one of the most important documents of that age. It is Mendelssohn, however, who is pre-eminent for his social significance. He was the reformer of the German Israelites, his co-religionists; he overthrew the authority of Talmudism and founded pure Mosaism. This man, called the German Socrates by his contemporaries and so reverently admired for the nobility of his soul and the power of his intellect, was the son of a poor attendant in the synagogue at Dessau. Besides this misfortune of birth, providence had also burdened him with a hump, as though to give the rabble a blatant lesson that people should be judged by their inward merit and not by their outward appearance. Or did providence give him a hump out of kindly caution, so that he might ascribe much maltreatment that he suffered at the hands of the rabble to a misfortune for which a wise man can easily be consoled?

As Luther overthrew the Papacy, so Mendelssohn overthrew the Talmud, and he did so in the same way, that is, by rejecting tradition, declaring the Bible to be the source of religion, and translating the most important part of it. He thus destroyed Jewish Catholicism, as Luther had destroyed Christian Catholicism. In fact, the Talmud is the Catholicism of the Jews. It is a Gothic cathedral, which, though overloaded with childish squiggles, still astonishes us by its heaven-aspiring boldness and gigantic dimensions. It is a hierarchy of religious laws which often deal with the drollest and most ridiculous subtleties, but which are so ingeniously arranged to sustain and support one another, and interact with such fearsome logical consistency, that they form a terrifyingly stubborn and colossal whole.

After the decline of Christian Catholicism, its Jewish counterpart, the Talmud, had also to perish. For by then the Talmud had lost its significance: that is, it had served only as a bulwark against Rome, enabling the Jews to stand up to Christian Rome as heroically as they once did to pagan Rome. And they not only stood up to it; they defeated it. The poor rabbi of Nazareth, above whose dying head the pagan Roman wrote the spiteful words 'King of the Jews' – this carnival king of the Jews, crowned with thorns and robed in ironic purple, became in the end the god of the Romans, and they were obliged to kneel down before him! Like pagan Rome, Christian Rome too was conquered, and indeed paid tribute. If, dear reader, you make your way just after the beginning of the quarter to the rue Lafitte, number 15, you will see a fat man descending from a ponderous coach that has stopped in front of a lofty archway. The fat man goes upstairs to a little room where there sits a fair-haired young man, who is nevertheless older than he looks, and who combines the aristocratic nonchalance of a *grand seigneur* with a solid, positive, absolute air, as though all the world's money were in his pocket. And in fact all the world's money is in his pocket, and his name is Monsieur James de Rothschild, and the fat man is Monsignor Garibaldi, the emissary of His Holiness the Pope, in whose name he was bringing the interest on the Roman loan, the tribute from Rome.

Who needs the Talmud now?

Moses Mendelssohn thus deserves great praise for overthrowing this Jewish Catholicism, at least in Germany. For whatever is superfluous is harmful. Rejecting tradition, he nevertheless sought to maintain the ceremonial law of Moses as a religious obligation. Was this cowardice or cleverness? Was it a sad, lingering affection that held him back from laying destructive hands on objects which his forefathers revered most deeply, and for which the blood and tears of so many martyrs had flowed? I think not. The kings of the spirit, like the kings of matter, must be inexorable in the face of family affection; even on the throne of the idea one cannot give way to easygoing mildness. I am therefore more inclined to suppose that Moses Mendelssohn saw in pure Mosaism an institution that might serve as the last ditch of deism. For deism was his innermost faith and his deepest conviction. When his friend Lessing died and was accused of Spinozism, Mendelssohn defended him with the most anxious zeal, and died of vexation.

I have now mentioned for the second time the name that no German can utter without awakening a more or less powerful echo in his bosom. Not since Luther has Germany produced a greater or better man than Gotthold Ephraim Lessing. These two are our pride and joy. In the gloom of the present we raise our eyes to their statues for consolation, and they nod to us with a glorious promise. Yes, there shall come a third to accomplish what Luther began and Lessing continued. The third liberator – I can already see his golden armour gleaming forth from beneath his robe of imperial purple, 'like the sun from the daybreak!'

Lessing, like Luther, was effectual not only by his specific achievements but by stirring up the German people and by producing a salutary commotion of minds, through his criticism, through his polemics. He was the living criticism of his age, and his whole life was a polemic. His criticism applied throughout the widest domains of thought and feeling, in religion, in scholarship, in art. His polemics overcame every opponent and grew stronger after every victory. For, as he himself admitted, Lessing needed conflict in order to develop his own mind. He resembled that famous Norman who inherited the talents, knowledge and strength of the men he slew in single combat and thus ended up being endowed with every possible advantage. It is understandable that such a doughty fighter should have made no small stir in Germany, in quiet Germany, which in those days enjoyed an even deeper Sabbath peace than today. Most people were staggered by his literary boldness. But this redounded greatly to his benefit: for 'Oser!'[29] is the secret of success in literature, as in revolution – and in love. Everyone trembled at Lessing's sword. No one's head was safe from him. Indeed, he split many skulls from sheer high spirits, and would then be malicious enough to pick up the skull and show the public that it was hollow. Anyone out of reach of his sword would be slain by the arrows of his wit. His friends admired his arrows' bright feathers; his foes felt their points in their hearts. Lessing's wit is not like the *enjouement*, the gaiety, the sudden sallies, that are familiar in this country. His wit was not a little French greyhound that runs after its own shadow: his wit was more like a great German tom-cat that plays with the mouse before throttling it.

Yes, polemics were our Lessing's greatest pleasure, and therefore he seldom paused to consider whether his opponent was worthy of his steel. Thus his very polemics rescued many names from well-deserved oblivion. There were numerous tiny writers round whom he spun a web, as it were, made of the wittiest mockery and the most delicious humour, and they are preserved for all time in Lessing's works, like insects caught in a piece of amber. By slaying his opponents, he also made them immortal. Who would ever have heard otherwise of Klotz,[30] on whom Lessing expended so much scorn and ingenuity! The rocks he hurled against that poor antiquary to crush him now form Klotz's imperishable monument.

It is curious that Lessing, the wittiest man in Germany, was at the same time the most honest. There is nothing to match his love of truth. Lessing did not make the slightest concession to falsehood, even if, in the usual manner of the worldly-wise, it would have enabled him to promote the victory of truth. He could do anything for the sake of truth, except lie. 'Anyone who wants to render truth attractive by masks and make-up,' he once said, 'may be her pimp, but has never been her lover.'

Buffon's fine remark that 'style is the man himself' fits no one better than Lessing. His manner of writing is exactly like his character: truthful, firm, plain, beautiful, and impressive thanks to its indwelling strength. His style is just the style of Roman buildings, combining the utmost solidity with the utmost simplicity; the sentences rest upon one another like ashlars, held together invisibly by logical cohesion, as ashlars are by the law of gravity. That is why Lessing's prose contains so little of the padding and pompous phrasing that we use as mortar in constructing our periods. Much less do we find in it those intellectual caryatids that you call 'la belle phrase'.

You will readily understand that a man like Lessing could never be happy. Even if he had not loved truth and had not defended her cause everywhere so stubbornly, he must have been unhappy; for he was a genius. 'Everything can be forgiven,' sighed a poet not long ago; 'wealth, high birth, good looks can be forgiven, even talent may be allowed to pass, but genius can expect no mercy.' Alas! even if genius did not meet with outward ill-will, it would still find in itself the enemy that renders it miserable. For this reason the history of great men is always a tale of martyrdom; even if they did not suffer for humanity, they at least suffered for their own greatness, for their great mode of existence, their lack of philistinism, for being uncomfortable with the ostentatious vulgarity and smiling meanness that surround them, a discomfort that naturally leads them to extravagances, such as the playhouse or even the gaming-den – as happened to poor Lessing.

Scandal, however, has managed to report nothing worse of him than this, and from his biography we learn only that he found beautiful actresses more entertaining than Hamburg clergymen, and that he derived more enjoyment from silent cards than from talkative Wolffians.

It is heart-breaking to read in this biography how fate denied Lessing any joy, and did not even permit him to relax from his daily combats in the shelter of a family. Only once did Fortuna seem to smile on him, giving him a beloved wife and a child – but this happiness was like the sunbeam that gilds the wing of a passing bird, and it vanished just as quickly: his wife died from the effects of childbirth, the child died soon after its birth, and he wrote the following hideously witty words to a friend concerning his child's death:

> My joy was but short. And I was sorry to lose this son! For he was so intelligent! so intelligent! Do not think that a few hours of fatherhood made me into a besotted father! I know what I am talking about. Was it not intelligent of him that he had to be drawn into the world with iron tongs? that he smelt a rat so quickly? Was it not intelligent of him to take the earliest opportunity of making his escape? I once wanted to be as happy as other people. But that has turned out very badly.[31]

There was one misfortune which Lessing never mentioned to his friends: that was his appalling loneliness, his intellectual isolation. He was loved by a few contemporaries, understood by none. Mendelssohn, his best friend, was zealous in his defence when he was accused of Spinozism. The defence and the zeal were as ridiculous as they were superfluous. Rest peacefully in your grave, old Moses; your Lessing was indeed heading towards this frightful error, this lamentable misfortune of Spinozism – but the Highest, the Father in heaven, saved him just in time through death. Rest assured, your Lessing was no Spinozist, as slander claimed; he died a good deist, like you and Nicolai and Teller and the *Universal German Library*!

Lessing was only the prophet who pointed the way from the second testament to the third. I have described him as continuing Luther's work, and it is really this aspect of him that I have to describe here. His importance for German art can be discussed only later. Not only by his criticism, but also by his example, he effected a salutary artistic reform, and it is this side of his activity which as a rule receives the greatest emphasis and attention. We, however, are considering him from a different standpoint, and his philosophical and theological combats concern us more than his dramaturgy and his dramas. The latter, however, like all his writings, have a social significance, and *Nathan the Wise* is at bottom not merely a good comedy, but also a philosophical and theological treatise in favour of pure deism. Art gave Lessing yet another platform, and when he was thrust down from the pulpit or the lecture podium, he would jump into the theatre, where he spoke a still clearer language and gained a still more numerous public.

I say that Lessing continued Luther's work. After Luther had freed us from tradition and elevated the Bible to the sole source of Christianity, a rigid cult of the word came into being, as I recounted earlier, and the letter of the Bible ruled as tyrannically as tradition had formerly done. It was Lessing who did most to free us from this tyrannical letter. Just as Luther was not the only one to combat tradition, so Lessing was not the letter's only antagonist, though certainly the most powerful. Here his battle-cry rings out loudest; here he brandishes his sword most joyously, and it shines and slays. But here, too, Lessing was most mightily assailed by the black host, and when hard pressed by them he once cried:

> *O sancta simplicitas!* But I have not yet reached the place where the good man who uttered this cry was able to say nothing else. [Huss uttered this cry when being burnt alive.] Let us first be heard and judged by him who is able and willing to listen and judge!
>
> O that he could do so, he whom I would most like to have as my judge! Luther, you great, misunderstood man! And by no one more misunderstood than by the short-sighted bigots who stroll along the road you built, with your slippers in their hands, noisy but indifferent! You freed us from the yoke of tradition; who will free us from the more intolerable yoke of the letter! Who will finally give us a Christianity as you would teach it now; as Christ himself would teach it![32]

Yes, the letter, said Lessing, was the last covering of Christianity, and only when this covering was destroyed would the spirit step forth. This spirit, however, is precisely what the Wolffian philosophers tried to demonstrate, what the philanthropists felt in their hearts, what Mendelssohn found in Mosaism, what the Freemasons sang, what the poets whistled, what exerted its influence in every form in Germany at that time: pure deism.

Lessing died at Brunswick in 1781, misunderstood, hated, and abused. In the same year, at Königsberg, Immanuel Kant published his *Critique of Pure Reason*. This book, by a strange time-lag, did not become generally known until the end of the 1780s; it initiated an intellectual revolution in Germany which offers the most remarkable analogies with the material revolution in France, and must strike the profound thinker as equally important. It develops in the same phases, and the most curious parallelism exists between the two. On either side of the Rhine we see the same breach with the past; tradition is denied its tribute of respect: just as here in France every privilege is required to justify itself, so in Germany the same is required of every idea; and the overthrow of the monarchy, the keystone of the old social order, corresponds to that of deism, the keystone of the intellectual *ancien régime*.

This catastrophe, deism's twenty-first of January,[33] will be dealt with in the following chapter. A strange unease, a mysterious piety, prevents us from writing any more today. Our bosom is filled with hideous compassion: old Jehovah himself is preparing for his death. We have known him so well ever since he lay in his cradle, in Egypt, where he was brought up among divine calves, crocodiles, sacred onions, ibises, and cats. We saw him bid farewell to these childhood playmates and to the obelisks and sphinxes of his native Nile valley, and become a little god-king in Palestine among a poor shepherd tribe, where he lived in a temple-palace of his own. We saw later how he encountered Assyrian and Babylonian civilization and put aside his all-too-human passions, no longer spitting anger and revenge, at least not uttering thunder on account of every trifle. We saw him emigrate to Rome, the capital, where he abandoned all local prejudices, and proclaimed the heavenly equality of all the nations, and, with the aid of such fine slogans, formed an opposition party against old Jupiter, and kept intriguing until he attained power and governed the city and the world, *urbem et orbem*, from the Capitol. We saw how he became yet more spiritual, how he whimpered mildly, how he became a loving father, a friend of humanity, a universal benefactor, a philanthropist – none of it helped him –

Do you hear the bell ringing? Kneel down – They are bringing the sacraments to a dying God.

BOOK THREE

THE story goes that an English mechanic, who had already devised the most ingenious machines, at last hit on the idea of constructing a human being. In this he finally succeeded: the work of his hands could act and behave just like a human being, and in its leather bosom it even had a kind of human feeling, not all that different from the normal feelings of Englishmen. It could convey its sensations in articulate sounds, and the noise of its internal wheels, rasps, and screws, which then became audible, gave these sounds a perfect English accent. In short this automaton was a complete gentleman, and it lacked nothing but a soul in order to be a real human being. A soul, however, was more than the English mechanic could give it, and the poor creature, aware of this deficiency, tormented its creator night and day, pleading with him to give it a soul. This plea was repeated ever more insistently, till at last the artist could endure it no longer and took flight from his own artefact. The automaton, however, promptly took a special mail-coach, pursued him to the Continent, and now perpetually travels after him. Sometimes it catches up with him, and then it croaks and grunts at him: 'Give me a soul!'[1] These two figures are to be met with in every country, and only those who know the peculiar relation between them can understand why they are in such haste and in such a state of fearful ill-temper. Those who do not know their relationship, however, see in it something more general: they see how part of the English people has grown weary of its mechanical existence and is demanding a soul, while the remaining part, terrified by this desire, is driven hither and yon, and neither of them can stand being at home any longer.

That is a horrible story. It is appalling when the bodies we have created ask us for a soul. Yet it is far more horrible, appalling, and uncanny when we have created a soul which then demands its body and pursues us with this demand. The idea we have thought is such a soul, and it will not let us rest until we have given it its body, until we have enabled its sensory manifestation. The idea wants to become a deed, the word to become flesh. And, wonderful to relate! like the God of the Bible, man has only to voice his idea, and the world takes shape, there is light or darkness, the waters divide themselves from the dry land, or wild beasts appear. The world is the signature of the word.

Mark this well, you proud men of action. You are no more than the unwitting servants of the men of ideas, who have often, humbly and quietly, drawn up distinct plans in advance for everything you do. Maximilian Robespierre was no more than the hand of Jean-Jacques Rousseau, the bloody hand that drew forth from the womb of time the body whose soul Rousseau had created. The restless terror that plagued Rousseau's life – did it originate from his premonition of what a midwife his ideas would need in order to be born in bodily shape?

Old Fontenelle[2] may have been right in saying: 'If I held all the world's ideas in my fist, I would take care not to open it.' For my part, I think differently. If I had all the world's ideas in my fist, I might ask you to chop my hand off there and then, but I certainly would not keep my fist clenched. I am not cut out to be a gaoler for ideas. By God! I let them go. They may take shape as the most alarming phenomena, they may rage through every country like a wild train of Bacchantes, they may shatter our most innocent flowers with their ivy-wreathed staves, they may burst into our hospitals and force the sick old world out of its bed – of course that will grieve my heart and I myself will come to grief! For alas! I myself belong to this sick old world, and the poet rightly says: 'One may mock one's crutches, but one can walk none the better for that.' I am more sick than any of you and the more to be pitied, since I know what health is. But you, you enviable ones, you do not know this! You could die without even noticing. Indeed, many of you have long been dead and buried, and your true life is only now beginning. If I contradict such madness, people are cross with me and scold me – and, terrible to tell, the corpses leap up at me, and abuse me, and their odour of decay offends me worse than their insults . . . Away, you ghosts! I am now speaking of a man whose very name has the power of exorcism, I am speaking of Immanuel Kant!

It is said that nocturnal spirits are frightened by seeing an executioner's sword. How frightened they must be if one brandishes Kant's *Critique of Pure Reason* at them! This book is the sword with which deism was executed in Germany.

In all honesty, you Frenchmen, by comparison with the Germans you are tame and moderate. The most you could achieve was to kill a king, and he had already lost his head before you beheaded him. And in the process you had to drum, and shout, and stamp your feet so much that it shook the entire globe. It is paying Maximilian Robespierre too much honour to compare him to Immanuel Kant. Of course Maximilian Robespierre, the great philistine of the rue Saint-Honoré, had fits of destructive fury when the monarchy was at stake, and the convulsions of his regicidal epilepsy were terrible enough; but as soon as the Supreme Being was mentioned, he wiped the foam from his lips and the blood from his hands, and put on his blue Sunday suit with shiny buttons, and, what is more, placed a bunch of flowers in his broad lapel.

It is hard to recount Immanuel Kant's life-history. For he had neither life nor history. He led a mechanically ordered, almost abstract bachelor's existence in a quiet, remote back street in Königsberg, an old town on the north-eastern border of Germany. I do not believe that the great clock on the cathedral there went about its daily business more tranquilly and regularly than its fellow-countryman Immanuel Kant. Getting up, drinking coffee, writing, giving lectures, eating, going for walks – everything had its appointed time, and the neighbours could be certain that it was half-past three when Immanuel Kant, wearing his grey surtout and carrying his malacca cane, stepped out of his front door and betook himself to the little avenue of lime-trees which is still called the Philosopher's Walk in his memory. He would walk up and down the avenue eight times, at every season, and if the weather was gloomy or grey clouds gave warning of rain, his servant, old Lampe, could be seen following him with anxious concern, carrying a long umbrella under his arm, like an image of providence.

Strange contrast between the outward life of this man and his destructive ideas that pounded a world to smithereens! Truly, if the citizens of Königsberg had suspected the significance of his ideas, they would have felt far deeper horror of this man than of an executioner, an executioner who only executes people – but these good folk saw in him nothing more than a professor of philosophy, and when he walked past at the appointed time, they bade him a kindly good-day, and adjusted their watches by him.

But if Immanuel Kant, that great destroyer in the realm of ideas, far surpassed Maximilian Robespierre in terrorism, he still has many similarities with the latter, which invite a comparison between the two men. Firstly, we find in both the same inexorable, cutting, unpoetic, sober honesty. Then we find in both the same talent for suspicion, except that the former exercises it upon ideas and calls it criticism, while the latter applies it to people and dubs it republican virtue. Both, however, exhibit in the highest degree the typical features of the small-town philistine. Nature intended them to weigh out coffee and sugar, but fate meant them to weigh other things, and placed a king on one set of scales and a God on the other . . .

And they gave the right weight!

The *Critique of Pure Reason* is Kant's main work, and we must give it our special attention. None of all Kant's writings is of greater importance. The book appeared in 1781, but only became widely known in 1789. At first it was completely ignored; only two unimportant reviews of it appeared then; only at a late stage did articles by Schütz,[3] Schultz, and Reinhold direct the attention of the public to this great book. The reason for this delayed recognition no doubt lies in its unusual form and bad style. In the latter respect Kant deserves more censure than any other philosopher, especially when we consider that previously his style was better. The recently published collection of his minor writings contains his earliest essays, and we are surprised by their good and sometimes very witty style. He trilled these little essays to himself when he was already elaborating his great work in his head. He smiles in them like a soldier quietly arming for a battle where he is certain of victory. Among these minor writings, the following are particularly curious: 'Universal Natural History and Theory of the Sky', written as early as 1755; 'Observations on the Feeling of the Beautiful and Sublime', written ten years later, as was 'Dreams of a Spirit-Seer', full of good humour in the manner of French essays. The wit of a Kant, as he states his views in these short pieces, has something very peculiar about it. His wit grows aloft by clinging to his thought, and despite its weakness it thus attains a considerable height. Without such a support, indeed, the most abundant wit cannot thrive; like a vine deprived of a pole, it must crawl wretchedly on the ground and decay along with its most precious fruits.

But why did Kant write the *Critique of Pure Reason* in such a grey, dry, wrapping-papery style? I think that, having rejected the mathematical form of presentation adopted by the followers of Descartes, Leibniz, and Wolff, he feared that science might forfeit some of its dignity if it uttered its views in a light, agreeable, cheerful tone. He therefore gave it a stiff, abstract form, which coldly rebuffed any familiarity from the lower intellectual classes. He wanted to stand haughtily aloof from the popular philosophers of the day, who aimed at middle-class directness, and he clothed his ideas in the frosty officialese of the courtier. This reveals him as a philistine. But perhaps the carefully measured progress of Kant's ideas required a language that was even more carefully measured, and he was unable to create a better one. Only genius has a new word for a new idea. Immanuel Kant, however, was no genius. Being conscious of this deficiency, like the good Maximilian, Kant was all the more suspicious of genius, and in his *Critique of Judgement* he even asserts that genius has no business in science, as its efficacy belongs to the realm of art.

By the heavy, starchy style of his main work, Kant did a great deal of harm. For his unintelligent followers aped him in this external feature, and the superstition arose among us that if you wrote well, you were not a philosopher. After Kant, however, the mathematical form could not return to philosophy. In the *Critique of Pure Reason* he condemned this form mercilessly. Mathematical form in philosophy, he said, produced nothing but houses of cards, just as philosophical form in mathematics produced nothing but idle chatter. For in philosophy, he continued, there could be no definitions, as in mathematics where the definitions were not discursive but intuitive, that is, they could be demonstrated by immediate intuition; what were called definitions in philosophy were put forward only in a tentative, hypothetical manner; the correct definition appeared only at the end, as the result.

How is it that philosophers are so attached to the mathematical form of presentation? This attachment goes all the way back to Pythagoras, who denoted the principles of things by numbers. This was an idea of genius. From a number everything sensuous and finite has been stripped away, and yet it denotes a definite entity and its relation to another definite entity, while the latter, likewise denoted by a number, acquires the same non-sensuous and non-finite character. In this regard the number resembles ideas, which have the same character and the same relation to one another. The ideas that appear in our minds and in nature can aptly be denoted by numbers; but the number always remains the sign of the idea, not the idea itself. The master remains conscious of this distinction, but the pupil forgets it, and transmits to his own pupils nothing but a hieroglyphic system of numbers, mere ciphers, which are recited parrot-fashion with academic pride, while nobody any longer knows their living significance. The same applies to the other elements of mathematical form. Intellectual things are everlastingly in motion and cannot be pinned down; they are not to be pinned down by lines, triangles, rectangles, and circles, any more than by numbers. Thought can neither be counted nor measured.

Since my main concern is to assist the study of German philosophy in France, I always devote most of my discussion to those external features which can easily frighten off the layman if he has not been told about them beforehand. To any literary people who are thinking of editing Kant for the French public, I would especially point out that they can omit the part of his philosophy that merely serves to combat the absurdities of Wolffian philosophy. This polemic, which forces its way in everywhere, can bring the French no benefit, but only confusion.

As I have already said, the *Critique of Pure Reason* is Kant's main book, and his remaining writings can be regarded as to some degree dispensable, or at best as commentaries. The social significance of his main book will emerge from what follows.

Philosophers before Kant certainly pondered the sources of our knowledge, and, as we have already shown, they went in two different directions, depending on whether they assumed ideas *a priori* or ideas *a posteriori*; less attention was given to the faculty of knowledge itself, to the extent of our knowledge, or to the limits of our knowledge. This became Kant's task: he subjected our faculty of knowledge to a merciless examination, he plumbed the depths of this faculty and established all its boundaries. He found, of course, that we could know nothing at all about a great many things with which we previously supposed ourselves to be familiarly acquainted. That was very tiresome. But it was still useful to know which things we could know nothing about. Anyone who warns us against useless by-ways does us as good a service as someone who shows us the right way. Kant proved that we could know nothing about things as they are in themselves, but could know about them only in so far as they were reflected in our minds. Thus we are just like the prisoners whose melancholy situation Plato describes in the seventh book of the *Republic*. These unfortunates, chained by the necks and ankles, so that they cannot turn their heads, sit in a prison with an opening at the top, through which they get some light. This light, however, comes from a fire burning behind them, and separated from them by a low wall. Along this wall there walk people carrying all manner of statues and images made of wood and stone, and speaking to one another. The poor prisoners cannot see these people who are less tall than the wall, and of the statues being carried along, which project above the wall, they can see only the shadows moving on the wall opposite them; and they take these shadows to be real things, and, deceived by the echo in their prison, they think that it is the shadows that are speaking to one another.

Previous philosophy, which ran about sniffing at things, and collected and classified their characteristics, ceased on Kant's appearance. He made the human mind once more the subject of inquiry, and examined what manifested itself there. He is therefore not mistaken in comparing his philosophy with the method of Copernicus. Formerly, when the world was thought to stand still and the sun to go round it, astronomical calculations could not be made to agree; whereupon Copernicus made the sun stand still and the earth go round it, and behold! everything worked out perfectly. Formerly reason, like the sun, went round the world of appearances and tried to cast light on it; but Kant makes reason, the sun, stand still, and the world of appearances turns round it and is illuminated as it enters the realm of this sun.

After these brief words in which I have indicated Kant's task, everyone can understand why I consider the section of his book dealing with 'phenomena' and 'noumena', as he calls them, to be the most important part, the centre of his philosophy. Kant, you see, makes a distinction between the appearances of things and the things in themselves. As we can know about things only in so far as they manifest themselves in appearance, and as things do not show themselves to us as they are in themselves, Kant calls things, in so far as they appear, 'phenomena', and things as they are in themselves 'noumena'. It is only things as phenomena that we can know anything about; we can know nothing about things as noumena. The latter are merely problematic: we can say neither that they exist nor that they do not exist. Indeed, the word 'noumenon' is placed beside the word 'phenomenon' only to make it possible to talk about things that are knowable without referring to things that are unknowable.

Unlike many teachers whom I shall not name, Kant therefore did not divide things into phenomena and noumena, into things which exist for us and things which do not exist for us. That would be an Irish bull in philosophy. He intended only to provide a limiting concept.

God, according to Kant, is a noumenon. It follows from his argumentation that the transcendental ideal being whom we have hitherto called God is nothing but a fiction, produced by a natural illusion. Indeed, Kant shows that we can know nothing whatever about the noumenon God, and even that it will never be possible in future to demonstrate his existence. Above this section of the *Critique of Pure Reason* we shall inscribe Dante's words: 'Abandon hope!'

I am sure my readers will readily excuse me from giving a popular explanation of the part dealing with 'the proofs by which speculative reason may argue for the existence of a Supreme Being'. Although the actual refutation of these proofs does not take up much space and only appears in the second half of the book, it is introduced from the outset with the utmost calculation, and is one of the book's high points. It leads on to the 'critique of all speculative theology'. I must observe that when Kant attacks the three principal proofs for the existence of God, the ontological, the cosmological, and the physico-theological proofs, he succeeds, in my opinion, in confounding the latter two, but not the first. I do not know whether the terms I have just used are known here, and I therefore reproduce the passage from the *Critique of Pure Reason* in which Kant formulates the distinctions among them:

> *There are only three possible ways of proving the existence of God by means of speculative reason.* All the paths leading to this goal begin either from determinate experience and the specific constitution of the world of sense as thereby known, and ascend from it, in accordance with laws of causality, to the supreme cause outside the world; or they start from experience which is purely indeterminate, that is, from experience of existence in general; or finally they abstract from all experience, and argue completely *a priori*, from mere concepts, to the existence of a supreme cause. The first proof is the *physico-theological*, the second the *cosmological*, the third the *ontological*. There are, and there can be, no others.[4]

After working my way several times through Kant's main book I thought I could see the polemic against these established proofs for God's existence peeping out everywhere, and I would deal with this more fully if I were not restrained by a religious emotion. Even to see someone discussing the existence of God arouses in me such strange alarm, such uncanny unease, as I once felt at New Bedlam in London, when, surrounded only by madmen, I lost sight of my guide. 'God is everything that is,' and to doubt him is to doubt life itself; it is death.

However reprehensible it is to discuss the existence of God, it is all the more praiseworthy to reflect upon God's nature. Such reflection is a veritable religious ceremony: it draws our hearts away from what is transient and finite, and renders them aware of primal goodness and eternal harmony. This awareness makes the man of feeling tremble when he prays or contemplates ecclesiastical symbols; the thinker discovers this holy state of mind in the exercise of that sublime intellectual power which we call reason, and whose highest task is to study the nature of God. Particularly religious people are engaged in this task from childhood onwards; they feel a mysterious compulsion to do so as soon as reason first stirs in them. The author of these pages is joyously aware of such an early, innate religiosity, and it has never left him. God has always been the beginning and the end of all my thoughts. If I now ask: 'What is God? What is his nature?' I used to ask even as a small child: 'What is God like? What does he look like?' And at that time I could spend whole days gazing up into the sky, and in the evening I would be very downcast because I had never seen God's holy countenance, but only stupid grey cloud-masks. I was quite bewildered by the astronomical information which in those days, in the Enlightenment period, was inflicted even on the smallest children, and I could never get over my surprise that all these thousands of millions of stars were beautiful great globes just like ours, and that a single God ruled over this luminous swarm of worlds. Once, I remember, I saw God in a dream, high aloft in the remotest distance. He was looking cheerfully out of a little heavenly window, a pious old face with a little Jewish beard, and scattering a mass of seeds, which, as they fell from heaven, ripened and grew, so to speak, in infinite space, attaining an enormous size and turning into radiant, flourishing inhabited worlds, each of them as big as our own globe. I have never forgotten this vision, and in my dreams I often saw the cheerful old man scattering the seed of worlds from his little heavenly window; once I even saw him smack his lips, as our maid used to do when she threw barley to the hens. I could only see the falling seeds expanding into great luminous globes; but I could not see the enormous hens that I thought must be lurking somewhere with gaping beaks, to be fed with the scattered globes.

You smile, dear reader, at the enormous hens. Yet this childish view is not so very far removed from the view of the most mature deists. In order to supply some notion of the God outside the world, the Orient and the Occident have worn themselves out in childish hyperboles. With the infinity of space and time, however, the imagination of the deists has wearied itself in vain. This reveals their feebleness, the untenability of their world-view, of the idea of God's nature. We cannot therefore be very upset when this idea is confounded. Kant, however, actually caused them this grief by destroying their arguments for the existence of God.

Rescuing the ontological proof would bring no particular benefit to deism, since this proof can likewise be used for pantheism. To make myself more clearly understood I will remark that the ontological proof is the one which Descartes put forward and which was formulated long before, in the Middle Ages, in the form of a moving prayer, by Anselm of Canterbury.[5] Indeed, it could be said that St Augustine put forward the ontological proof in the second book *De libero arbitrio.*

As I said, I shall refrain from a popularizing explanation of Kant's polemic against these proofs. I shall content myself with asserting that deism has since faded away from the realm of speculative reason. The sorrowful news of its death may need a few centuries to penetrate everywhere – but we have long since gone into mourning for it. *De profundis!*[6]

Did you think we could go home now? By heaven! there is another play to be performed. After tragedy comes farce. So far Immanuel Kant has played the tragic part of the most inexorable philosopher, he has stormed heaven, he has put the entire garrison to the sword, the Supreme Lord of the world, unproved, is weltering in his blood, there is no longer any universal compassion, no fatherly love, no reward in the next life for self-denial in this one, the immortality of the soul is about to give up the ghost – it's gasping and groaning – and old

Lampe is standing by with his umbrella under his arm, a sorrowful spectator, sweating with terror, and the tears are running down his face. Then Immanuel Kant has mercy, showing that he is not only a great philosopher but also a good man, and he thinks for a bit, and he says with a mixture of kindness and irony: 'Old Lampe must have a God, otherwise the poor man can't be happy – but man is meant to be happy in this world – so says practical reason – all right then, practical reason may as well guarantee the existence of God.' In consequence of this argument Kant distinguishes between theoretical reason and practical reason, and with the latter, as though with a magic wand, he restores to life the corpse of deism, which theoretical reason had killed.

Did Kant undertake this resurrection, by any chance, not just for the sake of old Lampe, but also for the sake of the police? Or was he really following his convictions? By destroying all proofs of the existence of God, did he want to show us how unpleasant it is to know nothing about God's existence? He acted almost as wisely as my Westphalian friend who broke all the lights on Weender Street in Göttingen, and then, standing in the dark, delivered a long speech about the practical necessity of street-lights, which he had broken only theoretically, in order to prove to us that we could see nothing without them.

I mentioned earlier that the *Critique of Pure Reason* did not make the least sensation on its appearance. Only a few years later, when some acute philosophers had written elucidations of this book, did it arouse the public's attention, and in 1789 nothing was talked about in Germany save Kant's philosophy, and it already had a wealth of commentaries, chrestomathies, explanations, remarks, apologias, and so forth. You need only glance at the first catalogue of philosophical studies that comes to hand, and the prodigious number of writings about Kant that then appeared will testify sufficiently to the intellectual agitation that proceeded from this one man. Some people revealed wild enthusiasm, others bitter hostility, while many waited open-mouthed for the outcome of this intellectual revolution. We had insurrections in the intellectual world, just as you had in the material world, and in tearing down the old dogmatism we were as excited as you were at the storming of the Bastille. In our case, too, admittedly, there were only a couple of broken-down old soldiers to defend dogmatism, that is, Wolffian philosophy. It was a revolution, and it was not lacking in atrocities. Among the party of the past, it was the genuine good Christians who were least indignant at these atrocities. Indeed, they wished for still worse atrocities, so that things would come to a head and the counter-revolution could begin all the sooner as a necessary reaction. We had pessimists in philosophy, just as you had them in politics. Many of our pessimists carried self-deception so far that they fancied Kant was secretly in league with them and had only destroyed the previous proofs of God's existence so that the world might realize that knowledge of God could never be attained through reason, and that people should cling to revealed religion.

Kant brought about this intellectual commotion, not so much through the content of his writings, as through the critical spirit that prevails in them, and which now forced its way into all the sciences. All disciplines were seized by it. Indeed, even poetry was not spared its influence. Schiller,[7] for instance, was a mighty Kantian, and his aesthetic views are impregnated by the spirit of Kantian philosophy. This philosophy, because of its abstract dryness, was extremely harmful to literature and the fine arts. Fortunately it did not meddle with cookery.

The people of Germany are not easy to move, but if they have once been moved on to a particular track, they will follow that track to its end with the most stubborn perseverance. We revealed this character in religious matters. We have now shown it also in philosophy. Shall we move forward as consistently in politics?

Thanks to Kant, Germany had been drawn on to the philosophical track, and philosophy became a national affair. An array of great thinkers suddenly sprouted from the soil of Germany as if by magic. One day, when German philosophy, like the French Revolution, finds its Thiers and its Mignet,[8] its history will provide equally remarkable reading, and the German will read it with pride and the Frenchman with admiration.

Among Kant's pupils, the pre-eminence soon belonged to Johann Gottlieb Fichte.

I almost despair of being able to convey an accurate idea of this man's significance. In Kant's case we had only a book to consider. Here, however, we have to consider not only the book but also a man, in whom thought and personality are one, and it is in this magnificent unity that they affect posterity. We therefore have not only a philosophy to discuss, but also a character which, so to speak, determined it, and to understand the influence of both, an account of the historical setting would probably be required as well. What an immense task! We shall undoubtedly be fully forgiven for offering only meagre scraps of information.

Even Fichte's thought is very hard to explain. Here, too, we encounter peculiar difficulties. They concern not only its content, but also its form and method: two things which we should be glad to introduce to foreigners at the outset. First, therefore, a few words about the Fichtean method. Initially it is entirely borrowed from Kant. Soon, however, this method is modified by the nature of its subject-matter. Kant, you see, had only offered a critique, that is something negative; Fichte, however, put forward a system, hence something positive. Because of its lack of a definite system, some people have tried to deny Kantian philosophy the title of philosophy. With respect to Immanuel Kant himself, they were right, but certainly not with respect to the Kantians, who constructed quite a number of definite systems from Kant's theorems. In his earlier writings, as I said, Fichte remains faithful to the Kantian method, so that when his first treatise appeared anonymously it could be mistaken for a work by Kant. When, however, Fichte later puts forward a system, he finds himself involved in a zealous and obstinate programme of construction, and when he has constructed the entire world, he begins, just as zealously and obstinately, to provide logical demonstrations for his construction, starting at the top and working down. In this constructing and demonstrating, Fichte manifests what might be called an abstract passion. His presentation, like his system itself, soon becomes dominated by subjectivity. Kant, on the other hand, places the idea in front of himself, dissects it, and analyses it into its finest fibres, and his *Critique of Pure Reason* is, as it were, the anatomical theatre of the mind. He himself remains cold and impassive throughout the operation, like a true surgeon.

The form of Fichte's writings corresponds to their method. It is a living form, but with all the defects of life: it is restless and bewildering. In order to remain alive, Fichte spurns the usual terminology of philosophy, which seems to him like something dead; but without it he is much harder to understand. In general, he has some very odd notions about being understood. When Reinhold agreed with him, Fichte declared that nobody understood him better than Reinhold.

When the latter came to differ from him, Fichte declared that he had never understood him. When he differed from Kant, he asserted in print that Kant did not understand himself. Here I am touching on the comic side of our philosophers. They constantly complain of not being understood. When Hegel was on his death-bed, he said: 'Only one man ever understood me,' and then added crossly: 'and he didn't understand me either.'

As regards its intrinsic content, Fichte's philosophy has no great significance. It has given society no results. The content of Fichte's teaching is of some interest in so far as it is one of the most curious phases that German philosophy ever passed through, as it manifests the sterility of idealism when taken to its ultimate consequences, and as it forms the necessary transition to the contemporary philosophy of nature. Since its content is of more historical and scholarly than social interest, I shall summarize it as briefly as possible.

The problem Fichte proposes is this. What grounds have we for supposing that our conceptions of things correspond to things outside ourselves? And he solves this problem by maintaining that all things have reality only in our minds.

Just as Kant's main work is the *Critique of Pure Reason*, so Fichte's main work is the *Science of Knowledge*. The latter book is, so to speak, a continuation of the former. The science of knowledge likewise refers the mind back to itself. But where Kant analyses, Fichte constructs. The science of knowledge begins with an abstract formula (I = I), it brings forth the world creatively from the depths of the mind, it rejoins the parts which analysis had separated, it goes back along the path of abstraction until it arrives at the phenomenal world. This phenomenal world can then be explained by the mind as necessary actions on the part of intelligence.

There is still the special problem in Fichte that he claims that the mind observes itself while active. The 'I', or the self, is supposed to reflect upon its intellectual actions while carrying them out. Thought is supposed to overhear itself thinking, as it gradually becomes warmer and warmer until it is cooked. This operation reminds us of the monkey that sat by the fire in front of a copper cauldron and cooked its own tail. For it argued that the true art of cookery consists not in mere objective cooking, but also in becoming subjectively aware of cooking.

It is a curious fact that Fichte's philosophy has always had to endure many satirical attacks. I once saw a caricature depicting a Fichtean goose. Its liver was so big that it no longer knew whether it was the goose or its liver, and on its belly was written 'I = I'. Jean Paul satirized Fichte's philosophy mercilessly in a book entitled *Clavis Fichteana* (*The Key to Fichte*). The claim that idealism, taken to its logical conclusion, must end by denying the reality of matter seemed to the great public a joke that had gone too far. We laughed heartily at the Fichtean self that produced the entire phenomenal world merely by thinking. Our scoffers were encouraged by a misconception that became too widespread for me to overlook it. The vast majority supposed that the Fichtean self was the self of Johann Gottlieb Fichte, and that this individual self denied the existence of anything else. 'What impertinence!' exclaimed the good people, 'this fellow doesn't believe that we exist, though we are much stouter than he is, and, as mayors and actuaries, we are actually his superiors!' The ladies asked: 'Doesn't he at least believe in his wife's existence? No? And Madame Fichte puts up with that?'

The Fichtean self, however, is not any individual self, but the universal world-self which has attained full consciousness. Fichtean thinking is not the thinking done by an individual, a particular person called Johann Gottlieb Fichte; rather, it is a universal thinking that manifests itself in an individual. Just as we say 'It is raining', 'It is snowing', and so forth, Fichte ought not to say 'I am thinking', but rather 'It is thinking', 'The universal world-thought is thinking in me.'

Once, when I was drawing a comparison between the French Revolution and German philosophy, I compared Fichte, more in jest than in earnest, with Napoleon. But there are in fact significant similarities. Fichte appears on the scene after the Kantians have completed their terrorist work of destruction, just as Napoleon appeared after the Convention, likewise employing a critique of pure reason, had demolished the whole of the past. Napoleon and Fichte represent the great, inexorable self in which thought and deed are one, and the colossal edifices that both can construct testify to a colossal will. But since this will acknowledges no limits, its edifices immediately perish, and both the science of knowledge and the Napoleonic Empire collapse and disappear as quickly as they sprang up.

The Empire is part of history, but the commotion that the Emperor produced in the world has not yet died down, and the present age still lives on this commotion. The same is true of Fichte's philosophy. It has entirely perished, but people's minds are still agitated by the ideas to which Fichte gave voice, and the effect of his words is incalculable. Even if transcendental idealism was wholly mistaken, Fichte's writings still contained a proud independence, a love of freedom, a manly dignity, which exercised a salutary influence, especially on young people. Fichte's conception of the self was in perfect accord with his unbending, obstinate, iron character. The doctrine of such an all-powerful self could perhaps stem only from such a character, and by taking root in such a doctrine, such a character could only become yet more unbending, yet more obstinate, yet more iron-clad.[9]

I have shown how Fichte's philosophy, though constructed from the flimsiest abstractions, nevertheless revealed an iron inflexibility in its arguments as they ascended to the most daring pinnacle. Early one morning, however, we observe a great change in it. It becomes meek and mild, flowery and tearful. The Titan of idealism, who climbed up to heaven on an intellectual ladder and poked about in its empty rooms with a bold hand, now dwindles into a prostrate Christian creature that sighs about love. This is Fichte's second period, which concerns us here very little. His entire system undergoes the most disconcerting modifications. At that time he wrote the book which you have recently translated, *The Vocation of Man*. A similar book, *Directions for a Holy Life*, belongs to the same period.

Naturally Fichte, that stubborn man, would never confess to this great transformation. He claimed that his philosophy was the same as ever, only with its terminology changed and improved, and that nobody had ever understood him. He claimed also that the philosophy of nature, which was emerging in Germany at that time and supplanting idealism, was basically his own system, and that his pupil Herr Joseph Schelling, who had abandoned him and introduced this new philosophy, had merely altered its terminology and extended his old doctrine by some unedifying additions.

Here we arrive at a new phase of German thought. We have mentioned the name Joseph Schelling and the term 'philosophy of nature'; since the former is almost entirely unknown here, and since the term 'philosophy of nature' is not generally understood, I must explain the significance of both. We cannot, of course, do so exhaustively in these pages; a later book will be devoted to such a task. We want only to rebut some persistent errors, and to pay some attention to the social importance of the above-mentioned philosophy.

It should be mentioned at the outset that Fichte was not so far wrong in asserting that Herr Joseph Schelling's teachings were really his own, with some reformulations and elaborations. Like Herr Joseph Schelling, Fichte also taught that there was only one being, the self, the absolute; he taught the identity of the ideal and the real. In the *Science of Knowledge*, as I have shown, Fichte tried to construct the real from the ideal by an intellectual construction. Herr Joseph Schelling, however, did things the other way round: he sought to educe the ideal from the real. To express myself yet more clearly: starting from the principle that thought and nature are one and the same, Fichte arrives at the phenomenal world by means of a mental operation; he creates nature from thought, the real from the ideal. Conversely, while Herr Schelling starts from the same principle, for him the phenomenal world becomes pure ideas, nature becomes thought, the real becomes the ideal. Thus both directions, that taken by Fichte and that taken by Herr Schelling, complement each other after a fashion. For, according to the above-mentioned supreme principle, philosophy could be divided into two parts, and in one part would be shown how nature, starting from the idea, acquires phenomenal reality; in the other part would be shown how nature dissolves into pure ideas. Philosophy could thus be divided into transcendental idealism and philosophy of nature. These two tendencies have indeed been recognized by Herr Schelling, and he pursues the former in his *System of Transcendental Idealism* and the latter in his *Ideas for a Philosophy of Nature*.

I mention these works, one of which appeared in 1797 and the other in 1800, only because these two complementary tendencies are already formulated in their titles, not because they contain any kind of complete system. No, such a thing is not to be found in any of Herr Schelling's books. Unlike Kant and Fichte, he has no principal work that can be regarded as the centre of his philosophy. It would be an injustice to judge Herr Schelling by the size of a book and by the rigour of the letter. Instead one must read his books in chronological order, pursuing the gradual development of his thought, and holding firmly to his basic idea. In fact, it often seems to me necessary also to distinguish where his thinking ends and his poetry begins. For Herr Schelling is one of those creatures whom nature has endowed with more of an inclination for poetry than poetic potency, and who, unable to satisfy the daughters of Parnassus, have fled into the forests of philosophy, where they live in sterile wedlock with abstract hamadryads. Their feelings are poetic, but their instrument, the word, is weak; they labour in vain to find an artistic form in which to communicate their thoughts and insights. Poetry is Herr Schelling's forte and his weakness. This is the main difference between himself and Fichte, both to his advantage and to his disadvantage. Fichte is only a philosopher, and his power consists in dialectic and his strength in demonstrative argument. The latter, however, is Herr Schelling's weak point: he prefers intuitive awareness, he does not feel at home on the chilly heights of logic, he likes to stray into the flowery vales of symbolism, and his philosophical strength consists in construction. This, however, is an intellectual ability which is found as often among mediocre poets as among the best philosophers.

After this last hint, it will be readily understandable that in the part of philosophy which is mere transcendental idealism Herr Schelling neither did nor could do anything more than parrot the words of Fichte, while in the philosophy of nature, where he could busy himself with flowers and stars, he could not help flowering and shining mightily. This tendency, therefore, was not confined to him, but was also pursued by his like-minded friends, and the boisterous behaviour that resulted was, so to speak, simply the reaction of poetasters against the abstract intellectualism of previous philosophy. Like boys let out of school after groaning all day in fusty classrooms under their burden of Latin vocabulary and mathematical figures, Herr Schelling's pupils rushed out into nature, into fragrant, sunny reality, and shouted with joy, and turned somersaults, and kicked up no end of a racket.

The expression 'Herr Schelling's pupils' is likewise not to be taken in its usual sense. Herr Schelling himself says that it was only in the manner of the ancient poets that he wanted to form a school, a school of poets, in which nobody is bound to a particular doctrine or by a particular discipline, but everyone obeys the spirit and reveals it in his own way. He could also have said that he was founding a school of prophets, in which inspired persons would begin to prophesy as the fancy took them, and in whatever language they pleased. This is exactly what his disciples did when prompted by the Master's spirit:

even the dullest minds began to prophesy, each in a different tongue, and there was a great Pentecost in philosophy.

The philosophy of nature here permits us to observe how the most portentous and magnificent matters can be used for mere mummery and buffoonery, and how a great idea can be compromised by a horde of cowardly rogues and melancholy clowns. But the philosophy of nature cannot be blamed for the ridicule brought to it by Herr Schelling's school of prophets or poets. For the idea of the philosophy of nature is at bottom none other than Spinoza's idea – pantheism.

The teaching of Spinoza and the philosophy of nature, as put forward by Schelling in his better periods, are essentially one and the same. After the Germans had spurned Locke's materialism and taken Leibniz's idealism to extremes, only to find it likewise unfruitful, they eventually reached Descartes's third son, Spinoza. Philosophy has once again completed a great cycle, and one could say that this is the same cycle that it passed through two thousand years ago in Greece. A closer comparison of these two cycles, however, reveals an essential difference. The Greeks had just as bold sceptics as we have; the Eleatics[10] denied the reality of the external world quite as positively as our recent transcendental idealists. Plato, as well as Herr Schelling, rediscovered the intellectual world in the phenomenal world. But we have an advantage over the Greeks, as well as over the Cartesian schools; we have an advantage over them, namely:

We began our philosophical cycle with an examination of the sources of human knowledge, with the *Critique of Pure Reason* by our Immanuel Kant.

Having mentioned Kant, I can add to the above reflections that the proof of God's existence which Kant left intact – that is, what is known as the moral proof – was demolished with great éclat by Herr Schelling. I have already remarked, however, that this proof was not particularly strong, and may have owed its survival only to Kant's kindness. Herr Schelling's God is the God-Universe of Spinoza. At least, this was so in 1801, in the second volume of the *Journal of Speculative Physics*. Here God is the absolute identity of nature and thought, of matter and spirit, and absolute identity is not the cause of the universe but the universe itself, hence it is the God-Universe. In it there are no oppositions or divisions: hence absolute identity is also absolute totality. A year later Herr Schelling had developed his God still further; this occurred in a work entitled *Bruno, or the Divine or Natural Principle of Things*. This title recalls the noblest martyr for our doctrine, Giordano Bruno of Nola, of glorious memory. The Italians maintain that Herr Schelling borrowed his best ideas from old Bruno,[11] and they accuse him of plagiarism. They are wrong; for there is no plagiarism in philosophy. In 1804 Herr Schelling's God at last appeared fully fledged in a work entitled *Philosophy and Religion*. Here we find the doctrine of the absolute completely worked out. Here the absolute is expressed in three formulae. The first is categorical: the absolute is neither the ideal nor the real (neither spirit nor matter), but the identity of both. The second formula is hypothetical: if there is a subject and an object, the absolute is the essential equality of both. The third formula is disjunctive: there is only one being, but this one being can simultaneously or alternately be regarded as wholly ideal or as wholly real. The first formula is entirely negative; the second presupposes a condition which is harder to grasp than what depends on it; and the third formula is entirely that of Spinoza, to the effect that absolute substance can be known either as thought or as extension. Herr Schelling could therefore get no further than Spinoza along the philosophical path, since the absolute can only be grasped in the form of these two attributes, thought and extension. But Herr Schelling is now leaving the path of philosophy and seeking to attain to the contemplation of the absolute itself by a kind of mystical intuition; he is trying to contemplate it in its centre, in its essence, where it is neither something ideal nor something real, neither thought nor extension, neither subject nor object, neither spirit nor matter, but . . . how can I tell!

It is here that Herr Schelling's philosophy ends and his poetry, or rather folly, begins. It is here too, however, that he is most eagerly listened to by a host of windbags who are only too happy to abandon the calm pursuit of thought and to imitate the whirling dervishes. The dervishes, as our friend Jules David[12] recounts, spin round and round until they lose sight of the objective and the subjective worlds and both coalesce into a white nothingness that is neither real nor ideal; until they see what is invisible, hear what is inaudible, hear colours and see sounds; until the absolute becomes manifest to their senses.

With the attempt to apprehend the absolute intellectually, Herr Schelling's philosophical career has, I think, come to an end. A greater thinker now appears on the scene, one who develops the philosophy of nature into a complete system, uses this synthesis to explain the entire world of phenomena, extends the great ideas of his predecessors by greater ideas, pursues them through all the disciplines, and thus gives them a scientific foundation. He is a pupil of Herr Schelling, but a pupil who gradually usurped all his master's power in the realm of philosophy, came to dwarf the latter in his greed for power, and finally cast him into obscurity. This is the great Hegel, the greatest philosopher Germany has produced since Leibniz. There is no question that he is far superior to Kant and Fichte. He has the sharpness of the one and the strength of the other, and at the same time he has a constitutive calmness, an intellectual harmony, that we do not find in Kant and Fichte, since it is more the revolutionary spirit that prevails in them. To compare this man with Herr Joseph Schelling is flatly impossible; for Hegel was a man of character. And even if, like Herr Schelling, he provided some very disturbing justifications for the existing order in church and state, he after all did this for a state that, at least in theory, acknowledges the principle of progress, and for a church that regards the principle of free inquiry as the element in which it lives; and he made no secret of what he was doing, he was frank about all his intentions. Herr Schelling, on the other hand, twists like a worm in the ante-rooms of an absolutism which is both practical and theoretical, and he does menial tasks in the Jesuit cave where fetters are forged for the mind; and at the same time he would like us to believe that he is still the same enlightened man he once was, he denies his denial, and to the disgrace of apostasy he adds the cowardice of lying!

We must not conceal it, whether out of piety or calculation, and we shall not suppress it: the man who was once bolder than anyone else in Germany in enunciating the religion of pantheism, who proclaimed the sanctification of nature and the restoration of man to his divine rights, this man has become a renegade from his own teachings, he has abandoned the altar that he himself consecrated, he has crept back into the believers' stable of the past, he is now a good Catholic and preaches a transcendent, personal God, 'who committed the folly of creating the world'. Let the old believers ring their bells and sing the Kyrie Eleison to celebrate such a conversion: it still does nothing to confirm their opinions, it proves only that man leans towards Catholicism when he grows old and weary, when he has lost his physical and intellectual powers, when he can no longer enjoy pleasures or think. So many free-thinkers have been converted on their death-beds – but don't make a song and dance about it! These conversion stories belong, at most, to pathology, and would provide only poor testimony for your cause. In the end they prove only that you were unable to convert these free-thinkers as long as they were walking about under God's free sky with unimpaired senses and had full command of their reason.

I think Ballanche[13] says that it is a law of nature that initiators must die as soon as they have completed their work of initiation. Alas, my dear Ballanche, this is only partially true, and I would sooner say that when the work of initiation is complete, the initiator dies – or becomes a renegade. And thus we may be able to alleviate somewhat the harsh judgement that the thinking part of Germany has passed on Herr Schelling; we may be able to transform the heavy, thick contempt that weighs upon him into quiet compassion, and to explain his apostasy from his own teachings only as a consequence of a law of nature. This law states that anyone who has devoted all his powers to uttering an idea, or to putting it into practice, will afterwards, once the idea has been uttered or put into practice, collapse with exhaustion – will collapse either into the arms of death or into the arms of his former opponents.

After such an explanation we can perhaps comprehend certain phenomena of our day which are even more blatant and which cause us deep distress. We may comprehend why men who have sacrificed everything for their opinion, who have struggled and suffered for its sake, at last, when they are victorious, abandon that opinion and go over to the enemy's camp! After such an explanation I may also be permitted to point out that not only Herr Joseph Schelling, but also Fichte and Kant, in a certain sense, may be accused of apostasy. Fichte died in good time, before his apostasy from his own philosophy could become glaringly obvious. And Kant betrayed the *Critique of Pure Reason* by writing the *Critique of Practical Reason*. The initiator dies – or becomes a renegade.

I do not know why it is, but my feelings are so saddened and subdued by this last sentence that at present I am unable to utter the remaining bitter truths that concern the Herr Schelling of today. Let us rather praise the former Schelling, whose memory will remain green and imperishable in the annals of German thought; for the former Schelling, like Kant and Fichte, represents one of the great phases of our philosophical revolution, which I have compared in these pages with the phases of the political revolution in France. Indeed, if one sees Kant as the terrorist Convention and Fichte as the Napoleonic Empire, then one can see Herr Schelling as the reactionary Restoration which followed. But initially it was a restoration in the good sense. Herr Schelling restored nature to its legitimate rights, he strove to reconcile spirit and nature, he wanted to reunite both in the everlasting world-soul. He restored that great philosophy of nature that we find in the ancient Greek philosophers and that needed Socrates to guide it further into the human heart, after which it dissolved into ideality. He restored that great philosophy of nature that, surreptitiously sprouting from the old pantheistic religion of the Germans, displayed its finest flowers in the age of Paracelsus, but was crushed by the introduction of Cartesianism. Alas! in the end he restored things which enable us to compare him in the bad sense, too, with the French Restoration. Yet the public's reason would no longer put up with him, and he was cast down in disgrace from his intellectual throne. Hegel, his palace mayor, took the crown from his head, and shaved his pate, and thereafter the deposed Schelling led the life of a miserable little monk in Munich, a city whose priest-ridden character is evident from its very name: in Latin, *Monacho monachorum*. There I saw him tottering about in ghostly fashion with his great pale eyes and his dismal, apathetic face, a lamentable image of decayed magnificence. Hegel, however, accepted the crown – and some royal ointment as well, unfortunately – in Berlin, and ruled over German philosophy thereafter.

Our philosophical revolution has come to an end. Its great circle was closed by Hegel. Since then we have seen only the development and elaboration of the philosophy of nature. The latter, as I said, has forced its way into all the sciences and has produced extraordinary and splendid achievements. A great deal that was less admirable, as I have likewise indicated, was bound to emerge as well. These phenomena are so diverse that it would take a whole book to list them all. This is the really interesting and colourful part of our philosophical history. I am convinced, however, that it is more beneficial for the French to learn nothing at all about this part. For such information might help to make people's minds in France yet more confused; many propositions of the philosophy of nature, torn from their context, could do great damage among you. I know this much, that if you had known about the German philosophy of nature four years ago, you could never have made the July Revolution. This deed required a concentration of your thoughts and energies, a noble one-sidedness, an arrogant frivolity, such as only your old school of thought permitted. Your enthusiasm would have been dampened and your courage paralysed by the philosophical absurdities with which legitimacy and the Catholic doctrine of the Incarnation could have been upheld. I therefore consider it important for the history of the world that your great eclectic[14] who at that time wanted to instruct you in German philosophy did not understand the first thing about it. His providential ignorance was salutary for France and for the whole of mankind.

Alas! though the philosophy of nature has produced the most splendid fruits in many areas of knowledge, especially the natural sciences proper, in others it has engendered the most pernicious weeds. While Oken,[15] a thinker of the utmost genius and one of Germany's greatest citizens, was discovering new worlds of thought and arousing the enthusiasm of young Germans for the basic rights of man, for freedom and equality, at the very same time, alas! Adam Müller was lecturing on how the nations should be stabled and fattened according to principles derived from the philosophy of nature. Meanwhile Herr Görres was preaching the obscurantism of the Middle Ages, taking from the philosophy of nature the view that the state is only a tree whose organic articulation requires a trunk, branches and leaves, all of which can so readily be found in the hierarchical corporations of the Middle Ages. At the same time Herr Steffens was proclaiming the philosophical law whereby the peasant estate is distinguished from the noble estate by the fact that nature intends the peasant to work without enjoyment, while the noble is entitled to enjoyment without work. Indeed, I am told that a few months ago a squireen from Westphalia, a jackanapes named Haxthausen,[16] I think, published a book in which he urges the royal government of Prussia to consider the consistent parallelism demonstrated by philosophy in the entire organism of the world, and to introduce sharper distinctions between the political estates; for he claims that just as there are four elements –

fire, air, water, and earth – in nature, so there are four analogous elements in society – nobility, clergy, townsfolk, and peasants.

When such depressing follies were seen sprouting from philosophy and producing the most pernicious blossoms; when it was observed that young Germans, immersed in metaphysical abstractions, forgot the most pressing demands of the age and were rendered unfit for practical life; then patriots and friends of liberty could hardly fail to feel justly irritated with philosophy, and a few went so far as to condemn it outright as idle and useless shadow-boxing.

We shall not be so foolish as to make a serious attempt to refute these malcontents. German philosophy is a matter of importance that affects the entire human race, and only our last descendants will be able to decide whether we deserve praise or censure for elaborating our philosophy first and our revolution only afterwards. I rather think that a methodical nation like ourselves had to begin with the Reformation; only then could we transfer our attention to philosophy, and only after completing our philosophy could we turn to the political revolution. I find this sequence very sensible. The heads that philosophy has used for thinking can be chopped off later by the revolution and used for whatever purpose it likes. Philosophy, however, could never have done anything with the heads that the revolution would have chopped off if it had come first. But don't worry, you German republicans; although the German revolution will follow Kant's critiques, Fichte's transcendental idealism, not to mention the philosophy of nature, it will not turn out any milder or gentler for all that. These doctrines have assisted the development of revolutionary forces which are only waiting for the day when they can burst forth and fill the world with horror and admiration. Kantians will emerge who are as devoid of piety for the phenomenal world as Kant was towards God; they will ravage the soil of our European life mercilessly with swords and axes in order to root out the last vestiges of the past. Armed Fichteans will appear on the scene, whose fanatical wills cannot be restrained by either fear or selfishness; for they live in the spirit and defy matter, like the early Christians, who likewise could not be overcome by physical torments or physical pleasures. Indeed, in a social upheaval such transcendental idealists would be even more inflexible than the early Christians; for the latter endured earthly torments in order to attain to the bliss of heaven, while the transcendental idealist regards the torments themselves as mere illusion and is inaccessibly entrenched behind his own ideas. More terrible than any of these, however, would be the philosophers of nature, if they intervened actively in a German revolution and identified themselves with the work of destruction. For if the Kantian's hand strikes strongly and surely, because no traditional veneration stirs his heart; if the Fichtean courageously defies every danger, because for him it has no existence in reality; then the philosopher of nature will be frightful because he will enter into an alliance with the primeval forces of nature, because he can summon up the demonic powers of ancient Germanic pantheism, and because he will feel anew that lust for battle that we find in the ancient Germans – one that does not fight to destroy, nor to win, but only for the sake of fighting. Christianity, and this is its finest achievement, quietened this brutal Germanic lust for battle to some degree, but could not eradicate it entirely, and if one day that subduing talisman, the cross, is broken, then the savagery of the ancient warriors will rattle its weapons afresh in the senseless rage of the Berserkers of which the Nordic poets tell in song and story. The talisman is rotten, and the day will come when it collapses lamentably; then the old stone gods will arise from the forgotten rubble, and Thor with his gigantic hammer will spring aloft and smash the Gothic cathedrals. When you hear the thunder and crashing, you children next door, you French people, then take care not to meddle in the work that we will be accomplishing in Germany; or else it might be the worse for you. Take care not to fan the fire, take care not to extinguish it; you could easily burn your fingers in the flames.

Do not laugh at my advice, the advice of a dreamer warning you against Kantians, Fichteans, and philosophers of nature. Do not laugh at the visionary who expects the same revolution to occur in the phenomenal realm as has happened in the realm of the mind. Thought precedes action as lightning precedes thunder. German thunder, of course, being German, is not very agile, and rolls along rather slowly; but it will arrive in due course, and when you hear such a crash as has never yet been heard in the history of the world, then you will know that German thunder has finally reached its goal. When its sound is heard, the eagles will drop down dead from the sky, and the lions in the remotest deserts of Africa will draw in their tails and creep into their royal caves. A play will be performed in Germany, compared with which the French Revolution will seem a mere inoffensive idyll. At present, indeed, things are fairly quiet; and even if this or that person gesticulates somewhat vigorously, do not believe that, when the day comes, they will step forward as real actors. These are only the little dogs running about in the empty arena, barking and snapping at each other, until the moment comes for the host of gladiators to arrive and fight to the death.

And that moment will come. Other nations will surround Germany, as though sitting on the steps of an amphitheatre, to watch the great combat. I advise you, you French people, to keep very quiet, and, as you value your lives, take care not to applaud. We might well misunderstand you and silence you somewhat roughly, in our impolite manner; for if we were sometimes able to overcome you in our state of servile discontent, we should be much better able to do so when drunk with the exhilaration of freedom. You know yourselves what one is capable of in such a state; and you are no longer in such a state. Have a care! I have your welfare at heart, and that is why I am telling you the harsh truth. You have more to fear from a liberated Germany than from the entire Holy Alliance with all its Croats and Cossacks. For, firstly, you are not liked in Germany, which is almost incomprehensible, since you are so likeable, and when you were in Germany you took so much pains to appeal at least to the better and fairer half of the German nation. And if this half did like you, it is the half that does not bear arms and whose friendship can therefore do you little good. I have never been able to understand the charges that are actually brought against you. Once, in a Göttingen beer-cellar, a young Old German declared that we must be revenged upon the French for Conradin von Staufen, whom they beheaded at Naples. No doubt you have long since forgotten this. We, however, forget nothing. You can see that if we feel like picking a quarrel with you, we shall be at no loss for good reasons. At all events I advise you therefore to be on your guard. Whatever happens in Germany, whether the Prince of Kyritz[17] or Dr Wirth attains power, maintain your weapons and stay at your posts with your rifles at the ready. I have your welfare at heart, and I was almost terrified when I learnt recently that your ministers intended to disarm France.

Since you are innately classical, despite the Romantic phase you are going through, you know Mount Olympus. Among the naked gods and goddesses who disport themselves there amid nectar and ambrosia, you can see one goddess who, though surrounded by such joys and delights, always wears a breastplate and keeps a helmet on her head and a spear in her hand. She is the goddess of wisdom.

MEMOIRS

I HAVE indeed, dear lady, endeavoured to record the memorable events of my time, in so far as I myself encountered them either as spectator or as victim, as truthfully and faithfully as possible. However, I was obliged to destroy wellnigh half of these notes, which I had complacently entitled *Memoirs*, partly from unfortunate family considerations, and partly from religious scruples. Since then I have taken pains to fill out the resulting gaps as best I could, but I fear that posthumous obligations or a self-tormenting depression may force me to subject my *Memoirs* to a new *auto-da-fé* before my death, and whatever is then spared by the flames may never see the daylight of publication. I shall be sure not to name the friends whom I am entrusting with the care of my manuscript and the execution of my last will and testament in regard to it; I do not wish to expose them, after my demise, to the importunity of the idle public and thus tempt them to disobey their instructions. Such disobedience is something I have always found inexcusable; it is an immoral and improper action to publish even a line by a writer that he himself did not intend for the public at large. This applies particularly to letters addressed to private individuals. Anyone who prints or publishes them commits a felony that deserves to be despised.

After these confessions, dear lady, you will readily understand that I cannot permit you to read my memoirs and correspondence as you desire. However, a courtier of your charm, such as I have always been, cannot refuse any of your wishes outright, and as testimony of my good will I shall find another way of satisfying the gracious curiosity that springs from an affectionate concern for my fortunes. It is for this purpose that I wrote the following pages, and here you will find an ample amount of the biographical information that interests you. Everything significant and characteristic has here been faithfully reported, and the interaction of external occurrences and inward psychological events will reveal to you the *signatura* of my very being. The veil falls from my soul, and you may contemplate it in its beautiful nakedness. It has no stains, only wounds. Alas! and only wounds inflicted by friends, not by enemies!

The night is mute. There is nothing but the rain outside splashing on the roofs and the autumn wind sighing sorrowfully. At this moment my wretched sick-room is almost voluptuously cosy, and I am sitting, free from pain, in my big arm-chair. Then, though the latch does not move, your lovely image enters, and you lie on the cushions at my feet. Lay your beautiful head on my knee and listen without looking up. I will tell you the fairy-tale of my life. If large drops should sometimes fall on your curly head, stay calm; it is not the rain trickling through the roof. Do not cry, just squeeze my hand in silence.

What a sublime emotion must animate a Church dignitary as he gazes down upon the seething market-place where thousands of people are kneeling before him, their heads bared, devoutly awaiting his blessing! In the Italian travel-book by Counsellor Moritz[1] I once read a description of such a scene, including a circumstance that now recurs to my mind. Moritz recounts how, among the country people whom he saw kneeling there, one in particular attracted his attention. It was one of the rosary-pedlars from the mountains, who carve the most beautiful rosaries from a variety of brown wood and sell them throughout the Romagna at a price which reflects their ability to have the rosaries consecrated by the Pope on Church festivals. The man was kneeling with the utmost devotion, but he was holding up the broad-brimmed felt hat containing his wares, the rosaries, and as the Pope uttered the blessing with outstretched hands, he shook his hat and agitated the beads in it, as chestnut-sellers do when they are roasting their chestnuts on the gridiron; he seemed to be conscientiously ensuring that the rosaries at the bottom of the pile got a bit of the papal blessing, so that all were equally consecrated.

I could not forbear to insert this touching instance of naive piety at this point, and now take up once more the thread of my confessions, all of which refer to the intellectual and spiritual development that I had later to undergo. The most recent phenomena can be explained by the earliest beginnings. It is certainly significant that when I was only thirteen the systems of all the free-thinkers were expounded to me, and that this was done by a venerable clergyman who did not neglect the duties of his sacerdotal office in the slightest. Thus I saw at an early age how religion and doubt can go side by side without any hypocrisy, and this imbued me not only with scepticism, but also with the most tolerant indifference. Time and place are also important factors: I was born at the end of the sceptical eighteenth century and in a town which during my childhood was ruled not only by the French but also by the French spirit.

The Frenchmen I got to know introduced me, I must confess, to very unsavoury books, which instilled in me a prejudice against the whole of French literature. Even later I never loved it as it deserves, and I have always been most unjust towards French poetry, which since my childhood I have never been able to stand. This must be chiefly the fault of the confounded Abbé Daulnoy, who taught the French language in the secondary school at Düsseldorf and insisted on forcing me to make French verses. He came close to giving me a distaste not just for French poetry but for poetry in general. The Abbé Daulnoy, an émigré priest, was a little elderly man with extremely mobile facial muscles and a brown wig which tilted to one side whenever he became angry. He had compiled several French grammars as well as literary anthologies, containing extracts from the French and German classics, for his various classes to translate. For the top class he also published an *Art oratoire* and an *Art poétique*. The first of these little books contained directions for eloquence taken from Quintilian[2] and illustrated by examples from the sermons of Fléchier, Massillion, Bourdaloue, and Bossuet, which I did not find too insufferably boring – But the other book, containing definitions of poetry as 'l'art de peindre par les images', the dreary scrapings of the old Batteux[3] school, French prosody, and the whole of French metrics – what a terrible nightmare! Even now I know nothing more inane than the metrical system of French poetry, that 'art of painting by images', as the French define it, a preposterous notion which may help to explain why they always end up in picturesque paraphrases. Their metrics must have been invented by Procrustes:[4] it is a real straitjacket for ideas which are surely too tame to need one. The idea that the beauty of a poem consists in surmounting metrical difficulties is a ludicrous principle, derived from the same idiotic source. I detest the French hexameter, that rhyming belch. The French themselves have always been aware of this revolting offence against nature, a much more heinous sin than the horrors of Sodom and Gomorrah, and their good actors are instructed to deliver the verses with pauses, as though they were in prose – but why then the unnecessary trouble of versification?

That is what I think now, but I sensed this even as a boy, and you can well imagine that when I explained to the old brown wig that it was impossible for me to make French verses, our relations must have become openly hostile. He denied me any feeling for poetry and called me a barbarian from the Teutoburg Forest. I still recall with horror how I had to translate Caiaphas's address to the Sanhedrin from the hexameters of Klopstock's *Messiah*[5] into French alexandrines, using the Professor's anthology! It was a refinement of cruelty which surpassed even the torments of the Messiah's own Passion, and which he himself would not have endured without complaint. God forgive me, I cursed the world and the foreign oppressors who wanted to impose their metrics upon us, and I nearly became a fire-eating Francophobe. I could have died for France, but make French verses – never!

The quarrel was settled by the headmaster and my mother. The latter did not like my making verses, even if they were only French ones. You see, she was terrified that I might become a poet; she always used to say that that was the worst thing that could happen to me. For the notions that at that time were associated with the word 'poet' were not very honourable, and a poet was a poor devil in rags, who would compose an occasional poem for a couple of dollars and end up dying in hospital.

My mother, however, had great and lofty things in store for me, and all her educational plans served this end. She played the main part in my development, she drew up the entire programme of my studies, and her plans for my education began even before my birth.

At first it was the splendour of the Empire that dazzled my mother, and since a close friend[6] of hers, the daughter of a local iron-worker, had become a duchess and had reported that her husband had won a great many battles and would shortly rise to the rank of king – oh dear! my mother dreamt of my boasting the most golden epaulettes or the most richly embroidered honorary offices at the court of the Empire, to whose service she intended to devote me. For this reason I was obliged to concentrate on the studies that might lead to such a career, and although my school made ample provision for the mathematical sciences, and I was crammed by the kindly Professor Brewer with geometry, statics, hydrostatics, hydraulics, and so forth, till I nearly burst, and was almost drowned in logarithms and algebra, nevertheless I had to take private lessons in such disciplines, so that they might equip me to become a great strategist or, if necessary, the administrator of conquered provinces. With the fall of the Empire my mother had to abandon the magnificent career she had dreamt of for me; the studies directed towards it came to an end, and, strange to say, they left not the slightest trace in my mind, so completely alien were they. It was only a mechanical acquisition which I discarded as useless rubbish.

My mother now began to dream of a quite different kind of brilliant future for me. At that time the house of Rothschild, with whose head my father was on familiar terms, had already begun its fabulous flourishing; other princes of banking and industry had also arisen in our neighbourhood, and my mother maintained that the moment had come when a gifted person could attain extraordinary success in business and reach the supreme pinnacle of worldly power. She accordingly decided that I should become a great financier, and now I had to study foreign languages, especially English, geography, book-keeping, in short, all the branches of learning that deal with trade by land and sea and with the secrets of commerce. In order to learn something about the bill business and overseas imports, I was later obliged to attend the counting-house of one of my father's bankers and the warehouses of an important spice-dealer; the former set of visits lasted at most three weeks, the latter four weeks, but I did learn how to draw up a bill of exchange, and what nutmegs look like.

A well-known merchant with whom I wanted to become an apprentice millionaire observed that I had no talent for money-making, and I confessed to him, laughing, that he was probably right. Since a great commercial crisis occurred soon afterwards and my father, like many of our friends, lost his savings, the mercantile soap-bubble burst even more quickly and more lamentably than the imperial one, and my mother had to dream up another career for me. She now thought that I must unquestionably study law. For she had noticed how the legal profession, which had long been all-powerful in England, had also become so in France and in the parts of Germany that enjoyed constitutional government; in particular, advocates, used to public speaking, played the loquacious leading roles, and thus attained the highest offices of state. My mother's observation was perfectly accurate. As the new University of Bonn had just been founded, and its law faculty staffed with the most distinguished professors, my mother promptly dispatched me to Bonn, where I was soon sitting at the feet of Mackeldey and Welcker[7] and gulping down the manna of their learning. Out of the seven years that I spent at German universities, I wasted three beautiful years of my life's spring with the study of Roman case law and jurisprudence, that most illiberal of all sciences. What a frightful book is the *Corpus Juris*, the Bible of selfishness! I always hated the Roman legal code as much as the Romans themselves. Those thieves wanted to secure their booty, and what they had gained by the sword, they sought to protect by the laws; that is why the Roman was simultaneously a soldier and an advocate, producing the most disgusting combination. Truly, it is to those Roman thieves that we owe the theory of property, something that previously existed only as a fact, and the development of this doctrine right down to its basest conclusions is that much-praised Roman law that forms the basis of all our modern legislation and indeed of all modern institutes of state, although it flies in the face of religion, morality, humane feeling, and reason. I managed to complete those accursed studies, but I could never bring myself to make any use of such an accomplishment, and, perhaps in part because I felt that others would easily surpass me in the arts of *avocasserie* and pettifoggery, I bade a less than fond farewell to the legal profession.

My mother looked even graver than usual. But I was very grown-up, and at an age when one must do without maternal protection. The good woman had likewise grown older, and in giving up the supervision of my life after so many fiascos, she regretted, as we have already seen, that she had not devoted me to the clerical profession. She is now a matron of eighty-seven, and her mind has not been impaired by age. She has never presumed to control my actual way of thinking, and has always been the very embodiment of kindness and love towards me. Her creed was a strict deism that was wholly appropriate to her predominant rationalism. She was a pupil of Rousseau, had read his *Émile*,[8] breast-fed her children, and education was her hobby-horse. She had herself enjoyed a scholarly education, sharing the studies of a brother who became a distinguished doctor but died young. Even as a young girl she had to read Latin dissertations and other scholarly writings aloud to her father, and often astonished the old man with her questions. Her reason and her feelings were completely sound, and it was not from her that I inherited my taste for fantasy and Romanticism. As I have already mentioned, she was afraid of poetry, confiscated every novel she found me reading, never allowed me to visit the theatre, forbade me to take part in popular festivals, kept a close eye on the company I frequented, scolded the maids for telling ghost-stories in my presence – in short, she did all she possibly could to keep me well away from superstition and poetry. She was thrifty, but only as concerned herself; when other people's enjoyments were involved she could be extravagant, and as she did not love money but only valued it, she readily gave it away, and often astonished me by her active charity and generosity. How much she sacrificed herself for her son, when times were hard, by providing not only the plan of his studies but also the means of pursuing them! When I went up to university, my father's business affairs were in a sorry state, and my mother sold her jewellery, a necklace and ear-rings of great value, in order to support me for my first four years of study.

I was, incidentally, not the first member of our family to eat jewels and swallow pearls at university. My mother's father, as she once told me, attempted the same feat. The jewels that had adorned the prayer-book of his departed mother had to pay for the costs of his attendance at university after his father, old Lazarus de Geldern, had been reduced to extreme poverty by a lawsuit with a married sister. Yet old Lazarus had inherited from *his* father an immense fortune about which an old great-aunt told me amazing stories. It always sounded to the boy like something from the *Arabian Nights* when the old woman talked of the great palaces and the Persian hangings and the massive gold and silver plate which the old man forfeited in such a lamentable fashion, after enjoying so many honours at the court of the Elector and the Electress. His town house was the big hotel in Rhine Street; what is now the hospital in the New Town belonged to him, as did a mansion at Gravenberg, yet in the end he scarcely had anywhere to lay his head.

At this point I will insert a story that forms a counterpart to this one, since it should rehabilitate the much-maligned mother of one of my fellow-writers in the eyes of the public. I once read in the biography of poor Dietrich Grabbe[9] that the vice of drunkenness, which proved his downfall, was implanted in him at an early age by his own mother, who, when he was a boy, indeed a child, gave him brandy to drink. This charge, which the author of the biography heard from the lips of hostile relatives, seems entirely false when I recall the words in which the late Grabbe often described how his mother had warned him emphatically against 'the bottle'. She was a rough lady, the wife of a prison warder, and when she caressed her young Wolf-Dietrich she may often have scratched him a little with her she-wolf's paws. But she had a true maternal heart, and proved it when her son set off for Berlin in order to study there. Grabbe told me how, at their leave-taking, she pressed a parcel into his hands which turned out to contain half a dozen silver spoons, six small coffee-spoons *ditto*, and a large soup-spoon *ditto*, wrapped in soft cotton – a glorious domestic treasure such as women of the people never relinquish without a bleeding heart, since it is a kind of silver decoration which they think distinguishes them from the common pewter rabble. When I first met Grabbe, he had already consumed the soup-spoon, the Goliath, as he called it. When I occasionally asked him how things were going, he would frown and reply laconically: 'I'm on my third spoon', or 'I'm on my fourth spoon.' 'The big ones are almost all gone,' he once sighed, 'and when it is the turn of the little ones, the coffee-spoons, I shall get very slender portions, and when they are used up, I shall have no more portions at all.' Unfortunately he was right, and the less he had to eat, the more he took to drinking, ending up as a hopeless drunkard. It was his misery first of all, and later his domestic sorrow, that drove the poor fellow to seek cheerfulness or oblivion in intoxication, and in the end he probably picked up the bottle as others pick up a pistol, in order to put an end to a wretched existence. 'Believe me,' one of Grabbe's naive fellow-Westphalians once said to me, 'he could carry a lot, and he didn't die because he drank, but drank because he wanted to die; he drank his life away.'

The above tribute to a mother can surely never be out of place; I put off writing it down until now, because I wanted to include it in an account of Grabbe's life and character; but that never got written, and even in my book *De l'Allemagne* I was able to mention Grabbe only briefly.

This remark is intended for German rather than French readers, and for the latter's benefit I will only observe that this Dietrich Grabbe was one of the greatest German poets and, of all our dramatic poets, may well be called the one who had the greatest affinity with Shakespeare. He may have fewer strings on his lyre than others who perhaps outrank him by their broader range, but the strings he does have utter notes found only in the great Briton. He has the same abrupt effects, the same natural tones, with which Shakespeare terrifies, overwhelms, and delights us. But all his fine qualities are overshadowed by his lack of taste, his cynicism, and his wild freedom, all of which surpass the craziest and most revolting fantasies that any brain ever created. What produced them, however, was not illness, such as fever or dementia, but a spiritual intoxication of the genius. Just as Plato very aptly called Diogenes a mad Socrates, so our Grabbe could – with twofold justification, alas – be called a drunken Shakespeare. In his published dramas these monstrosities are very much toned down, but in the manuscript of his tragedy *Duke Theodore of Gothland* they were hideous and glaring. When he was still quite unknown to me, he once gave me this play, or rather threw it at my feet, with the words: 'I wanted to know whether I was any good, so I took this manuscript to Professor Gubitz. He shook his head at it, and in order to get rid of me he sent me to you, because you had just as crazy fancies in your head as I did, so you'd understand me much better. Well, here's the abortion!' Having uttered these words, and without waiting for an answer, the crack-brained fellow went on his way. As I was going to Frau von Varnhagen, I took the manuscript with me, to give her the first sample of a new poet; for the few passages I had read showed me that there was a poet here. Poetic game can be recognized by its scent alone. But this time the smell was too strong for female nerves, and much later, almost at midnight, Frau von Varnhagen summoned me and urged me for heaven's sake to take back that awful manuscript, since she claimed that she could not sleep so long as it was in her house. Such was the impression made by Grabbe's creations in their original form.

To pay tribute to a mother is always appropriate, and the feeling reader will not consider Grabbe's words about the poor, much-maligned woman who gave him birth to be an idle digression. Now, however, having done my pious duty towards an unhappy poet, I shall return to my own mother and her kindred, in order to say more about the influence exerted from this direction upon my intellectual development. This subject was of absorbing concern not only to my mother but also, in almost equal measure, to her brother, my uncle Simon de Geldern. He has been dead for twenty years. He was an eccentric, though unassuming, indeed comical, in his outward appearance: small and stout, with a pale, severe face and a nose which was Greek in its straightness, but longer by at least one third than the Greeks used to wear their noses. In his youth, it was said, this nose had been the normal size, and had been so unduly lengthened only by his bad habit of constantly tugging at it. Whenever we children asked our uncle if this was true, he reprimanded us vigorously for such disrespectful remarks and then tugged at his nose once more. He dressed like an eighteenth-century French gentleman, with breeches, white silk stockings, buckled shoes, and an old-fashioned, fairly long pigtail. When the little manikin tripped through the streets, this pigtail flew from one shoulder to the other, cut all kinds of capers, and seemed to be making fun of its own master behind his back. Often, when my good uncle was sitting deep in thought or reading the newspaper, I was overcome by the criminal impulse to seize his pigtail and pull it, as though it were a bell-pull. This likewise made my uncle very cross: he would wring his hands and expostulate about the younger generation that no longer respected anything, could not be controlled by human or by divine authority, and would end up by desecrating whatever was most sacred.

If the man's outward appearance was not apt to inspire respect, his inner being, his heart, deserved all the more respect: it was the finest and noblest heart that I ever encountered on this earth. The man had a sense of honour that recalled the rigorous code of honour in old Spanish plays; and he also resembled the heroes of those plays in his loyalty. He never had the chance to become 'the physician of his own honour',[10] but he was a 'steadfast prince' on an equally chivalrous scale, though he did not declaim in trochaic tetrameters, let alone thirst for the palm of death, and instead of the knight's shining armour he wore a modest black swallow-tail coat. He was far from being a puritanical ascetic; he loved country fairs and the wine-house kept by Rasia, where he especially liked eating fieldfare with juniper berries – but he was proudly and unhesitatingly prepared to sacrifice all the fieldfares in the world, and all its enjoyments, when an idea that he considered true and good was at stake. And he made this sacrifice so unassumingly, indeed so bashfully, that nobody noticed the secret martyr concealed in his comical exterior.

By worldly standards his life was a failure. Simon de Geldern had pursued humane studies, known as Humaniora, in the Jesuits' college, but when his parents' death left him entirely free to choose a career, he did not choose any. Instead of embarking on any professional studies at foreign universities, he preferred to stay at home in Düsseldorf in 'Noah's Ark'. This was the name of the little house which his father had left him and which displayed above its door a very prettily carved and brightly painted image of Noah's Ark. Here, being indefatigably active, he abandoned himself to all his learned hobbies and crazes, to his bibliomania and, in particular, to his obsession with writing, which found its main outlets in political newspapers and obscure periodicals. Incidentally, not only writing, but thinking as well, cost him great efforts. Did his compulsive writing, I wonder, originate from an urge to help the community? He was interested in all current affairs, and his reading of newspapers and pamphlets came close to mania. His neighbours called him the Doctor, not because of his erudition, but because his father and brother had been doctors of medicine. And the old women were firmly convinced that the son of the old doctor who had so often cured them must have inherited his father's remedies, and whenever they fell ill they came running to him with their bottles of urine, tearfully begging him to inspect the bottles and tell them what was wrong with them. When my poor uncle was interrupted in this way amid his studies, he was capable of flying into a rage, telling the old biddies to go to the devil with their bottles of urine, and sending them packing.

It was this uncle who exerted a great influence on my intellectual development, and to whom I owe an enormous amount in this respect. However our views differed, and however limited his literary efforts were, they may well have inspired in me the desire to try my hand at writing. My uncle wrote in a stiff, old-fashioned chancellery style, such as is taught in Jesuit schools where the main subject is Latin, and had difficulty in reconciling himself to my mode of expression, which struck him as too light, too playful, too irreverent. But I benefited immensely from the eagerness with which he directed me to books that could help my intellectual progress. Even when I was a boy, he gave me beautiful and expensive works as presents; he gave me the run of his own library, which was rich in classical books and important pamphlets on current events, and he even allowed me to rummage about in the chests in the attic of Noah's Ark that contained the old books and writings of my late grandfather.

What mysterious bliss rejoiced in the boy's heart when he was able to spend whole days in this attic, which was really a large loft. It was not exactly a pleasant place to spend one's time, and its only inhabitant, a fat Angora cat, did not bother much about cleanliness, and only rarely used her tail to sweep some of the dust and cobwebs from the old lumber that lay there in stacks. But my heart was in the bloom of youth, and the sun shone so cheerfully through the little skylight that everything seemed bathed in the light of fantasy, and the old cat herself seemed like an enchanted princess who would suddenly be freed from her animal shape and reveal herself in her previous beauty and magnificence, while the attic would turn into a splendid palace, as happens in all fairy-tales. But the good old age of fairy-tales is no more, cats remain cats, and the attic of Noah's Ark remained a dusty lumber-room, a geriatric home for broken-down household objects, a Salpetrière[11] for old pieces of furniture that had reached the utmost degree of decrepitude and yet could not be thrown out, because of sentimental affection and the pious memories associated with them.

There was a rickety, broken cradle in which my mother had once been rocked; it now contained the wig that my grandfather used to wear on grand occasions, which had completely mouldered and seemed to have entered a second childhood in its old age. My grandfather's rusty dress-sword, half a pair of fire-tongs, and other disabled pieces of ironmongery were hanging on the wall. Beside them, on a wobbly shelf, stood my dear departed grandmother's stuffed parrot, which, having lost all its feathers, was no longer green but ashen-grey, and looked extremely sinister with its one remaining glass eye. There was also a large green china pug-dog, which was hollow inside; part of its hindquarters was broken off, and the cat seemed to hold this Chinese or Japanese ornament in great respect, for she kow-towed before it and may even have considered it a divine being – cats are so superstitious. In one corner lay an old flute which had once belonged to my mother; she used to play it when she was still a young girl, and she chose that very attic as her concert-hall, so that the old gentleman, her father, should not have his work disturbed by music nor be annoyed by the sentimental time-wasting of which his daughter was guilty. The cat had now chosen this flute as her favourite toy, and would roll it to and fro on the floor with the aid of the faded pink ribbon that was attached to it.

The antiquities in the attic also included some globes, curious maps of the planets, and flasks and retorts, recalling astrological and alchemical studies. Among my grandfather's books in the chests there were many that dealt with such occult sciences. Most of the books, admittedly, were trashy works on medicine. There was no lack of books on philosophy, but alongside the arch-rationalist Descartes there were also fantasists like Paracelsus,[12] van Helmont and even Agrippa of Nettesheim, whose *Philosophia occulta* I here laid eyes on for the first time. Even as a boy I was amused by the dedicatory epistle to Abbot Trithemius, printed together with the latter's reply, in which this rogue pays back the other charlatan's bombastic compliments with interest. However, the best and most precious find that I made in these dusty chests was a notebook written by one of my grandfather's brothers, who was known as the Chevalier or the Easterner, and about whom the old grannies had a never-ending fund of tales.

This great-uncle, who was likewise called Simon de Geldern, must have been an odd customer. He was nicknamed 'the Easterner' because he had travelled widely in the East and always wore Oriental costume after his return. He seems to have spent the greater part of his time in the cities of the North African coast, especially in the Moroccan states, where a Portuguese taught him the trade of an armourer, which he practised successfully. He made a pilgrimage to Jerusalem, and when praying ecstatically on Mount Moriah[13] he had a vision. What did he see? He never revealed it. An independent Bedouin tribe which professed a kind of Mosaism instead of Islam, and had a sort of *pied à terre* in one of the unknown oases of the North African desert, elected him its leader or sheik. This warlike little nation was at feud with all the neighbouring tribes and was a terror to caravans. To speak in European terms, my great-uncle, the pious visionary of the sacred mountain of Moriah, became a robber chief. In this beautiful region he also acquired the knowledge of horse-breeding and the skilled horsemanship with which he aroused so much admiration after his return to the West.

At the various courts where he spent long periods, he made a brilliant impression by his personal beauty and dignity, as well as the splendour of his Oriental garb, which enchanted women in particular. No doubt he impressed people most by the occult knowledge to which he laid claim, and nobody dared to lower the standing of the all-powerful necromancer in the eyes of his lofty patrons. The spirit of intrigue fears the spirits of the Kabbalah. Nothing could ruin him but his own overweening pride, and the old gossips would shake their grey heads with a strange air of mystery when they muttered about the amorous relations between the Easterner and a very high-born lady, and how their discovery forced him to leave the court and the country post-haste. Only by flight and by abandoning all his possessions could he avoid certain death, and it was his well-tried horsemanship that ensured his safety. After this adventure he seems to have found a safe but ill-provided refuge in England. I gather this from a pamphlet which my great-uncle had printed in London, and which I once found by chance when I climbed up to the highest bookshelves in the Düsseldorf library. It was an oratorio in French verse entitled 'Moses on Mount Horeb', referring perhaps to the vision I have mentioned; its preface, however, was written in English and dated from London. The verses, like all French verses, were lukewarm water set to rhyme, but the English prose of the preface betrayed the anger of a proud man who finds himself in need. From my great-uncle's notebook I could not learn much that was reliable; it was, perhaps as a precaution, written mostly in Arabic, Syriac, and Coptic characters, interspersed, strangely enough, with French quotations, such as the frequently recurring verse 'Où l'innocence périt c'est un crime de vivre'.[14] I was also struck by many remarks that were likewise written in French; this seemed to be the writer's customary idiom.

This great-uncle was a strange, perplexing phenomenon. He led one of those peculiar lives that were possible only in the early and mid eighteenth century; he was partly an enthusiast who propagated cosmopolitan, utopian ideas intended to benefit humanity, partly a soldier of fortune who, conscious of his individual strength, broke down or leapt over the decaying barriers of a decaying society. At all events, he was wholly human. His charlatanry, which we do not dispute, was not of the common sort. He was not the ordinary charlatan who extracts peasants' teeth in the market-place; instead he boldly forced his way into the palaces of the great and extracted their strongest wisdom teeth, as Sir Huon of Bordeaux[15] once did to the Sultan of Babylon. You must cry your wares if you want to sell them, as the proverb says, and life is a matter of selling one's wares. And what notable person is not something of a charlatan? Modest charlatans are the worst of all, with their arrogance masked as humility! Anyone who wants to move the crowd, in particular, needs a dose of charlatanry.

The end justifies the means. After all, when God promulgated his Law on Mount Sinai, he himself did not disdain to give a display of thunder and lightning, though the Law was so excellent, so divinely good, that it could well have dispensed with the flashing of pine-resin and the thunder of kettle-drums. But the Lord knew his public: they were standing at the bottom of the mountain with their oxen and sheep and gaping mouths, and were doubtless more disposed to admire a physical marvel than all the miracles of eternal thought.

However that may be, this great-uncle had an absorbing effect on the boy's imagination. Everything I was told about him made an indelible impression on my young heart, and I became so immersed in his wanderings and fortunes that sometimes in broad daylight I would be seized by an uncanny feeling, as though I were myself my late great-uncle, living only a continuation of the life of this long-dead relative! At night this sensation would be reflected retrospectively in my dreams. My life at that time resembled a great newspaper, the upper section of which contained the present, the day with its daily news and debates, while in the lower section the poetic past was fantastically proclaimed in continuous nocturnal dreams, like the episodes of a serialized novel. In these dreams I identified completely with my great-uncle, feeling simultaneously with horror that I was a different person and belonged to a different age. There were localities I had never seen before, there were situations of which I had previously had no inkling, yet I walked among them sure-footedly and always knew how to behave, I met people with strange, garish costumes and wild, weird physiognomies, yet I shook hands with them as if they were old acquaintances; I understood their alien tongue, though I had never heard it before, and to my own astonishment I replied in the same tongue, while gesticulating with a violence that was never natural to me, and even saying things that formed a repulsive contrast to my normal way of thinking.

This peculiar state must have lasted for a year, and though I regained my unity of consciousness, secret traces nevertheless remained in my soul. Many idiosyncrasies, many fateful sympathies and antipathies that do not accord with my nature, indeed many actions that conflict with my way of thinking, can only be explained as after-effects of that period of dreaming in which I was my own great-uncle. When I make mistakes whose causes I cannot understand, I readily ascribe them to my Eastern double. Once, when I put such a hypothesis to my father in order to excuse some small oversight, he remarked mischievously that he hoped my great-uncle had not signed any bills of exchange which might one day be presented to me for payment.

I have not been presented with any such Oriental bills of exchange, and I have a hard enough time with my own Occidental ones. But there are worse debts than financial ones, left by our ancestors for us to clear. Each generation is a continuation of the others, and is responsible for their deeds. The Scripture says: 'The fathers have eaten sour grapes, and the children's teeth shall be set on edge.'[16] There is a solidarity among successive generations; indeed, the nations that succeed one another in the arena share such a solidarity, and in the end the whole of mankind will liquidate the assets of the past – perhaps through a universal bankruptcy.

I shall not conduct any inquiries into this matter, but, continuing my personal confessions, I shall simply take this opportunity of showing by a further example how the most innocent facts have sometimes been used for the most malicious insinuations by my enemies. The latter claimed to have discovered that, in giving biographical information, I had a great deal to say about my maternal family but nothing about my paternal kith and kin, and they described this as deliberate emphasis and concealment and accused me of the same vain motives as those with which my late fellow-writer Wolfgang Goethe was charged.

It is of course true that in Goethe's memoirs he talks much and with particular pleasure about his paternal grandfather, who held the solemn office of mayor in Frankfurt town-hall, while his maternal grandfather, an honest little tailor who squatted at his table in Bockenheim Lane and mended the republic's old trousers, is never once mentioned. I hold no brief for Goethe as regards this omission, but speaking for myself, I should like to correct these malicious and much-exploited interpretations and insinuations by pointing out that it is not my fault if my writings never mention my paternal grandfather. The reason is quite simple: I know scarcely anything about him. My late father came to Düsseldorf, my birthplace, as a complete stranger, and had no relatives here. He had none of these old grannies and aunties, who are the female bards who recite old family legends day in, day out, with epic monotony, replacing the bagpipe accompaniment which was obligatory among the Scottish bards by blowing their noses. This source could inform my young heart only about the great heroes of my maternal clan.

My father himself was by nature very taciturn and reluctant to talk. Once, when I was a little boy spending my weekdays in the dreary Franciscan monastery school but my Sundays at home, I took an opportunity of asking my father who my grandfather had been. He replied to this question with a mixture of amusement and surliness: 'Your grandfather was a little Jew with a long beard.' The next day, on entering the class-room, where my little comrades were already assembled, I could not wait to tell them this important piece of news – that my grandfather was a little Jew with a long beard. No sooner had I announced this information than it flew from one pair of lips to another and was repeated in every key, accompanied by animal imitations. The boys leapt on to the desks and benches, tore the counting-frames from the walls and let them tumble alongside the ink-wells, while laughing, bleating, grunting, barking, crowing, and generally kicking up an almighty row, the recurrent refrain of which was my grandfather who was a little Jew with a long beard. The teacher in charge of the class heard the din, entered the room, red in the face with fury, and demanded at once who had started this riot. As always happens in such cases, everyone became subdued and professed complete innocence, and the inquiry ended with poor me being found guilty of causing the din with my news about my grandfather, and I expiated my guilt with a prolonged beating.

It was the first beating I ever received on this earth, and even on this occasion I reflected philosophically that God, the creator of beatings, had in his wisdom and benevolence also provided that he who does the beating must eventually grow tired, for otherwise the beating would be unbearable. The stick with which I was beaten was a yellow cane, but the stripes it left on my back were dark blue. I have never forgotten them. Nor did I forget the name of the teacher who beat me so unmercifully: it was Father Dickerscheit; he was soon removed from the school for reasons which I have not forgotten either, but which I will not pass on. The priesthood has often been unjustly vilified by liberalism, and may deserve some lenience when one of its unworthy members commits crimes which are ultimately only natural, or rather unnatural. Along with the name of the man who gave me my first beating, I also remembered the reason, that is, my unfortunate piece of genealogical information, and the after-effect of these youthful impressions was so strong that whenever I heard little Jews with long beards being mentioned, a sinister recollection would make my flesh crawl. 'The burnt child fears the fire,' says the proverb, and it will be readily understood that I felt little inclination to make further inquiries about this troublesome grandfather and his family tree, nor to transmit such information to the great public, as I had once done to a small public.

I cannot say much either about my maternal grandmother, but I would not like to omit her. She was an exceptionally beautiful woman, the only daughter of a Hamburg banker who was famous far and wide for his wealth. These circumstances incline me to think that the little Jew who married the beautiful girl and took her from her prosperous parents' home to his house in Hanover must have possessed some admirable qualities in addition to his long beard, and must have been worthy of great respect. He died young, leaving a young widow with six children, all of them boys of tender years. She returned to Hamburg, where she died at no great age. I once saw my grandmother's portrait in the bedroom of my uncle Salomon Heine at Hamburg. The painter, striving for Rembrandtesque effects of light and shade, had given her black, monastic-looking headgear, a dark robe of almost equal severity, and a completely pitch-black background, so that her round-cheeked face with its double chin shone forth like a full moon from nocturnal clouds. Her features still bore the traces of great beauty, mild and serious at the same time, and the *morbidezza* of her skin, in particular, gave the whole face a remarkably refined expression. If the painter had shown a large diamond-studded cross on her bosom, the portrait would have been taken for that of some princely abbess of a Protestant retreat for noble ladies.

Of my grandmother's children only two, so far as I know, inherited her exceptional good looks: my father and my uncle Salomon Heine, the deceased head of the Hamburg banking house of that name. My father's good looks had something excessively soft, characterless, almost womanish about them. His brother had more masculine good looks, and he was indeed a man; his noble, regular features revealed his strength of character in an imposing, indeed sometimes breathtaking fashion. All his children, without exception, grew up to be enchantingly beautiful, but death swept them away in the flower of their youth, and only two members of this beautiful human bouquet are still alive: the present head of the banking house and his sister, my [. . .][17]

I was very fond of all those children, and also of their mother, who was also so beautiful and died so early, and they all cost me many a tear. Truly, at this moment I must shake my cap and bells to drown out my tearful thoughts.

I said earlier that my father's good looks had something feminine about them. It is not my intention to suggest any lack of manliness: he gave ample evidence of this, especially in his youth, and I, after all, am living proof of it. This is not supposed to be an improper remark: I meant only the contours of his physique, which was soft and gently rounded rather than upright and burly. His features were not strongly marked, but faded into indefiniteness. In his later years he put on weight, but even in his youth he does not seem to have been exactly skinny. This conjecture is confirmed by a portrait which has since been lost in a fire in my mother's house, but which showed my father as a young man of eighteen or nineteen, in a red uniform, with his hair powdered and tied into a ball at the back. The portrait was fortunately painted in pastels. I say 'fortunately' because pastels are much better than oils, with their additional glossy varnish, for conveying that fine pollen-like dust that we see on the faces of people with powdered hair, advantageously veiling the indefiniteness of their features. By framing my father's rosy face in his white powdered hair and his white neckerchief, the painter increased its colouring by contrast and enabled it to make a stronger impression. Similarly, the scarlet colour of the coat, which grins at us so hideously in oil-paintings, here has instead a good effect, by pleasantly softening the rosy complexion of the face. The type of beauty expressed in my father's features recalled neither the chaste, severe ideality of Greek sculpture nor the devoutly spiritualistic Renaissance style, impregnated with pagan good health. Instead, his portrait bore all the character of an age that had no character, and that loved prettiness, daintiness, and coquettish delicacy rather than beauty; an age that elevated insipidity to poetry, the sweet, decorative Rococo period, which was also known as the age of the hair-bag and whose emblem was a hair-bag worn at the nape of the neck instead of the forehead. If my father's portrait had been more of a miniature, one might have thought that the admirable Watteau had painted it in order to parade, framed in fantastic arabesques of precious stones and gilded tinsel, on one of Madame de Pompadour's fans.

It is perhaps noteworthy that even in his later years my father remained faithful to the eighteenth-century French fashion for powder and had his hair powdered every day until his death, although he had the most beautiful hair imaginable. It was blond, almost golden, and softer than anything I know except Chinese floss silk. He would doubtless have liked to retain his hair-bag as well, but the advancing spirit of the age was remorseless. In this quandary, however, my father found a satisfying compromise. He sacrificed only the form, that is, the little black bag containing the hair, but he wore his long locks like a loosely plaited chignon attached to his head with tiny combs. Since his hair was so soft, and covered in powder, this plaiting was almost imperceptible, and so my father was not really a renegade from the cult of the hair-bag, but, like many crypto-orthodox believers, he had merely complied outwardly with the harsh spirit of the age.

The red uniform in which my father is depicted in this portrait suggests that he was in the Hanoverian service. At the beginning of the French Revolution my father was part of the retinue of Prince Ernest of Cumberland,[18] and took part in the campaign in Flanders and Brabant as a commissary or quartermaster, or as the French call such people, an *officier de bouche*; the Prussians call them 'mealworms'. My father, who was very young at that time, was really employed as one of the favourites of the Prince, a miniature Beau Brummel without a starched collar, and he ended up sharing the fate of such playthings of princely favour. He retained a lifelong conviction that the Prince, who later became King of Hanover, had not forgotten him, but he was at a loss to explain why the Prince never sent for him, never inquired after him, since for all the Prince knew his former favourite might be living in circumstances where he needed his help.

This campaigning period introduced my father to some worrying hobbies, from which my mother could only gradually wean him away. For example, he liked gambling for high stakes, patronized the art of drama or rather its priestesses, and had a positive passion for horses and dogs. When he went to Düsseldorf, where his love for my mother induced him to settle down as a businessman, he brought twelve of the finest nags with him. However, he disposed of them at the express wish of his young wife, who pointed out that this four-legged capital consumed too much oats and brought no money in. My mother had more difficulty in getting rid of the stable-man, a sturdy rogue who was always lying in the straw and playing cards with some disreputable companion. In the end he departed of his own accord, accompanied by my father's gold repeating watch and some other valuable objects.

Once my mother was rid of this scoundrel, she also dismissed my father's hounds, except for one who, though called Joly, was hideously ugly. He found grace in her eyes because he was really quite unsuitable for hunting and was well fitted to become a loyal and virtuous bourgeois house-dog. He lived in my father's old barouche, which was kept in the empty stable, and whenever my father met him here, each would give the other meaningful glances. 'Yes, Joly,' my father would sigh, and Joly would wag his tail sorrowfully. I suspect that the dog was a hypocrite, and once, when my father was in a bad mood and his pet was whimpering rather too miserably at having been kicked, he admitted that the rascal was putting on an act. In the end Joly became very mangy, and as he was now a walking barracks of fleas, he had to be drowned; my father let this happen without raising any objection. People sacrifice their four-legged favourites with as much indifference as princes do their two-legged ones.

The period my father spent in army camps doubtless also gave rise to his boundless enthusiasm for soldiers, or rather for playing soldiers: his delight in their merry, idle life, in which tinsel and scarlet patches conceal inner emptiness, and intoxicated vanity assumes the role of courage. Among the country gentlemen in his neighbourhood there was no serious devotion to military matters, or any real thirst for fame; of heroism there was no question. For him, the essentials of military life were the changing of the guard, the ringing sword-belt, and the close-fitting uniform that looks so well on handsome men. How happy my father was, therefore, when the citizens' guard was set up in Düsseldorf, and as one of its officers he was able to wear its handsome dark-blue uniform with sky-blue velvet facings and to march past our house at the head of his columns. He would salute my mother, who stood blushing at the window, with the most charming courtesy; the plume on his three-cornered hat fluttered proudly, and his epaulettes gleamed joyously in the sunshine.

My father was even happier when, as commanding officer, it was his turn to mount guard and ensure the town's safety. On days like these the guard-post would flow with the finest Rüdesheimer and Assmannshäuser vintages, all at the expense of the commanding officer, and the guards under his command, his Tom, Dick and Harry, could never praise his generosity too highly. My father enjoyed a popularity among them that must have been quite as great as the enthusiasm with which the Old Guard hailed the Emperor Napoleon. The latter, indeed, had a different way of intoxicating his followers. My father's guards were not lacking in a certain sort of bravery, especially when they had to storm a battery of wine-bottles, and the more massive the better. But their heroic temper was of a different kind from that of the old Imperial Guard, who remained bolt upright until their deaths, whereas my father's guards stayed alive but could never remain upright for long. As for the safety of the town of Düsseldorf, this was probably not best provided for on the nights when my father commanded the guard. He certainly took care to send out patrols, who roamed through the town in diverse directions, singing and rattling their weapons. On one occasion two such patrols met, and in the darkness each wanted to arrest the others as drunken disturbers of the peace. Fortunately my countrymen are cheerful and inoffensive, they are good-humoured when drunk, 'ils ont le vin bon', and no misfortune occurred; each surrendered to the other.

The principal feature of my father's character was a boundless *joie de vivre*. He was pleasure-loving, light-hearted, disposed to see everything in a roseate glow. In his heart there was always a party going on, and even if sometimes the dance-music was rather subdued, the violins were always tuned. Sky-blue merriment, fanfares of jollity, a carefree temperament that forgot yesterday and took no thought for the morrow. This disposition formed a most curious contrast to the gravity displayed on his calm and severe countenance and proclaimed in the posture and in every movement of his body. Anyone who did not know him, and saw this serious, powdered figure and his portentous expression for the first time, must surely have taken him for one of the seven sages of Greece. On closer acquaintance, however, it became apparent that he was neither a Thales[19] nor a Lampsacus, brooding over problems of cosmogony. Although his gravity was not feigned, it nevertheless recalled those ancient bas-reliefs on which a merry child holds a great tragic mask in front of its face. He was in reality a great child, with a child-like naivety which dull virtuosos of the intellect could easily mistake for simple-mindedness, but which now and again, by some profound observation or other, betrayed a remarkable gift of intuition. With his mental antennae he picked up things which clever people took a long time to grasp by reflection. He thought with his heart, rather than his head, and had the kindest heart you can imagine. The smile that sometimes played around his lips, forming a drolly charming contrast with the gravity above mentioned, was the sweet reflection of his kind-heartedness. His voice, too, though manly and resonant, had something child-like about it; I might almost say that it recalled bird-song, say the chirping of the robin redbreast. When he spoke, his voice penetrated so directly to one's heart as though it had not had to travel via one's ears.

He spoke the dialect of Hanover, where German is pronounced best, as it is also in the countryside south of the town. It was a great advantage for me that even in childhood, thanks to my father, my ear grew accustomed to a good German pronunciation, whereas in our town itself people speak the terrible jargon of the Lower Rhine, which, though more or less tolerable in Düsseldorf, becomes truly loathsome in nearby Cologne. Cologne is the Tuscany of a classic mispronunciation of German, and Jake canoodles with Meg in a patois that sounds, and almost smells, like bad eggs. The language spoken in Düsseldorf has some transitional features connecting it with the croaking frogs of the Dutch marshes. Not that I have the slightest wish to deny the Dutch language its distinctive beauties, but I confess that I have no ear for them. It may even be true that our own German language, as patriotic linguists in the Netherlands have maintained, is only a corrupt form of Dutch. It is possible. This reminds me of the view put forward by a cosmopolitan zoologist who claims that the ape is the ancestor of the human race. In his opinion, human beings are only educated, indeed over-educated apes. If apes could speak, they would probably maintain that human beings are only degenerate apes and humanity a corrupt simianity, just as, in the opinion of the Dutch, the German language is a corrupt form of Dutch.

I said 'if apes could speak', though I am by no means convinced that they cannot. The Senegalese declare roundly that apes are human beings like us, only wiser, since they refrain from speech in order not to be recognized as human beings and forced to work; their comical antics are a sly device to persuade the great ones of the earth that they are unfit to be exploited like the rest of us. Such an abnegation of vanity would give me a very high opinion of those people who retain a mute incognito and perhaps make fun of our simplicity. They remain free in their forests, never renouncing the state of nature. They would indeed be justified in claiming that human beings are degenerate apes. Perhaps our eighteenth-century forefathers suspected something of the sort, and in feeling instinctively that our polished over-civilization is mere polished rottenness, and that we should go back to nature, they were trying to return to our primordial prototype of the natural ape. They did all they could to this end, and when at last they needed only tails to be complete apes, they supplied this deficiency by wearing pigtails. Hence the fashion for pigtails is not a frivolous game, but a significant symptom of a serious need – but it is in vain for me to shake my cap and bells in order to drown out the melancholy that affects me whenever I think of my late father.

He was the person whom I loved more than anyone else on this earth. He has now been dead for more than twenty-five years. It never occurred to me that I would lose him one day, and even now I can scarcely believe that I have really lost him. It is so hard to convince ourselves of the death of somebody whom we have loved so deeply. But they are not dead: they live on in us and dwell in our souls. Since then there has never been a night when I was not forced to think of my late father, and when I wake up in the morning, I often imagine that I can hear the sound of his voice, like the echo of a dream. Then I feel as though I should dress hastily and hurry downstairs to my father in the big parlour, as I did as a child. My father used always to get up very early and attend to his business, winter and summer, and I usually found him already at his desk, where without looking up, he would give me his hand to kiss. A beautiful, finely chiselled, elegant hand, which he always washed with almond bran. I can still see it, I can still see each one of the tiny blue veins that ran through its dazzling white marble. I feel as though the scent of almonds were rising and tickling my nose; and my eyes grow moist. Sometimes my father did more than let me kiss his hand: he would take me between his knees and kiss me on the forehead. One morning he embraced me with particular tenderness and said: 'Last night I had a lovely dream about you, and I am very pleased with you, my dear Harry.' As he uttered these naive words, a smile played about his lips, and seemed to be saying: 'However naughty Harry may be in reality, I shall always have lovely dreams about him, so that I may love him unreservedly.'

Among the English, Harry is the familiar form of the name 'Henry', and it corresponds precisely to my German baptismal name, Heinrich. In my home dialect the familiar forms of this name are extremely cacophonous, almost grotesque, such as 'Heinz', 'Heinzchen', 'Hinz'. 'Heinzchen' is also the name often given to brownies, and 'Hinz' is the name of Puss in Boots in the puppet-play, and indeed of all cats in folk-tales. However, it was not to remove this discomfort, but to honour one of his best friends in England, that my father anglicized my name. Mr Harry was my father's business correspondent in Liverpool; he knew the best factories making velveteen, a commodity about which my father cared deeply, though from ambition rather than self-interest. For although he claimed that this article earned him large sums of money, this was highly problematic, and my father might well have paid more in order to dispose of velveteen of a higher quality and in greater quantities than his competitors. Generally, indeed, my father lacked the mercantile spirit of calculation, though he was always doing sums, and business was more of a game for him, just as children play at soldiers or cooking. His activity was really a way of constantly keeping himself busy. Velveteen was his favourite toy, and he was happy when the great goods-carts were unloaded and, even before they were unpacked, all the Jewish traders of the district filled his hallway; for these were his best customers, and among them his velveteen found not only the best market, but also honourable appreciation. Since, dear reader, you may not know what velveteen is, I will take the liberty of explaining that it is an English word meaning 'velvet-like' and referring to a kind of cotton velvet from which very fine trousers, waistcoats, and even camisoles are made. This material is also called 'Manchester' after the manufacturing city of that name, where it was first made.

Since my father's friend who was an expert on the purchase of velveteen bore the name Harry, I too was given this name, and was known as Harry at home and among neighbours and friends of the family. Here in France my German name 'Heinrich' was translated into 'Henri' as soon as I arrived in Paris, and I was obliged to accept this and use the name myself, since the word 'Heinrich' did not appeal to the French ear, and since the French change everything in the world to suit themselves. They could never get their tongues round the name 'Henri Heine', either, and most of them call me 'Monsieur Enri Enn'; many contract this to 'Enrienne', and some have called me 'Monsieur un rien'. This does me some harm as far as literature is concerned, but also has its advantages. For example, my noble fellow-countrymen who come to Paris include many who would like to blacken my reputation, but since they always pronounce my name in the German fashion, it never occurs to the French that the villainous poisoner of the wells of innocence who is denounced so frightfully is none other than their friend Monsieur Enrienne, and it is in vain for those noble souls to unleash their virtuous zeal; the French do not realize that they are referring to me, and trans-Rhenan virtue shoots all the darts of slander in vain.

As I said, however, it is irritating to have one's name mispronounced. There are people who display great sensitivity in such cases. I once amused myself by asking old Cherubini[20] if it were true that the Emperor Napoleon always pronounced his name 'Sherubini' instead of 'Kerubini', although the Emperor's command of Italian was quite sufficient for him to know when the Italian 'ch' should be pronounced 'k'. This question produced an outburst of highly comical rage from the old maestro. I have never had such feelings. Heinrich, Harry, Henry – all these names sound well when they are uttered by beautiful lips. Admittedly, the version that sounds best is Signor Enrico. This was the name given to me in the bright blue summer nights, embroidered with great silver stars, of that noble and unhappy country, the home of beauty, that produced Raphael Sanzio of Urbino, Joachimo Rossini, and the Princess Cristina Belgiojoso.[21]

Since my physical condition deprives me of any hope of ever again living in society, and society really does not exist for me any longer, I have also cast off the fetters of that personal vanity that encumbers everyone who mixes with humanity in the so-called social world. Hence I can now speak without embarrassment of the misfortune connected with my name 'Harry' that spoiled the spring-tide of my life. It was like this. In my home town there lived a man called 'Mucky Mick' because he went through the streets of the town every morning, with a cart drawn by a donkey, in order to collect the rubbish which the girls had swept into neat piles and transport it to the dump outside the town. The man resembled his calling, and the donkey, which in turn resembled its master, would stand still in front of the houses or begin trotting, according to the modulation in which Mick called out the word 'Haarüh!'. Was this a real name or only a catchword? I do not know, but this much is certain, that because of the similarity between this word and my name Harry, I had an extraordinary amount of suffering to endure from schoolmates and neighbours' children. In order to tease me, they would pronounce it just as Mucky Mick called to his donkey, and if I were annoyed by this, the rogues would sometimes assume an air of complete innocence and ask me to clear up the confusion by teaching them how my name and that of the donkey should be pronounced. They were very awkward pupils, however, claiming that Mick stretched out the first syllable and snapped out the second very abruptly, but that at other times he did the opposite, so that his cry sounded exactly like my name; and when the boys mixed up all these ideas, confusing me with the donkey and the donkey with me, a wild *coq à l'âne*[22] arose which made all the others laugh but made me cry. When I complained to my mother, she told me I should try to learn a great deal and become clever, and then no one would mistake me for a donkey.

Nevertheless, my homonymity with that shabby jackass continued to torment me. The big boys called out 'Haarüh!' as they went past; the smaller ones issued the same greeting, but from some distance. At school this theme was exploited with refined cruelty; if a donkey was mentioned at all, people squinted at me, and I always blushed. It is incredible how schoolboys can discover or invent barbed remarks wherever they look. For example, one would ask the other: 'What is the difference between Balaam's ass and a zebra?' The answer was: 'One spoke Hebrew and the other speaks Zebrew.' Then came the question: 'What's the difference between Mucky Mick's donkey and his namesake?' and the impertinent answer was: 'We don't know.' I would then be about to hit them, but the others would calm me down, and my friend Dietrich, who made exceptionally beautiful pictures of saints and later became a famous painter, tried to comfort me on one such occasion by promising me a picture. He painted a St Michael for me – but the villain held me up to scorn in the most shameful fashion. The archangel had the features of Mucky Mick, his steed looked exactly like the latter's donkey, and his lance, instead of wounding a dragon, transfixed the remains of a dead cat. Even gentle, fair-haired, girlish Franz, whom I was so fond of, once betrayed me: he folded me in his arms, rested his cheek tenderly upon mine, clung sentimentally to my bosom, and – suddenly laughed and shouted 'Haarüh!' in my ear! As he ran away, he kept modulating the vile word so that it echoed far and wide through the cloisters of the monastery.

I received still rougher treatment from some neighbours' children, street-urchins of the lowest class known in Düsseldorf as *Haluten*, a word which etymology-hunters would doubtless derive from the Helots of the Spartans. One such *Halut* was little Jupp, that is, Joseph, whom I shall refer to by his family name of Flader so that nobody will confuse him with Jupp Rörsch, a good child who, as I happened to learn, now works for the post office in Bonn. Jupp Flader always carried a long fishing-rod with which he struck at me every time he met me. He also used to throw lumps of horse-dung at my head, having picked them up from the street piping hot, just as they came from nature's oven. But then he never failed to shout that dreadful 'Haarüh!' in every modulation. This bad boy was the grandson of old Frau Flader, who was one of my father's clients. His poor grandmother was as good-hearted as the boy was bad; she was an image of poverty and misery, but heart-rending rather than repulsive. She must have been over eighty, with a big, trembling body, a white leathery face with colourless, worried eyes, a soft, gasping, whimpering voice, and begging in completely straightforward language, which always sounds frightful. My father always gave her a chair to sit on when she came to collect her monthly allowance on the days when he officially dispensed poor-relief.

Of my father's sessions as poor-relief officer I remember only those that took place in winter, early in the morning, when it was still dark. My father would sit at a big table, covered with money-bags of every size. Instead of the silver candlestick with wax candles which my father customarily used, but which, having such a tactful heart, he did not want to display to the poor, there would be on the table two copper candlesticks with tallow candles which cast a dismal light on the assembled company with the red flame of their thick, blackened wicks. Those present were the poor of all ages, queueing in a line that stretched back to the ante-room. One after another came up to receive his bag of money, and some received two; the big bag would contain alms given privately by my father, the small one the money from the poor-relief fund. I sat on a high chair beside my father and handed him the bags. For he wanted me to learn how to give, and on this subject one could learn a sound lesson from my father. Many people whose hearts are in the right place do not know how to give, and it takes a long time for the will of the heart to make its way to the pocket; between the good resolution and its accomplishment time crawls at a snail's pace. My father's heart and his pocket, however, seemed to be linked by a railway line. It goes without saying that his shares in this railway did not make him rich; more money was earned from the Northern Railway or the Lyons Railway.

Most of my father's clients were old women, and later too, even when his circumstances were becoming very unbrilliant, he had a similar clientele of elderly females to whom he doled out small pensions. They used to lie in wait wherever he had to go, and thus he had a secret bodyguard of old women like the late Robespierre before him. This old, grey guard included many an old biddy who pursued him, not from need, but from genuine attachment, because of his kindly and invariably pleasant manner. He was charm personified, not only to young women but also to older ones, and the old women who are so savage when injured are the most grateful class of humanity when shown some attention and courtesy; anyone who wants to be paid in flattery will find them unstinting, while pert young chits scarcely think us worthy of a nod in return for all our civilities. Since handsome men who specialize in being handsome have a great need for flattery and do not care whether the incense comes from rosy or withered lips, provided it spurts forth in dense clouds, it may be understood how my beloved father, without any deliberate speculation, nevertheless profited richly from his dealings with the old ladies. The quantity of incense in which they enshrouded him, and the ease with which he endured the strongest dose, are incredible. This was by no means due to simplicity, but to his happy temperament. He knew very well that he was being flattered, but he also knew that flattery, like sugar, is always sweet, and he was like a child saying to its mother: 'Flatter me a bit, even a bit too much.'

My father's relation to the aforementioned women, however, also had a more serious basis. For he was their adviser, and it is curious that a man whose own behaviour was so ill-advised was the embodiment of worldly wisdom when he had to advise others in awkward predicaments. He would take in the position at a glance, and when his sorrowful client had explained how her trade was getting worse and worse, he would finally utter a remark that I often heard him pronounce when things were going badly: 'In such a case one must tap another barrel.' He meant that one should not persist stubbornly in a lost cause, but start something new, launch out in a new direction. It is better to knock out the bottom of the old barrel, which yields only scanty drops of sour wine, and 'tap another barrel'! Instead, however, people prefer the lazy option of lying with open mouths under the dry bung-hole and hoping that the wine will flow more strongly and sweetly.

When old Hanne complained to my father that her customers were dwindling and that she had neither a crust to eat nor (what was more painful for her) a drop to drink, he first gave her a dollar and then pondered. Old Hanne had formerly been one of the leading midwives, but in later years she took rather to drinking and still more to snuff; and since there was a perpetual thaw in her red nose and the falling drops turned the white sheets of the expectant mothers brown, her services were everywhere dispensed with. When my father had carefully reflected, he finally said: 'You must tap another barrel, and this time it must be a barrel of brandy; I advise you to open a little liquor-shop, selling schnapps, in one of the better streets frequented by sailors near the harbour.' The ex-midwife followed this advice, set herself up selling schnapps at the harbour, did a good trade, and would undoubtedly have made a pile, if she had not unfortunately been her own best customer. She also sold tobacco, and I often saw her standing in front of her shop with her nose red and bloated from snuff-taking, a living advertisement that appealed to many a soft-hearted sailor.

Prominent among my father's pleasing qualities was the extreme politeness which, being a truly noble-minded man, he showed to the poor as much as to the rich. I noticed this particularly in the sessions I have described, in which he always said a few polite words to the poor people as he was handing over their money-bags. I learnt something from this, and indeed many a famous benefactor who used to throw money-bags in poor people's faces so hard that every dollar gave them a bruise could have learnt something from my polite father. He asked most of the poor women how they were keeping, and he was so used to the formula 'Good to see you' that he even used it when showing discontented and defiant old biddies the door. He was especially polite to old Frau Flader, and always offered her a chair. She was indeed very unsteady on her legs, and it was all she could do to hobble away with the aid of her crutch. The last time she called on my father to collect her monthly dole she was so decrepit that her grandson, Jupp, had to guide her. He gave me a strange look when he saw me sitting at the table beside my father. Besides her little bag, the old woman also received from my father a big private money-bag, and she burst into a flood of blessings and tears. It is terrible when an old grandmother weeps so copiously. I was close to tears myself, and the old woman probably noticed it. She could not say enough about what a pretty child I was, and she added that she would pray to the Virgin to ensure that I would never be hungry and have to beg. My father was a little annoyed by these words, but the old woman meant them sincerely; there was something eerie, but also devout and loving, in her gaze, and finally she said to her grandson: 'Jupp, go and kiss that dear child's hand.' Jupp pulled a sour face, but he obeyed his grandmother's order; I felt his lips burning on my hand like the bite of a viper. I could hardly say why, but I pulled all the farthings out of my pocket and gave them to Jupp, who counted them up with an expression of blank stupidity and put them calmly in his trouser pocket.

The bad boy remained unchanged. The very next day after our encounter in my father's presence, I met him in the street. He was walking along with his familiar fishing-rod. He struck me with it once more, threw some more lumps of horse-dung at me, and repeated his dreadful 'Haarüh!' so loudly and with such a faithful imitation of Mucky Mick's voice that the latter's donkey, which happened to be in a neighbouring alley along with the cart, thought it heard its master's voice and uttered a joyous and resonant 'Hee-haw'.

As I said, Jupp's grandmother died soon afterwards, and what is more, she died with the reputation of being a witch, which she certainly was not, although our Zippel firmly maintained the contrary. Zippel was the name of a female, still quite young, whose real name was Sibylle; she was my first nursemaid, and remained in our house afterwards. She happened to be in the room on the morning when the scene took place which I have just described, when old Frau Flader lavished so much praise on me and admired my beauty. When Zippel heard these words, they aroused in her the old popular delusion that it is harmful for children to be praised so highly, and that they may fall ill or be afflicted by some misfortune; and in order to ward off the misfortune by which she thought I was threatened, she had recourse to one of the remedies recommended as tried and tested by popular belief, which consisted in spitting three times on the child who has been praised. She immediately bounded up to me and spat three times on my head. This, however, was only a provisional spitting, for the cognoscenti claim that if the dangerous praise is conferred by a witch, then the evil spell can only be broken by someone who is likewise a witch. So Zippel resolved to go that same day to a woman who was known to her as a witch and who, as I later learnt, had done her many favours through her mysterious and prohibited arts. This witch wetted her thumb with spittle and ran it over the crown of my head, from which she had cut off a few hairs; she touched me similarly in a few other places, muttering all manner of mumbo-jumbo, and so I may have been ordained at an early age as a priest of the Devil. At any rate, I kept up my acquaintance with this woman, and later, when I was already grown up, she initiated me into the secret arts. I myself did not become a wizard, but I know how to play tricks, and to see through others' trickery. The woman was known as the Mistress or the Göcherin, because she had been born in Goch, where her late husband was also domiciled; he plied the hateful trade of an executioner, and was called to exercise his office far and wide. It was known that he had bequeathed sundry arcana to his widow, and she was well able to exploit her reputation.

Her best customers were pub landlords to whom she sold dead men's fingers which she said had been left to her by her husband. These are the fingers of thieves who have been hanged, and they serve to make the beer in the barrel tastier and more plentiful. For if you tie the finger of a hanged man, especially of one who was hanged unjustly, to a piece of string and let it hang down inside the barrel, this not only makes the beer tastier, but from this barrel you can tap off twice or even four times as much as from an ordinary barrel of the same size. Enlightened landlords have a more rational method of increasing the quantity of their beer, but it loses in strength.

The Mistress also had plenty of custom from young people of romantic inclinations, and she supplied them with love-potions. Having a charlatan's love of Latin, and wanting to make the Latin sound even more Latin, she called this a philtrarium; the man who gave the potion to his fair one was called the philtrarius, and the lady was the philtrariata. Now and again the philtrarium was ineffectual, or even produced the opposite effect to the one intended. Thus an unloved lad who had talked his reluctant beloved into drinking a bottle of wine with him poured a philtrarium into her glass without her noticing, and as soon as his philtrariata had drunk, he noticed a remarkable change in her behaviour, a certain discomposure, which he took for the outbreak of amorous passion, and he thought the great moment was at hand. But alas! as he forcibly embraced the blushing fair, his nose was assailed by a scent that was not one of Cupid's perfumes; he perceived that the philtrarium had instead acted as a laxative, and his passion was cooled in a most repellent manner. The Mistress saved the reputation of her art by claiming to have misunderstood the unfortunate philtrarius and to have thought he wanted to be cured of his love. Better than her love-potions were the pieces of good advice with which the Mistress accompanied her philtraria. She advised one always to carry some gold in one's pocket, as gold was very healthy and brought good luck, especially to a lover. Who does not recall at this point the words of honest Iago in *Othello* when he tells the lovelorn Rodrigo: 'Take money in your pocket!'[23]

Our Zippel was on intimate terms with this great Mistress, and though she no longer bought love-potions from her, she sometimes called on the arts of the Göcherin when she wanted to avenge herself on a happy rival who had married her own former lover by casting a spell that made the woman infertile or horribly emasculated the unfaithful man. Infertility was produced by magic knots. This is very easy: you enter the church where bride and groom are being married, and just as the priest is declaring them man and wife, you snap shut an iron lock concealed under your apron; and the womb of the newlywed woman closes like the lock. The ceremonies observed in order to produce emasculation are so filthy, hair-raising, and horrible that I cannot possibly reveal them. Suffice it to say that the patient is not rendered impotent in the usual sense, but, in the full sense of the word, deprived of his sexual organs, and the witch who remains in possession of the booty has the following method of preserving the *corpus delicti*, the thing without a name, which is simply called 'the thing'; the Göcherin, with her passion for Latin, always called it a Numen Pompilius, probably a reminiscence of King Numa,[24] the wise law-giver and pupil of the nymph Egeria, who undoubtedly never suspected how shamefully his honest name would one day be abused.

The witch proceeds as follows. She places the thing she has seized in an empty bird's nest, which she fastens high up between the leafy twigs of a tree; additional things which she subsequently wrests from their owners are placed in the same nest, but in such a way that there are never more than half a dozen in it. At first the things are very sickly and wretched, perhaps from emotion and homesickness, but the fresh air strengthens them, and they utter sounds like the chirping of cicadas. The birds fluttering round the tree are deceived thereby into mistaking them for fledglings, and compassion makes them bring food in their bills to feed the motherless orphans; the latter accept this readily, grow strong, fat, and healthy, and twitter loudly instead of chirping softly. This delights the witch, and in cool summer nights, when the moon shines down with true German sentimentality, she sits under the tree and listens to the song of the things, which she calls her sweet nightingales.

Sprenger[25] in his *Malleus Maleficarum* or *Hammer of Witches* mentions these fiendish women's foul deeds with reference to spells like the above, and an old author cited by Scheible in his *Monastery*, but whose name I have forgotten, tells how witches are often compelled to return their booty to the emasculated men. However, the witch mostly performs the theft of manhood in order to extort a ransom by restoring it to the emasculated. When the misappropriated object is returned, comical confusions sometimes occur, and I know the tale of a cathedral canon who was given the wrong Numa Pompilius, one which, according to the reverend gentleman's housekeeper, his nymph Egeria, must have belonged to a Turk rather than a Christian.

I kept up my acquaintance with the Göcherin, and I must have been about sixteen when I went to her dwelling oftener than before, drawn by a spell that was stronger than any of her bombastic Latin philtraria. For she had a niece who was likewise barely sixteen, but, having suddenly shot up and become a tall, slender figure, seemed much older. Her sudden growth was also responsible for her being extremely thin. She had the narrow waist that may be seen among the quadroons in the West Indies, and as she did not wear a corset, nor a dozen petticoats, her tightly-fitting garments resembled the wet drapery of a statue. No marble statue, indeed, could have rivalled her for beauty, since she was a revelation of life itself and every movement revealed the rhythms of her body, I might almost say the music of her soul. None of Niobe's daughters[26] had a face of nobler form; its colour, like her skin generally, was a somewhat changeable white. Her great, deep, dark eyes looked as though she had propounded a riddle and were calmly waiting for the solution, while her mouth with its small, pursed lips and its chalk-white, rather long teeth seemed to say: 'You are too stupid, and it's no good your guessing.' Her hair was red, blood-red, and hung down in long locks over her shoulders, so that she could tie it under her chin. This, however, made her look as if her throat had been cut and her blood were welling forth in red streams.

Josepha, or 'Red Sefchen', as the Göcherin's beautiful niece was called, did not have a particularly melodious voice, and her vocal organs were sometimes so husky as to be toneless; but suddenly, when passion made its appearance, an extremely resonant tone would burst out, which I found especially moving since Josepha's voice bore so great a resemblance to my own. When she spoke, I would sometimes be frightened and think I heard myself speaking, and her singing also reminded me of dreams in which I had heard myself singing in exactly the same way. She knew many old folk-songs, and may have awakened my feeling for this genre; she certainly exercised considerable influence on my poetic beginnings, so that the first poems in my 'Dream Pictures', which I wrote soon afterwards, had a grim and gloomy colouring, like the relationship that was then casting its bloodstained shadow over my young life and thought. Among the songs Josepha sang there was a folk-song which she had learnt from Zippel, and which the latter had often sung to me in my childhood, so that I remembered two verses; I will communicate these here all the more readily, since I have not found the poem in any of the available collections of folk-songs. They run like this. First the wicked Tragig speaks:

'Otilje mine, Otilje dear,
You will not be the last, I fear –
Say, will you hang on the lofty tree?
Or will you swim in the blue sea?

Or will you kiss the naked sword,
Decreed by the almighty Lord?'

And Otilje replies:

'I will not hang on the lofty tree,
I will not swim in the blue sea,
But I will kiss the naked sword,
Decreed by the almighty Lord!'

Once, when Red Sefchen was singing the song and came to the end of this verse, I noticed her inner turmoil and was myself so deeply moved that I suddenly burst into tears, and we fell sobbing into each other's arms and did not speak a single word for at least an hour, while the tears flowed from our eyes and we looked at each other as if through a veil of tears. I asked Sefchen to write these verses down for me, and she did so, but she wrote them in her blood instead of ink; afterwards I lost the red autograph, but the verses remained indelibly in my memory.

The Göcherin's husband was the brother of Sefchen's father, who was likewise an executioner, but as he died at an early age, the Göcherin adopted the child. Soon afterwards, however, when her husband died and she settled in Düsseldorf, she handed the little girl over to her grandfather, who was also an executioner and lived in Westphalia. Here, in the 'free house', as the executioner's dwelling was known, Sefchen remained until her fourteenth year, when her grandfather died and the Göcherin again took in the orphan. Because of her illegitimate birth Sefchen led an isolated life from her childhood till she was a young woman, and in her grandfather's 'free house' she was completely cut off from social intercourse. Hence her shyness, her sensitive shuddering at unfamiliar contact, her mysterious brooding, allied to stubborn defiance, headstrong obstinacy and wildness. Strange! even in her dreams, as she once confessed to me, she did not live with human beings, but dreamt only of animals.

In the solitude of the executioner's dwelling she could occupy her time only with her grandfather's old books; he taught her to read and write, but was exceedingly taciturn. Sometimes he was absent with his assistants for several days, and the child would stay in the 'free house', which was in a very lonely situation among the woods near the gallows. There was nobody else at home except three doddering old women, whose spinning-wheels were continually whirring as they coughed, squabbled, and drank brandy. Poor Sefchen felt very uneasy in the lonely house, especially on winter nights, when the wind outside shook the old oaks and the wind howled so weirdly in the chimney where the fire was flickering; for it is then that a visit from thieves was to be feared – not living ones but dead men, hanged men, who had torn themselves free from the gallows and knocked at the low window-panes of the house and demanded to be let in to warm themselves a little. They look so frozen and miserable, and they can only be driven away if you fetch the executioner's axe from the store-room and threaten them with it; then they rush away like a whirlwind. Sometimes what attracts them is not only the fire on the hearth, but also the desire to steal back the fingers that the executioner stole from them. If the door has not been properly bolted and barred, then their old thievishness works on them even in death, and they steal the sheets from the cupboards and beds. One of the old women, noticing such a theft just in time, ran after the dead thief, whose sheet was fluttering in the wind, and, seizing one corner, tore his booty from him, just as he had reached the gallows and was about to flee to its cross-beam.

It was only on days when Sefchen's grandfather was preparing for a great execution that his fellow-workers would come from the neighbourhood to visit him, and then there was boiling, roasting, feasting, drinking, little talk and no singing. They would drink from silver tankards, whereas in inns they visited the despised 'free-master', let alone his 'free-hands', would be given only a mug with a wooden lid, while all other guests would be served from mugs with tin lids. In some places they break the glass from which the executioner has drunk; nobody speaks to him, everyone shuns even the slightest contact with him. This disgrace rests on his entire clan, which is why the executioners' families always intermarry.

When Sefchen was already eight, as she told me, one fine autumn day an unusual number of guests came to her grandfather's cottage, though there was no execution or any other grave official duty to be performed. There must have been over a dozen of them, almost all of them very old, shrunken men with iron-grey hair or bald heads, carrying their swords under their long red cloaks, and dressed in their best Sunday clothes of old French cut. They had come, they said, to hold a session, and the finest provisions that kitchen and cellar could offer were served up for their lunch. They were the oldest executioners from the most distant regions. It was a long time since they had seen one another; they kept shaking hands, said little, often used a mysterious sign-language, and amused themselves in their own way – that is, 'moulct tristement', as Froissart[27] said of the Englishmen who held a banquet after the battle of Poitiers. When night was falling, the master of the house sent his assistants away, and told the old housekeeper to fetch three dozen bottles of his best Rhine wine from the cellar and place them on the stone table that stood outside in front of the semicircular space formed by the great oak-trees; he also told her to set up the iron holders for the pine-wood torches on this table, and at last he found a pretext for sending the old woman and her two aged companions out of the house. Even the opening in the planks of the dog-kennel was stuffed with a horse-blanket, and the dog was carefully chained up. Red Sefchen was kept in the house by her grandfather, who told her to rinse out the big silver cup that had pictures of the sea-gods with their dolphins and conches on it, and to put the cup on the stone table that was mentioned earlier, but then, he added with some embarrassment, she was to go to bed at once in her little bedroom.

Red Sefchen obediently rinsed out the cup with the picture of Neptune, and put it on the stone table beside the wine-bottles, but she did not go to bed, and, impelled by curiosity, she hid herself behind some bushes near the oak-trees, where, though she could hear little, she could see clearly everything that happened. The strangers, with her grandfather at their head, approached solemnly, two by two, and sat down on big blocks of wood in a semicircle round the stone table, where the lighted resin cast a terrifying light on their grave, stony faces. For a long time they sat in silence, or rather muttering to themselves, perhaps in prayer. Then Sefchen's grandfather filled the cup with wine; each man emptied the cup and passed it to his neighbour once it had been refilled; after each drink they also shook hands in a frank and honest manner. Finally Sefchen's grandfather made a speech; she could make out little and understand nothing, but it seemed to deal with very sorrowful matters, for great tears dropped from the old man's eyes, and the other old men also began to weep bitterly. This was a fearful sight, since these people looked as hard and weatherbeaten as the grey stone figures carved above a church doorway – and now tears were gushing from their stony, expressionless eyes, and they were sobbing like children. The moon meanwhile was looking down in such a melancholy fashion through its veils of vapour in the starless sky that the little eavesdropper felt her heart almost breaking with pity. She was especially moved by the grief of a little old man who was weeping harder than the others and lamenting in such a loud voice that she could clearly make out some of his words. He cried incessantly: 'O God! O God! Our misfortune has already lasted so long that a human soul can no longer endure it. O God, thou art unjust, yea, unjust.' His comrades seemed to have great difficulty in pacifying him.

Finally the assembled men rose once more from their seats, threw off their red cloaks, and, each of them with his sword under his arm, they went two by two behind a tree. Here an iron spade was in readiness, and one of them took the spade and within a few minutes he had dug a deep pit. Now Sefchen's grandfather approached the pit; unlike the others, he had not removed his red cloak, and from under it he drew forth a white package, which was very thin, but at least an ell long, and wrapped in a sheet; he placed this carefully in the open pit, which he filled up once more in great haste.

Poor Sefchen could not bear to stay in her hiding-place any longer; at the sight of this mysterious burial her hair stood on end, and the poor child was driven away by mortal terror; she ran to her little bedroom, crept under the blanket, and fell asleep.

The next morning Sefchen thought it must all have been a dream, but when she saw the freshly turned soil behind the well-known tree, she perceived that it was real. She spent a long time wondering what might be buried there: a child? an animal? a treasure? – but she did not breathe a whisper about the nocturnal event to anyone, and as the years went by it slipped into the recesses of her memory. It was not until five years later, when her grandfather was dead and the Göcherin had come to take the girl to Düsseldorf, that she ventured to open her heart to her aunt. The latter, however, was neither frightened nor surprised by the strange story, but extremely pleased, and told Sefchen that what lay buried in the pit was neither a child, nor a cat, nor a treasure, but her grandfather's old sword, with which he had cut off the heads of a hundred condemned men. She explained that it was a custom among the executioners that a sword that had done the fatal office a hundred times could no longer be kept, let alone used; for such a sword was not like other swords, it had gradually acquired a kind of consciousness, and needed to rest in the grave at last, like a human being. Many people think, too, that so much bloodshed makes these swords cruel in the end, and that they sometimes thirst for blood. It is said that at midnight they can be heard rattling and rumbling in the cupboards where they are hung; indeed, some grow spiteful and malicious, just as we do, and so bemuse the person holding them that he wounds his best friends with them. In the Göcherin's own family, she claimed, one brother once stabbed another with such a sword. Nevertheless, the Göcherin confessed that a sword that had taken a hundred lives could be used for the rarest magic, and that very night she lost no time in digging up the sword buried under the tree Sefchen had indicated, and after that she kept it in her lumber-room with her other magic tools.

Once, when the Göcherin was away from home, I asked Sefchen to show me this curiosity. She did not need to be asked twice; she went into the lumber-room and came out immediately with a huge sword, which she swung mightily despite her thin arms, singing in a mischievous and menacing tone:

'Will you kiss the naked sword,
Decreed by the almighty Lord?'

I replied in the same tone: 'I will not kiss the naked sword – I'll kiss Red Sefchen!' And since she was too afraid of wounding me with the deadly steel to defend herself, she had to let me put my arms boldly round her slender body and kiss her defiant lips. Yes, despite the sword that had beheaded a hundred poor rogues, and despite the infamy attached to any contact with this dishonourable kindred, I kissed the executioner's beautiful daughter. I kissed her, not merely because I was fond of her, but also to mock the old order of society and all its obscure prejudices, and at that moment there flared up in me the first flames of the two passions to which my subsequent life was to be devoted: the love of beautiful women and the love of the French Revolution, the modern *furor francese*, which seized on me too when I was fighting the troopers of the Middle Ages.

I shall not enter into further detail about my love for Josepha. Let me simply confess that she was, after all, only a prelude to the great tragedies of my maturer period. Thus Romeo is infatuated with

Rosalind before he sees his Juliet. In love, as in the Roman Catholic religion, there is a provisional purgatory, in which one is supposed to get used to being roasted, before entering the real everlasting hell. Hell? Can one speak of love so abusively? Well, if you wish, I'll also compare it to heaven. Unfortunately one can never quite establish at what point love begins more to resemble hell or heaven, just as one cannot tell whether the angels we encounter are really devils in disguise, or whether the devils down there may not sometimes be disguised angels.

You will have noticed, dear reader, that my mother's attempt to inoculate me against love as a child failed of its effect. It was written that I should be afflicted by the great evil, the pox of the heart, worse than other mortals, and my heart bears so many unhealed scars that it looks like the plaster cast of Mirabeau, or the façade of the Palais Mazarin after the glorious July days, or even the reputation of the greatest tragic actress. But is there no remedy at all against this dreadful ailment? Recently a psychologist claimed that one could overcome it by using some suitable medicine at the beginning of the attack. However, this prescription recalls the naive old prayer-book containing prayers for all the misfortunes that threaten mankind, including a prayer several pages long which is to be recited by a roofer if he feels dizzy and in danger of falling off the roof. It is equally foolish to advise a lovesick man to flee the sight of his fair one and seek recovery in solitude, at the bosom of nature. Alas, nature's green bosom will only bore him, and he would be better advised, unless all his energies are exhausted, to turn to other and whiter bosoms and seek, if not rest, then salutary unrest; for the most effectual antidote against women is women; of course that means using Beelzebub to drive out Satan, and in such cases the medicine often does more harm than the disease. But it is always a chance, and in states of hopeless love a change of inamorata is undoubtedly the most advisable course, and here my father would be entitled to say: 'You must tap a new barrel.'

Yes, let us return to my dear father, who was informed by some charitable old woman of my frequent visits to the Göcherin and my fondness for Red Sefchen. These denunciations, however, had no effect, beyond that of giving my father the opportunity to manifest his charming politeness. For Sefchen told me, soon afterwards, that a very fine man with his head powdered, accompanied by another, had met her on the promenade, and after his companion had whispered to him, he gave her a kind look and greeted her in passing by taking off his hat to her. From the description I recognized the man who greeted her as my dear, kindly father.

He did not show such indulgence when some irreligious mockery I had uttered was reported to him. I was accused of denying the existence of God, and my father delivered a speech, probably the longest he had ever made, which ran as follows: 'My dear son! Your mother lets you study philosophy with Rector Schallmeyer. That is her business. For my part, I do not like philosophy, for it is mere superstition, and as a merchant I need my head for my business. You can be a philosopher as much as you please, but I beg you not to say publicly what you think, for you would damage my business if people found out that I had a son who did not believe in God. The Jews, in particular, would buy no more velveteen from me, and they are honest people who pay promptly, and are therefore right to stick to religion. I am your father, so I am older than you, and hence more experienced; you can take my word for it when I take the liberty of telling you that atheism is a great sin.'

NOTES

The Harz Journey

1 (p. 31). *Börne*: from 'Memorial Oration for Jean Paul' (1825) by Ludwig Börne (1786–1837), the German-Jewish radical journalist who was later the subject of a contentious book by Heine (*Ludwig Börne: A Memorial*, 1840). Jean Paul Friedrich Richter (1763–1825) was a very popular humorous novelist whose convoluted and allusive style was probably one model for Heine's.

2 (p. 33). *Lüder*: Wilhelm Lüder, a Göttingen student famous as an athlete.

3 (p. 34). *Guelph Orders*: the Guelphs or Welfs were a powerful medieval family, based from 1286 to 1387 at Göttingen, and rivals of the Hohenstaufen emperors. The Guelph Order was founded in 1815; Heine mentions it as an example of politically regressive medievalism. *Graduation-day coaches*: coaches in which successful doctoral candidates paid ceremonial visits to their professors.

4 (p. 34). *Marx*: Karl Friedrich Heinrich Marx, a lecturer in medicine at Göttingen, compiled a survey entitled *Göttingen described from medical, physical and historical viewpoints* (1824), the pedantic style and structure of which Heine is parodying.

5 (p. 35). *the learned —*: most probably Johann Friedrich Blumenbach, professor of natural science and medicine at Göttingen from 1776 to 1835, who was famous partly for his vast collection of index cards.

6 (p. 35). *Pandects*: a collection of Roman laws completed in A.D. 534, forming part of the *Corpus juris civilis*, compiled by the lawyer Tribonian on the orders of the Byzantine Emperor Justinian (reigned 527–65). *Hermogenian* was a fourth-century Roman lawyer who compiled the *Codex Hermogenianus*, the other major Roman law code. The 'Pandects' stable' was a nickname for the Göttingen law faculty.

7 (p. 35). *Shepherd and Doris*: two university disciplinary officers, P. H. Schäfer and C. C. Dohrs. As the name 'Schäfer' means 'shepherd' and the name 'Doris' often occurs in pastoral poetry, Heine associates them with the famous pastorals of Salomon Gessner (1730–88).

8 (p. 36). *Fusia Canina*: another, rather obscure student joke, connected with the Roman *lex Fusia Canina* which restricted the liberation of

slaves. Jost Hermand points out that Heine associates yellow leather with surreptitious sex: cf. the yellow leather trousers on p. 75.

9 (p. 37). *Nebuchadnezzar*: see Daniel 4:33.

10 (p. 37). *Pharaoh's fat kine*: see Genesis 41:18–19.

11 (p. 38). *Themis*: goddess of justice. *Rusticus* is Anton Bauer, professor of criminal law at Göttingen; *Lycurgus* was the legendary law-giver of Sparta; *Cujacius* is Gustav Hugo, whose lectures on Roman law Heine found particularly boring, and whom he ironically equates with the humanist lawyer Cujacius (Jacques de Cujas, 1522–90). Hugo had taken part in a controversy about whether a passage in the *Corpus Juris*, requiring that trees marking the border of a field should be clipped to the height of fifteen feet, meant the bottom fifteen feet or (as Hugo maintained) the top fifteen feet.

12 (p. 39). *Münchhausen*: the Hanoverian statesman G. A. von Münchhausen (1688–1770), first curator of Göttingen University.

13 (p. 40). *Duke Ernest*: a medieval epic poem, combining history and legend, about Duke Ernest of Swabia who was exiled by the Emperor for refusing to take up arms against a friend.

14 (p. 40). *'Full of joy ... free!'*: Goethe's poem (sung by Klärchen in *Egmont*, Act III) runs: 'Freudvoll und leidvoll,/Gedankenvoll sein ...' ('Full of joy, full of sorrow,/Full of pensiveness ...'). The supposed journeyman was actually a quite well-educated travelling salesman named Carl Dörne, who had had a drop too much and decided to pull Heine's leg. After reading the description of himself in *The Harz Journey* Dörne published an account of his meeting with Heine, in which he recounted how he simply sang folk-songs, deliberately changing the words, in order to maintain his disguise as a journeyman. But it appears that Heine also tried to pull *his* leg, though less successfully, for according to Dörne Heine introduced himself as Peregrinus and claimed to be an emissary of the Sultan of Turkey, travelling through Germany to recruit soldiers.

15 (p. 40). *Lotte ... grave*: this anonymous poem, which appeared in 1775, describes a scene that does not in fact occur in Goethe's novel.

16 (p. 41). *Hoffmann*: E. T. A. Hoffmann (1776–1822), the Romantic author of *The Golden Pot*, *The Sandman*, and many other tales and novels.

17 (p. 44). *Lafayette*: the French nobleman Marie-Joseph Motier de Lafayette (1757–1834) had fought in the American War of Independence and supported the French Revolution; in the autumn of 1824 he was being enthusiastically welcomed on a tour of the United States.

18 (p. 45). *Duke of Cambridge*: Adolphus Frederick, Duke of Cambridge

(1774–1850), youngest son of King George III, and ruler of Hanover from 1814 onwards.

19 (p. 45). *Eckart*: in this legend, adapted by Ludwig Tieck (1773–1853) and other Romantics, Eckart, despite his maltreatment by his lord the Duke of Burgundy, saves the latter's life and lays down his own life for the Duke's sons.

20 (p. 47). *Aulic Counsellor B.*: Friedrich Bouterwek, professor of aesthetics at Göttingen, whom Heine read and admired.

21 (p. 47). *Chamisso*: author (1781–1838) of poetry, travel books, and fiction, including *The Wondrous Tale of Peter Schlemihl* (1814) about a man who sells his shadow to the Devil.

22 (p. 52). *Austrian Observer*: government newspaper in Vienna, strongly reactionary and hence afraid of the 'ghosts' of the French Revolution.

23 (p. 52). *Saul Ascher*: a Berlin Jewish book-seller and philosopher (1767–1822).

24 (p. 53). *Varnhagen von Ense*: Karl August Varnhagen von Ense (1785–1858), officer, diplomat, and writer; married to the literary hostess and convert from Judaism Rahel Varnhagen, *née* Rahel Levin (1771–1833); both were close friends of Heine.

25 (p. 65). *St Genevieve*: the heroine of Tieck's Romantic drama *Life and Death of St Genevieve* (1799). Unjustly accused of adultery by her steward Golo, Genevieve is sent by her husband into the wilderness, where her son Sorrowful (Schmerzensreich) is suckled by a deer.

26 (p. 66). *Evening News*: a literary paper published in Dresden; Heine also mocks literary salons in the famous poem *Lyrical Intermezzo* No. 50, which begins (in Hal Draper's translation): 'They talked of love and devotion / Over the tea and the sweets'.

27 (p. 68). *'The Blocksberg . . . philistine!'*: from the 'Rheinweinlied' ('Rhenish Wine Song') by Matthias Claudius (1740–1815).

28 (p. 68). *'Schierke' and 'Elend'*: villages near the Brocken, mentioned in the 'Walpurgisnacht scene' of Goethe's *Faust*. 'Elend' means 'misery'.

29 (p. 70). *Elise von Hohenhausen*: writer and translator (1789–1857), whose literary salon in Berlin Heine frequently attended. She introduced Heine to Byron's works and described him as 'the German Byron'.

30 (p. 70). *Schütz*: C. F. Schütz, professor of literature at Halle.

31 (p. 71). *Wisotzki*: the owner of a restaurant and a puppet-theatre in Berlin.

32 (p. 71). *'The tongue . . . words'*: from Schiller's play *Wallenstein's Death* (1800).

33 (p. 71). *'colour . . . play in'*: Shakespeare, *A Midsummer Night's Dream*, I, ii, 80. This passage refers to Count von Brühl, director of

the Royal Theatre in Berlin, and his obsession with historically accurate costumes.

34 (p. 71). *Professor Lichtenstein*: professor of zoology at Berlin, responsible for establishing the Zoo.

35 (p. 71). *Hatred and Penitence*: a popular tragedy (1789) by August von Kotzebue (1761–1819).

36 (p. 71). *Spontini's Janissary opera*: the opera *Olympia* by Gaspare Spontini (1774–1851), who in 1820 became general musical director at the Prussian court. It was first performed in Berlin in 1821, with vast numbers of dancers and singers, deafening music, and a live elephant on stage.

37 (p. 72). *Hoguet*: an outstanding solo dancer at the Berlin Opera; *Bucholz*: a political writer in Berlin, despised by liberals.

38 (p. 72). *friend in the East*: Tsar Alexander I of Russia.

39 (p. 72). *Lemière* and *Röhnisch*: female dancers at the Berlin Opera, whom Heine would have seen in *Olympia*.

40 (p. 72). *Cervantes*: see *Don Quixote*, Book I, Ch. 2.

41 (p. 72). *Greifswald*: since no student from Greifswald, on the Baltic coast, is recorded in the Brocken visitors' book for the night Heine stayed there, this nationalist is evidently invented, especially as he comes from the same university as E. M. Arndt (see Introduction, and note 43 below).

42 (p. 73). *Blücher*: the Prussian general who had been a hero of the nationalist student movement since his defeat of Napoleon at Waterloo.

43 (p. 73). *'The Father of our Country'*: a patriotic student song, composed by A. C. H. Niemann in 1782. *Wilhelm Müller* (1794–1827) was a lyric poet, author of *Winter Journey* (1823); Friedrich *Rückert* (1788–1866) was famous first for his patriotic verse, and later for his poetry in Oriental styles. Ludwig *Uhland* (1787–1862) was among the best-known Romantic poets, though his reputation has faded. Albert Gottlieb *Methfessel* (1786–1869), composer and friend of Heine's, composed a book of student songs and also set some of Heine's early poems to music. Ernst Moritz *Arndt* (1769–1860) was a leading anti-French propagandist; the quotation is from his rousing 'Song of the Fatherland' (1813).

44 (p. 73). *Guilt*: a fate-tragedy (published 1816) by Adolf Müllner (1774–1829).

45 (p. 75). *'Hast thou halls like unto me?'*: a not quite translatable pun on 'Halle', meaning both the university town and 'hall'.

46 (p. 76). *Falcidia*: the Roman *lex Falcidia* limited the freedom of testators; Eduard *Gans* (1798–1839), a Berlin friend of Heine's, was an authority on the law of inheritance; J. F. L. *Göschen*, here lampooned as

servile and asinine, was a conservative law professor at Göttingen, as was C. F. *Elvers*, here ironically given the forenames of the Roman orator Cicero. The dream recalls Spontini's extravagant opera *The Vestal Virgin* set in ancient Rome.

47 (p. 78). *The Prince of Pallagonia's palace*: a bizarrely constructed building in Palermo, described in Goethe's *Italian Journey*.

48 (p. 78). *Clauren*: pseudonym of Carl Gottlieb Samuel Heun (1771–1854), author of mildly prurient novels which Heine often mentions distastefully.

49 (p. 79). *Theophrastus*: not the Greek prose-writer, but Theophrastus Bombastus von Hohenheim, known as Paracelsus: see p. 252 below.

50 (p. 82). *our late cousin . . . Mölln*: Till Eulenspiegel, a folk-hero famous for practical jokes; he died at Mölln, not far from Hamburg, in 1530.

51 (p. 83). *Evening News*: see note 26 above; the poem was by Theodor Hell (pseudonym of K. G. T. Winkler, 1775–1856). L. F. *Niemann* published a *Guidebook for Travellers in the Harz* (1824).

52 (p. 83). *Lüneburg Chronicle*: Heine's memory seems to have fused a number of medieval chronicles; this one cannot be precisely identified. Klaus Briegleb substitutes 'Limburg Chronicle', a chronicle of the city of Limburg begun in 1336 and published in 1617.

53 (p. 84). *Georg Sartorius*: professor of history at Göttingen, noted for his mildly liberal political opinions.

54 (p. 85). *Paris*: son of King Priam of Troy; he had to judge which of the three goddesses, Hera, Athena, and Aphrodite, was the most beautiful, and gave the prize, an apple, to Aphrodite.

55 (p. 86). *Jungfernstieg*: a street in Hamburg, beside the Alster Lake; cf. the poem 'Recollection of Hammonia'.

Ideas: The Book of Le Grand

1 (p. 89). *Stalwart race . . . fall*: part of the crucial, twice-repeated prophecy from Müllner's *Guilt*: see *The Harz Journey*, note 44.

2 (p. 91). *Jagor's*: an outstanding restaurant on Unter den Linden in Berlin.

3 (p. 93). *Via Burstah*: the Great Burstah, a major shopping street in Hamburg.

4 (p. 93). *Susannah*: see the Book of Susannah in the Apocrypha; *Leda* was raped by Zeus in the guise of a swan; the primeval Romans are said to have abducted the neighbouring *Sabine women* to provide themselves with wives; Friederike *Bethmann* (1760–1815) was a famous actress; *la belle ferronière* is a portrait in the Louvre, supposedly by Leonardo da Vinci, depicting a mistress of François I of France.

5 (p. 94). *Strada San Giovanni*: the Johannisstrasse in Hamburg.

6 (p. 96). *Life . . . death*: Heine corrects the conclusion of Schiller's play *The Bride of Messina* (1803): 'Life is *not* the highest good,/But guilt is the greatest evil.' *Kleist*: an allusion to Act III, scene 5 of *Prince Friedrich von Homburg* (completed 1810, published 1821) by Heinrich von Kleist (1777–1811), in which the Prince, having glimpsed the grave that has been prepared for him, passionately expresses his longing to stay alive at whatever cost. Kleist himself committed suicide at the Wannsee in Berlin. Heine democratically omits the 'von' indicating nobility. *Egmont*: the eponymous hero of Goethe's play *Egmont* (completed 1787) speaks these words after being condemned to death. Heine's last quotation comes from the tragedy *Edwin* by his friend Karl Immermann (1796–1840).

7 (p. 96). *O shining Odysseus . . . dead*: quoted from Richmond Lattimore's translation of the *Odyssey*, Book 11.

8 (p. 96). *Duvent* and *Löwe*: invented names, meaning 'windy' and 'lion'; Löwe was a common Jewish name. See Ecclesiastes 9:4.

9 (p. 98). *Valmiki*: the author of the Indian epic *Ramayana*, whose hero is the divine *Rama*; *Kalidasa* was the author of the play *Sakuntala*, which Heine knew in Georg Forster's German translation.

10 (p. 98). *a kind lady*: Amalie von Helvig, whose mother was the second wife of Warren Hastings (1732–1818), Governor-General of India until his recall from office in 1785.

11 (p. 98). *Franz Bopp*: an outstanding philologist (1791–1867), whose lectures on Sanskrit literature Heine had attended at Berlin. In 1819 he published a Latin translation of *Nalus*, an episode from the epic *Mahabharata*.

12 (p. 99). *Tiotio . . . tototinx*: the nightingales' song from the translation of Aristophanes' comedy *The Birds* by Johann Heinrich *Voss* (1821).

13 (p. 99). *Görres*: Joseph Görres (1776–1848), nationalist writer, associated with some of the leading Romantics, and founder and editor of the *Rhenish Mercury*, which from 1814 to 1816 advocated the unification of Germany.

14 (p. 101). *seven cities*: six of these towns are traditionally associated with fools; Heine has maliciously inserted Göttingen among them.

15 (p. 102). *Wilhelm*: Heine's schoolmate Fritz von Wizewsky, who was apparently drowned as Heine describes; cf. the later poem about this incident, 'Memory', with its refrain 'But the kitten, the kitten was rescued'.

16 (p. 102). *Elector Jan Wilhelm*: Elector Palatine (1658–1716), who made Düsseldorf his capital from 1690 to 1716 and founded an art gallery there in 1710.

17 (p. 104). *'Ça ira'*: a French revolutionary song: 'Oh, we'll manage it, we'll manage it, we'll manage it,/The aristocrats to the lamp-post!'

18 (p. 107). *Niebuhr*: the historian Barthold Georg Niebuhr (1776–1831), whose *Roman History* (1810–11) exposed some of the early history of Rome recounted by Livy as legend.

19 (p. 107). *Haman*: see Esther 3.

20 (p. 107). *Wadzeck*: Franz Daniel Wadzeck, who died in 1823, was a Hamburg philanthropist who, having founded an orphanage, liked to describe himself as 'father of 360 children'; Heine therefore links him with the promiscuous Cleopatra.

21 (p. 107). *Hamlet*: see I, ii, 187–8.

22 (p. 107). *Vis ... sinapis*: strength, wood, thirst, cough, gherkin, ruler, hemp, and mustard. It is hard to imagine that Heine used any of these words in the Latin disputation on five legal topics that earned him his doctorate.

23 (p. 108). *katal ... pik*: forms of the Hebrew verbs meaning 'kill' and 'seek'.

24 (p. 108). *Adelung's grammar*: Johann Christoph Adelung (1732–1806) compiled a famous dictionary and numerous grammars of German.

25 (p. 110). *apprendre par cœur*: learning by heart; *bête allemande*: German beast.

26 (p. 110). *Hans Michel Martens*: probably the Prussian diplomat Friedrich von Martens.

27 (p. 111). *Goethe*: a mistake: Goethe does not mention this march, either in his *Campaign in France* or elsewhere.

28 (p. 112). *Schmalz*: a Berlin lawyer of conservative views.

29 (p. 112). *Becker*: author of a textbook on world history for schoolchildren, incongruously juxtaposed with the Greek travel-writer Pausanias and the classic Roman historians Livy and Sallust.

30 (p. 112). *Professor Saalfeld*: J. C. F. Saalfeld, professor of history and politics in Göttingen, and author of violent denunciations of Napoleon.

31 (p. 114). *et la Prusse n'existait plus*: 'and Prussia no longer existed'.

32 (p. 114). *Indian Ocean*: St Helena, where Napoleon was exiled and buried, is actually in the Atlantic Ocean. His remains were transferred to Paris in 1840.

33 (p. 115). *Sir Hudson*: Sir Hudson Lowe, Governor of St Helena. After Waterloo, Napoleon hoped to find refuge on the British ship the *Bellerophon* which delivered him into captivity. The Comte de *Las Cases* accompanied Napoleon to St Helena; Barry *O'Meara* was Napoleon's doctor there till 1818, when he was replaced by Francesco *Antommarchi*. All three published memoirs of Napoleon.

34 (p. 115). *Londonderry*: the Marquess of Londonderry (1769–1822), better known as Lord Castlereagh, British foreign secretary from 1812 to 1822, committed suicide.

35 (p. 116). *Very like leaves . . . away*: from Homer's *Iliad*, Book 6, translated by Robert Fitzgerald.

36 (p. 120). *Du sublime . . .*: 'From the sublime to the ridiculous it is only a step': Napoleon made this remark to the French ambassador in Warsaw on 10 December 1812, during his retreat from Russia.

37 (p. 122). *Leda*: having been raped by Zeus in the guise of a swan, Leda laid an egg from which was born Helen, whose beauty gave rise to the Trojan War.

38 (p. 122). *My friend G.*: Eduard Gans; see note 46 to *The Harz Journey*.

39 (p. 122). *Michael Beer*: dramatist (1800–1833) and brother of the composer Meyerbeer.

40 (p. 123). *Ponce de Leon*: a comedy (1804) by Clemens Brentano (1778–1842); the text actually runs: 'These bad musicians and good people.'

41 (p. 123). *Lucullus*: the famous Roman general and gourmet.

42 (p. 123). *Steinweg*: a street in Hamburg with many Jewish restaurants.

43 (p. 124). *Tacitus*: Roman historian who alleges in his *Histories*, Book 5, that the Jews once worshipped a donkey in their temple at Jerusalem.

44 (p. 124). *Balaam's ass*: see Numbers 22:28.

45 (p. 124). *Gesneri . . .*: an actual treatise, 'On the ancient honesty of donkeys', by the Göttingen philologist Johann Matthias Gesner (1691–1761).

46 (p. 124). *Jacob*: see Genesis 49:14; *Ajax*: see Homer, *Iliad*, Book 11, l. 558; *Herr von ....*: as Heine leaves nine dots, he may mean the dramatist Friedrich von Uechtritz, who is also alluded to below. *Abelardum*: Heine took most of the following references almost verbatim from a little-known and eccentric work by Johann Adam Bernhard entitled *Brief and Curious History of Scholars, wherein an account is given of the birth, education, manners, destinies, writings, etc., of learned persons . . .* (1718), including the quotation from Mabillon's *German Journey* (*c.* 1680) in which the author complains 'that the stench of filthy tobacco was very unpleasant'.

47 (p. 125). *Lot*: see Genesis 19:17. *Madame de Staël* (1766–1817), author of *De l'Allemagne* (1810), fled from France to Switzerland in 1792 to escape the guillotine; Heine often satirizes her and accuses her of mannishness. The Hungarian Count *Benjowsky* escaped in 1771 from captivity in Siberia and described his adventures in a widely read book. The *Prussian army* retreated in disorder after being defeated at Jena in 1806. Pope *Gregory VII* had to flee from Rome to Salerno in 1084 during his

conflict with the Emperor. *Rabbi Yitskhok Abarbanel* had to leave Aragon in 1482 to escape the King's displeasure. *Rousseau* fled from France to Geneva, and thence to England, to escape punishment for publishing *Émile*.

48 (p. 126). *Pastor S.*: apparently L. C. G. Strauch, a strictly orthodox clergyman, chosen here for his incongruity.

49 (p. 126). *Heeren*: A. H. L. Heeren, professor of history at Göttingen, the fourth impression of whose *Ideas on the Politics, Traffic and Commerce of the Principal Nations of the Ancient World* appeared in 1824.

50 (p. 127). *Gubitz*: Friedrich Wilhelm Gubitz (1786–1870), editor of the *Companion*, in which several of Heine's early writings, including *The Harz Journey*, were first published.

51 (p. 127). *Horace*: his *Art of Poetry* recommends that whatever one writes should be 'stored up for eight years in your notebooks at home' (D. A. Russell's translation). *Maecenas* was Horace's patron.

52 (p. 128). *Pangloss*: the invincibly optimistic philosopher in *Candide* (1759) by Voltaire (1694–1778).

53 (p. 129). *Schupp*: Johann Balthasar Schupp (1610–61), a Hamburg clergyman, wrote satirical descriptions of the Germany of his day.

54 (p. 129). *Damascus*: see the Song of Solomon 7:4.

55 (p. 131). *obscurest man*: a Hamburg broker, Joseph Friedländer, thought he was the 'dark broker, not yet hanged' mentioned in *The Harz Journey* (p. 86), jostled Heine in the street, and then put it about that he had beaten Heine up. Having emphasized his dark looks, Heine then calls him 'Herr von Weiss' ('white'), and continues the play on darkness and light by quoting *'Mais . . . alors'*: 'But will you see any more clearly?' This reply was given during the French Revolution by the reactionary Abbé Maury to a crowd that was threatening to hang him from a lamp-post.

56 (p. 131). *'On the Rhine . . . growing'*: from 'Rhenish Wine Song' by Matthias Claudius (see *The Harz Journey*, note 27). *'This picture . . .'*: Tamino's aria in Mozart's *Magic Flute* (1791). *'O white lady'*: a slightly confused allusion to a song from the opera *The White Lady* (1825) by François Adrien Boieldieu (1775–1834).

57 (p. 132). *a sorrowful tragedian*: Friedrich von Uechtritz (1800–1875), author of *Alexander and Darius* (1826).

58 (p. 132). *Clauren*: see note 48 to *The Harz Journey*; because of his sentimentally erotic novel *Mimili* (1815), Heine links him with the prostitutes of Friedrich Street in Berlin. Celery and asparagus were supposed to be aphrodisiacs.

59 (p. 133). *Willibald Alexis*: pseudonym of the novelist H. G. W. Häring (1798–1871); hence, herring salad.

60 (p. 133). *5,588 years*: in Jewish chronology, 1827 is the 5,588th year since the creation of the world.

61 (p. 134). *Fouché*: Joseph Fouché (1759–1820), minister of police under Napoleon; his posthumously published *Memoirs* were widely, though wrongly, thought to be a forgery. The saying ascribed to him ('Words are made to conceal our thoughts') goes back to classical antiquity.

62 (p. 136). *Agur*: see Proverbs 30:2.

63 (p. 136). *Haude and Spener Gazette*: a leading daily newspaper in Berlin. *Livy*, *Curtius*, and *Cornelius Nepos* are Roman historians. For the *Companion*, see note 50 above.

64 (p. 137). *'God d—n, . . . 'F—e'*: thus in the original.

65 (p. 139). *Thomas Paine*: English republican (1737–1809), active as a revolutionary politician in France, author of *The Rights of Man* (1791). *Système de la Nature*: a materialist and atheist work of philosophy by Paul D'Holbach (1723–89). The *Westphalian Advertiser*: a newspaper which was at first liberal but became increasingly conservative throughout the 1820s. F. D. E. *Schleiermacher* (1768–1834) was a Protestant theologian closely associated with the Romantics.

66 (p. 140). *Vous pleurez . . .?*: 'You are crying . . .?'

67 (p. 142). *Ganesha*: the Indian god of intelligence. In the *Ramayana*, the divine maiden *Maneka* descends from heaven to distract King *Visvamitra* from his penitential exercises.

68 (p. 143). *Barthold Schwarz*: the fourteenth-century German monk credited with inventing gunpowder.

The Town of Lucca

1 (p. 145). *Letters from a Dead Man*: by Prince Pückler-Muskau (1785–1871), witty travel-writer and diarist.

2 (p. 147). *Fido*: Heine's friend Eduard Gans (see *The Harz Journey*, note 46) who, by converting from Judaism to Protestantism, had obtained a professorship in the law faculty of Berlin University and was in conflict with the ultra-conservative Professor Savigny.

3 (p. 149). *Breihahn*: a kind of beer, named after the brewer.

4 (p. 149). Nanette *Schechner*-Waagen and Henriette *Sontag*: two singers, regarded as rivals for the favour of the Berlin public.

5 (p. 150). *Lyonnet*: Pierre Lyonnet (1707–89), French naturalist.

6 (p. 151). *'Occhie, stelle mortali'*: 'Eyes, mortal stars!'

7 (p. 153). *neo-German school*: the Nazarenes, a quasi-religious order of painters founded in 1809 by Franz Overbeck (1789–1869) and Franz

Pforr (1788–1812), who aimed to revive German religious art by modelling themselves on Dürer and the young Raphael.

8 (p. 153). *Sakuntala*: see *Ideas*, note 9. *Vasantasena*: a play ascribed to King Sudraka and translated into German (1828) by O. L. B. Wolff, concerning the love of the prostitute Vasantasena for a poor Brahmin.

9 (p. 154). *Krug*: Wilhelm Traugott Krug, professor of philosophy at Leipzig, published in 1829 an attack on the celibacy of Catholic priests.

10 (p. 154). *The Maid of Orleans*: a tragedy by Schiller (1801); on Count von Brühl and his passion for theatrical authenticity, see *The Harz Journey*, note 33.

11 (p. 154). *Church Times*: a strictly orthodox Lutheran paper in Berlin, edited by Ernst Wilhelm Hengstenberg (a frequent target of Heine's satire); in 1830 it condemned the Hebrew scholar Wilhelm *Gesenius* for his liberal approach to the Bible.

12 (p. 157). *Denon*: Dominique Vivant Denon accompanied Napoleon to Egypt and in 1802 published an account of his travels with pictures of Egyptian monuments. In Count von Brühl's production of Mozart's *The Magic Flute* Sarastro wore a tall cap in Egyptian style. Giovanni Battista *Belzoni*, an Egyptologist, published in 1821 an illustrated account of his excavations.

13 (p. 160). *Then . . . sang*: from the *Iliad*, Book I, in Fitzgerald's translation. The *Vulgate* is the Latin translation of the Bible approved by the Catholic Church. Heine is implying that Homer is the Bible of Sensualism (see Introduction).

14 (p. 163). *Kyrie Eleison*: 'Lord, have mercy.'

15 (p. 164). *'Delightful!'*: in English in the original.

16 (p. 164). *Catalani*: Angelica Catalani, an internationally renowned opera singer.

17 (p. 168). *'I like this man'*: in English in the original.

18 (p. 169). *Plutarch*: (*c.* A.D. 46–120), Greek biographer and moral philosopher, author of *Lives of the Noble Greeks and Romans*. The anecdote is not in fact from Plutarch, but from Joinville's *Histoire de Saint Louis*, and is set in medieval Damascus, not ancient Alexandria.

19 (p. 170). *'Dem Zefardeyim Kinnim'*: refers to three of the Egyptian plagues (Exodus 7 and 8): the turning of water into blood, the plague of frogs, and the swarms of flies.

20 (p. 171). *Carbonari*: a secret society which aimed to liberate and unify Italy.

21 (p. 174). *tulip*: an allusion to Heine's campaign against the poet Count Platen (1796–1835), which dominates the later chapters of *The Baths of Lucca*. The tulip, a scentless flower which is a frequent image in Platen's

poetry, symbolizes his homosexuality. Matilda also shows her aversion to tulips in *The Baths of Lucca*, Ch. 2.

22 (p. 175). *Tamar*: see Genesis 38; *Lot*: Genesis 19:32–8; *Potiphar's wife*: Genesis 39:11–13; *Susannah*: Apocrypha; *Jacob*: Genesis 25:29–34, 27:6–41; 30:31–42; *David*: 2 Samuel 11:14–17; *Solomon*: 1 Kings 11:3.

23 (p. 176). *Austrians*: much of Northern Italy, including Tuscany (where Lucca is situated), was under Austrian rule from the Congress of Vienna (1815) until Austria's unsuccessful war in Italy (1859).

24 (p. 176). *The Bear and the Bassa*: a musical play by Karl Ludwig Blum, director of the Königstädter Theatre in Berlin.

25 (p. 176). *sore head*: the original exploits the idiom 'to tie a bear [to somebody]', which in Heine's day meant 'to avoid paying one's bill', and runs literally: 'but this often costs them more money than they have brought with them, and in such cases one of the bears is tied up until his comrades come back and pay, whence the expression "to tie up a bear"'.

26 (p. 179). *'fault-finding with humanity'*: a quotation from Lessing's philosemitic play *Nathan the Wise* (1779), referring to the extreme moralism that originated with the Jews.

27 (p. 180). *Montesquieu*: (1689–1755), French political philosopher; the quotation is from his *On the Spirit of the Laws* (1748).

28 (p. 180). *Mel . . . factis*: 'Honey in the mouth, words of milk, gall in the heart, deceit in deeds.'

29 (p. 182). *Falstaff*: Shakespeare, *Henry IV Part 2*, IV.ii.64.

30 (p. 183). *roturier*: a commoner as opposed to a nobleman.

31 (p. 184). *Marcus Brutus*: the assassin of Julius Caesar; *Stoa*: the Athenian colonnade which gave its name to the Stoic school of moral philosophers.

32 (p. 186). *Knight of the Silver Moon*: in *Don Quixote*, Part II, Ch. 64.

33 (p. 187). *Agis*: Plutarch tells how he tried to restore equality in Sparta but was killed by a conspiracy of wealthy men. *Gaius and Tiberius Gracchus* tried to alleviate poverty in republican Rome by redistributing land, but were likewise killed.

34 (p. 187). *toga virilis*: the gown assumed by a Roman on attaining manhood.

35 (p. 188). *Ham*: see Genesis 9:21–2.

36 (p. 189). *Maritorne*: a hideous maidservant in *Don Quixote*, Book 3, Ch. 2.

37 (p. 190). *third Hegira of the Bourbons*: the flight of the Bourbon king Charles X during the July Revolution in 1830. The previous flights

were Louis XVI's unsuccessful flight from Paris in 1791 and Louis XVIII's flight in 1815 on learning of Napoleon's escape from Elba. The Hegira is Muhammad's flight from Mecca to Medina in 622.

38 (p. 190). *Gottfried Bassen*: a publisher of chivalric novels, hence associated with the anachronistic nobility.

39 (p. 191). *ex ungue leonem*: 'from a claw [you may paint] the lion.'

40 (p. 191). *Barbaroux*: Charles Barbaroux, the revolutionary who led the Girondists to Paris in July 1792, singing the Marseillaise; they were guillotined in the Reign of Terror in 1794.

Differing Conceptions of History

1 (p. 195). *'There is . . . sun'*: Ecclesiastes 1:9.

2 (p. 195). *well-known government*: that of Prussia, which sent the historian Leopold von Ranke (1795–1886) to study in Vienna and Italy. The original contains some untranslatable puns on Ranke's name, as part of a polemic against his anti-liberal views and historical detachment. On Goethe and the Historical School of law, see Introduction.

3 (p. 195). *fever of liberty*: the July Revolution of 1830 in France.

4 (p. 196). *philosophers of humanity*: eighteenth-century German thinkers associated with the Enlightenment who believed that history was the gradual development of mankind's capacity for reason, wisdom and justice, and hence of its true humanity: see, for example, Lessing's *The Education of the Human Race* (quoted in Introduction).

5 (p. 196). *'Le pain . . . peuple'*: 'Bread is the people's first right', ascribed to the French revolutionary leader Antoine de Saint-Just (1767–94).

On the History of Religion and Philosophy in Germany

PREFACES

1 (p. 199). *a law*: the decree of the German Federal Diet, issued on 3 July 1832, which required books consisting of less than twenty unbound sheets to be submitted to censorship before publication in Germany.

2 (p. 200). *Count Molé*: Prime Minister of France from 1836 to 1839.

3 (p. 200). *playthings for monkeys*: see the 'Witch's Kitchen' scene of Goethe's *Faust*, Part One.

4 (p. 201). *Ruge*: Arnold Ruge (1802–80), German journalist of the Young Hegelian school who founded the radical *Halle Yearbooks* in 1837 and,

when in political exile in Paris, edited the *German–French Yearbooks* jointly with Karl Marx.

5 (p. 202). *Marx*: Heine became friendly with Karl Marx (1818–83) during the latter's stay in Paris in 1844. Ludwig *Feuerbach* (1804–72), philosopher and author of *The Essence of Christianity* which explained God away as a projection of human wishes. Georg Friedrich *Daumer* (1800–1875) and Bruno *Bauer* (1809–82) were likewise left-Hegelians and opponents of Christianity. The orthodox theologian *Hengstenberg* (see *The Town of Lucca*, note 11) is placed among them out of malice.

6 (p. 202). *'If ye eat . . . God'*: see Genesis 3:5.

7 (p. 202). *Damascus . . . Capuchins*: after the unexplained murder of a Capuchin monk in Damascus in 1840, the Jews there were accused of having committed the murder for ritual purposes. Heine took up the Jews' cause in his *Lutetia* articles.

8 (p. 203). *Second Temple*: in A.D. 70 Titus Vespasian (later Emperor of Rome, 79–81) suppressed the Jews' uprising and destroyed the Temple at Jerusalem.

9 (p. 204). *All these . . . great deep*: Ecclesiasticus 24:23–9.

BOOK ONE

1 (p. 206). *Sanson*: the Parisian executioner who beheaded Louis XVI in 1793.

2 (p. 206). *Dictionnaire*: an allusion to Voltaire's *Philosophical Dictionary* (1764).

3 (p. 206). *Baronius*, etc.: church historians; Heine took their names, and most of the following information about early Christianity, from Spittler's *Outline of the History of the Christian Church* (1814).

4 (p. 207). *homousios*: the doctrine that the Word was identical with (not just similar to) God. *Investiture*: the medieval Holy Roman Emperors waged a long conflict with the Pope over the right to appoint ('invest') bishops.

5 (p. 207). *Eudoxia*: Byzantine Empress who in the early fifth century supported Nestorius, Archbishop of Constantinople, against Cyril, Patriarch of Alexandria, in a dispute about whether Christ's human nature was separable from his divine nature; Cyril enjoyed the backing of the later Empress *Pulcheria*, who, according to Heine's source, hated Nestorius for betraying her love-intrigues.

6 (p. 207). *'after . . . provinces'*: quotation from Heine's *The North Sea* (1826).

7 (p. 207). *Isidore's Decretals*: a ninth-century collection of laws, including some forgeries designed to strengthen the authority of the Pope.

8 (p. 208). *Cerinthus*: the first Christian Gnostic (second century).

9 (p. 210). *the Council*: the Council of Basle lasted from 1431 to 1448. Heine found this story, and much other German folklore, in F. L. von Dobeneck's *Popular Beliefs and Heroic Legends of the German Middle Ages* (1815).

10 (p. 210). *annates*: the first year's revenue of an ecclesiastical benefice, paid to the Papal curia; *expectatives*: rights of succession to a profitable office; *reservations*: the restriction of certain sins to the jurisdiction of bishops.

11 (p. 210). *Thomas Aquinas* (1225–74), *Bonaventura* (1221–74): leading theologians.

12 (p. 211). *'adjuro . . . mortuos'*: 'I command you by Him who will come to judge the living and the dead'.

13 (p. 212). *'O Venus . . . thou art!'*: from the fifteenth-century 'Song of Tannhäuser'. Heine uses the medieval form 'Tanhüser'.

14 (p. 213). *Melusine*: a water-nymph in Southern French legend; *Morgan Le Fay*: sister of King Arthur, said to rule the island of *Avalon*. What Heine says about the character of French and Breton mythology has recently been borne out by its imaginative use in A. S. Byatt's *Possession* (1990).

15 (p. 213). *Berlioz*: an allusion to his Symphonie Fantastique (1830).

16 (p. 213). *Remigius*: Nicolas Remy (1530–1612) prosecuted accused witches in Lorraine and defended his actions in his *Daemonolatriae libri tres* (1595); Heine read about him in Dobeneck. The account of his death given below also comes from Dobeneck, but is not supported by any other source.

17 (p. 214). *Praetorius*: Johannes Praetorius (1630–80) published *Anthropodemus Plutonicus, that is, a new description of the world including all* manner of wondrous people (1666).

18 (p. 217). *Andersen*: Hans Christian Andersen (1805–75), whom Heine got to know in Paris in 1833.

19 (p. 217). *'We're flitting!'*: there is a close parallel to this story in Tennyson's poem 'Walking to the Mail'.

20 (p. 219). *Politian*: Angelo Poliziani (1454–94), Italian humanist.

21 (p. 220). *Bossuet*: French bishop and historian (1627–1704), author of a *History of the Variations of the Protestant Churches* (1688).

22 (p. 221). *Queen of Navarre*: Marguerite de Navarre (1492–1549), author of a collection of tales, the *Heptameron* (1559), modelled on Boccaccio's *Decameron* and likewise including stories about priestly misdemeanours (cf. *The Town of Lucca*, Ch. 5).

23 (p. 221). *Le ciel . . . accommodements*: 'Heaven, it is true, forbids some

pleasures, but one can come to an arrangement with it'; from *Tartuffe* (1669), IV, v.

24 (p. 221). *Jansenism*: a Catholic reform movement founded by Cornélius Jansen (1585–1638).

25 (p. 222). *John of Leyden*: Jan Bockelson (1510–36), leader of the Anabaptists who seized power in Münster in 1535 and introduced community of goods and polygamy.

26 (p. 225). *Jung-Stilling's treatise on ghosts*: Johann Heinrich Jung (1740–1817), known as Stilling, Pietist autobiographer, believed in the existence of spirits and published a *Theory of Spiritualism* (1808).

27 (p. 225). *Erasmus*: the humanist scholar Desiderius Erasmus of Rotterdam (1466–1536); *Melanchthon*: Philipp Melanchthon (1497–1560), close associate of Luther.

28 (p. 225). *St Boniface*: missionary to the pagan Germans in the eighth century.

29 (p. 226). *Bosco*: Bartolommeo Bosco (1793–1863), a conjurer.

30 (p. 226). *Père Olinde*: Olinde Rodrigues (1794–1851), a French banker with the title of 'Father' in the Saint-Simonian movement (see Introduction); this incident occurred on 15 January 1832.

31 (p. 228). *Marquis of Brandenburg*: a punning allusion to King Frederick II of Prussia; the Mark Brandenburg was Prussia's central territory.

32 (p. 228). *Dr Hoffmann*: official censor in Hamburg from 1822 to 1848; Heine introduces him into *Germany: A Winter's Tale*.

33 (p. 230). *Septuagint*: the oldest Greek translation of the Old Testament.

34 (p. 230). *Reuchlin*: the humanist and Hebrew scholar Johannes Reuchlin (1455–1522) prevented the destruction of Jewish books demanded by the ex-Jewish convert Johann Pfefferkorn of Cologne. Reuchlin was opposed by the Dominican Jakob von *Hoogstraeten* and supported by the humanist *Ulrich von Hutten* (1488–1523), author of the satirical *Litterae obscurorum virorum* ('Letters of Obscure Men', 1515–17).

35 (p. 231). *preacher on the Mountain*: Heine fuses Christ's Sermon on the Mount with the speeches of the French revolutionary Danton, leader of the radical faction known as the Mountain.

36 (p. 232). *'A sure stronghold'*: in the original Heine quotes the whole of this hymn.

37 (p. 232). *Hans Sachs*: a cobbler and poet in Nuremberg (1494–1576), whom Tieck and A. W. Schlegel had claimed as the initiator of modern German literature. His *Meistergesang* was a form of poetry, both secular and religious, set to music and sung solo.

BOOK TWO

1 (p. 236). *Bacon*: the English essayist, philosopher and politician Francis Bacon (1561–1621).

2 (p. 239). *Condillac*: Condillac (1715–80), *Helvétius* (1715–71), *Holbach* (1723–89), and *La Mettrie* (1709–51), author of *L'homme-machine* ('Man the Machine', 1748), were philosophers of the French Enlightenment, more or less closely identified with materialism.

3 (p. 239). *Benthamites*: followers of Jeremy Bentham (1748–1832) and his philosophy of utilitarianism ('the greatest good of the greatest number').

4 (p. 243). *Maimon*: Salomon Maimon (1753–1800), a Polish Jew who joined the Berlin Enlightenment and became a devotee of Kant, recounts this incident in his highly readable autobiography (1792–3).

5 (p. 244). *political crimes*: Franz van der Ende (or van Ende), an Amsterdam physician with whose daughter Spinoza is unreliably said to have been in love, was executed in Paris in 1674 for his part in a conspiracy against Louis XIV.

6 (p. 245). *natura naturans*: 'active, creating nature', which Spinoza contrasts with *natura naturata*, 'created nature'.

7 (p. 245). *Madame du Deffand*: Parisian salon hostess; the quotation comes from Voltaire's letter to her of 3 April 1769.

8 (p. 245). *'living interpenetration ... models'*: quoted from Schelling's *Philosophical Inquiries into the Essence of Human Freedom* (1809).

9 (p. 246). *St Augustine*: this comparison is not to be found in his works.

10 (p. 246). *'God ... is everything there is'*: Spinoza's formula, 'whatever is, is in God', was adapted in this way by the Saint-Simonians and often quoted by Heine, for example in the poem 'Auf diesem Felsen bauen wir' ('Upon this rock we'll build a church')

11 (p. 247). *Some priests*: especially the proto-socialist Félicité-Robert de Lamennais, whose *Words of a Believer* (1834) had been translated into German by Heine's antagonist Börne.

12 (p. 248). *Purusa*: according to Hinduism, the world is composed of matter (*prakriti*) and soul (*purusa*).

13 (p. 250). *'Dost ... ale?'*: Shakespeare, *Twelfth Night*, II, iii, 110.

14 (p. 250). *F. H. Jacobi*: philosopher (1743–1819) who identified Spinozism with atheism.

15 (p. 250). *penseur téméraire*: 'daring thinker'.

16 (p. 251). *Johannes Tauler*: preacher and mystic (*c.* 1300–1361).

17 (p. 252). *Paracelsus*: professor of medicine (1493–1541), with unconventional views on natural healing; the first academic to lecture in German instead of Latin.

18 (p. 252). *Jakob Böhme*: mystic (1575–1624) whose main works were translated into French by L. C. de *Saint-Martin* at the beginning of the nineteenth century.

19 (p. 254). *Eriugena*: Johannes Eriugena (*c*. 810–77), Irish theologian who translated the works of the fifth-century Neoplatonist known as Dionysus the Areopagite or Pseudo-Dionysus.

20 (p. 255). *Happy French . . . dying breath*: this passage was not in Heine's manuscript of *History*; he wrote it in 1834, inserted it into the French version, and later retranslated it for the second edition of *History* (1852). I have omitted an untranslatable passage which turns on the two meanings of *vergeben* ('forgive' and 'poison').

21 (p. 255). *Hegel's saying*: 'Whatever is rational is real; and whatever is real is rational', from the preface to his *Introduction to the Philosophy of Right* (1821).

22 (p. 256). *Aeschylus*: a reference to his tragedy *Prometheus*.

23 (p. 256). *Semler*: J. S. Semler (1725–91), W. A. *Teller* (1734–1804), and K. F. *Bahrdt* (1741–92) were all rationalist theologians. By arguing that Jesus's teachings were adapted to the contemporary outlook of his audience, Semler made an important contribution to the historical study of the Bible.

24 (p. 256). *Nicolai*: Friedrich Nicolai (1733–1811), a Berlin bookseller, journalist and novelist, a friend of Lessing and Mendelssohn, and a leading proponent of Enlightenment rationalism.

25 (p. 257). *Gellert*: Christian Fürchtegott Gellert (1715–69), poet, remembered especially for his fables and his novel *Life of the Swedish Countess G.* (1747–8).

26 (p. 288). *letter to a friend*: from Lessing's letter to J. J. Eschenburg of 26 October 1774.

27 (p. 258). *a revised* Werther: Nicolai's *The Joys of Young Werther* (1775).

28 (p. 259). *Mendelssohn*: Moses Mendelssohn (1729–86), Jewish philosopher of the Berlin Enlightenment; the most important of the authors listed here, along with Karl Philipp Moritz (1756–93), author of the outstanding autobiographical novel *Anton Reiser* (1785–90).

29 (p. 262). *'Oser!'*: 'Dare!'

30 (p. 262). *Klotz*: Christian Adolf Klotz, a professor of philosophy and eloquence, whose book on ancient brooches Lessing demolished in his *Letters on Antiquarian Subjects* (1768–9).

31 (p. 264). *My joy . . . badly*: from Lessing's letter to Eschenburg, 31 December 1777. Lessing's son died soon after birth on 25 December 1777, his wife on 10 January 1778.

32 (p. 265). *O sancta . . . teach it!*: from 'A Parable' (1778), one of Lessing's

polemics against the Hamburg clergyman Goeze. John *Huss* or Jan Hus (1370–1415), Czech religious reformer, was burnt at the stake during the Council of Constance; he uttered this cry ('O holy simplicity!') on seeing an old woman adding fuel to his pyre in order to ensure her own salvation.

33 (p. 266). *twenty-first of January*: Louis XVI was executed on 21 January 1793.

BOOK THREE

1 (p. 267). *'Give me a soul!'*: in English in the original.

2 (p. 268). *Fontenelle*: Bernard de Fontenelle (1657–1757), the French Enlightenment author.

3 (p. 270). C. G. *Schütz*: Schütz publicized Kantian philosophy in the *General Literary Journal* of Jena from 1785 on; Johann *Schulz*, a colleague and friend of Kant, published an interpretation of the *Critique of Pure Reason* in 1784; C. L. *Reinhold*'s *Letters on the Kantian Philosophy* (1786–7) did most to make Kant known.

4 (p. 274). *There are . . . no others*: quoted from the *Critique of Pure Reason*, 'Transcendental Doctrine of Elements', First Part, Second Division, Book II, Ch. III, Section 3 (Kemp Smith's translation).

5 (p. 276). *Anselm of Canterbury*: scholastic theologian and philosopher (1033–1109), argued that the greatest being we can imagine must also exist, otherwise it would lack an attribute of greatness. *St Augustine* wrote in his *On Free Will*: 'I can acknowledge as God only that to which there is nothing superior.'

6 (p. 276). *De profundis*: part of the opening words of Psalm 130, 'Out of the depths have I cried unto thee, O Lord', used in prayers for the dead.

7 (p. 278). *Schiller*: Friedrich Schiller (1759–1805), dramatist and philosopher; see especially his *Letters on the Aesthetic Education of Mankind* (1795).

8 (p. 278). *Thiers* and *Mignet*: historians of the French Revolution.

9 (p. 282). I have here omitted a very long and circumstantial passage about Fichte's relations with Goethe and Kant.

10 (p. 285). *Eleatics*: early Greek philosophers active in Elea in southern Italy from 540 to 460 B.C., who taught that the essence of things could be grasped only by thought, not by perception.

11 (p. 286). *Bruno*: Giordano Bruno (1548–1600), Dominican monk and philosopher, burnt by the Inquisition for supporting the astronomical findings of Copernicus.

12 (p. 286). *Jules David*: French journalist with a special interest in Oriental subjects.

13 (p. 288). *Ballanche*: Pierre-Simon Ballanche (1776–1847), French philosopher, says this in his *Orpheus* (1827–8).

14 (p. 290). *eclectic*: Victor Cousin (1792–1867), who had already described the philosophy of Schelling and Hegel for French readers.

15 (p. 290). *Oken*: Lorenz Oken, pseudonym of L. Ockenfuss (1779–1851), a leading Romantic scientist who, inspired by Schelling, believed in the continuous evolution of beings from primeval slime to man; he taught and influenced Georg Büchner. He was dismissed from his professorship at Jena in 1819 for opposing the restrictions on freedom introduced by the Carlsbad Decrees. Adam *Müller* (1779–1829) was a reactionary political philosopher who advocated the restoration of feudal hierarchy. For *Görres*, see *Ideas*, note 13. Henrik *Steffens* (1773–1845), a Norwegian natural scientist who taught in Berlin, similarly advocated the maintenance of social hierarchy.

16 (p. 290). *Haxthausen*: Werner Freiherr (i.e. baron) von Haxthausen, a Westphalian doctor and journalist, uncle of the poetess Annette von Droste-Hülshoff, put these ideas forward in *On the Foundations of our Constitution* (1833).

17 (p. 293). *Prince of Kyritz*: the then Crown Prince of Prussia, who in 1840 became King Frederick William IV; Kyritz is an unimportant village near Potsdam. *Dr Wirth*: Johann Georg Wirth (1798–1848), a leading German liberal and republican.

Memoirs

1 (p. 298). *Moritz*: *Travels of a German in Italy in the Years 1786–1788*, by Karl Philipp Moritz (see *History*, Book Two, note 28).

2 (p. 299). *Quintilian*: Roman orator (*c.* A.D. 30–96) and author of an influential treatise on rhetoric.

3 (p. 299). *Batteux*: Charles Batteux, author of *The Fine Arts Reduced to a Single Rule* (1746).

4 (p. 299). *Procrustes*: character in Greek legend who made all his guests fit his bed, by stretching them if they were too short, or lopping off part of their legs if they were too tall.

5 (p. 300). *Klopstock*: Friedrich Gottlob Klopstock (1724–1803), major poet, known especially for his epic about Christ, *The Messiah* (1748–73).

6 (p. 300). *a close friend*: Louise Berg, daughter of a swordsmith in Solingen, not far from Düsseldorf; in 1796 she married Nicolas Soult, who, as one of Napoleon's generals, in 1807 received the title of Duke of Dalmatia.

7 (p. 302). *Mackeldey and Welcker*: Ferdinand Mackeldey and Karl Theodor Welcker were lecturers in law at Bonn University.

8 (p. 302). *Émile* (1762): Rousseau's novel setting out a scheme of education which permits the natural development of the child's character.

9 (p. 303). *Grabbe*: Christian Dietrich Grabbe (1801–36), dramatist, whose works include *Duke Theodor of Gothland* (1827), *Napoleon or the Hundred Days* (1831) and *Hannibal* (1835). Heine knew Grabbe in Berlin in 1822.

10 (p. 306). *The Physician of his own Honour* and *The Steadfast Prince* are plays by Pedro Calderón de la Barca (1600–1681).

11 (p. 308). *Salpetrière*: a famous hospital in Paris.

12 (p. 309). *Paracelsus*: see *History*, p. 252. Johann Baptist *van Helmont* (1577–1644), physician and naturalist; Heinrich Cornelius (1486–1535), known as *Agrippa of Nettesheim*, was the author of a treatise on *Occult Philosophy* which he sent to the abbot Johannes Tritheim (1462–1516) or *Trithemius*.

13 (p. 309). *Mount Moriah*: cf. Genesis 22:2.

14 (p. 310). *'Où l'innocence ... vivre'*: 'Where innocence perishes, it is a crime to live.'

15 (p. 310). *Huon of Bordeaux*: hero of an old French epic; Heine knew the German version, *Oberon* (1780), by Christoph Martin Wieland (1733–1813).

16 (p. 312). *'The fathers ... edge'*: Jeremiah 31:29; Ezekiel 18:2.

17 (p. 315). *my /.../*: the gap in the text was formerly attributed to censorship by Heine's brother Maximilian, but the most recent editor attributes it merely to the unfinished state of Heine's manuscript.

18 (p. 316). *Prince Ernest of Cumberland*: (1771–1851) became King of Hanover in 1837.

19 (p. 318). *Thales*: the ancient Greek thinker (*c.* 640–543 B.C.) who maintained that the world arose from water; *Lampsacus* is not a person but a place.

20 (p. 322). *Cherubini*: Luigi Cherubini (1760–1842), composer.

21 (p. 322). *Princess Cristina Belgiojoso*: (1808–71) a friend of Heine's in Paris, and advocate of Italian independence.

22 (p. 323). *coq à l'âne*: turmoil.

23 (p. 329). *'Take money ... pocket'*: misquoted from *Othello*, I, iii, 340.

24 (p. 330). *Numa*: Numa Pompilius was a legendary king of Rome, who was counselled by the nymph Egeria; confused with Latin *numen*, 'divine power'.

25 (p. 330). *Sprenger*: the Dominican monk Jakob Sprenger (1436–95), author (with Heinrich Institoris) of the *Hammer of Witches*. Scheible's

Monastery was a series of books on folklore, some of which Heine consulted while writing his *Memoirs*.

26 (p. 331). *Niobe's daughters*: in Greek legend, Niobe's six daughters and six sons were killed by the gods to punish her for her pride: see the *Iliad*, Book 24, ll. 600ff.

27 (p. 334). *Froissart*: an inaccurate recollection of an episode in the *Chronicles* of Jean Froissart (*c.* 1337–1410) after the English victory over the French in 1356.

WITHDRAWN

READ MORE IN PENGUIN

A CHOICE OF CLASSICS

Jacob Burckhardt	**The Civilization of the Renaissance in Italy**
Carl von Clausewitz	**On War**
Friedrich Engels	**The Origins of the Family, Private Property and the State**
Wolfram von Eschenbach	**Parzival**
	Willehalm
Goethe	**Elective Affinities**
	Faust Parts One and Two (in 2 volumes)
	Italian Journey
	The Sorrows of Young Werther
Jacob and Wilhelm Grimm	**Selected Tales**
E. T. A. Hoffmann	**Tales of Hoffmann**
Henrik Ibsen	**The Doll's House/The League of Youth/The Lady from the Sea**
	Ghosts/A Public Enemy/When We Dead Wake
	Hedda Gabler/The Pillars of the Community/The Wild Duck
	The Master Builder/Rosmersholm/Little Eyolf/John Gabriel Borkman
	Peer Gynt
Søren Kierkegaard	**Fear and Trembling**
	The Sickness Unto Death
Georg Christoph Lichtenberg	**Aphorisms**
Friedrich Nietzsche	**Beyond Good and Evil**
	Ecce Homo
	A Nietzsche Reader
	Thus Spoke Zarathustra
	Twilight of the Idols and **The Anti-Christ**
Friedrich Schiller	**The Robbers** and **Wallenstein**
Arthur Schopenhauer	**Essays and Aphorisms**
Gottfried von Strassburg	**Tristan**
August Strindberg	**The Father/Miss Julie/Easter**